The Dawning of Desire

Nathaniel flung himself from his horse and ran to the inert figure.

"Gabrielle! Dear God!" He dropped to his knees beside her, tearing at the snowy cravat to bare her throat, his fingers feeling for her pulse. It was strong but fast. He sighed with relief and then frowned. The black lashes formed half-moons on the pale skin, her lips were slightly parted, her chest rising and falling with each regular breath.

Her pulse was far too vibrant for an unconscious person.

"Gabrielle," he said in a near whisper. "If this is a trick, so help me, I'll make you sorrier than you've ever been in your life."

"Try it," she said. Her eyelids swept up, revealing utterly mischievous charcoal eyes, and in the same moment she sat up. Her arms went around his neck before he realized what was happening and her mouth found his.

A wildness swept through him. His arms went around her. For a minute their tongues fenced, and then he moved his hands to grasp her head, holding it strongly as he drove deep within her mouth on a voyage of assertion that in some faint part of his brain seemed long overdue.

Gabrielle had believed she could fake sufficient response to satisfy him. She had not expected to find herself responding from some deep passionate well within herself.

It wasn't supposed to happen. But it was happening. And Nathaniel Praed was matching her every step of the way. And it was going to play merry hell with her schemes of revenge. . . .

JANE FEATHER

Velvet

BANTAM BOOKS
New York   Toronto   London   Sydney   Auckland

VELVET

A Bantam Book / August 1994

PUBLISHING HISTORY

All rights reserved.

Copyright © 1994 by Jane Feather.

Cover art copyright © 1994 by George Bush.

No part of this book may be reproduced or transmitted in any form or by any means, electronic or mechanical, including photocopying, recording, or by any information storage and retrieval system, without permission in writing from the publisher.

For information address: Bantam Books.

ISBN 0-553-56469-2

Published simultaneously in the United States and Canada

Bantam Books are published by Bantam Books, a division of Random House, Inc. Its trademark, consisting of the words "Bantam Books" and the portrayal of a rooster, is Registered in U.S. Patent and Trademark Office and in other countries. Marca Registrada. Bantam Books, 1540 Broadway, New York, New York 10036.

PRINTED IN THE UNITED STATES OF AMERICA

OPM   17   16   15   14   13   12   11   10   9   8

Richard: This one's for you.

Velvet

Prologue

The gibbous moon hung low in the sky over the forest of St. Cloud. A fox moved sleekly through the bracken, a rabbit sat on its hind legs, eyes fixed and staring, nose twitching as it caught the scent of the predator. Then it was gone, a flash of white scut vanishing into the undergrowth. An owl's hollow hoot hung over a glade where a deer drank at a trickling stream falling over flat stones.

The rustic pavilion in the small clearing was in darkness, or so it appeared to the figure cleaving to the trunk of a copper beech at the edge of the glade. Black-clad, he merged with his surroundings, a darker shadow in the shadows of the forest. His eyes stretched into the darkness toward the single-story building humped in the center of the clearing. Long glass doors opened onto a colonnaded porch encircling the pavilion, and a wisp of white fluttered from the open door facing the watcher as the night breezes caught the muslin curtains.

He wore soft-soled leather moccasins and made no

sound as he slipped from concealment and approached the portico. Black britches, black shirt, hair concealed under a black cap, pale complexion darkened with burnt cork, the only touch of color came from the gleam of the long double-bladed knife he held at his side. He was an assassin who knew his work well.

In a book-lined room on the far side of the circular pavilion, a single candle burned low in its socket, its light so negligible as to be invisible to anyone outside.

Charles-Maurice de Talleyrand-Perigord dozed beside the empty hearth, a book lying open, facedown on his lap. A soft snore bubbled from the slightly open lips of a thin aristocratic mouth. His head jerked on his chest as if some sound had pierced his sleep, then the breathing deepened again.

The assassin moved on his leather soles to the open window on the other side of the pavilion. His night's work was no concern of Monsieur de Talleyrand, Minister for Foreign Affairs to the Emperor Napoleon—or so he believed.

The bed in the room was a sumptuous affair, high and hung with filmy white curtains that rose and fell in the breeze as if the bed were a ship on the high seas. Amid rumpled white silk sheets and damask coverlets, two naked figures slept entwined, their bodies heavy with the deep relaxation of fulfillment. The woman lay sprawled on her back, one arm falling loosely around the neck of her partner, whose dark head was pillowed on her breast, one leg flung over her thighs, pressing her into the deep feather mattress with his weight. His back curved toward the French window, his neck open and vulnerable, the ribs sharply delineated beneath the taut skin.

The knife slid between the third and fourth ribs. Guillaume de Granville stirred as sharp pain invaded his sleep, his dreams of love. A small sound came from him, a sound of protest, of confusion, that faded into a tiny sigh and his body lost the tautness of living flesh, sinking into his mistress's body with a flaccid heaviness that bore no relation to the relaxation of a moment before.

Gabrielle should not have woken, the killing had been so silent, but her body was still in tune with Guillaume's after long hours of love, and as life left him she woke and sat up in the same instant. Her lover's body slid sideways and her sleep-filled eyes stared disbelieving at the crimson stain on the smooth pale flesh of his back. It was a small blemish and yet not for one minute, even in the dumb trance of new awakening, did she think it was insignificant. The deadly stain began to spread in a slow, inexorable flush.

It had been a matter of seconds since the assassin had entered, and as Gabrielle's stunned gaze lifted she met the cold, blank stare of pale eyes in a blackened countenance. Eyes without life, without emotion. She opened her mouth on a scream and the man lunged, the knife aimed to puncture her throat. She flung herself sideways, heaving the dead body of Guillaume de Granville aside with the superhuman strength of terror. Her scream ripped through the chamber, shattered the silence of the elegant pavilion.

For a second of uncharacteristic hesitation the assassin stood poised on the balls of his feet, his knife hand raised. Gabrielle's scream continued as if she would never run out of breath. Suddenly her cry was met and matched by the clanging of a bell, the violent barking of hounds. The assassin spun on his toes toward the French door and leaped with the agility of a woodland creature through the opening.

Talleyrand had woken from his doze at the first skirling scream, his hand going immediately to the bellrope beside his chair. At the loud summons, men trained to respond with the speed of thought were moving at a run through the pavilion toward the source of the screaming. In the kennels outside, the keeper, following standing orders, released the hounds.

The door to the bedchamber burst open. The men barely glanced at the bed, where the woman cradled the body of her lover, her eyes wild, her mouth still open on a continuing shriek. They ran for the open door onto the portico, pistols in their hands.

Gabrielle's scream died as her breath finally failed. She gazed down at Guillaume's body, where the blood now pumped thickly from between his ribs. Her hand stroked his hair, feeling the curious deadness of him almost as if it were a purely intellectual sensation.

Talleyrand came into the room. With his halting limp, he crossed to the bed. Taking up the coverlet, he draped it around the woman's shoulders, covering her nakedness before he examined the body of Guillaume de Granville, feeling for a pulse at the throat.

"Who?" Gabrielle spoke the one word on a whisper. The wildness had gone from her eyes and her body was taut with a fierce energy that Talleyrand, who had known her from babyhood, recognized and understood.

"Will you avenge his death, Gabrielle?" he asked quietly.

"You know I will." The response was as direct as he had expected.

He walked over to the open French door. The baying of the hounds was fainter as they pursued their quarry deeper into the forest. But they had been on his heels within minutes and would catch him in the end, unless, like some spirit, the assassin had no scent and left no footprint.

Monsieur de Talleyrand had no truck with spirits. He dealt in the corporeal world, where cunning and intrigue were the only efficient defenses and the only sure means of advancement and influence, both personal and political. And Napoleon's Minister for Foreign Affairs was undoubtedly the preeminent exponent of those arts in Europe.

He turned back to the bed, his cool gaze holding a spark of compassion as it rested on the young woman's set white face. But compassion was not a useful emotion, and Gabrielle had been in the business long enough to know that. She wanted the tool of revenge in her hands. A revenge that would, not coincidentally, benefit both France and Monsieur de Talleyrand-Perigord.

He began to speak, his well-modulated voice quiet yet crisp in the now-silent chamber of death.

1

"Who's the titian, Miles?" Nathaniel Praed put up his eye glass for a closer scrutiny.

Miles Bennet followed his friend's gaze, although the description could apply to only one woman in Lady Georgiana Vanbrugh's drawing room.

"Comtesse de Beaucaire," he replied. "A distant cousin of Georgie's on her mother's side. They've known each other almost since the cradle."

Nathaniel let his glass fall, commenting dryly, "Presumably there's a Comte de Beaucaire."

"Not anymore," Miles said, somewhat surprised at this show of interest. In general, Nathaniel was indifferent to the charms of Society women. "He died tragically soon after their marriage, I believe. Taken off by some fever very suddenly—all over in a couple of days, as I understand it." He shrugged. "Gabrielle's officially out of mourning now, but she still wears black much of the time."

"She knows what suits her," observed Lord Praed, putting up his glass again.

Miles had no fault to find with the observation. Gabrielle stood out in a room full of women in diaphanous pastels. Her dress of severely cut black velvet accentuated her unusual height and threw into startling relief the mass of dark red hair tumbling in an unruly cloud of ringlets around a pale face.

"Magnificent emeralds," Nathaniel now mused, assessing with a connoisseur's eye the jewels at throat, ears, wrist, and hair.

"Part of the treasure chest of the Hawksworths, I imagine," Miles said. "Her mother was Imogen Hawksworth ... married the Duc de Gervais ... they were both victims of Madame Guillotine in the Terror. Gabrielle was the only child. There wasn't much to inherit after the Revolution, but her mother's jewels were saved somehow."

He glanced curiously at his friend. "Why the interest?"

"You have to admit, she's a striking woman. She must have been a child in the Terror. How did she survive?"

Miles withdrew a Sèvres snuffbox from his pocket and took a delicate pinch. "Her parents were killed at the height of the Terror, the end of 'ninety, I believe. Family friends managed to smuggle Gabrielle out of France. She must have been about eight. That's when she and Georgie became inseparable; they're much of an age, and Gabrielle became part of the family until it was safe for her to return to France. She has powerful connections—Madame de Staël and Talleyrand, to name but two. She's been living in France for the last six or seven years, with occasional visits to Georgie and Simon."

"Mmmm. That would explain why I know nothing about her ... and why you, my friend, as always, know everything." Nathaniel laughed slightly. Miles was well known for the sharpness of the ear he kept to the ground and the reliability of his information.

"Georgie *is* my cousin by marriage," Miles said as if defending the source of his information.

"Then you are perfectly placed to effect an introduction." A silvery eyebrow quirked.

"But of course," Miles agreed promptly. "You can hardly spend the entire houseparty without meeting each other. I own I'm interested to see what you make of each other."

"Now, just what does that mean?"

Miles chuckled. "You'll see. Come."

Nathaniel followed his friend across the drawing room to where Gabrielle de Beaucaire stood in a small group by the window.

Gabrielle watched his approach over the rim of her champagne glass. She knew perfectly well who he was. Nathaniel Praed was her reason for being there, just as she was his, although, if Simon had kept his word, he didn't know that yet. It pleased her that she should have the upper hand in this respect. It gave her the opportunity to make some assessments of the man unhindered by the role he would undoubtedly adopt once he knew exactly who and what she was.

"Gabrielle, may I introduce Lord Praed." Miles bowed, smiled, gestured to his companion.

"My lord." She gave him a silk-gloved hand as cool as her smile. "Delighted."

"Enchanté, countess." He bowed over her hand. "I understand you're recently arrived from France."

"My parentage makes me persona grata on both sides of the Channel," she said. "An enviable position, I'm sure you'll agree."

Her eyes were the color of dark charcoal, framed in thick black lashes beneath black eyebrows. It was a startling contrast to the red hair and the very white skin.

"On the contrary," Nathaniel said, nettled by an indefinable hint of mockery in her gaze. "I would consider it uncomfortable to have a foot in both camps during wartime."

"You're surely not questioning my loyalty, Lord Praed?" The black brows rose. "The only family I have are in England . . . in this room, in fact. Both my parents and all my father's family perished in the Terror." A chilly smile touched the wide, generous mouth, and she put her head on one side, waiting to see how he would respond to being put in quite such an uncomfortable spot.

Nathaniel didn't miss a beat, and not a hint of his annoyance showed on the lean, ascetic face. "I would hardly be so impertinent, madame, particularly on such a short acquaintance. May I offer my condolences on your husband's death. I'm sure he was a loyal supporter of the Bourbons even if expediency required token submission to the emperor."

Now, that had taken the wind out of her sails. Satisfied, he watched the flash of surprise at this hard-hitting return of serve.

"He was a Frenchman, sir. A man who loved his country," she replied quietly, and her eyes held his for a moment.

Nathaniel was of middle height, and the tall woman's charcoal eyes were almost on a level with his own; despite this proximity, he couldn't read the message they contained. But he had the unshakable conviction that Gabrielle de Beaucaire was toying with him in some way—that she knew something he didn't. It was an unfamiliar sensation for Lord Praed, and he didn't care for it in the least.

"Oh, I'm so glad you two have been introduced." Lady Georgiana Vanbrugh glided toward them, a beautiful woman, her daintily rounded figure delicately clad in lilac spider gauze. She slipped her arm through Gabrielle's and smiled with the genuine warmth and pleasure she always felt when she believed her friends were enjoying themselves.

"It's such a pity Simon had to go up to town so suddenly, Lord Praed. He charged me most expressly to tell you how sorry he is not to be here to greet you. But when duty calls . . ." She smiled, lifted round white shoulders so that the graceful swell of her breasts rose from her décolletage. "He assured me he'd do everything possible to be here in time for dinner tomorrow."

Two more different women would be hard to find, Nathaniel reflected, as they stood arm in arm, severe black velvet against lilac gossamer. The tall, white-skinned redhead with high cheekbones, cleft chin, and retroussé nose could only be called striking, if a man found clearly defined irregular features, a crooked smile, and a tall, willowy figure attractive. If he didn't, then one would be inclined to dismiss her as without charm. Georgiana, on the other hand, by any standards, was conventionally lovely with soft feminine curves, a peaches and cream complexion, small regular features, and gleaming golden hair.

"Members of the government are not their own masters, particularly in wartime," Nathaniel said easily.

"You speak as one who knows, Lord Praed," Gabrielle said. "Are you also involved in government work?"

Why did it sound as if she had some underlying point to make? He looked sharply at her and met a calm, cool gaze and that crooked little smile. "No," he said brusquely. "I am not."

Her smile widened as if again she was relishing some secret knowledge before she turned to Miles, a highly entertained but so far silent observer of the exchange.

"Do you hunt tomorrow, Miles?"

"If you do," he said with a gallant bow. "Although I doubt I'll keep up with you." He gestured to Nathaniel. "Gabrielle's a bruising rider to hounds, Nathaniel. You'd do well not to let her give you a lead."

"Oh, I'm sure Lord Praed will take any fence that presents itself," Gabrielle said, still smiling.

"I've never failed a fence yet, countess." He made a curt bow and walked away, annoyed that he'd allowed her to provoke him, yet intrigued despite himself . . . almost like a rabbit fascinated by the cobra, he thought irritably as he accepted a fresh glass of champagne from a hovering footman. A distinct aura of trouble clung to Gabrielle de Beaucaire.

"You don't appear to like Lord Praed, Gabby." Georgiana looked half reproachful, half anxious. "Did he upset you?"

Oh, he merely killed the man whose life was dearer to me than my own. "Of course not," Gabrielle said. "Was I rude? You know what my tongue's like when it runs away with me."

"I thought you'd find a sparring partner in Nathaniel," Miles remarked. "And I suspect you'll find him a worthy opponent." He grinned. "However, I think you won that round, so perhaps I'd better go and smooth his ruffled feathers." He went off chuckling with the slightly malicious pleasure of one who enjoys stirring up the complacent.

"Miles is wicked," Georgie declared. "Nathaniel Praed's his closest friend, I don't know why he so relishes making mischief."

"Oh, dear," Gabrielle said. "Should I beg Lord Praed's pardon?" Her expression had changed completely. There was warmth in her eyes as she smiled at her cousin and a vibrancy to the previously bland expression. "I didn't mean to disgrace you, Georgie, by offending your guest."

"Stuff!" Georgie declared. "I don't like him myself, really, but he's a most particular friend of Simon's. They seem to have a kind of partnership." She shrugged. "I expect he's something to do with the government, whatever he might say. But he's such a cold fish. He

terrifies me, if you want the truth. I always feel tongue-
tied around him."

"Well, he doesn't intimidate me," Gabrielle declared. "For all that his eyes are like stones at the
bottom of a pond."

The butler announced dinner at this point and
Gabrielle went in on the arm of Miles Bennet.
Nathaniel Praed was sitting opposite her, and she was
able to observe him covertly while responding to the
easy social chatter of her dinner partners on either side.
His eyes were definitely stonelike, she thought.
Browny-green, hard and flat in that lean face, with its
chiseled mouth and aquiline nose. He reminded her of
some overbred hunter. There was the same nervous energy to the slender athletic frame, supple and wiry
rather than muscular. His hair was his most startling
feature: crisp and dark, except for silver-gray swatches
at his temples, matching the silver eyebrows.

She became abruptly aware of his eyes on her and
understood that her own observation had ceased to be
covert ... in fact, not to put too fine a point on it,
she'd been staring at him with unabashed interest.

Thankful, not for the first time in her life, that she
rarely blushed, Gabrielle turned her attention to the
man on her left with an animated inquiry as to whether
he was familiar with Sir Walter Scott's poem "The Lay
of the Last Minstrel."

In the absence of their host, the men didn't sit long
over their port and soon joined the ladies in the drawing room. To his irritation, Nathaniel found himself
looking for the titian, but the Comtesse de Beaucaire
was conspicuous by her absence. He wandered with apparent casualness through the smaller salons, where
various games had been set up, but there was no sign of
the redhead among the exuberant players of lottery
tickets or the more intense card players at the whist
tables.

He examined the faces of the men at the whist tables. One of them at some point in the week would be revealed as Simon's candidate ... once Simon decided to stop playing silly undercover games. He'd dragged him down here with the promise of a perfect candidate for the service, refusing to divulge his identity, choosing instead to play a silly game with a ridiculous form of introduction.

It was typical Simon, of course. For a grown man, he took a childish delight in games and surprises. Nathaniel took his tea and sat in a corner of the drawing room, frowning at the various musical performances succeeding each other on harp and pianoforte.

"Miss Bayberry's performance doesn't seem to find favor," Miles observed, wandering over to his friend's corner. "Her voice is a trifle thin, I grant you."

"I hadn't noticed," Nathaniel said shortly. "Besides, I'm no judge, as well you know."

"No, you never have had time for life's niceties," Miles agreed with a tranquil smile. "How's young Jake?"

At this reference to his small son, Nathaniel's frown deepened. "Well enough, according to his governess."

"And according to Jake ... ?" Miles prompted.

"For heaven's sake, Miles, the lad's six years old; I'm not about to consult him. He's far too young to have an opinion on anything." Nathaniel shrugged and said dismissively, "From all reports, he appears obedient enough, so it's to be presumed he's happy enough."

"Yes, I suppose so." Miles didn't sound too convinced, but he knew which of his friend's tender spots were better left without exacerbation. If the child didn't bear such an uncanny resemblance to his mother, maybe it would be different.

He changed the subject. "So what inducements bring you to Vanbrugh Court? Country houseparties aren't your usual style of entertainment."

Nathaniel shrugged with an appearance of nonchalance. Not even Miles knew how Nathaniel Praed served his country. "Quite frankly, now that I'm here, I don't know. Simon was at his most pressing and just wore me down. Agreeing seemed the only way to achieve peace. He seemed to think it would amuse me. You know what he's like." Nathaniel shook his head in mingled exasperation and resignation. "He's never taken no for an answer, not even at Harrow." He glared around the room. "You'd think in the circumstances, he'd manage to be here himself."

"He does have a fairly lofty position in Portland's ministry," Miles pointed out mildly. "Anyway, he'll be here tomorrow."

"And in the meantime we have to endure this tedium with an appearance of good grace."

Miles chuckled. "You're an ill-tempered bastard, Nathaniel. The most thoroughgoing misanthropist." He glanced around the room. "I wonder where Gabrielle's disappeared to."

"Mmmm," responded Lord Praed, taking snuff.

Miles cast his friend a sharp look. For some reason the indifferent mumble didn't ring true. Nathaniel hadn't always been a misanthropist. It had taken Helen's death to turn him into this introspective, chilly character who seemed to delight in rebuffing all friendly overtures. Most of his friends had given up by now; only Miles and Simon persevered, partly because they'd known Nathaniel since boyhood and knew what a stout and unstinting friend he was when a man needed a friend, and partly because they both knew that despite his attitude, Nathaniel needed and relied on their loyalty and friendship, that without it he would retreat from the world completely and be utterly irreclaimable.

A man couldn't grieve forever, and the old Nathaniel would one day inhabit his skin again. Perhaps this concealed interest in Gabrielle de Beaucaire was a hopeful sign.

"I expect she decided to have an early night," he commented. "Be fresh for the hunt tomorrow."

"Somehow, I doubt that. The countess didn't strike me as a woman in need of much sleep in any circumstances." Nathaniel's tone was disapproving; but then, he made a habit of disapproval, Miles reflected.

Nathaniel went up to his own room shortly after, leaving the sounds of merriment behind. He had some work to do, and reading reports struck him as an infinitely more rewarding way of spending the shank of the evening.

Around midnight the house fell silent. House-parties kept early hours, particularly with a hunt on the morrow. Nathaniel yawned and put aside the report from the agent at the court of Czar Alexander. The czar had appointed a new commander in chief of his army. It remained to be seen whether Bennigsen would do better than the enfeebled Kamensky when it came to engaging Napoleon's troops in Eastern Prussia. Ostensibly the czar was fulfilling his promise to support Prussia against Napoleon, but Nathaniel's agent reported the vigorous opposition of the czar's mother to a policy that could sacrifice Russia for Prussia. It remained to be seen which way the czar would jump in the end. It was hard to second-guess a man who, according to this latest report, was described by his closest associate as "a combination of weakness, uncertainty, terror, injustice, and incoherence that drives one to grief and despair."

Nathaniel swung out of bed and went to open the window. Whatever the temperature, he was unable to sleep with the window closed. Several narrow escapes had given him a constitutional dislike of enclosed spaces.

It was a bright, clear night, the air crisp, the stars sharp in the limitless black sky. He flung open the window, leaning his elbows on the sill, looking out over the expanse of smooth lawn where frost glittered under the starlight. It would be a beautiful morning for the hunt.

He climbed back into bed and blew out his candle.

He heard the rustling of the Virginia creeper almost immediately. His hand slipped beneath his pillow to his constant companion, the small silver-mounted pistol. He lay very still, every muscle held in waiting, his ears straining into the darkness. The small scratching rustling sounds continued, drawing closer to the open window. Someone was climbing the thick ancient creeper clinging to the mellow brick walls of the Jacobean manor house.

His hand closed more firmly over the pistol and he hitched himself up on one elbow, his eyes on the square of the window, waiting.

Hands competently gripped the edge of the windowsill, followed by a dark head. The nocturnal visitor swung a leg over the sill and hitched himself upright, straddling the sill.

"Since you've only just snuffed your candle, I'm sure you're still awake," Gabrielle de Beaucaire said into the dark, still room. "And I'm sure you have a pistol, so please don't shoot, it's only me."

Nathaniel was rarely taken by surprise, and when he was, he was a master at concealing it. On this occasion, however, his training deserted him.

"*Only!*" he exclaimed. "What the hell are you doing?"

"Guess," his visitor challenged cheerfully from her perch.

"You'll have to forgive me, but I don't find guessing games amusing," he declared in clipped accents. He sat up, his pistol still in his hand, and stared at the dark shape outlined against the moonlight. That aura of trouble surrounding Gabrielle de Beaucaire had not been a figment of his imagination.

"Perhaps I should be flattered," he said icily. "Am

I to assume unbridled lust lies behind the honor of this visit, madame?" His eyes narrowed.

Disconcertingly, the woman appeared to be impervious to irony. She laughed. A warm, merry sound that Nathaniel found as incongruous in the circumstances as it was disturbingly attractive.

"Not at this point, Lord Praed; but there's no saying what the future might hold." It was a mischievous and outrageous statement that rendered him temporarily speechless.

She took something out of the pocket of her britches and held it on the palm of her hand. "I'm here to present my credentials."

She swung off the windowsill and approached the bed, a sinuous figure in her black britches and glimmering white shirt.

He leaned sideways, struck flint on tinder, and relit the bedside candle. The dark red hair glowed in the light as she extended her hand, palm upward, toward him, and he saw what she held.

It was a small scrap of black velvet cut with a ragged edge.

"Well, well." The evening's puzzles were finally solved. Lord Praed opened a drawer in the bedside table and took out a piece of tissue paper. Unfolding it, he revealed the twin of the scrap of material.

"I should have guessed," he said pensively. "Only a woman would have come up with such a fanciful idea." He took the velvet from her extended palm and fitted the ragged edge to the other piece, making a whole square. "So you're Simon's surprise. No wonder he was so secretive."

He sat back against the pillows, an expression of boredom now on the lean features. "This is a tedious waste of time, madame. I don't employ women in my business, and Simon knows it."

"How very definite you sound," Gabrielle said, seemingly unperturbed. "Women make good spies.

They have different assets and techniques from men, I would imagine."

"Oh, they're tricky enough, I grant you," he declared as indifferently as before. "But they're more vulnerable . . . they hurt more easily."

Gabrielle shrugged. "If a woman decides to take the risk and accept the consequences, it's hardly your responsibility, Lord Praed."

"On the contrary. Each agent is part of an interlocking network . . . dependent upon one another. In my experience, women are not good team members. And they don't stand up well to pressure." His lips thinned. "You understand me, I'm sure."

Gabrielle nodded. "Women are more likely to talk under torture."

"Not more likely," he said with a shrug. "Just more quickly. In the end, everyone talks. But the lives of an entire cell can depend on the extra hour a man can hold out."

"I believe I have as much fortitude as most men," Gabrielle declared. *And certainly as much experience in your business, Sir Spymaster*—but that was a private reflection. "I can move freely between England and France," she continued. "I speak both languages without accent." She sat on the edge of his bed with an air of calm assurance that Nathaniel found supremely irritating. It seemed calculated to increase the disadvantages of his position, huddled in bed in his nightshirt like some invalid.

"You'll have to forgive me," he said sardonically, "but I don't trust women." He began to count off on his fingers. "As I said, they don't make good team members; they lack concentration; they can't focus on one task; and in general they fail to grasp the significance of information. I do not employ women."

Clearly a man of blind and stupid prejudice. It was amazing he was as successful and highly regarded as he was.

"I also know Talleyrand very well." She continued

to enumerate her credentials as if she hadn't heard him. "He was a close friend of my father's and his house is always open to me. I move in political circles in Paris and have entrees at court. I even know Fouché quite well. I could be very useful to you, Lord Praed. I don't think a spymaster can afford to indulge his prejudices about women in general when faced with such advantages in a potential agent."

Nathaniel hung on to his temper by a thread. "I am not prejudiced toward women in general," he said in frigid accents. "As it happens——"

"Oh, good," she interrupted cheerfully. "I'm glad we've established that. Working together could be tricky if you really dislike women. Simon seemed to think that I could be put to good use discovering the identities of the French agents in London."

"Simon is not responsible for selecting agents, madame." Why did he have this almost desperate feeling of facing an immovable object?

"No," she agreed. "You are. But I'm sure you take advice. And Simon is a very senior minister in Lord Portland's government." She examined her fingernails with an air of great interest.

Her hands were long and narrow, he noticed, the nails short, the fingers white and slender. He pulled himself up sharply. She had just made the outrageous suggestion that he was bound to submit to the instructions of Simon Vanbrugh. Only the prime minister had the power of veto over the affairs of the secret service . . . and even that was open to question.

"You are greatly mistaken, madame, if you think I can be influenced against my better judgment by anyone. My word is the last one, countess, and the only one that counts. I do not employ women agents."

"There are exceptions to every rule, my lord," she pointed out with a tranquil smile. "My credentials are impressive, don't you think?"

They were, of course. Simon hadn't exaggerated

when he'd described the potential usefulness of this candidate to the service. Her sex, of course, explained the elaborate setup. Simon knew that if he'd been honest, Nathaniel would have refused point blank even to see her. But presumably Simon had tasted the mettle of Gabrielle de Beaucaire and was no more capable of convincing her to take no for an answer than he himself seemed to be.

He spoke now with calculated hostility, flavoring the words with insult. "Oh, yes, very impressive, madame. As impressive in the service of France as in the service of England. As I understand it, you've spent most of the last few years in France, and now I'm supposed to believe you're eager to betray France to her enemy? It's testing my credulity a little too far, I'm afraid."

He watched her expression, looking for the slightest telltale signs of hesitation, of shiftiness—a slide of the eye, a touch of color to the cheek, a quiver of the lips. The candid charcoal gaze didn't waver, however, and the pale skin remained translucent.

"It's not an unreasonable question," she said steadily. "Let me explain. I've always felt closer to my mother's side of the family." Her voice was no longer light but quiet and somber. "I spent most of my childhood here with Georgie's family during the Terror. My father was a supporter of reform before the Revolution, but he was always a royalist and would have supported the Bourbons if they'd survived the Terror. I can best serve my parents' memories and my own loyalties by helping to defeat Napoleon and restore the Bourbon monarchy to the throne of France."

She put her head on one side, and a smile enlivened the somber countenance. "So, Lord Praed, I am at the service of the English secret service."

"Your husband . . . ?"

Shadows darkened her eyes to black. "He loved France, sir. He would agree to anything that would benefit his beloved country . . . and Napoleon is not good for France."

"No." Nathaniel found himself agreeing, forgetting for a moment the reason for this discussion. "In the long run, I'm sure that's true. Although military victories seem to indicate otherwise," he added wryly.

Her explanation was convincing. His reports indicated these days that many concerned, thinking Frenchmen were beginning to understand that Napoleon's increasing megalomania was detrimental to his country. He wanted to control the whole of Europe, but the time would come when the countries he'd subjugated and humiliated would form alliances and rise up against the tyrant because they'd have nothing further to lose. And when that happened, it would be ordinary French men and women who would pay the price for one man's overweening ambition. Working to bring down Napoleon was not necessarily the act of a traitor to France.

And Gabrielle de Beaucaire was superbly placed to gather the kind of information it could take another agent months to discover.

But he didn't employ women.

He regarded her in brooding silence. She lacked something essential to femininity, he thought, some weakness or vulnerability that he associated with the female sex. She was tensile, strong, unwavering. But with a sense of humor. And something else, something he'd learned to recognize in a good spy a long time ago. He believed she had that indefinable and essential quality of bending, like the willow tree in a wind. A spy had to bend, to adapt, to switch rapidly from stance to stance.

And there were exceptions to every rule, but not this one.

"I don't deny your credentials, but I do not employ women. There is nothing more to be said. Now, perhaps you'd do me the favor of removing yourself. I don't mean to be inhospitable . . ." He tried another heavily ironic smile, lifting one eyebrow. But if he'd hoped to disconcert her, he was disappointed again.

"Very well." She rose from the bed. "Then I'll bid you good night, Lord Praed." She went toward the door. "You won't mind if I go out this way?"

"No," he said, seizing on a legitimate complaint. "On the contrary. Perhaps you'd like to explain why you chose to arrive in such unorthodox fashion. What the devil was wrong with the door in the first place? The house is asleep."

"It seemed more interesting . . . more amusing," she said with a shrug.

"And more dangerous." His voice was harsh. "This is not a game. We're not in this business for amusement. We don't take unnecessary risks in the service. You may have the credentials, madame, but you obviously do not have the wisdom or the intelligence."

Gabrielle stood still, her hand on the doorknob, her lower lip clipped between her teeth as she fought to conceal the violent upsurge of anger at such stinging scorn. He didn't know how far off the mark he was. She *never* took unnecessary risks, and this one had been *entirely* justified in terms of her plan. But Nathaniel Praed was not to know that, of course.

With a supreme effort she conjured up a tone of dignified defense. "I'm no fool, Lord Praed. I can tell the difference between games and reality. Nothing was at stake tonight, so I could see no reason not to indulge myself in a little unorthodox exercise."

"Apart from compromising your reputation," he remarked aridly.

At that she laughed again, and again he was attracted to the deep, warm sound. "Not so," she said. "The house is asleep, as you said. And even if anyone saw me scaling the walls, they'd hardly recognize the Comtesse de Beaucaire in this outfit." She passed a hand in a sweeping gesture down her body, delineating her frame. "Would they?"

"It would depend on how well they know you," he said, as aridly as before, reflecting that once seen like this, Gabrielle would be impossible to forget.

"Well, no harm's done," she said with a dismissive shake of her head. "And I do take your point, sir."

"I'm relieved. Not that it makes any difference to anything. Good night." He blew out his candle.

"Good night, Lord Praed." The door closed behind her.

He lay on his back, staring up into the darkness. Hopefully that was the end of any involvement with Gabrielle de Beaucaire. He'd give Simon a piece of his mind tomorrow. What the hell had he thought he was doing, encouraging that troublesome woman to see herself as an agent? She presumably had some romantic, glamorous conception of what was at best a dirty and dangerous business, and Simon was always susceptible to female persuasion.

Gabrielle stood for a second in the corridor outside, hugging the shadows while she slowly unclenched her fists and breathed deeply until her tight muscles relaxed. He hadn't guessed her tension, she was sure of it. But her entire body ached as if she'd been tied in knots. He'd accept her in the end, he had to. Simon had said it would take time and she'd have to appeal to the most unorthodox aspects of his nature if she was to overcome his resistance. She'd certainly tried that tonight, and tomorrow was another day.

But how difficult it was to conceal her rage and the longing to hurt him as he had hurt Guillaume. Oh, it hadn't been his hand that had wielded the knife, but it had been at his orders. He hadn't known Guillaume, not even known his real name, and yet he'd had him murdered.

How could she possibly seduce such a man? But she had to. She would remember Guillaume, relive his death, and then she would be able to do what had to be done.

2

There were two men in the comfortable study at the back of the tall house on rue d'Anjou. They were an ill-matched pair, Napoleon's Minister for Foreign Affairs and his Minister of Police. Talleyrand, the elegant aristocrat, and the brutal-featured Fouché were as unlike physically as they were in their choice of methods and techniques. But they were both experts at working in the shadows, at achieving their purposes along the tortuous winding paths of secrecy and intrigue, diplomatic in the one case, mercilessly pragmatic in the other.

After Napoleon, they were the two most influential and powerful men in France and, by extension, Napoleonic Europe. In general, they rarely collaborated, each leaving the other his sphere of operations, each courting the ear of Napoleon in his own way. But on this cold January night in Paris, with Napoleon preparing to face the Russian army in Eastern Prussia, they had come together to discuss the progress of a plan where both their interests meshed.

"She was making contact this weekend at the Vanbrugh house in Kent." Talleyrand sipped cognac, gesturing to his guest that he should refill his own glass.

Fouché's fingers around the delicate crystal decanter were thick and coarse, the nails ragged, tufts of hair sprouting on the red knuckles. Talleyrand tapped the tapering white soft-skinned fingers of a pampered aristocrat on the polished wooden arm of his chair.

"What does she know of Praed?" Fouché asked before taking a deep swallow from his liberally recharged glass.

"That he's the cleverest spymaster the English have yet produced . . . that so far we haven't been able to get close to him . . . that it's her assignment to do so."

"And provide us with the means to remove him permanently," Fouché declared, smacking his lips as he savored his cognac.

Talleyrand winced slightly. Fouché was so unsubtle. As it happened, removing Nathaniel Praed was the last thing the Minister for Foreign Affairs wanted, but Fouché didn't need to know that. It suited both of them to have Gabrielle infiltrating the English secret service, and they had combined their resources to achieve it. Fouché wanted a double agent in England to enable him to wreak havoc with that nation's secret service, and Talleyrand, much more devious, wanted a line of communication directly into the ear of the English government. Nathaniel Praed via Gabrielle was to be that ear.

For the moment the two men could work together toward their differing goals. If Fouché's goal interfered with Talleyrand's at some future point, then the Minister for Foreign Affairs would deal with it.

"You believe the woman will succeed in infiltrating their system?" Fouché regarded his host with shrewd eyes as he posed the question.

Talleyrand nodded. "Gabrielle's been one of our most resourceful and intrepid couriers for the last five years, throughout her liaison with *le lièvre noir*. This mission requires different skills, of course, but she's a woman of passionate convictions and determination, intent on avenging her lover's murder. She *will* succeed."

"I wish to God I knew who'd betrayed him," Fouché declared with a savage twist to his mouth. "To lose our top agent in such fashion! *Mon dieu*, it makes me want to spit!"

His mouth pursed and Talleyrand grimaced, thinking he was about to suit action to words, but Fouché restrained himself, draining the contents of his brandy goblet in one gulp.

There was a moment's silence. The fire spurted and a candle flared as a needle of frigid air found its way under the door.

"However," Talleyrand said finally, "as we agreed, there's a way to pull the chestnuts out of this fire. Gabrielle will turn disadvantage to advantage. Once she's gained Praed's trust, she will bring us, among other information, a list of the English agents presently working in France. If Guillaume was betrayed by an English double agent in our own ranks, we'll discover it."

"You're sure there's nothing to connect Gabrielle de Beaucaire with *le lièvre?*"

"Nothing," Talleyrand said firmly. "Their love affair was known only to myself. Gabrielle, as you know, is my goddaughter. Her father was one of my dearest boyhood friends. It was natural that I should offer her my protection when she returned from England after the Revolution. She met Guillaume one night when he was visiting me in secret. They became lovers almost immediately."

A shadow fell over the haughty countenance as Talleyrand remembered the passion of the two young people, the overpowering attraction that had swept them into one of the most turbulent and intense love affairs he'd ever been privileged to promote.

Fouché made no comment. Such liaisons were much more frequent than the fashionable world officially recognized.

"Inevitably with such a passionate affair, Gabrielle discovered the truth about Guillaume and how he served France. I felt he had perhaps yielded up his secrets rather too easily . . ." Talleyrand shrugged with a half-smile, remembering how he'd rebuked the young man for unprofessional indiscretion. Guillaume had most vigorously defended both himself and his mistress, and he'd been proved right.

"Gabrielle insisted on playing her own part in the service and *le lièvre* trained her as a courier. As her cover, she took part in society as my goddaughter and the widow of the completely fictional Comte de Beaucaire, who, it's believed, died tragically and very suddenly on his estates in the Midi. But her real life she lived in the shadows."

He spread his hands wide. "They met only in the deepest secrecy and waited for the moment when they could live again in the open . . . marry, have children." He shook his head. "It was not to be."

"No," said Fouché with a touch of impatience. He was a man devoid of sentiment. "And she will seduce this Praed?"

"If necessary."

The bland statement drew a smile from the policeman. "You're as cold-blooded as I am," he commented, rising to his feet. "Notwithstanding the bishop's miter, Talleyrand."

"An excommunicated bishop," Talleyrand corrected calmly, rising with his guest. "One who loves his country. You will leave by the back entrance?" His eyebrows lifted.

"How else?" Fouché agreed. "There are sharp eyes around, and our emperor would not be happy to hear that his Minister for Foreign Affairs and his Minister of Police have secret conferences."

Talleyrand smiled. "*D'accord.* I suspect that our master would regard an alliance between us as more formidable than another Trafalgar."

"And he'd be correct," Fouché said with another dry smile.

Talleyrand returned to the fire as the door closed on the policeman. He and Fouché made uneasy bedfellows, but they played a game of intrigue where the stakes were of the highest: The Emperor Napoleon was to be toppled from his imperial throne. They would work together toward this goal, using their different techniques and spheres of influence, and one day they would succeed. And when that day came, their uneasy alliance would be shattered as they became rivals for the power vacuum thus created.

Talleyrand sipped his cognac thoughtfully. Fouché knew this as well as he did himself, but until then he was as prepared as Talleyrand to use his arch rival in the interests of expediency.

The world didn't lack for interest, he reflected, taking a copy of Voltaire's *Candide* from the bookshelves. He riffled through it, chuckling at Pangloss's eternal passive optimism: *All's for the best in the best of all possible worlds.* Disagreement with that particular philosophy was one belief Napoleon's Minister for Foreign Affairs and his Minister of Police had in common. There was always room for change.

At Vanbrugh Court, Gabrielle slept the sleep of the just, her dreams untroubled by the obstinacy of Lord Nathaniel Praed. She awoke before the maid brought her hot chocolate, feeling as refreshed as if she hadn't spent a part of the night scaling the walls. She sprang from bed and flung open the curtains, looking out on a perfect winter morning with pale early sun sparking off the hoarfrost on the lawn beneath her window.

She craned her neck outside, looking along the creeper-thick façade of the house toward Nathaniel Praed's window, wondering if he'd decided to close it after his nocturnal visitor had left. In the cold light of day, the climb from the gravel path below looked rather more daunting than it had in the night, but she'd been too set on her goal for apprehension then.

She turned away from the window as the maid knocked and entered with a tray of chocolate and sweet biscuits.

"You're up betimes, madam," the girl said, setting the tray beside the bed. "Cold as the grave it is in 'ere. Best close that window, and I'll get the fire goin'."

"Thank you, Maisie." Gabrielle, shivering in her thin nightgown, closed the window and jumped back into bed, watching as the girl bent to the hearth, expertly raked the ashes, and threw on kindling.

"Shall I lay out your habit, ma'am?" The maid straightened, dusting off her hands as the fire blazed in the grate.

"Please." Gabrielle poured chocolate in a rich aromatic stream from the silver pot.

"The boot boy blacked your boots nicely," Maisie observed, holding Gabrielle's riding boots of cordovan leather up to the light, examining them for any residual sign of scuff marks.

Gabrielle murmured vague assent. It had been agreed with Talleyrand that she should travel without her own maid, relying on Georgiana's staff. The fewer people close to her, the less dangerous any inadvertent errors would be, and she'd have much more freedom of movement if she had only herself to consider.

Maisie bustled around with jugs of hot water, lacing, buttoning, brushing hair, all the while chatting cheerfully about her pregnant sister's latest ailments and the poacher the gamekeeper had caught during the night. Gabrielle allowed the chat to wash over her, murmuring vaguely when it seemed required. Her own thoughts were fixed on the day ahead and how best to renew her attack on Nathaniel Praed.

An hour later she made her way down to the breakfast parlor, humming an old nursery rhyme softly

to herself: *A-hunting we will go, a-hunting we will go.
We'll catch a fox and put him in a box. A-hunting we will
go.*

But her quarry today would be more than just Rey-
nard.

A footman jumped to open the door to the breakfast parlor and she went in to find herself alone with
Lord Praed.

"Good morning, sir." She greeted him with a casual
smile as if she had never climbed into his bedchamber
and sat on the edge of his bed in the middle of the
night. "We seem to be ahead of the others."

"Yes," he agreed shortly, barely looking up from his
plate.

"A lovely day," she persevered, lifting the lids of
the chafing dishes on the sideboard.

"Yes."

"Perfect for hunting."

There was no reply.

"Oh, forgive me. Are you one of those people who
hates to talk at the breakfast table?" The crooked smile
was faintly mocking.

Lord Praed's response was something between a
grunt and a snort.

Gabrielle helped herself to a dish of kedgeree and
sat down at the far end of the long table, as far from
her taciturn breakfast companion as she could manage.
She hummed the silly nursery rhyme to herself as she
buttered toast, studiously avoiding looking at
Nathaniel.

"Must you?" Lord Praed demanded abruptly, a deep
frown corrugating his forehead, the greenish-brown eyes
filled with irritation.

"Must I what?" She looked up in innocent, puzzled
inquiry.

"Sing that damn song," he said. "It's getting on my
nerves."

"Oh, yes," she said with a serene smile. "It's getting

on mine too, but I can't get it out of my head. It's going round and round. You know the way these silly songs do."

"No, I'm happy to say I don't know," he snapped.

Gabrielle shrugged and reached for the coffeepot. "I must say, Lord Praed, that if I disliked company at breakfast as much as you do, I'd make quite certain I breakfasted alone."

"That was exactly what I was trying to do. Most people don't appear in the breakfast parlor before half past seven, by which time I'm long gone."

"My, that was a long speech," Gabrielle observed admiringly. "Could you pass the milk, please."

Nathaniel pushed back his chair with a noisy scrape on the polished floor, picked up the silver creamer, and marched the length of the table, depositing it beside her coffee cup with such force that milk slurped over the top.

"Thank you," she said sweetly, mopping at the spill with her table napkin.

Nathaniel stared down at her for a minute in impotent exasperation. Then he spun on his heel and marched out of the room, narrowly avoiding a collision with Miles Bennet and Miss Bayberry, who were deep in chatter as they entered the breakfast room.

"Morning, Nathaniel." Miles greeted his friend cheerfully. "I suppose you've breakfasted already in splendid isolation."

"On the contrary," Nathaniel said, and went on his way.

Grinning, Miles held out a chair for Miss Bayberry. "Good morning, Gabby. I gather you've disturbed our friend's need for solitude at break of day."

"So it would seem," Gabrielle agreed tranquilly. "He should eat in his room if he hates company that much."

The table filled rapidly with avid hunters, and Gabrielle went up to her room soon after to fetch her hat, gloves, and whip. Nathaniel Praed had been in riding britches and coat, so presumably he intended joining the hunt. Although, if he was as morose on the field as at the breakfast table, it might prove difficult to engage him in pointful discourse. But it was always possible that the opportunity for some more unconventional contact might present itself.

Nathaniel also traveled without personal servants, for much the same reasons as Gabrielle. He straightened his stock in front of the mirror and dusted off his top hat against his thigh. He looked neat and conventional, but unremarkable. The Comtesse de Beaucaire, on the other hand, had taken his breath away when she'd first walked into the breakfast parlor, although he trusted he hadn't given her the satisfaction of seeing it.

If ever a woman knew how to dress to advantage, the countess did. Most tall women tried to disguise their height, Gabrielle made the most of it. The black riding habit had been as severely cut as her gown of the previous evening, clinging to the lines of her body in a most seductive fashion. Emerald-green braiding was the only adornment, and he seemed to remember that at her throat she'd worn a snowy white muslin cravat with an emerald pin.

How the hell had he managed to notice all that while she'd been disturbing his peace with inane prattle?

He'd obey the dictates of courtesy and wait for Simon to join them, and then he'd tell him exactly what he thought of his underhand scheming, and then he'd leave . . . go into Hampshire for some peace and quiet. Check on Jake.

Jake. Just thinking about the child produced a surge of unease and dismay. What had Miles been getting at last evening, when he'd asked what Jake thought of his life? What right did a six-year-old child have to an opinion on such a matter?

The boy's brown eyes hung in his father's internal

vision. Thick-lashed, liquid, emotional. Helen's eyes. His hair, curly, fair, with even fairer streaks. Helen's hair. The dimple on his chin. Helen's dimple; Helen's chin.

Helen's exhausted face on the pillow . . . so white, whiter than it was possible for living flesh. The glazing mist in the eyes gazing up at him with such desperate dependent need . . . trusting that Nathaniel wouldn't let anything bad happen to her.

And he'd failed her. She'd been dead when they pulled Jake with their ghastly instruments from her body. She'd never looked upon the child whose life had taken her own.

It was six years in the past, and yet it felt like yesterday. Would the torment ever cease? Surely a merciful God had some statute of limitations on the emotional agonies of memory, the devastating misery of an unreasonable guilt that couldn't be absolved.

The imperative summons of a hunting horn broke into the bleak circular thoughts. He picked up his gloves and whip and left the room. A day on the hunting field would banish the memories, at least temporarily. A tired body was a great panacea.

He saw Gabrielle de Beaucaire when he stepped through the front door and stood looking down at the milling throng of huntsmen, dogs, riders congregated on the circular gravel sweep before the house. The countess wore a tricorn hat with a silver plume sweeping her shoulder, and she sat a black hunter, her skirts blending with the animal's glossy coat.

As if aware of his observation, she turned slightly and looked directly at him. He was too far away to see her expression clearly, but it was all too easy to imagine the mocking glimmer in the charcoal eyes, the small, crooked smile—he'd seen them often enough. For a moment he felt as if she were holding him with her gaze, as if she'd robbed him of the will to move. Then she bent to take the stirrup cup being proffered by a footman; a groom brought Nathaniel's rat-tailed gray and the spell was broken. He mounted swiftly and eased his horse to the edge of the throng away from the animated conversations and shouted greetings, the curses of the huntservants as they whipped in the hounds.

Gabrielle tossed the hot spiced wine in the stirrup cup down her throat in approved fashion and handed the cup back to the footman before remarking to her neighbor, "Lord Praed really doesn't care for his fellow man, does he, Miles?"

Miles chuckled. "You've noticed."

"Hard to miss. Look at him hovering on the outskirts." She frowned. "Any special reason?"

"He's been like that since his wife died in childbirth six years ago. He adored her."

"Oh." Gabrielle was silent. Talleyrand had given her no personal details about the man she was here to seduce and betray. Simon, dear, kind Simon, drawn all unwitting into the plan, had said only that Nathaniel was a difficult man and Gabrielle would have to find her own way of dealing with him.

But she didn't want to feel sorry for him. She didn't want to understand him or know anything about the secret nooks and crannies of his soul. She was going to use him, pure and simple, and avenge Guillaume's death in the process. Seeing the man as human with a tragedy in his past would clutter up the purity of her plan and its motives.

"There's a lad ... Jake ..." Miles was continuing, not party to Gabrielle's thoughts. "Nice child, but withdrawn from his father. Nathaniel doesn't seem to know how to handle him. I imagine because the boy's the spitting image of his mother."

No, she definitely didn't want to hear this. "I expect he'll get over it," she said with a shrug. She could hear how cold and callous she sounded and was aware of Miles's disapproving surprise. But there was nothing she could do about it.

"The huntsman was saying they're going to draw Dunnet's Spinney," she said, changing the subject. "They usually find there."

"Let's hope it's a good day." Miles offered her a half-bow and moved away with a touch of frost to his smile.

The huntsman blew up for the start and the hounds set off in a baying, snapping exuberant pack, the whippers-in bawling at them in a language only they and the dogs could understand. The meet moved down the long driveway, Gabrielle expertly ensuring herself a position in the front just behind the hounds, the huntsman, and the huntservants.

Nathaniel watched her maneuvering with an eye of reluctant respect as he edged to the front himself. Gabrielle de Beaucaire was clearly an aggressive rider who knew her way around the hunting field. Something he was obliged to admit that they shared. Even if he had to ride beside her, he wasn't prepared to hang back. He drew alongside her mount, offering a brief nod of greeting.

"Are you as reluctant for conversation on horseback as at the breakfast table, Lord Praed? Or may I venture to address you without having my head bitten off?"

The question was asked in dulcet tones, accompanied by a sideways glance of glinting amusement and more than a hint of challenge. Some force seemed to emanate from her. He'd felt it the night before, but it seemed even stronger now. Again he had the sense that she had marked him for something, that she knew something he didn't. He'd thought the purpose of her nighttime visit had explained that feeling, but it was just as powerful now.

"So long as you don't sing that damned song," he said, and found himself smiling.

The smile was a revelation. Instead of brown stone, his eyes became a warm, merry hazel. The lean features softened, little crinkly lines appeared at the corners of his eyes, and his mouth lost its harshness.

Gabrielle realized with a flash of astonishment that Nathaniel Praed was a very attractive man when he wanted to be.

"A-hunting we will go; a-hunting we will go," she sang softly, laughing. "It's your fault, Lord Praed, for reminding me. Now I can't get it out of my head again. We'll catch a fox—"

"Gabrielle, stop it!"

"I'll need an inducement, sir."

Pure mischief. But suggestive mischief. He could hear the suggestion as clearly as if she'd articulated it. His mind whirled. The woman was flirting with him. He hadn't flirted with a woman for eight years, not since he'd met Helen. It wasn't Helen's style, she'd been too innocent and straightforward.

He realized that he no longer knew how to respond with the right touch, and the realization made him feel as tongue-tied and embarrassed as a schoolboy.

"I was thinking," she said, her voice now serious, offering welcome distraction from his ineptitude. "I was thinking that you could give me some kind of test so that I could prove how useful I could be to you."

"*What?*" His exclamation was low but nonetheless forceful.

"A test," she said patiently. "A task to perform . . . some information to get . . . or—"

"Quiet!" he said, making a chopping movement with his hand. "Of all the indiscreet—"

"No," she interrupted. "Not indiscreet at all. How could anyone know what we're talking about? Even if anyone was listening. We're well ahead of the field." She gestured behind them. It was true they were riding alone at the moment.

This fact, however, did nothing to defuse

Nathaniel's outrage. He cursed Simon for exposing his identity to this loose-tongued woman who clearly thought that the deadly serious business in which he was involved was some kind of game.

"I don't know what the hell Simon thought he was doing," he said with low-voiced fury. "No one, I repeat, no one, outside the government and the service knows what I do. Not even Miles. And now you have the temerity to chat with total insouciance about a matter of life and death in the middle of a goddamned hunting field!"

"You exaggerate," she said, not a whit put out by this attack. "I've already proved to Simon how useful I can be, which is why he agreed to present me to you. You can ask him all about it."

"Oh, I intend to, believe me," Lord Praed said grimly.

"Besides," Gabrielle continued as if she hadn't heard him. "I'd have thought it made good sense to have conversations where secrecy is vital in such public places. No one would ever suspect anything. And no one can hear a thing. It seems like a very sensible tactic to me. One could pass on a nugget of precious information in the middle of a dinner party without anyone being any the wiser if it was done cleverly." She shot him a sideways glance, one black eyebrow raised quizzically.

Nathaniel ground his teeth. It was perfectly true and a tactic he favored himself. But to hear it expounded in self-defense by a spoiled, bored society woman was almost too much to endure.

"Cry truce," she now said. "You know I'm right. And I can safely promise you that I am never indiscreet. I'll not betray your confidence. Simon knows that. But then, he knows me rather better than you do, although I hope that will soon be remedied," she added pensively.

"Madame, that is a hope I am afraid I do not share." With compressed lips he fell back as they reached a hunting gate leading into a covert. The hounds surged forward and the hunt followed in relatively slow single file.

Nathaniel hung back, allowing Gabrielle to get well ahead. There were only two ways to deal with trouble: confront it or run from it. The latter struck him as the only sensible course when dealing with the trouble embodied in the Comtesse de Beaucaire.

Gabrielle rode on, wondering if she'd moved one step forward or two steps back. There'd been that moment of warmth and humor, but had she negated it by moving too quickly? But she had to move quickly. She had only this week. Once the spymaster left Vanbrugh Court, there was no knowing when she'd be in his vicinity again, let alone under the same roof. Certainly it was unlikely she'd have such a good opportunity another time to work on him.

The huntsman's strange vocalizing among his baying, searching pack suddenly changed tenor and her head snapped up, all thoughts of anything but the fox banished with the familiar surge of excitement that curled her toes in her boots.

The huntsman's horn blew, a long two-note resonance in the frosty air. The hounds in full cry tore across the covert, and then came the bellow from one of the huntservants that sent the blood coursing through Gabrielle's veins.

"Gone away!" Someone had seen the fox break from the covert.

The huntsman blew the note for any who'd failed to grasp the message and the entire field surged forward, breaking out of the trees, hooves pounding the frozen ground, breath steaming in the frosty air.

A long slope of meadowland lay ahead, and Gabrielle abruptly pulled her mount aside as the riders plunged past her.

"Nathaniel!" she yelled as she saw him pulling ahead of the main body. "This way!"

She was unaware that she'd used his name in her urgent need to attract his attention. She was aware now only that he was as eager and intrepid a huntsman as she was and she would share with him her own private knowledge garnered from hunting this land in childhood.

He veered toward her without conscious reflection of his own, and she charged ahead of him, giving him a lead to the far corner of the meadow.

He registered the massive bramble-studded thicket hedge in a kind of daze as Gabrielle's horse gathered itself for the jump.

It was impossible, he thought. A suicide jump. And then his own mount was collecting himself, adjusting his stride, and he was sailing through the air. Only when they landed on the other side did Nathaniel absorb the wide ice-covered ditch they'd also had to clear at the base of the hedge behind them.

Of all the wild, reckless madwomen! But he had no time for further thought. She was racing ahead of him across a flat field toward a mercifully lower hedge at the bottom, and the excitement of the chase was in his blood, the frantic baying of the hounds sounding ever closer, the squall of the huntsman's horn filling his ears.

They sailed over the hedge and he saw they were way ahead of the field, right up behind the huntsman and his hounds, and the fox was a smudge of reddish-brown streaking toward a spinney to the right of them.

Neck and neck, they pounded behind the hounds and into the spinney, the rest of the field some hundred yards behind them. The pack of hounds abruptly lost direction and began rushing around in confused circles, yipping frantically.

Gabrielle drew rein just in time to stop herself from overtaking the hounds and committing the cardinal sin of destroying any scents in the process.

"He's gone to ground," she gasped. "I don't know

whether to be glad or sorry. Wasn't that a wonderful run?"

Her hat was slightly askew, dark red ringlets escaping from its confines. The translucent pallor of her complexion had taken on a rosy glow and the dark eyes were alight. Nathaniel's head spun again.

"You're mad," he declared. "Of all the crazy, reckless pieces of riding! There had to be an easier way over that hedge."

Gabrielle looked at him as if he'd taken on some strange, alien shape. "Of course there was. But we wanted to be ahead of the field."

"That's no excuse."

She continued to stare at him in incomprehension. "What are you saying?"

"That it was a piece of the most foolhardy risk-taking I've ever witnessed," he said flatly.

"Well, why did you follow me if you were scared?"

"I was not scared. It was all right for me to take the fence; my mount is bigger and more powerful than yours."

"Oh, wait a minute," she said softly. "This is nothing to do with horses, is it, Lord Praed? This is to do with what men can do and women can't ... or do I mean *shouldn't?*"

"You can mean what you wish," he said. "But you've demonstrated yet again that you lack the qualities to join the service. I told you last night that reckless endangerment of oneself and others is unacceptable."

"Nonsense," Gabrielle said stoutly. "There was nothing reckless about that. My mount is one of Simon's hunters. He's well up to the weight of a grown man, let alone mine, and very powerful. Besides, I've jumped that fence hundreds of times. Georgie's family estates march with the Vanbrughs' and I hunted this land almost every winter until a few years ago."

"You don't stop to contemplate consequences,

madame," he declared. "Such habits make for a dangerous and untrustworthy partner."

Impatiently he glared around at the frustrated pack of hounds, the cursing huntsman, and the milling riders as they straggled into the spinney. "This is going nowhere. Why don't they move on and draw another covert?"

"They'll move to Hogart's Wood in a minute," Gabrielle said thoughtfully. There was no point defending herself verbally against such a wealth of misguided prejudice. They'd end up in a shouting match that would achieve nothing. A different, more challenging approach was needed.

"If you'll excuse me, Lord Praed, I think I'll make my way to the wood now. There's a shortcut. You won't wish to take it, of course, since it involves another rather sizable hurdle. But I'm sure you won't miss anything if you follow the body of the field."

She turned her horse and cantered off down the ride leading out of the spinney. Hooves sounded behind her with satisfying immediacy, and she smiled to herself, leaning low over the horse's neck as they emerged onto a stretch of gorse-strewn common land. She nudged his flanks and the animal broke into an easy gallop. She hadn't exaggerated when she'd said he was well up to a weight considerably more than her own. It gave her the advantage of speed in this race she was running with Nathaniel Praed.

They raced across the common, up a relatively steep hill, and then down the other side. The obstacle she intended to jump was a ten-foot stone wall at the bottom of the hill bounding the orchard of a sizable farmhouse. Hogart's Wood lay on the far side of the orchard and the hounds would have to be taken around the wall. An intrepid rider could thus ensure he was on the spot when the hounds drew the wood.

Nathaniel didn't know why he was following her. Except that she'd needled him again with that derisive challenge. Except that he couldn't seem to keep his distance. Except that he seemed in her company to follow impulse in as headstrong a fashion as the Comtesse de Beaucaire.

He saw the wall ahead—mellow golden stone in the crisp sunlight, dwarfing the horse and rider pounding toward it. He wanted to yell at her not to be a fool, but the black was already gathering himself for the effort and he knew he couldn't risk putting the animal off his stride by startling him. A hesitation would be enough to throw him off balance, and if his hooves so much as clipped the top of the wall at that height and terrifying speed, he would go down, hurling his rider to the ground like a cannonball from the breach of a gun.

He closed his eyes involuntarily and when he opened them again the wall was almost upon him and it was too late to bring his own hunter to a halt even if he'd wanted to. The animal, like all horses, simply followed his leader in blind trust.

For a dizzying moment they were in the air and then landed with a jolt on solid ground amid the apple trees of Farmer Gregson's orchard.

Gabrielle's horse stood panting, reins hanging loose from his neck. On the ground beside him lay the still figure of his rider, her hat flung several feet from her body, her black habit spread over the damp, dark green grass beneath the trees.

3

Nathaniel flung himself from his horse and ran to the inert figure.

"Gabrielle! Dear God!" He dropped to his knees beside her, tearing at the snowy cravat to bare her throat, his fingers feeling for her pulse. It was strong but fast beneath his fingertip. He sighed with relief and then frowned. The black lashes formed half-moons on the pale skin, her lips were slightly parted, her chest rising and falling with each regular breath.

Her pulse was far too vibrant for an unconscious person.

"Gabrielle," he said in a near whisper. "If this is a trick, so help me, I'll make you sorrier than you've ever been in your life."

"Try it," she said. Her eyelids swept up, revealing utterly mischievous charcoal eyes, and in the same moment she sat up. Her arms went around his neck before he realized what was happening, and he could smell her warm skin tinged with the freshness of the winter air. Her mouth found his and he could taste her sweetness as the pliant lips opened beneath his and her tongue ran lightly over his mouth. Her body was pressed to his, her gloved hands palming his scalp. He could feel her heart beating against his chest.

And a wildness swept through him. His arms went around her, and his hands spread over her back, feeling her supple slenderness, the rippling play of her muscles as she obeyed the pressure and reached against him. For a minute their tongues fenced, half in play half in war, and then he moved his hands to grasp her head, holding it strongly as he drove deep within her mouth on a voyage of assertion that in some faint part of his brain seemed long overdue.

Gabrielle had believed she could fake sufficient response to satisfy him. She had been prepared for revulsion and had trusted she would be able to control it sufficiently for her purposes. She had expected to take her pleasure in the satisfaction of fooling him, of achieving her goal.

She had not been prepared for what was happening. She had not expected to find herself responding from some deep, passionate well within herself as the red mist of arousal engulfed her and she could smell him and feel him and taste him ... and she wanted him. She wanted him as vitally as she had ever wanted Guillaume. She wanted him in the same way, wanton and unthinking, the visceral responses of her body overtaking, suppressing any possible restraints of the brain.

It wasn't supposed to happen. But it was happening. And Nathaniel Praed was matching her every step of the way. The knowledge was in her blood, transmitted from his skin to hers.

And it was going to play merry hell with schemes of revenge.

At long last his grip on her head slackened, his flat palm passed in a soft, caressing motion over her hair, and he raised his head. Her mouth felt bereft, and she knew her face was open and vulnerable, the truth of her responses naked in her eyes, but she could no more dissemble than she could cut her own head off.

Nathaniel's expression was as bewildered and as open as her own, his eyes no longer hard and flat but deep and luminous, desire burning like a candle in their misty depths.

"How the *hell* did that happen?" he said softly, touching his own mouth with a wondering finger before running the same finger over Gabrielle's lips.

"It seemed ... seems ... as if it *had* to happen," she said with much the same bemused wonder.

Nathaniel hadn't kissed a woman for six years. He'd had women, fly-by-night encounters for the most part, satisfying a sharp bodily need and then forgotten, not the kind of encounters to include lingering, passionate kisses.

Sitting back on his heels, he regarded Gabrielle with a puzzled frown. She returned the look with a slight quizzical smile in her eyes, no hint of the mockery he was accustomed to. Then he shook his head in an abrupt irritable gesture of dismissal. The grass beneath his knees was unpleasantly damp and cold, and he'd just indulged in a piece of flagrant idiocy, allowed himself to be manipulated by a spoiled woman who had nothing better to do with her life than play silly games. Or so he told himself.

He stood up, brushing at the damp patches on his knees, just as the huntsman's horn sounded from the far side of the orchard.

"*Merde!*" exclaimed the countess inelegantly, springing to her feet. "After all that, they've reached Hogart's Wood ahead of us. Help me to mount, please. I can't manage Simon's hunters without a mounting block."

"It'll serve you right to walk home," Lord Praed declared unhelpfully. "I'm damned if I'm going to encourage you to play any more tricks." With which unfriendly statement, he swung onto his own mount and cantered toward the gate out of the orchard.

"Well, of all the—" Gabrielle swallowed the expletive. It was of no practical use in her present predicament. She'd have her revenge on Lord Praed in her own good time. She looked around the orchard for a substitute mounting block. Dismounting from the black had been a simple operation, and she'd been so fired with her plan that she hadn't thought about the logistics of the reverse maneuver. But then, it hadn't occurred to her that Nathaniel Praed would be so bloody-minded.

She picked up her hat, crammed it on her head, led the black back to the wall, found a toehold made by an uneven stone a couple of feet off the ground, and scrambled somehow into the saddle, thankful that there were no witnesses to the undignified process. She took a minute to adjust the plume of her hat on her shoulder, smooth her skirts over the pommel, and retie her cravat. She remembered the rough haste with which he'd pulled it free of her throat, and for a second her fingers touched her skin where Nathaniel had touched her and a shiver crept down her spine, her skin tingling with memory.

Dear God! Fate had really stirred the pot with a busy hand. But maybe it could be turned to good account. If he found the attraction as hard to resist as Gabrielle knew she did, then matters could well proceed apace.

It hadn't occurred to Nathaniel that Gabrielle would be defeated by his own lack of assistance, and he wasn't surprised when she trotted into the wood some five minutes after he'd reached the hunt. The hounds were making a cast, trying to pick up the scent of the fox, and the field milled around, waiting for something to happen.

"It's not like Gabrielle to turn up in the rear of the

field," Miles observed, unscrewing the silver cap of a hip flask and offering it to Nathaniel.

"Isn't it?" Nathaniel managed to sound indifferent as he took a swig of the cognac and handed back the flask.

"You really haven't taken to each other, have you?" Miles observed, drinking in his turn before returning the flask to his pocket. "It's funny, but I'd have thought her spirit might have appealed to you. She's unusual, and you're always bored by the conventional."

"She's trouble," Nathaniel stated without compromise.

Miles's eyebrows shot into his scalp. His friend's reaction to the Comtesse de Beaucaire was clearly far from indifferent, even if it wasn't warm. However, he only said lightly, "She's always been something of an *enfant terrible*, I grant you."

The hounds caught a scent and with a great hue and cry set off after it, the field following with rather less enthusiasm than they'd shown at the beginning of the morning.

"The problem with hunting," Miles observed as he and Nathaniel cantered side by side, "is that it alternates frantic bursts of energy and excitement with long periods of boredom and idleness in the cold. How about peeling off here for some sustenance? There's an inn across the next field which does a very tolerable shepherd's pie. And an excellent stilton."

Nathaniel shook his head, his eyes on the black horse and his black-clad rider ahead of them. He realized with a sense of the inevitable that he had no intention of leaving the field before Gabrielle de Beaucaire. "I'll see what this run brings, Miles."

"As you wish. I'm for a tankard of ale and some nuncheon. My toes are frozen." Miles turned his horse aside and galloped away from the hunt.

A few minutes later the fox broke cover and the hounds were in full cry. Nathaniel gave his horse his

head and came up with Gabrielle as they charged hell
for leather across a plowed field. She shot him a quick
sideways glance as he reached her and he called, "This
time, Madame Reckless, I am going to give you a lead."

Her laugh was rich and exultant. "You won't lose
me, Lord Praed, I can assure you."

"Oh, I know that," he called back, his eyes glittering. And neither of them missed the underlying meaning of their words. Something had been started that
would not soon be finished. But neither of them was as
yet prepared to put a name to what it was.

The chase took them across four fields and
Gabrielle was at his heels throughout. They sailed over
hedge and stream and he could almost feel her breath
on his back. The frigid January air whistled past their
ears; the hooves crashed over the hard-ridged furrows of
the plowed fields; they plunged into a copse and he
heard her laughing curse as a branch whipped her
cheek and she dropped low on the horse's neck.

And at the kill she sat her panting horse steadily,
with no sign of flinching from the swift and bloody
slaughter.

Nathaniel felt again the power emanating from the
tall, taut figure. He was responding to the wildness, the
passion, the force that drove her, and he couldn't help
himself. Fearless and unconventional, Gabrielle de
Beaucaire spelled a form of trouble he didn't think he
could resist, not if he stayed in her vicinity.

He waited for her to show some fatigue as the day
wore on. Or at least to say that she was hungry. But she
stayed at the head of the field, unflagging and uncom-
plaining. He was famished and knew she must be too,
but he couldn't bring himself to admit a need that his
indomitable companion ignored. They exchanged few
words but their paths never veered. Sometimes
Gabrielle took the lead, sometimes he did. And
Nathaniel began to feel they were engaged in an un-

spoken competition. Which of them would call a halt first?

In the end it was Gabrielle who said, "We'd better turn back. We're about ten miles from Vanbrugh Court and we'll be lucky to make it home before dusk."

"The horses are tired," he offered in assent.

Gabrielle shot him a quick glance at this bland observation and her lips twitched. "So am I."

"Oh, are you? I feel as fresh as I did this morning."

"That's a Banbury story if ever I heard one," she said, refusing to rise to provocation. "If we go this way, we can clip a mile off the ride." She gestured with her whip across a style.

"And how many times do we risk breaking our necks?"

She seemed to consider the question. "Twice." Chuckling, she turned her horse and jumped the style.

It was nearly dusk when the weary horses trotted up the drive of Vanbrugh Court. A postchaise with the Vanbrugh arms on its panels was being driven away from the front door. "Simon must have just arrived," Gabrielle observed.

Nathaniel made no comment. Once he'd spoken his mind to his host, he would be free to leave the trouble and temptation resident in Vanbrugh Court before matters became any worse. He'd be on the road by dawn.

Gabrielle swung down from her mount without assistance, but Nathaniel's sharp eyes noticed that she wavered for a second as her feet touched solid ground and the straight back curved slightly, her shoulders drooping.

So she wasn't completely invincible. It was a small satisfaction. He put a hand lightly under her elbow as they went up the steps to the open front door. The touch was electrifying, and he heard her sharp indrawn breath.

"Oh, there you are!" Georgie came out of the library. "You're the last to come back. I was beginning to worry."

"Gabby's always the last to return from a hunt," her husband commented, following her into the hall.

Simon Vanbrugh was a rotund man with a genial expression enlivened by a pair of very shrewd gray eyes. His assessing gaze ran over the new arrivals. Had Gabrielle managed to win over the prejudiced spymaster? It was hard to tell, but they'd presumably spent the day together and there was a promising informality to Nathaniel's supporting hand beneath her elbow.

"Did she wear you out, Nathaniel?" He laughed lightly as he bent to kiss his wife's cousin. He and Georgie had grown up as neighbors and had been childhood sweethearts, so Simon had known Gabby almost as long as his wife had.

"Did I, Lord Praed?" Gabrielle turned to look at her escort with a cool arch smile.

"I don't believe so, madame," he said, suddenly stiff and formal. His hand dropped from her elbow. "If you have a minute, Simon, I'd like a word with you."

"Georgie, will you come and talk to me in my bath?" Gabrielle asked as the two men disappeared into the library. "Or must you play hostess for the next hour?"

Georgie shook her head, interest sparkling in her eyes. "Everyone's dressing for dinner. Besides, nothing can take precedence over an account of your day with Nathaniel Praed."

Gabrielle laughed, linking her arm through her cousin's as they mounted the stairs. "I've a tale to tell, Georgie."

In the library Nathaniel flung himself onto a leather sofa with an audible sigh. He stretched out his legs to the fire and examined his mud-splattered boots.

He came to the point with customary lack of ceremony. "What the devil do you mean by foisting that wild woman on me, Simon?"

"Wild? Gabby?" Simon turned from the sideboard, a cut-glass decanter in his hand. "She's not wild, Nathaniel. Oh, a trifle spirited, I grant you, but she's got as cool a head on her shoulders as anyone I know."

"Oh, is that so? And it's a cool head that leads a woman to climb through my bedroom window at one o'clock in the morning? It's a cool head that leads her to jump a ten-foot stone wall as if it's a stack of fire-wood?"

"Claret?" Simon inquired, a chuckle in his voice. "Did she really climb through your window?"

"Thank you." Nathaniel took the proffered glass. "Yes, she did, presenting me with that ridiculous scrap of velvet . . . of all the absurd, fanciful notions. Obviously she thinks the business of the service is some great game of secret signs and amusing clandestine excursions. I tell you, Simon, you had no right, no right at all, to compromise me by revealing my identity to a headstrong, reckless, *wild* woman."

Having thus unburdened himself, Nathaniel drank deeply of his claret.

Simon sat down in a wing chair opposite him and thoughtfully sipped his own wine. "You're not compromised, Nathaniel. You should know better than to imagine I would reveal your identity without good cause."

He leaned back in his chair and took a pinch of snuff. "Gabby came to me some weeks ago. You remember that interesting piece of information we received about Napoleon's intention to attack Sicily?"

Nathaniel nodded, his eyes sharp with attention. The piece of intelligence from a hitherto unknown source had enabled the government to strengthen the British fleet protecting the Bourbon king in Sicily. The show of strength had changed Napoleon's mind somewhat abruptly.

"Well, it came from Gabby." Simon permitted himself a satisfied smile as he saw his companion's reaction. "She learned it from Talleyrand and brought it to me as an indication of her ability and her desire to act as an intelligence agent for England. I discussed it with Portland, of course, and we decided you should make the decision. Even if you decide against her, I will vouch absolutely for her discretion. I've known her since she was eight years old. She's unusual. She's clever. She has wit and courage. And she most desperately wants to be of service to England."

"Even if I grant she has some of those qualities, you know I do *not* employ women." Nathaniel stood up and went to refill his glass.

"There are exceptions to every rule," his host reminded him. "Tell me where you would find another agent so perfectly placed, so impeccably qualified? She has entrees into every diplomatic, political, and social circle in Paris. Talleyrand is her godfather, man!"

"And she's prepared to betray him?" Nathaniel looked skeptical.

"She grew up in England," Simon explained. "When Talleyrand insisted she return to France, she was very unhappy. But he was in essence in loco parentis, and she really had no choice but to obey him. But she's always been clear where her true loyalties lie. They lie here."

Simon leaned forward and kicked a fallen log back into the grate. "After her husband's death, she became very depressed . . . listless. Her letters had none of the usual spark and vitality. Georgie was worried about her. She invited her to stay for a while and Gabby came to me with the suggestion that she use her position and contacts in France to work for England. She was very convincing." He shrugged lightly. "Her information was *most* convincing."

He looked across at his now-silent companion. "She's always had a political mind, unlike Georgie, who most of the time couldn't tell you the members of the cabinet. It doesn't interest her. But Gabby's very different. Her upbringing, perhaps. Losing her parents to the Terror. Talleyrand's influence—whatever. But she knows a great deal. She can sift the wheat from the chaff when it comes to information. And she needs something to absorb her mind." He examined his friend shrewdly as he hammered the nail on the head. "You've been looking for an insider in Paris. Gabby's the best placed."

"I don't deny that." Nathaniel, as Simon knew, could never resist logic and fact. Even his prejudices gave way before such potent persuaders.

Simon sat back, crossing his ankles, his eyes narrowed as they assessed Nathaniel's reaction.

"It won't do." Nathaniel got to his feet again. "Even if she is what you say, I can't see a way to working with her. She's not disciplined and I'll not jeopardize my other people by taking on an unknown quantity."

"Very well." Simon inclined his head courteously. "The decision was always yours. We know you know your own business best."

"Oh, in this respect, Simon, believe me, I do."

There was something about the way Nathaniel said this that struck Simon as a little curious.

Nathaniel put down his glass. "I must change for dinner. I'll leave first thing in the morning, since my business here is done." The door closed behind him.

And what of friendship? Simon thought sadly. Is that done too? Nathaniel saw everything these days in terms of business, and the dictates of friendship meant nothing to him. It hadn't always been the case. Like Miles Bennet, Simon Vanbrugh hoped for the day when the old Nathaniel would emerge from this cold, distant carapace. He'd had the faintest hope that Gabby might have some effect. Few people could come within her orbit and remain unaffected by her personality or her out-

look on life. But it seemed he'd been indulging himself
in wishful thinking.

Upstairs, Gabrielle embalmed her weary muscles in
hot water before a blazing fire in her bedchamber and
told Georgie the details of her day with Lord Praed.

Her cousin was too worldly to be shocked at the
picture of two near strangers locked in an ardent embrace in a deserted orchard. She did, however, somewhat tentatively question Gabrielle's taste.

"I thought you didn't like him. You said his eyes
were like stones at the bottom of a pond."

"So they are sometimes." Gabrielle raised one leg
and soaped it languidly. "But they can also be warm
and merry . . . and *very* passionate," she added with deliberation, switching legs.

"And you're in the market for passion?" Georgie
took a sip from her sherry glass, watching her friend
closely.

"In the market and in the mood," Gabrielle said
calmly. "I've played the grieving widow long enough."

"Gabby!" This did shock Georgie. "You were desolated after your husband's death."

"No, I wasn't," Gabrielle said. "Roland was a
deeply unpleasant man who managed to hide it until
our wedding night. When he died, I was not desolated
in the least. It seemed to me I'd suffer a lot fewer
bruises as his widow than as his wife."

"Oh." Georgie was silent, absorbing this new light
on her cousin's past. "But your letters were so depressed
. . . so listless."

Gabrielle sat up and picked up her own glass of
sherry from the carpet beside the hip bath. Frowning
slightly, she traced a pattern in the condensation on
the glass. "I was depressed, not at Roland's death, but
at the thought that I'd allowed myself to be treated as
badly as he treated me. I'd misread him, fallen for the
façade. I felt a fool . . . and worse." She sipped and put
the glass down again. "It's humiliating to be ill-treated,

Georgie. Not the kind of thing you want people to know about. You begin to think you deserved it in some way."

"Oh, Gabby, I wish you'd said something. . . ." Georgie stumbled in inarticulate sympathy. Such situations were not uncommon, but that didn't make them any less horrifying.

Gabrielle looked up and gave her a reassuring smile. "It's over and done with, and I'm my old self now. And I find the prospect of a little dalliance with Lord Praed very enticing . . . or do I mean challenging?" Her damp shoulders rose in a light shrug. "Either way, I want to go into dinner with him, if you can arrange it."

Georgie laughed, only too glad to let go of the disturbing image of her strong and self-determining cousin suffering beneath the thumb of a violent husband. "Of course I can. But I must say, I don't see what you see in him."

"But you don't like rocky roads," her cousin pointed out. "Whereas I've always chosen them over the smooth path."

And loving Guillaume was the rockiest road she could ever have chosen. Rocky, wonderful, desperate—no middle ground ever. He was either in her bed or facing death and danger somewhere. There was either love or fear. No chance for the contentment of ordinary happiness, the possibility of boredom, no time to learn the irritating little habits as well as the glorious.

"That's true, I suppose." Georgie stood up. "Simon's a very smooth path. I'd better go down to the drawing room. Lady Alsop always appears well before the other guests and feels very slighted if I'm not there to look after her and see she's immediately ensconced by the fire, protected from the blaze by a screen, with a glass of ratafia beside her."

"I don't know why you let yourself be bullied by the old besom," Gabrielle said irreverently.

Georgie shook her head. "She's Simon's great-aunt. And anyway, I don't mind."

No, of course you don't, Gabrielle thought affectionately as the door closed on her friend. Georgie had the sweetest nature.

It was decidedly unpleasant to deceive her friends, Gabrielle reflected, but the cause was too important to let personal scruple get in the way. She'd had to produce some credible reason for her willingness to jump into a liaison when she was officially supposed to be a grieving widow. Georgie would tell Simon the *real* reason for Gabrielle's apparent depression and neither of them would question subsequent events.

Subsequent events. She stood up, dripping, and wrapped herself in the towel. First she had to maneuver herself into Nathaniel Praed's bed. Guillaume would understand, she knew. He'd approve of the reasons behind her actions; they belonged to the world of dark secrets that he'd made his own. But how would he feel about the other thing, about the sexual current between herself and the man who'd ordered his death? She thought he'd understand it. He was a man of such passions himself and he knew her own. But Gabrielle wished with all her heart that she felt only revulsion for Nathaniel Praed. To go willingly—no, not just willingly, eagerly and filled with excitement—to his bed was a betrayal of Guillaume, however pure the motives.

But Guillaume was dead. She was twenty-five and the years ahead stretched into a bleak wasteland.

She reached for the bellrope and rang for Maisie to help her dress.

Nathaniel was waiting for her to enter the drawing room. He tried to tell himself he wasn't, but his eyes were constantly on the door. When his vigil was rewarded, he was again breathless at the bold statement of her appearance. Black velvet fell open over a flame satin underdress. Her hair was piled high on her head, held by a diamond-studded comb. A diamond pendant nestled in the deep cleavage of her gown. They were her only adornment.

She walked directly across the room to his side as if she saw no one else, as he saw no one but her. Heads turned, but Gabrielle appeared unaware.

"Good evening," she said softly, reaching him.

"Good evening." He smiled at her and brushed a fingertip over her cheek where the faintest scratch marred the pale translucence. "The tree branch scratched you."

"Yes," she said. "Battle scars."

They were alone in the crowded room, oblivious of the startled looks, the whispers, the nudges.

"We have to do something," Georgie whispered urgently to Simon, who, having heard the details of Gabrielle's bath-time confession, was watching the encounter with amused fascination. "Everyone's staring at them."

She crossed the room swiftly, her husband at her heels. "So what do you think of our hunt country, Lord Praed?"

Her voice broke the charmed circle, but Nathaniel's eyes were glazed for a split second as he turned to respond. "Rough on occasion, Lady Vanbrugh," he said, recovering smoothly.

"Georgie doesn't hunt," Gabrielle said, recovering her own senses as swiftly and smoothly. "So when she talks about hunting, you have to realize that she's only being polite. She trots out the terms but doesn't have the faintest idea what they mean."

"Oh, unjust," Georgie said, laughing. "I've listened to you and Simon most of my life. Of course I know what they mean, don't I, Simon?"

Her husband smiled down at her. "It doesn't matter, my love, one way or the other. Why should you need to know what they mean?"

"Well, I own I dislike hunting excessively," Georgie agreed. "I feel so sorry for the fox."

"There is that," Gabrielle agreed.

"Oh, come now, countess," Nathaniel put in. "You made absolutely certain you were in at the kill, and I'll swear you didn't flinch."

"I'm not squeamish," Gabrielle said. "But that doesn't mean I can't feel sorry for the fox."

The conversation rapidly became general, and when Gabrielle went into the dining room on Nathaniel's arm, the strange and disconcerting moment of intimacy was forgotten by most of the guests, if not by its participants.

4

"It's been a long time since I've heard that sound," Miles observed to Simon as they entered the drawing room after dinner.

Simon needed no expansion of the remark. The deep, warm sound of Nathaniel Praed's laughter seemed to fill the corners of the long, high-ceilinged room. He was leaning over the back of Gabrielle's chair; her head was tilted upward, turned against the taffeta cushions as she spoke to him. Whatever she was saying seemed to be amusing his lordship mightily.

"He says she's trouble," Miles continued thoughtfully. "But I'm getting the impression the gentleman doth protest too much."

"Does it surprise you, my friend?" Simon chuckled. "If I weren't happily leg-shackled to Georgie, I could almost be tempted myself."

"Not I," Miles said. "Gabby's too much of an *enfant terrible* for me. A man would never know whether he was on his head or his heels with her. She's got the devil's own sense of humor, always mocking. Half the time I don't know whether she's serious or not."

"But one would never be bored," Simon commented. "Perhaps that's what Nathaniel needs."

"Perhaps." Miles took snuff with an indolent flick of his wrist. "It certainly won't hurt him to cross swords with someone who can give as good as she gets. A lesson in humility might be the saving of him. Gabby's not one to be intimidated by Nathaniel's particular brand of arrogance."

Simon laughed. "She has more than her own share of imperiousness—much as I love her. Maybe they'll take each other down a peg or two."

"Well, it'll certainly be an interesting spectator sport. Let's suggest a game of whist. I'd dearly love to see them partner each other."

They sauntered over to the engrossed pair and Miles said cheerfully, "Gabby ... Nathaniel ... you have to rescue us from certain disaster. Lady Alsop and Colonel Beamish are looking for another pair to make up a whist table. If you don't agree to play with us, Georgie will volunteer us the minute she looks in our direction."

Gabrielle examined Lord Praed with an air of speculation that was as mischievously inviting as it was challenging. "How well do you play, sir?"

"Well enough, ma'am," he responded without a blink of an eyelid. "But I might ask you the same question."

"I play as well as I hunt," she asserted glibly.

"But not, I trust, as recklessly."

"I take no unnecessary risks."

"You'll have to forgive me if I doubt that." His eyes held hers and that charmed circle enclosed them again.

Simon cleared his throat. "I can vouch for Gabby's cardplay, Nathaniel. She's not a conservative bidder, certainly, but she'll not leave you in the lurch."

"No," Gabrielle agreed with a sweet smile at her prospective partner. "I am an utterly reliable partner,

Lord Praed. In whist as in other things. Perhaps it's time I proved it to you."

Nathaniel's head was whirling, his scalp tight, as if he were in the grip of a fever. And perhaps he was, he thought distantly. The woman was drawing them both to the brink of the devil's own inferno. Somehow he had to keep from toppling in. He looked for the cold, formal response so much a habit with him.

For a moment nothing would come to his lips, and he knew he was smiling and his eyes were warm. Gabrielle's crooked smile and dark eyes hung like the moon in a mist before his rapt gaze, wisps of dark red hair escaping from the diamond comb. She was scarlet and black—she was trouble. Helen's soft features came suddenly to his rescue—the liquid eyes, the tentative expressions, the gentle hand.

"I'm not in the mood for cards," he said, his voice clipped, his eyes now cold and harsh. "I must ask you to forgive me, madame, I couldn't do you justice as a partner." He bowed and turned away, walking with undue haste to the drawing room door.

Simon sighed. "For a minute there I thought I spied the old Nathaniel."

"The old Nathaniel?" Gabrielle's eyebrows quirked.

"I told you this morning that he lost his wife in childbirth," Miles reminded her with a touch of his earlier stiffness.

"We all have tragedies," Gabrielle said quietly, and to the surprise of both men for once there was no mockery in her voice. Her eyes were dark pools of unhappiness, and then it was gone. "Well, if Lord Praed won't play, you must find me another partner."

She smiled in her usual fashion and took Simon's arm as they went into the cardroom.

Nathaniel lay fully dressed on his bed, listening to the voices from below, the strains of dance music as a few couples took the floor in an impromptu country dance. He'd left instructions with the stables that his postchaise be at the front door at five o'clock, well before dawn. Now all he had to do was get through the night and he'd be on his way to Hampshire and safe from the devil's inferno embodied in a pair of charcoal eyes.

After a while the noise died down and he heard the called good nights as his fellow guests made their way to bed. He undressed and tried to sleep. But all the usual tricks he used to bring about oblivion when he was keyed up failed him. When the handful of gravel flew through the open window and rattled on the polished wooden floor, he understood what he'd been waiting for.

To question the inevitable was an exercise in futility. He relit his beside candle, then got up, shrugged into his dressing gown, and went to the window. Gabrielle de Beaucaire stood on the pathway below, hands on her hips, her head thrown back as she looked up at his window, every line of her body both a question and an invitation.

Nathaniel leaned out into the moon-washed night. He said nothing, merely crooked a finger at the still figure. For the barest moment she seemed to hesitate, then she was swarming up the creeper, hand over hand, toes searching for a foothold, gripping where they could. Leaning his elbows on the broad sill, he watched her progress, trying to conceal his anxiety from himself.

When her head came level with the windowsill, he reached for her, taking her strongly beneath the arms and lifting her bodily through the window.

Gabrielle was so surprised at this evidence of more than ordinary strength in a man whose physique indicated wiriness and agility rather than muscle power that she made no sound until her feet made firm contact with the bedroom floor and she was released.

Then she drew breath and brushed the hair away from her forehead, offering him a small smile.

"I was a little scared of the climb tonight. But one shouldn't give in to fear, should one?"

He regarded her, unsmiling. "And temptation?" he inquired softly. "What of temptation, Gabrielle?"

"Ah." She put her head on one side, considering. "Resisting temptation is a different matter. A matter best left to individual consciences, I believe, according to circumstance."

"Yes," he said, still softly. What reason did he have for resisting this temptation just this once? He'd be away from there in a few short hours, away from Gabrielle de Beaucaire, and he'd never see her again. She wanted this as much as he did. This was an ephemeral temptation, not one that need be resisted.

His hands went to the buttons of her shirt. In leisurely fashion, one by one, they came undone. Gabrielle stood motionless under the purposeful unfastening, although her blood flowed swiftly and her heart was beating fast.

Lifting and turning her wrists, he unfastened the tiny pearl buttons before pulling the shirt-sleeves off her arms. He tossed the shirt aside and stood looking at her, bared to the waist in the moonlight. She held still for the long, unhurried scrutiny, her skin prickling, her nipples lifting and hardening with the cool breeze from the window.

He held the generous swell of her breasts in the palms of his hands, his thumb flicking the nipples, his eyes holding hers before he lowered his head and drew his tongue in a slow, easy stroke first over the right breast and then over the left. It was a caress so full of promise that Gabrielle caught her breath, but she obeyed the unspoken rule of silence that held them both.

In the same silence Nathaniel caught her waist and lifted her onto the windowsill before pulling off her boots and stockings in turn. Slowly, he unfastened the waistband of her britches, lifted her down again, and pushed the garment off her hips. Then, smiling, he hitched her back onto the cold stone windowsill and pulled the britches clear of her feet.

Gabrielle shivered, but it was not with cold, although the stone was hard and chill beneath her bottom and thighs as she sat naked in the window.

Nathaniel lifted her with the ease of before, cradled her in his arms, and carried her to the bed, laying her gently on the rumpled coverlet.

"Why do you keep carrying me around?" she inquired, her voice sounding strange as the intense silence was at last broken. She tried for a lightly amused tone, but there was a quiver in her voice that spoke of much more than amusement.

Nathaniel stood looking down at her as she lay on the bed, vulnerable in her nakedness. Her limbs were long and straight as hazel wands, and the generous curve of hip and bosom surprised and delighted him. Clothed, her height masked the richness of her body. "I suppose because it makes you more manageable," he said. "Or at least it gives me that illusion."

"And you need me to be manageable?"

"I have my share of masculine pride." A glimmer of self-mockery touched his eyes, and it was as if the harsh, isolated coldness he so often evinced belonged to a different man. He threw off his dressing gown and came down on the bed beside her.

"I'd never have believed it," Gabrielle murmured, brushing her fingertips over his chest. "Such a modest and unassuming man, I thought you were."

Nathaniel chuckled, flinging a leg over her thighs, drawing her close against the warmth of his body. "I must have been too delicate in my approach. I've never had dealings with a devil woman before."

They both knew the banter was a delaying tactic, a last-ditch attempt to bridle the heady swirl of passion wrapping tight around them.

Gabrielle closed her eyes, and the scent of his skin

filled the air around her. She inhaled greedily, her hands running over his back, learning the curve of hip and buttock, the swell and ripple of muscle, the knobs of his spine. She palmed his scalp, her fingers twisting in the crisp, wavy thatch.

Nathaniel felt the press of her breasts against his chest, the tautness of her erect nipples as he tasted the sweetness of her mouth with a questing tongue. His need rose hard and urgent, eclipsing all else but the immediacy of desire. With a soft moan of assenting urgency Gabrielle moved against his rising flesh, her thighs tightening as she held him in the warm furrow of her body, the earthy words of uninhibited passion on her lips, whispering against his mouth.

"I want you," he said with low-voiced ferocity, his palms flattening against the insides of her thighs, opening her. He touched her heated core and she cried out.

"Come into me, love, *now*."

Despite her fervent imperative, he tried to hold back, to keep control for both of them, knowing that delay could only enhance their pleasure, afraid also that he might make an error of judgment if he yielded to hasty need, and knowing with aching certainty that this loving was going to be unique and must not be jeopardized by rash, unvarnished lust.

He gazed down at her as she sprawled beneath him in wanton abandon, her hips lifting unconsciously, her thighs parted, a sheen of moisture on the satiny inner slopes glistening in the soft glow of the bedside candle. Her tongue touched her lips and she repeated the demand. "*Now*, Nathaniel."

He was lost, irretrievably. With a shuddering breath he came over her, sliding his hands beneath her to lift her to meet his surging entry into the moist and welcoming sheath. With each deep thrust he probed her body and her eyes held his, a glow of wonder in the charcoal depths as she gloried in the presence of his flesh within her own.

There was a brief moment of awareness when she touched his lips with her finger and whispered, "You will be careful?"

"Of course," he responded simply.

A slow smile spread over her face and her eyes widened as the wondrous pleasure built deep, the strong rhythm of his body in hers becoming a part of her self.

And at the last, she chuckled, an exultant little sound of pure pleasure that drew an answering ripple of delighted amusement from Nathaniel. And then the coil burst asunder and for a magical instant they existed as one flesh before, with a wrenching sense of loss, Nathaniel kept his promise; but she held him tightly against her, her legs wrapped around his hips, her heels pressing into his buttocks as if he were still within her body as his throbbing climax tossed him on the sea of ultimate sensation until he fell forward, lying beached upon her, and her arms fell back, her legs flung wide around him in the formlessness of fulfillment.

After a minute he made a supreme effort and rolled onto the bed beside her. His hand stroked the damp skin of her belly, his face buried in the curve of her neck. Gabrielle lifted one hand and let it fall heavily across his back in an attempt to return the languid caress of gratitude and acknowledgment.

"Wild one," Nathaniel murmured finally, his breath warm on her neck. "That was indecently fast. I like to take my time, not tumble headlong into ecstasy."

"We both had a powerful thirst to slake," Gabrielle replied with a somewhat complacent smile. "Next time we can take our time."

Nathaniel turned his head toward the window. The moon swung in the black sky and the stars were as bright as ever. Dawn was an eternity away, an eternity in which to indulge temptation.

"Then perhaps we should start next time now," he murmured, hitching himself on an elbow, feasting his eyes on her body, taking in every inch now that lust's driving power was curbed.

Her skin was milk-white and smooth, stretched taut over her rib cage, curving into the concave hollow of her belly. He lowered his head to dip his tongue into the delicate thimble of her navel, his fingers twisting in the silky dark red fleece at the apex of her thighs.

Gabrielle stretched luxuriously beneath the caressing hand that with a sure and easy touch drew her up from the torpid depths of satiation, rekindling the ashes of arousal.

"No, lie still," he commanded when she attempted to reciprocate his play. "I want to explore you, to find out what pleases you. I want your body to speak to me."

"It's very eloquent at the moment," she whispered, arching catlike beneath his touch, more than willing to offer herself to such skilled and knowing handling, postponing her own game of intimate discovery.

Nathaniel played with her, reveling in the supreme responsiveness that enabled him to bring her again and again to the brink of joyous extinction. Their voices mingled in murmured delight and sometimes surprise as the night wore on and the erotic voyage took unexpected turns.

Gabrielle felt that every inch of her skin had been charted, every crevice of her body become known to the man who loved with such exquisite sensitivity. He knew the lobes of her ears, the bones of her ankles, the two dimpled indentations in the small of her back, the spaces between her toes, each and every fingernail. Finally he yielded his own body and she learned him with the same thoroughness, recognizing dimly that such a knowledge forged links between two people that could not easily be broken.

The final fusion was a dreamlike joining of two separate entities who no longer acknowledged their individuality. They rose and fell together in slow cadences and his skin was hers as hers was his, and his flesh pressed against her womb, an inextricable part of her essence.

They lay together, recovering their separateness, as the stars began to fade and, with the coming of dawn, Nathaniel dragged himself free from the woods of enchantment. It was time to return to the real world of dark dangers and mired secrets. Time, too, to don the mantle of fatherhood for a while, however uncomfortable a garment it was.

He'd not made love since Helen's pregnancy had so enervated her that she could barely raise her head from the chaise longue—he wouldn't dignify subsequent hasty satisfactions of bodily need with the term *lovemaking*—and not once tonight had he thought of Helen. The realization struck like a sliver of ice through his warm lethargy, his peaceful contemplation of the rich, sensuous interlude he'd shared with the long, sinuous, creamy form lying beside him.

How could he not have thought of the woman who would be living now if he hadn't yielded with such incontinence to his body's urgencies? Helen had miscarried three times before she carried Jake to full term and gave her life for the child's. And yet he hadn't thought to be careful. He'd expected her to be a wife to him and the mother of his children, and she hadn't said otherwise. But then, Helen was not a woman to say a man nay—to renege on what she believed were her obligations. Knowing that, he should have thought, should have understood, should have made the decision for both of them. Instead . . .

The woman beside him shifted on the mattress, turning her head to look at him. Dark red ringlets pooled on the white lawn pillow, a rich ruddy stain, like Helen's blood flowing unstoppably from her body until she was drained, lifeless, bloodless.

"Something's the matter," Gabrielle said directly, sitting up. "What is it, Nathaniel?"

It wasn't her fault. She'd offered temptation, but he

had chosen to yield to it. He hung on to the thought grimly until the fierce need to strike out at her, to punish her for his own self-indulgence was blunted enough for him to speak if not warmly at least without overt hostility.

"The night is done," he said, swinging his legs over the side of the bed, stretching and yawning. "It's time you returned to your own bed before the household begins moving around."

Gabrielle regarded him for a moment through narrowed eyes. Whatever was troubling him ran deep. She'd shared enough of the man's spirit tonight to recognize that. But even such sharing didn't permit prying, and besides, she had no wish to pry. She had one object and only one where Nathaniel Praed was concerned. If an explosion of bodily joy came along as an extra, then all well and good. But the closeness had to stop there. There could be nothing more.

"You're right," she assented. "It's getting light. Perhaps I'd better leave by the window to be on the safe side."

"What *safe side?*" he scoffed. "You'll leave by that window over my dead body."

Gabrielle put her head on one side in the engaging and frequently infuriating way she had. "Now, that seems a little extreme, sir. An unnecessary sacrifice, surely."

His lips twitched. "Witch! Put your clothes on and leave by the door." He picked up her clothes. "Catch."

The garments flew toward her: shirt, britches, stockings, and boots. Gabrielle snatched them from the air with an instinctive accuracy, and Nathaniel enjoyed the supple play of her body as she stretched and bent in reactive rhythm. And then he remembered Helen again. He wanted to look away as Gabrielle pulled on her britches, buttoned her shirt, but he couldn't. His eyes were fixed wide as if someone had wedged sticks beneath his eyelids.

But to his relief, Gabrielle showed no signs of lingering once she was dressed. She showed none of the softness of the night either, not even offering a farewell kiss before going to the door.

"Sleep well, Lord Praed. I promise I won't disturb you at the breakfast table this morning."

Her laugh had the old mockery in it as she closed the door behind her.

With a speed akin to desperation, Nathaniel began to dress, throwing his few belongings into a portmanteau before hurrying down the stairs and outside to his waiting postchaise.

Gabrielle encountered a maidservant struggling with a scuttle of coal as she turned into the corridor to her own bedchamber. She offered a cheerful good morning, but the girl, tongue-tied, stared wide-eyed at the dawn apparition in britches and shirt.

Shrugging, Gabrielle went on her way. The girl was presumably a very lowly member of the household staff and wouldn't know the names of the Vanbrughs' guests even if she was inclined to gossip. Not that it mattered one way or the other. No servant would be able to guess in whose bed the Comtesse de Beaucaire had passed the night.

She gained her own room without further incident. The neatly turned down bed awaited her, mute evidence of where she had *not* spent the night. A sheet of paper on the plumped virgin pillow caught her attention immediately. She picked it up. Georgie's spidery writing weaved untidily over the paper:

Gabby, where are you? Or can I guess? Perhaps I won't try. Just to alert you: Simon says Lord Praed has ordered his carriage for dawn. Apparently he's decided his business here is over and he won't even stay for breakfast! He's such a rude man, Gabby, I can't see what you see in him. But then, there's no accounting for taste, is there? I don't know if you want to know his plans, but just in case ... Sleep well!!

Gabrielle scrunched the paper in her fist, staring out of the window at the rapidly brightening day. He'd said nothing about leaving. Was he still going? After such a night, could he simply get up and leave without a word of explanation or even farewell as if those glorious hours had never happened?

She remembered the way the shadows had returned to his face just before they'd parted. His eyes had become brown stones again. And she knew he was capable of walking away from an ephemeral erotic encounter without a backward glance.

But she couldn't allow that. The seduction of Nathaniel Praed had to go much deeper than one mutually enjoyable night. She was still as far as ever from persuading him to accept her into the service ... and as far as ever from avenging Guillaume's death.

With swift efficiency she began to move around the room, packing a cloakbag with necessities—her riding habit, clean linen, several day dresses. Evening gowns and her jewel casket would not be necessary; she couldn't carry them anyway. It would help, of course, if she knew where he was going. She tossed her hairbrushes and toothpowder on top of the contents of the bag, swung a dark velvet hooded cloak around her shoulders, dropped an ivory-mounted pistol and a black loo mask into the deep pocket, and drew on her gloves, picked up her whip and the bag, and headed for the door.

"*Merde!*" She couldn't go without a word to Georgie. Dragging off her gloves again, she went to the *secrétaire*, found paper and quill, and scrawled a few words of oblique explanation. Her cousin would read between the lines and would send on the rest of her belongings once Gabrielle knew where she was going.

Taking the note, she left the room and hurried

down the corridor. Outside Georgie's room she folded the paper carefully and slipped it beneath the door, where Georgie's maid would see it when she awoke her mistress in a few hours time.

Gabrielle ran down the stairs and out of the front door, noticing that it was already unlocked. Presumably, Lord Praed, damn his eyes, had wasted no time in making his departure. She hurried to the stables, her cloak snapping around her ankles with her long stride. She'd have to borrow one of Simon's horses, but he wouldn't mind.

A groom was sweeping the stableyard as she strode in. "Saddle Major for me," she ordered. "Do you know which direction Lord Praed took?"

"Not off 'and, milady," the lad said, tugging his forelock. "But I reckon as 'ow Bert will." He hurried into the stable block and a minute later the head groom emerged.

"Major's got a swollen fetlock, my lady. You'd best take Thunderer," he stated as he came over to her. He knew Lord Vanbrugh's stable was available to the countess without question, and her present unconventional dress came as no surprise to a man who'd known her since childhood and knew her fondness for the freedom of early morning rides astride.

"I may need to keep him for a few days, Bert. Lord Vanbrugh won't need to ride him himself?"

"Don't reckon so, my lady. 'Is lordship's got the new geldin' to try out."

Gabrielle nodded. "Do you know which direction Lord Praed's chaise took? I have an urgent message for him."

"The driver said they was goin' into 'Ampshire, my lady. To 'is lordship's estate. Reckon they'd take the Crawley road."

Gabrielle frowned, picturing the route. "How long ago did they leave?"

" 'Alf an hour, ma'am. The chaise was ready at five, but 'is lordship didn't come fer it until 'alf five."

"I see."

The lad brought Thunderer, saddled, into the stableyard and Bert gave Gabrielle a leg up. She settled in the saddle, waiting while Bert adjusted the stirrup leathers for her and fastened her bag behind her. If the head groom thought there was anything strange about the countess's unheralded crack-of-dawn departure, unaccompanied and dressed as she was, he kept it to himself and behaved as if this were just another of her lone early morning excursions to be over by breakfast time.

Gabrielle trotted Thunderer out of the stableyard and down the long driveway to the road. The Crawley road lay to the left, and if she cut across country, she could join it about five miles along, where, if she remembered aright, there was a small stand of poplar trees beside the road. It would be perfect for what she had in mind. At a good gallop across the fields, Thunderer would gain on the slower road-bound chaise with ease.

Her crooked little smile lifted the corners of her mouth as she imagined Lord Praed's surprise. He would probably be enraged, of course, but unless she had read him wrong, and after such a night how could she have, he would find her unorthodox approach ultimately irresistible.

5

——————

Nathaniel sat back against the leather squabs of the light vehicle, his arms folded across his chest, his expression more than usually forbidding. Something about this hasty if planned departure went against the grain. It felt like flight—flight from the enchantress.

His body sang with the memory of her. Her scent lingered on his own skin, her taste was on his tongue, her exultant laughter ringing in his ears. Who was she? What was she? Apart from what Simon had told him, he knew nothing about her except the furthest reaches, the deepest intimacies of her glorious body.

How was that possible? How could one plumb the erotic depths of another's body and yet know nothing of the personality, the spiritual makeup, the motivations, fears, and hopes of such a lover?

Frowning, he tried to put together what few facts he had. But they added little to the sum. Gabrielle was a widow, a grieving widow according to Simon, desperate for some activity to take her mind off her grief. But the woman in his bed had shown none of the reservations one would expect of a grieving widow. But then, he had exhibited none of the reservations of a grieving widower, and he knew himself to be that. The grief and remorse ran so deep, it flowed with his blood in his veins. It hadn't stopped him . . . had put no brake on the sensual excesses of the night.

She was reckless, and always had been according to Simon and Miles. She followed impulse and went after what she wanted. She climbed walls and rode like the devil. But why? What had made her like that?

He rubbed his eyes wearily, suddenly tired of this exercise. It was over. He wasn't interested in who or what she was. He wanted nothing more to do with her. Simon would have to reinforce the message that there was no possible way the spymaster was going to change his policy and bring a woman into the network, and she'd find some other game to play . . . and some other lover.

Such a woman couldn't remain without a lover for very long.

The reflection had the same effect as sucking on a lemon. His mouth dried, his lips pursed, his nose wrinkled, and his frown deepened. It was thoroughly unpalatable. But time and distance would have its usual effect. The sharp edges of memory would be smudged, the piercing knowledge of joy would be blunted.

Abruptly he changed the course of his thoughts to good purpose.

Jake. He had to make some decisions about his son. It was time for the governess to leave and a tutor to take her place. In two years time the boy would be going to Harrow and he had to be prepared. A childhood spent in the exclusive soft company of nurses and governesses was no preparation for the rigors of school. And Jake was all too timid as it was. He was frightened of any horse bigger than his Shetland. He hated to see a fish gutted or a rabbit in a trap. He quailed at the slightest reprimand.

And he shrank from his father.

Why? Nathaniel hunched deeper into his coat,

turning up the collar against the early morning chill. Why did Jake always regard his father with wide, tremulous eyes? Why did he find it near impossible to construct a complete sentence in response to a civil question? Why was his voice barely above a whisper when he spoke with him?

The boy had spent too long hiding in women's skirts. It was the conclusion Nathaniel always reached. There could be no other explanation. Oh, he'd frowned on the child occasionally, scolded him once or twice, required his presence in the library before dinner whenever he was at home, examined him regularly as to his progress with his lessons, but he'd never done anything to warrant fear from his son.

Or love either.

He pushed the thought aside as irrelevant. He hadn't loved his own father—in fact, Gilbert, sixth Lord Praed, had been a chilly, distant man who ruled his household and most especially his only son with a martinet's severity. Nathaniel had good reason to fear him, far more reason than Jake had to fear the seventh Lord Praed. But a son owed his father respect—love was not an appropriate emotion between fathers and sons. It was different for daughters. They had fewer responsibilities ahead of them and could safely be reared with the softer emotions. Indeed, tenderness equipped them for their adult roles as wives and mothers. A mother could lavish love and tenderness on a child of either sex and it was right and proper. It was a foil for the necessary distance between a father and his son. But Jake had no mother. . . .

Nathaniel muttered a soft execration. It always came down to the same issue. He closed his eyes and tried to sleep. God knows he needed it after a night with Gabrielle de Beaucaire. He didn't think she was a woman with too much softness and tenderness in her makeup. But then, she'd lost her parents to one of the bloodiest tyrannies since the Inquisition.

The crack of a pistol, the violent lurching of the coach, brought him upright out of momentary oblivion with his hand on his pistol, his senses alert, his eyes wide open. He'd yanked down the glass panel at the window, his pistol resting on the ledge, his eye squinting down the barrel faster than he could have thought through the sequence of actions.

"Your money or your life, Lord Praed."

The voice so filled with laughing mockery was unmistakable, even if his body hadn't surged with recognition as his eye fell on the tall, slender figure astride the chestnut stallion. She had a pistol in her hand, aimed in businesslike fashion at the coachman on the box. A hood concealed her distinctive hair and a black loo mask covered her face.

"What the *hell!*" Lord Praed exclaimed, but his own weapon remained unwavering, his eye steady. "Put that damn pistol away now!"

"Oh, I'm not about to fire it by mistake," she said with an insouciant shrug. "You need have no fears on that score, sir."

"*Put it away!*" For a second, flaring brown eyes held her calm charcoal gaze in a battle of wills and his finger remained on the trigger.

Would he press it? Gabrielle found herself considering the possibility with a curious detachment. He had said he didn't play games and she had no reason to dispute the statement. He didn't have the air of a playful man at the moment.

With what she hoped was a casual gesture, Gabrielle shrugged again and thrust the pistol into the waistband of her britches.

"Beggin' yer pardon, m'lord, but what the 'ell's goin' on." The coachman swiveled on the box and leaned out around the corner to address his master. "Is this an' 'oldup or not. I've got me blunderbuss." He gestured with the ugly weapon.

"Oh, it's a holdup, all right," Nathaniel said dryly. "But not one that need involve a blunderbuss, Harkin."

He laid his own pistol on the seat beside him and swung open the door of the chaise. He kicked the lever that let down the footstep and balanced easily on the top step. It put him on a level with the chestnut's shoulders.

Before Gabrielle understood what he was about to do, she'd been hauled unceremoniously from her mount and found herself bundled into the interior of the chaise rather in the manner of an unwieldy parcel.

"Pass that bag in here and tether the horse to the back of the chaise," Nathaniel instructed his coachman. "Then get moving again. I want to change horses at Horsham in an hour."

He waited while Harkin unfastened the cloakbag from Thunderer's saddle and handed it into him. The coachman was accustomed to obeying strange orders without question. Lord Praed demanded discretion and sharp wits from his servants and paid well for both. If he chose to accommodate a somewhat unusual highwayman in his chaise, it was no business of Harkin's.

Nathaniel tossed the bag onto the seat, closed the carriage door with a restrained slam, and turned to survey Gabrielle, who had scrambled up from the floor and was gathering herself together on the seat.

"Take that ridiculous mask off," he snapped. "I am sick to death of your games, Gabrielle."

He did look somewhat exasperated. Actually, that was an understatement, Gabrielle decided, but at least his eyes weren't brown stones at the bottom of a muddy pond anymore. In fact, they were positively lively, passionate even, although not exactly the type of passion she preferred. However, one mustn't cavil too much. She was skating on the thinnest ice, and anything short of complete withdrawal had to be a plus.

Obligingly, she threw back the hood of her cloak and untied the strings of the loo mask. "Why shouldn't

we play this game, Nathaniel? An interlude of passion
without promises . . . What harm could it do either of
us . . . or anyone else for that matter?" She ran her
hands through her loosened hair and leaned her head
back against the squabs, regarding him with a quizzical
lift of her eyebrows.

In dawning disbelief Nathaniel realized that he
couldn't think of a logical reason to say no. Looking at
her, he saw the invitation, the promise, and he remembered how she fulfilled such promises. She wasn't a
woman to be judged by ordinary standards, or to be
treated by such.

"What are you afraid of?" she asked. Leaning forward, she touched his knee.

The sexual current jolted him to his core.

"Not of you," he declared.

"Good." Smiling, she leaned back against the
squabs again. "I'm famished. Must we wait till Horsham
before we stop for breakfast?"

Nathaniel's eyes narrowed. "You," he said with soft
deliberation, "are a brigand, Gabrielle de Beaucaire."

He sat down opposite her as the coachman's whip
cracked and the chaise lurched forward again.

Gabrielle chose to take the characterization as a
compliment and smiled her crooked smile again.

Nathaniel leaned forward, hooking a finger into
the clasp of her cloak, pulling her toward him. "I do
not intend breakfasting with a brigand." His mouth met
hers in a hard kiss. Then he unclasped the cloak and
pushed it off her shoulders. His hands cupped the swell
of her breasts under the white lawn shirt and her nipples sprang upright in instant gratifying response.

"A shameless, wanton brigand," he murmured.
"Take those damn clothes off."

"But it's cold," she protested with a mischievous
chuckle.

"Serves you right." He leaned back, folding his
arms across his chest. "I refuse to be seen in public with

a shameless hussy, so if you want breakfast, you must change your clothes."

"Oh, well, if it's that serious," she said amiably, unbuttoning her shirt, pulling it out of the waist of her britches.

Nathaniel stretched and jerked the pistol loose at the same moment. "You won't need this either." He examined it with an expert's eye. It was no toy for all its small size and delicate mounting. He cracked the barrel. It was primed.

"Why do you carry a pistol?"

"One never knows when one might need protection," she said, unfastening her britches, lifting her hips to push them down. The full swell of her breasts shifted sensuously with the motion of the coach and her own actions. Then she was naked on the seat of a swaying carriage on the road to Horsham. The dark red hair tumbled over her shoulders and her long legs stretched across the narrow space between them.

A monk couldn't have resisted. Nathaniel reached for her, pulling her between his knees. Her skin was warm despite the winter morning and the unheated vehicle.

"You've a mind to play again?" Her black eyebrows rose. "It could prove something of a challenge in these circumstances."

"I've never been afraid of challenges," he replied, unfastening his britches with one hand. "And I know full well how you view them."

His roused body sprang free from constraint. Smiling, Gabrielle touched him and then, obeying the pressure of his hands on her hips, slowly lowered herself astride his lap, guiding his body within her own.

"Ahh," she whispered. "Why do you feel so good . . . so right?"

"Why do you?" he whispered back, closing his eyes.

The carriage jolted in a rut and his grip tightened, his fingers pressing into the flesh of her hips. The movement of the carriage slowly insinuated itself into the rhythm of their joined bodies as Gabrielle moved herself over and around him and he lifted his hips to meet her.

"I read somewhere that cossacks make love galloping on horseback," Gabrielle murmured, lowering her head to brush his lips with her own in a fleeting caress. "Maybe we should try it later."

Nathaniel groaned. "How much stamina do you think I have, woman?"

"Limitless," she replied with a smile of utter confidence.

"Your faith is touching." Smiling, he gripped her more tightly as he felt the internal movements of her body, the little ripples that told him she was nearing her pinnacle.

Gabrielle drew breath sharply, her head falling back, the pure white column of her throat arched. He thrust upward, his fingers biting into her flesh as she convulsed around him. She fell forward with a moan of joy, her forehead resting on the top of his head, and he held her as he fell slowly from his own peak and the carriage swayed and rocked beneath them.

"*Mon Dieu*, I think we're going through a village," Gabrielle gasped with a weak chuckle as she raised her head, glancing toward the window. "Do you think anyone can see in?"

"Don't tell me you're worried about appearances!" Laughter, wonderful and carefree, bubbled in his chest. He couldn't remember when he'd last felt so lighthearted, so unrestrained, so much in charity with his fellow man. Distantly, it occurred to him that the true seductive power of Gabrielle de Beaucaire lay in her ability to create this feeling.

"Get off, you wicked creature." He lifted her off his lap and deposited her on the seat opposite. He shook his head, taking in the wonderful untidy sprawl of her naked limbs, the unruly tangle of that dark red hair as she smiled her crooked smile, her eyes languorous with satiation.

"For God's sake, put some clothes on," he directed, his voice a husky rasp. "You'll catch your death."

"And whose fault would that be?" She made no move to obey, just continued smiling at him.

Nathaniel pulled the cloakbag toward him and opened it. "You're not, I trust, going to have the unmitigated gall to imply that I have any say in your actions." He riffled through the contents of the bag.

"Only to the extent that you're the cause of them," she responded. "I seem to find you irresistible. My riding habit's in there somewhere."

Nathaniel looked up, his eyes sharply appraising. Then he shook his head in resignation. "The feeling is reciprocal, it seems. Are there undergarments in here, or do you always go without them?"

"Only when they might be a hindrance," she said with a serene smile. "I couldn't see much point wearing them last night, and your departure was so precipitate, I didn't have time to change my clothes this morning."

There was a hint of reproof in her voice as she said this.

Nathaniel pulled out a silk chemise and a pair of pantalettes. "Put these on." He held them out to her. Then he said with some constraint, "I felt I'd yielded sufficiently to temptation. Perhaps I should have said something—"

"Running off like that was distinctly ungentlemanly . . . not to put too fine a point on it," Gabrielle interrupted as her head emerged from the neck of the chemise.

"Perhaps so." Nathaniel leaned forward and began to do up the buttons at her throat. "But you made it very clear that you were responsible for your own actions. I didn't feel it necessary to tell you of my plans. They were made well before you arrived in my bed."

She took the drawers he handed her and slipped

them over her feet, raising her hips to pull them up. "Well, have you agreed to amend them?" She pulled on the stockings he held out.

Nathaniel lifted her right leg and slipped a lace-trimmed garter up to her thigh, and then served the left leg similarly, his hands smoothing over the muscled roundness of her calves, the satin softness of her inner thighs.

"It would seem so," he said with a wry smile, handing her a clean shirt and the skirt of her habit.

"Good," Gabrielle declared with a nod of satisfaction. She fastened the buttons of the shirt and slipped into the skirt, buttoning the waistband. "We shall have a game of passion . . . an interlude. No promises."

"And where will people think you are?"

She shrugged into her jacket. "Georgie knows. She's the only person who needs to know. And she's no prude. I'm no virginal innocent, Lord Praed. And I rule my own life."

"I don't question it," Nathaniel said. "My neighbors will look askance, however, at a woman sharing my roof so flagrantly."

Gabrielle grinned. "Somehow, Lord Praed, I don't believe you give a tinker's damn what your neighbors think. And I certainly don't. They don't know me from Eve and never will."

It was perfectly true. Since Helen's death, Nathaniel had as little to do with his county neighbors as possible. He didn't encourage callers, and paid no calls himself. He had a reputation for being a somewhat surly recluse. There would be gossip, of course, but it wouldn't worry him.

But what of Jake? Oh, the boy was too young to hear the tittle-tattle, and certainly too young to speculate on his father's visitor. He'd be in the nursery and the schoolroom most of the time anyway.

Gabrielle said suddenly, "What of your son, though?"

It was as if she'd been in his thoughts. "What do you know of Jake?" he demanded sharply.

She shrugged. "Nothing, really. Miles simply mentioned him in passing."

"And did he tell you of Helen?" His tone was still sharp.

"Only that she'd died." She decided against telling him what Miles had told her of Nathaniel's grief and his difficulties with fatherhood. It was no concern of hers anyway. "It was a word in passing. I wasn't particularly interested, and in fact, I'm not now. Interludes should have no attachments to the past and no strings to the future. Don't you agree?"

"You're an extraordinary woman." Nathaniel frowned. "You have none of the softnesses of your sex."

How could you know? I saw my mother in the tumbril on the way to the guillotine. How much softness can survive in the soul of an eight-year-old after that? And what was left was leached from my soul with Guillaume's blood as he died in my arms. She turned her head away with a sudden movement to hide from him both the grief and the fierce anger in her eyes, and she spoke lightly, revealing nothing in her voice.

"One reason you might reconsider the question of employing me, Sir Spymaster," she said. "Since it's the softness of women you object to."

"Is that what this is about?" His voice was cold and flat as he suddenly suspected manipulation.

She shook her head. "No." She said this with so much conviction that she realized with dismay that a part of herself meant it. The seduction had taken on a life of its own, and she was as much a victim of her plan as Nathaniel.

She rested her head on the squabs and regarded him through narrowed eyes. "No, I'm as much taken by surprise as you are. But that doesn't mean I'm going to give up trying to persuade you to change your mind, sir."

Nathaniel's expression was inscrutable, showing nothing of his thoughts. A wise man recognized when to drop his prejudices. Gabrielle de Beaucaire had courage, ingenuity, nerve, and audacity—everything essential for a good spy—except that she was a woman. For several years he'd been trying to place someone in the inner circles of Napoleon's government. This woman could be the perfect answer.

But was she genuine? She had convinced Simon, but Nathaniel ultimately trusted no one's judgment but his own when so many lives were at risk. She could be a plant. Her contacts in France were every bit as strong as her contacts here. She was as much French as she was English. And seduction and betrayal were the oldest tricks in the business.

If she was genuine, then she was a gift that only a stubborn fool would refuse. At Burley Manor he would have all the time he needed to test her out.

Deliberately, his expression lightened and a glimmer of amusement appeared in his steady gaze. "Your powers of persuasion are fearsome, madame. I can see I shall have my work cut out to withstand them."

"I'll make a small wager that you won't succeed," she said with a mischievous grin.

"Stakes?"

"Oh . . ." She pursed her lips, considering. "Let's say at the end of two weeks the loser puts him or herself entirely at the disposal of the winner for twenty-four hours."

Nathaniel smiled slowly. "Now, those are stakes worth winning."

"They might even be worth losing," she murmured with a lascivious chuckle that sent the blood coursing hot and swift through his veins.

"You have a wager, my wanton brigand."

So far so good. Gabrielle inclined her head in silent acknowledgment as the chaise came to a halt in the yard of the Black Cock in Horsham.

6

Jake sat on the bottom step of the stone flight leading up to the front door of Burley Manor. He was scratching with a stick in the gravel at his feet. A square box of a house with rectangular windows appeared beneath the point of the stick as he frowned over his artwork.

The mid-morning sun highlighted the almost white streaks in his blond head and his lower lip was caught between his teeth. He was a slight child who had not yet lost the round face and dimpled hands of babyhood.

At the sound of carriage wheels on the driveway, he looked up. His father's chaise bowled around the corner onto the gravel sweep before the house. Jake dropped the stick and slowly stood up, wiping his hands on the seat of his nankeen trousers. A wary look appeared in the round brown eyes, but he remained where he was, standing with his hands behind his back as the carriage came to a halt and the door swung open.

He watched as his father kicked free the footstep and jumped lightly to the ground. Then he held out a hand and to Jake's surprise a woman stepped out beside him.

His father often had visitors although Jake was never presented to them. They usually arrived at night and left at night, remaining closeted in the library with his father throughout their visit. He only ever met with his godfather, Miles Bennet. And he didn't come very often. Jake never remembered a lady arriving at Burley Manor before.

This one stood smiling in the sunshine, looking up at the graceful weathered façade of the Queen Anne house. She was hatless and her hair was pinned somewhat carelessly in a knot at the nape of her neck.

Then Nathaniel saw his son and tiny frown lines appeared on his brow, his mouth stiffening in the way that Jake knew so well. The child felt his stomach tighten. He always hoped for something different, although he didn't know how to put such a wish into words, but his father's response to him never changed.

"Jake." Nathaniel stepped toward the child, extending his hand in greeting. Solemnly, the little boy shook it. "Why aren't you at your lessons?" His father released the small hand, his frown deepening.

"It's Sunday, sir. I don't have lessons on Sunday." Jake's voice was a little tentative as he wondered if that had changed and no one had told him.

Nathaniel looked down at his son, remembering the Sundays of his own boyhood. During those wonderful hours of liberty, he would have been in the stables or down by the river fishing, or climbing the big beech tree at the entrance to the park, or . . .

Anything but sitting in unimaginative idleness on the steps of the house.

"How do you do, Jake?" The lady came toward him, smiling. "Have you been drawing pictures in the gravel? I used to love to do that." She bent to examine the scratchings. "I always put two chimneys on my houses, one in each corner. May I?" Laughing up at him, she reached for his discarded stick and deftly added a second chimney pot while Nathaniel stood staring and Jake's eyes grew ever rounder.

He thought she had to be the most beautiful

woman with her smiling dark eyes and her hair glowing in the sunlight and her white white skin. He loved Primmy, his governess, with a fierce love and he tolerated the fussing attentions of Nurse because they made him feel warm and comfortable even when they were irritating, but he didn't think of those two as women. His father's companion was unlike any lady he'd ever seen. He thought of Mrs. Bailey, the housekeeper, but she was like Primmy and Nurse, really. Mrs. Addison, the vicar's wife, was more like this lady, and yet not at all like her. Mrs. Addison was stiff with bombazine and held her nose in the air and she had a sharp chin.

"Where are your manners, Jake?" His father spoke sharply. "Make your bow to the Comtesse de Beaucaire."

Blinking, Jake complied.

"Oh, you must call me Gabby," Gabrielle said, taking his hands in a warm clasp. "All my English friends do."

"Go up to the schoolroom, Jake," Nathaniel directed. "It may be Sunday, but I'm sure you have your collect to learn."

"Or some other improving work," Gabrielle murmured as the child turned and mounted the steps with obvious reluctance.

"It is not appropriate for him to call you Gabby," Nathaniel said in a fierce undertone. "It shows marked lack of respect."

"Stuff!" Gabrielle declared as quietly as he, watching until the child was safely out of earshot. "What's he to call me that wouldn't be a dreadful mouthful for such a babe?"

"In the first place, he's no longer a baby. And in the second, 'madame' will do very well and is far from a mouthful."

Gabrielle's nose wrinkled. "If he has my permission, I can't see why you should object. There's no disrespect in that."

"It's overly familiar." Nathaniel glared at her. "You said yourself it's what your friends call you. A six-year-old child doesn't come into that category."

"I sincerely hope he will," Gabrielle averred.

"If all your English friends call you Gabby and I do not, where does that place me?" Nathaniel switched the angle of the discussion to himself without knowing why. The issue of Jake was far from settled.

"Wherever you wish." Her eyelids drooped with a seductive indolence as she squinted against the sun, her eyebrows quirked, lips curved in mischievous invitation. "Lovers have a special position, one that transcends mere friendship."

"Transcends, perhaps," he said slowly, his eyes locked with hers. "But it can encompass it, presumably?"

"One would hope so," she replied. *But not in this case. Not with the man responsible for Guillaume's death.*

The bleak thought came nowhere near her expression. The years of loving in the shadows with Guillaume had taught Gabrielle well how to conceal true feelings from a watchful world.

Now she shook her head, still smiling, and said, "Let's not quarrel about something as simple and unimportant as what Jake calls me while I'm here. If *Gabby* really makes you uncomfortable, then tell him to call me *madame*. I shan't like it, but . . ." She shrugged. "He's your son."

"I suppose it isn't that important," Nathaniel, to his astonishment, heard himself saying. "You won't be seeing much of him in any case."

"Why not?"

"Because his place is in the schoolroom and the nursery. And as soon as I've found him a suitable tutor, then he'll be too occupied to hang around outside, playing silly games with sticks. Come inside now."

He cupped her elbow and ushered her up the steps

to the open front door, where the housekeeper stood waiting to greet them.

Gabrielle kept her own counsel on this flat, uncompromising statement. It really wasn't her business, but Miles had not been exaggerating. Matters certainly seemed awry between Nathaniel and his small son.

Mrs. Bailey did her best to hide her shock and amazement when Lord Praed introduced his guest and announced that the countess would be paying an extended visit and should be accommodated in the Queen's Suite adjacent to his own.

Covertly, the housekeeper examined the French countess and, apart from the fact that she was hatless, could find nothing at fault in either appearance or demeanor. Lord Praed's guest was affable but composed, showing no sign of embarrassment and no lack of familiarity with a gentleman's establishment. She responded to the staff's greetings with a quiet ease. And for all the French name, she spoke the King's English without any trace of accent.

The presence of a lone female in a bachelor household could only have one construction, but Mrs. Bailey decided that any presumption of familiarity on the part of Lord Praed's staff would receive a more than frosty reception from the countess, who was undoubtedly a lady. His lordship, of course, would have the offender's guts for garters, she thought with private vulgarity.

"If your ladyship would follow me, I'll show you to your apartments." She offered a friendly but deferential smile. "Bartram will bring up your luggage."

"Thank you, Mrs. Bailey."

Gabrielle followed the housekeeper upstairs, reflecting with inner amusement that the meager belongings contained in the cloakbag would add fuel to the inevitable fire of speculation in the servants' hall. But Georgie would send on the rest of her belongings as soon as she received a message.

Nathaniel went into the library intending to look

over the correspondence that had accumulated in his absence. He'd have to send for his bailiff shortly, also, and pick up the threads of the estate management again. And he'd need a report on Jake's progress from his governess. He'd have to tell Miss Primmer he wouldn't be needing her services once he'd employed a tutor. Was the boy doing any better with his riding lessons? He'd go down to the stables and talk with Milner about that as soon as he'd seen the bailiff.

"Mrs. Bailey said I'd find you here." Gabrielle's cheerful tones interrupted this reverie, and Nathaniel turned to the door, frowning.

"I beg your pardon," Gabrielle said, taken aback by the ferocity of his expression. "Should I not have come in without knocking? I didn't think it was a private room."

His whole house was private, Nathaniel thought with an irritation that he couldn't master. At least, since Helen's death it was. He wasn't used to people barging in on him unexpectedly, disturbing his thoughts. What on earth had possessed him to yield to Gabrielle de Beaucaire's outrageous impulses? He had a host of matters to deal with and couldn't possibly dance attendance on some woman who'd thrust herself unasked into his life.

"Oh, dear," Gabrielle said with instant comprehension. "You're regretting inviting me."

"I didn't invite you," he snapped. "You invited yourself."

"But you agreed." She closed the door softly behind her and came toward him. "Perhaps I should remind you *why* you agreed. We were rather rushed this morning. That inn was not exactly conducive to a leisurely waking, was it?"

Smiling, she touched his mouth with a fingertip. "I wish I knew what it was about you I find irresistible, Lord Praed, because you really are the most illtempered man. And when you frown like this, you're not even attractive. You just look hard and surly."

Nathaniel caught her wrist, his fingers circling the fragile bones, feeling the steady throb of her pulse. "You're a believer in home truths, I take it, madame."

"On occasion a person needs to hear the plain unvarnished truth," she said, only half teasing.

"Mmm. Well, I can administer it too. You're a shamelessly manipulative baggage, Gabrielle de Beaucaire, and I don't know what devil has possessed me since I met you."

She put her head on one side, observing with due consideration, "Lust, I think it's called."

Nathaniel gave in. His mouth curved beneath her caressing finger. Somehow, Gabrielle managed to circumvent his usual responses. She seemed to have no fear of his limits . . . indeed, seemed to want to find them. For both of them, he thought, reading the message in the charcoal eyes. She was not a woman who would be satisfied with ordinary experiences. She was always wanting to climb the next peak, test the waters of the next river, jump the highest fence.

A dangerous woman—trouble ran in her veins. But she was the most exciting woman he'd ever met, and he could no more resist her than he could have held back an avalanche with his fingertip.

Catching both her wrists in one hand, he clipped her hands behind her back as he jerked her hard against his body. She laughed beneath his mouth, her breath mingling with his, her teeth nipping his lower lip. The sensual sting sent the blood racing through his veins, pounding in his head, filling him with lascivious greed. Releasing her wrists, he gripped her buttocks, pressing her against his rising flesh, pushing one knee between her legs in a rough gesture of intemperate hunger.

"Dear God," he whispered, drawing a ragged breath as he raised his head but kept his hard grip on her lower body. "You make me feel like a sailor who's not seen a woman in a twelve-month!"

"And you make me feel like a whore on the waterfront," she responded with her exultant little chuckle. "All body and no mind . . . all desire and no thought."

There was a knock at the door. His hands fell from her as he spun away. Gabrielle turned to the bookshelves as Nathaniel bade the knocker enter.

"Oh, Lord Praed, I was wondering if you'd wish Jake to join you in the library this evening after his supper?"

Nathaniel cleared his throat and surveyed Miss Primmer with what he hoped was his customary impassive expression. "I usually do, ma'am, when I'm at home," he said indifferently.

"I beg your pardon. I wasn't sure whether . . . as you had a visitor . . ." The governess stammered to a halt, her face fiery as she struggled to avoid looking at Gabrielle, who remained with her back to the room, studiously examining the books in the shelves.

"The Comtesse de Beaucaire will not object to Jake's presence for half an hour before dinner," Nathaniel said.

"No, indeed not." Gabrielle judged it time to turn to acknowledge the arrival. "I wouldn't dream of interfering in his usual routine. Children rely on them so, don't they?" She smiled at the governess, who immediately forgot the scandalous implications of the countess's presence as retailed by the housekeeper.

"Well, yes, they do, countess," she agreed with a tentative answering smile. "And Jake finds change very unsettling."

"I think, Miss Primmer, in that case, that he should be exposed to more variety in his life," Nathaniel observed. "He needs to learn to adapt more readily. When he goes to school—"

"Yes, of course, my lord. But he is still very young." Miss Primmer glanced at Gabrielle as if hoping for an ally. She was a woman of middle years, thin and faded with timid pale eyes and the demeanor of one who has long been accustomed to snubs and for whom tiny mortifications were a way of life.

No match for her employer, Gabrielle summed up readily, recognizing the signs of Nathaniel's rising impatience. Miss Primmer seemed to also, and began to back toward the door.

"I beg your pardon for disturbing you, sir. I'll bring Jake to the library at half past five."

"There's no need for you to accompany him," Nathaniel said in bored tones. "He's quite capable of finding his own way to the library."

Miss Primmer stood in agonized indecision, clearly wanting to say something but unable to summon up the courage.

"Is there something else, ma'am?" Nathaniel demanded.

"No, my lord." The governess backed out of the room, closing the door softly.

"The sooner she goes, the better," Nathaniel observed. "She seems to think Jake will shrivel up if she's not there to protect him."

"Protect him from what?"

"God knows. Ghoulies and ghosties and long leggety beasties, and things that go bump in the night," Nathaniel said, shrugging. "The child's a milksop. He'll be eaten alive at Harrow if he doesn't toughen up."

"But he won't be going to school for a few years," Gabrielle pointed out.

"Two years isn't that long."

"No," she agreed. It took a minute of stern reflection to remind herself that she had neither rights nor interest in Nathaniel Praed's personal concerns. But something had most effectively doused the surging passion of a few minutes earlier.

"Would you like to see around the house?" Nathaniel asked abruptly.

"I'd love to, if you can spare the time," she said politely.

"I have an hour before I must meet with the bailiff." He held the door for her. "You'll be able to amuse yourself, I imagine?"

"Very easily." She stepped past him into the hall. "I wish to send for the rest of my clothes, so must write to Georgie."

"If you bring me the letter when it's written, I'll frank it for you," he offered with hostly courtesy.

"You're too kind, Lord Praed," Gabrielle murmured, offering a sweet mocking smile and then stopped on the stair, her eye caught by the painting hanging at eye level across the hall from her.

"What a beautiful woman." The portrait was of a young woman whose liquid-brown eyes, so full of sweetness and emotion, gazed out of the canvas with a vibrancy that seemed to bring the painting to life. Her fair hair curled in sunny ringlets on smooth bare white shoulders, and she held one hand to her throat in a gesture that was as appealing as her gaze.

"It's by Henry Raeburn," Nathaniel said shortly. "He painted it in Scotland. I have a house there." He put a hand on her waist, urging her up the stairs.

"It's Helen, of course," Gabrielle said, ignoring the encouraging hand. "Jake has her eyes and her hair."

"That's hardly unusual." There was an edge to his voice now, and the pressure on her waist increased. "Let's get on. I don't have very long."

Deciding she would spend some quiet private time at her leisure with the portrait, Gabrielle acceded and they continued up the stairs to the Long Gallery, where hung portraits of earlier Lord Praeds and their wives and children.

Gabrielle walked the length of the room, examining each picture. The men struck her as a forbidding lot, all with the same lean, ascetic features as the present incumbent. She stopped before the image of Gilbert, sixth Lord Praed.

"He doesn't look much fun," she observed. "I

wouldn't want to be answerable to him. He looks like a firm proponent of the spare-the-rod-and-spoil-the-child principle."

"He was," Nathaniel agreed. "He had a powerful right arm and didn't scruple to use it . . . not that it did me any harm," he added.

Gabrielle glanced at him, wondering how true that was. Harsh parents could produce harsh parents.

"Were you afraid of him?"

Nathaniel laughed shortly. "Yes, terrified."

"And that didn't do you any harm?"

"A little healthy fear builds character," he responded, shrugging.

But what kind of character does it build? Gabrielle kept the question to herself, reminding herself yet again that she wasn't interested in understanding the twists and turns of the spymaster's personality.

"Do your agents tell you that Napoleon has demanded that Talleyrand join him in Warsaw?" she inquired casually.

"Yes." It was a curt affirmative.

"Do they also tell you that Talleyrand intends to try to persuade Napoleon to support the Polish patriots?" She paused at another portrait, apparently giving it her undivided attention.

Nathaniel had not heard this. The inner workings of the mind of Napoleon's Minister for Foreign Affairs were as much a closed book to him as to everyone. However, it didn't suit him to admit that at this point. Gabrielle, although she didn't know it, was on trial.

"So what?" he said dismissively.

"Well, I should have thought it of some interest. Talleyrand's convinced Napoleon is simply interested in milking Poland of her wealth and her military resources while leading them on to believe he'll do something concrete for their independence."

"I should have thought that was obvious to anyone watching the way Napoleon conducts himself."

Gabrielle frowned at this snub. She had various little nuggets of information provided by Talleyrand to feed Nathaniel in order to gain his confidence, but if he was as indifferent to them as he appeared, she would have her work cut out for her.

"And I suppose it's also obvious why Talleyrand, unlike his emperor, is in favor of a strong, independent Poland?" She was still examining the portrait of Nathaniel's mother—a haughty-looking woman who seemed a perfect match for the intimidating Gilbert.

Nathaniel looked at her averted back. She held herself very straight, he noticed, her shoulders back, her head high. Her stance was as uncompromising as the rest of her, he reflected. "I can guess," he said. "Tell me your version."

She turned, laughing. "That's an underhand trick, sir. But I'm not about to fall for it. I have every intention of winning our wager."

He raised a skeptical eyebrow and said derisively, "Only fools are overconfident."

Gabrielle lowered her eyelids, hiding the burning anger in her eyes. They would soon see which of them was the fool.

She shrugged easily. "We'll see." Deliberately she dropped the topic of Talleyrand and Poland, walking over to the long windows looking out across the rolling lawns toward a river running between smooth banks. "What's the river?"

"The Beaulieu River. It flows into the Solent. If you like to sail, there's a boathouse." He came up behind her, lightly encircling her neck with his hands, massaging the soft skin beneath her chin with his fingers. He didn't seem to be able to keep his hands off her. The fragrance of her skin and hair seemed to seep into his pores and he dropped his head, burying his nose and mouth in her hair.

"I don't know how to sail." She bent her head beneath the pressure of his, her voice languorous as she slipped into the trance of arousal.

"I didn't think there was anything you didn't know how to do." His thumbs moved to trace the shape of her ears, his palms flattening against the curve of her cheeks.

"You don't know very much about me," she murmured, rubbing her face against his palms like a cat responding to a caress. How could he do this to her, reduce her to molten lava with the slightest touch? The depths of her bitterness toward him, the power of her need for revenge, were feathers in a gale compared to this physical reaction.

Fleetingly she saw Guillaume's face, the passionate black eyes, the wide, humorous mouth, the pointed chin. Fleetingly her skin remembered the feel of his hands on her body—the assured touch of a lover who knew the deepest recesses of her soul.

Sorrow washed through her as vivid, fresh, and piercing now as in the very early days of her loss. And she was breathless with the pain.

Nathaniel felt the change in her, felt her pain in his own body, transmitted through the warm, living skin beneath his fingers.

"What is it?" he whispered into her hair. "You're hurting, I can feel it."

"Just a memory," she said with an effort, moving away from his hands with a little shudder of revulsion that she couldn't suppress. She couldn't share *this* pain with *this* man. "I think that concludes the tour, don't you?"

He stood frowning at her, feeling that shudder of rejection, hearing the brusque dismissal. Where had it come from? Was she hiding something?

"Yes, I must go," he said. "I sent for my bailiff an hour ago. I'll leave you to amuse yourself. If you wish to write your letter in the library, you'll find paper and pen and ink in the *secrétaire*."

"Thank you. I'll stay up here for a little longer, though."

"As you wish." He offered a small bow in farewell and then strode from the gallery.

Gabrielle stood looking out the window until the pain had subsided and the grief was once more locked away in its corner of her soul, safe from invasion.

Then she turned and went briskly downstairs, pausing for a few minutes to examine Helen Praed's portrait more closely. Miles had said Nathaniel had adored her. It wasn't hard to see why—the goodness and sweetness seemed to shine out of her eyes. She was all soft curves, no harsh abrasions, none of the angles and sharpnesses that Gabrielle knew in herself.

Had the Nathaniel Helen had loved been very different from the man he now was? He must always have had the sternness, she thought. The forbidding side of his nature. From what she'd seen of his ancestors, it seemed to be a trait of the Praeds. He was an impatient man. But perhaps he had held back that part of himself around Helen.

He wouldn't need to be so careful with Gabrielle. She was as hard as he was—hardened, she amended. Hardened in the fire of revolution, of terror, of the loss of so many she loved. But it was a superficial toughness. Guillaume had known that. Nathaniel Praed would never discover it. He would never get close enough to do so.

In the library she began a methodical search of the room, looking for some indication of where the spymaster might keep his papers and his secrets. There was no point passing up any opportunity for gleaning information.

Her initial search turned up nothing promising beyond a locked drawer in the desk. But it was a shallow drawer and Gabrielle couldn't see how it could contain much more than a sheet or two of paper. Sliding the blade of a paper knife between the top of the drawer and the desk, she felt for the hinge of the lock with deft expertise.

The sound of the doorknob turning sent her spinning away from the desk. The paper knife fell to the carpet, and she dropped to her knees to pick it up, breathing regularly, noticing with satisfaction that her hands were completely steady.

"Gabrielle?" It was Nathaniel's voice. "What on earth are you doing on the floor?"

"I dropped the paper knife." She stood up, casually laying the knife on the blotter, and smiled easily.

"Oh." He looked at her in clear puzzlement. "Why would you need the paper knife? I thought you were writing to your cousin."

"I am, but I couldn't find the ink. I was looking on the desk and knocked the knife off."

She watched his expression closely, looking for a flash of suspicion or doubt, but Nathaniel appeared to accept her explanation.

"The ink's in the *secrétaire* with the paper and pen, isn't it?" He went to the mahogany *secrétaire* and dropped the desk leaf, reaching into one of the pigeon-holes. "Here it is."

"Oh, thank you. I forgot where you said I'd find everything." She hurried over to the *secrétaire*. "I'll get on with the letter now."

"Mrs. Bailey's laid a nuncheon in the oval parlor," he said. "I came to see if you were hungry."

"Oh, yes . . . yes, I am. Famished." She caught up a loosened lock of hair and twisted it into the pins at the nape of her neck. "It seems ages since breakfast."

"It is," he stated. "We left the inn at six o'clock this morning, and it's now past noon."

"Then that explains it. Have you concluded your business with the bailiff?"

"For the moment." He went to one of the book-cases and pulled out several volumes. "Perhaps you'd like to ride this afternoon. I can't offer you the excitement of the hunt today, but there's some hard riding to be done in the New Forest."

"That would be lovely," she responded coolly, her eyes riveted on what had been revealed behind the books Nathaniel dropped carelessly onto a side table.

Nathaniel's long fingers were manipulating the locks of a gray metal safe. His back was to her, so she couldn't see exactly what he did, but the door swung open. She stepped closer, looking over his shoulder. There were papers and an assortment of boxes and pouches inside.

He drew out a sheaf of papers and riffled through them rapidly before replacing them and closing the door again. Then he manipulated the lock once more and there was a click. He put the books back into the shelves and turned to Gabrielle.

"Is that where you keep your secrets?" she asked directly, her voice lightly teasing. She had to make some comment; to ignore it would be most peculiar.

"That's right," he agreed with cheerful nonchalance. "The spymaster's tools of his trade. Let's go in to nuncheon."

He had to be very certain of the impregnability of his safe, Gabrielle reflected, following him out of the library. He'd made no attempt to hide its whereabouts from her, although it was clearly kept hidden from casual observers. But then, why would he assume she'd have any special interest in his secrets? Or that she was in the least untrustworthy? She'd offered her services to the English government and had convinced Simon and Lord Portland of the genuineness of the offer. The spymaster's only objection to her was her sex. So why should he see a need to hide anything but the safe's contents from her?

He didn't know, of course, that his houseguest was an expert at safe-breaking. What Guillaume hadn't taught her, Fouché's policemen had.

7

Jake struggled with his tears as he watched Milner lead Black Rob from the stable. The pony was enormous—twice the size of Jake's Shetland that he'd been riding for the past two years. But Milner said he had to learn to ride a proper pony; his father had said so. But every time Milner put him in the saddle, Jake froze with terror and the tears would pour down his face however hard he tried to stop them.

"Now then, Master Jake, no tears today," Milner said with rough kindliness. " 'Is lordship's goin' to want to 'ear ye've been riding Black Rob like a regular trooper."

Jake stepped backward as the pony snorted, rolling his lips back over big yellow teeth.

" 'Ere, give 'im a piece of apple." Milner held out half an apple to the boy. "Put in on the palm of yer 'and, lad, and 'old it up to 'im. Gentle as a lamb, 'e is. He'll just snuffle it off smooth as you please."

Jake shook his head and sniffed. Then he took the apple and tentatively held out his hand toward the fiercesome lips. The pony's head bent and his rubbery lips parted. At the last minute Jake snatched his hand away and the apple fell to the cobbles. Black Rob calmly dropped his head and cropped the fruit from the ground.

"Oh, dear," Milner said, sighing. "What d'you go an' do that fer?"

"I'm sorry," Jake whispered miserably. "It fell off my hand."

Milner shook his head. "Well, up ye go, an' try to be a brave boy this time. We'll just walk once around the paddock."

He lifted the child's rigid form and ensconced him in the saddle. Jake was as white as a sheet as he clutched frantically at the pommel of the saddle and stared down at the ground, such a dizzying distance away.

It was at this point that his father and the Comtesse de Beaucaire entered the yard, returning from their afternoon ride.

"Come on, now, Master Jake," Milner said in an urgent undertone. "Show 'is lordship what ye can do." He started to lead the pony around the yard and Jake wailed, unable to help himself as his perch rocked and he could see himself tumbling to the ground beneath the pony's great iron-shod hooves.

"What on earth's the matter?" Nathaniel, still on his rat-tailed gray, rode over to him. "Why are you crying, Jake?"

Jake couldn't answer. The tears poured down his ashen cheeks and he clung desperately to the pommel.

"'E's a bit frightened, my lord," Milner explained. "Seein' as 'ow Rob 'ere's quite a bit bigger than the Shetland. Takes a bit o' gettin' used to is all."

"He's terrified," Gabrielle said. "Poor little mite."

"Now, don't be silly, Jake," Nathaniel said briskly. "There's nothing to be afraid of. Sit up straight, you look like a sack of potatoes. Let go of the pommel and press your knees into the saddle."

The instructions had no effect except to increase the child's silent stream of tears.

"Take him up with you," Gabrielle suggested in a low voice. "He has to get used to being so high up. He'll feel safe in front of you and he'll start to relax."

"Don't be absurd," Nathaniel said. "He's nearly seven. He's quite big enough to handle a pony of ten hands without being babied."

"Some people are frightened of horses," Gabrielle pointed out. "I don't understand why, but I think they're born that way. He can't help it." Before Nathaniel could respond, she moved Thunderer alongside Black Rob and scooped Jake off the pony's back and into the saddle in front of her.

"Come on, Jake, we'll go for a ride on Thunderer. He's much bigger than your pony, but I won't let you fall."

Nathaniel stared for an instant of disbelieving astonishment as Gabrielle walked her horse across the yard toward the gate to the paddock.

"Beggin' yer pardon, m'lord, but 'er ladyship might 'ave a point," Milner said. "At me wits end, I've been, sir, tryin' to get Master Jake used to the pony, but fair petrified 'e is. Mebbe this'll do the trick."

Nathaniel made no answer, but trotted his horse after Thunderer.

Jake lost his terrified rigidity as he felt the steady, warm pressure of Gabrielle's body against his back. When she told him to take the reins, he did so. Her hands covered his, guiding his movements as he directed the big horse in a circle around the paddock.

"Are you ready to trot?" Gabrielle asked.

Jake swallowed and nodded bravely. Obeying instruction, he nudged the gigantic gelding with his heels and the horse with a reinforcing signal from Gabrielle broke into a steady trot.

Grimly, Nathaniel kept pace with them. He was too angry and discomfited by Gabrielle's assumption of control to say anything, but he watched his son throughout this unorthodox lesson, noticing that Jake knew perfectly well how to ride, and once he relaxed, his posture improved. It was inconceivable to Nathaniel that his son should be frightened of horses. He himself had attended his first hunt at the age of eight and had basked in his father's rare approval when it came to horsemanship. Gabrielle had the same natural skills and fearlessness. Unlike Nathaniel, however, she didn't seem to think there was anything out of the ordinary about Jake's fear.

It was galling and yet, reluctantly, Nathaniel had to admit that her method showed some measure of success. Jake wasn't enjoying himself, but he'd stopped crying and was able to concentrate again on the fundamental techniques of horsemanship.

"Now, how about riding your own pony?" Gabrielle suggested when they'd cantered once around the paddock, Jake hanging on for dear life, white-faced but determinedly silent. "You'll find it's nowhere near as high up as Thunderer. Won't he, Nathaniel?"

"I should imagine so," Nathaniel said in frigid tones, turning his horse back to the stableyard.

Jake looked anxiously up over his shoulder at Gabrielle, who returned a reassuring smile, although she was beginning to realize how high-handed and presumptuous her behavior must seem to Nathaniel.

Back in the stableyard, she swung Jake down to the waiting groom and then dismounted herself. "Would you like me to lead your pony, Jake?"

"That's Milner's job," Nathaniel stated curtly. He lifted Jake onto the back of Black Rob. "Take the reins and put your feet in the stirrups." The instructions were brisk, but his hands were gentle enough as they straightened the child's back and slipped his small feet into the stirrups.

"How does that feel?"

Jake just nodded stiffly, his mouth set tight. "Take

him to the paddock, Milner." Nathaniel stepped back
and the groom took hold of the pony's bridle. He
clicked his tongue against his teeth and the animal
walked on, his small rider rigid in the saddle, but so far
dry-eyed and silent.

Nathaniel and Gabrielle watched for a minute,
then Nathaniel said, "Come into the house."

He walked ahead of her with a long, impatient
stride, and she followed, bracing herself for his anger.

Nathaniel didn't waste any time. He closed the library door with a sharp click and demanded, "Just what
gave you the right to interfere, Gabrielle?"

"Well, nothing, really," she said, drawing off her
gloves. "And I'm sorry if you thought that was what I
was doing. But it seemed to me that you weren't going
about it right." *Tactless!* But it was said now.

"How I choose to handle *my* son is *my* business,"
Nathaniel declared, a white shade around his mouth,
his lips thinned. "He's timid and overprotected and he
has to learn how to overcome his fear and I will *not*, I
repeat *not*, tolerate the interference of a managing
busybody who has no right whatsoever to presume any
authority in my household."

It was worse than she'd expected. She'd been perfectly prepared to apologize, but this humiliating casti-
gation was too much to endure in meek silence.

"Your son may well be your business, Lord Praed,
but if you think bullying him will overcome his fear,
then you've even less understanding of children than it
appears ... and that's saying something," she stated
with lamentable lack of finesse.

"You know nothing about it, madame," he said furiously. "You push your way into my life without so
much as a by-your-leave and then assume you have the
right to dictate—"

"That is not so!" Gabrielle interrupted, outraged.
"I didn't push my way into your life—"

"Into my bed, you did," he interrupted in turn.

"Well, that wasn't without so much as a by-your-leave!" They were getting rather off the point, but Gabrielle found herself simply following his lead, perfectly prepared to give as good as she got.

"I will not tolerate your interference with my son."

"So what were you going to do, beat the fear out of him?" she threw at him with ringing scorn. "That's what *your* father would have done, I imagine. Ensured that you were more frightened of him than the horse!"

A pulse throbbed in Nathaniel's temples and a dark flush spread over his high cheekbones. Yet he made no immediate comeback to Gabrielle's searing challenge and she waited uneasily through a long, tense silence. When he finally spoke, his voice was flat, no trace of the previous emotion.

"Yes, he would have, but I'm not about to follow his example." He turned away from her and bent to throw another log on the fire. There was a heaviness in the room, the residue of the bright, sparking fury that had flown between them.

"I could never hurt Jake," Nathaniel said, leaning one elbow along the mantelpiece, staring down at the fire. "It would be like striking Helen."

Gabrielle could think of nothing to say. The statement was too confiding, too intimate.

Nathaniel raised his head from his forearm and looked across at her. His expression was bleak, suddenly open and vulnerable, and then it closed again like the oyster over its pearl. He pushed himself upright. "I must ask you to excuse me. I have work to do."

It was a curt dismissal. Without a word she walked out of the room, closing the door behind her.

Nathaniel stood glowering for a minute, tapping his fingernails on the mantelpiece. Then he strode to the bookshelves and removed the volumes of Locke's *Treatise on Government*, revealing the safe. He spun the tumblers and opened the door. Taking out the papers, he slipped them into the breast of his coat and replaced them in the safe with a sheaf of documents from the *secrétaire* relating to estate business. Perfectly innocent material for any prying eyes. He plucked a silver hair from his temple and carefully inserted it between the door of the safe and the rim before closing the door. Satisfied that the hair was invisible from the outside, he replaced the books and left the library.

Gabrielle, still disturbed by that angry exchange, went up to her apartments to change out of her riding habit. She passed the housekeeper coming down the stairs with an armful of linens.

Gabrielle paused. "What time does his lordship dine, Mrs. Bailey?"

"At six o'clock, ma'am. His lordship keeps country hours here. He sees Master Jake in the library at five-thirty, in general, and then dines afterward."

"I see. Thank you."

"I'll send Ellie up to help with your dressing, my lady. She's ironed your gowns. They were rather crumpled from the cloakbag."

"Yes, I'm not surprised," Gabrielle said without blinking an eye, even as she wondered what Ellie and the housekeeper had made of the britches keeping company with the more respectable items of clothing in the cloakbag. "I'm expecting the rest of my traps to be sent on in the next few days, so I'll be most grateful if Ellie can do what she can for now with what I have with me."

"Of course, my lady." Mrs. Bailey went on her way, as curious as ever about the Comtesse de Beaucaire. A proper lady she was, despite certain odd items of clothing in her meager luggage, but what was a proper lady with a wedding ring doing in this scandalous situation? The gossip would be all over the county in no time. Not that it would trouble his lordship any.

Since her arrival that morning, Gabrielle had had little opportunity to examine the apartments allotted her. There was a large, sunny bedchamber with heavy winter velvet hangings to the bed and windows, a Turkish carpet on the highly polished floorboards, a fire burning in the grate beneath an elegant carved mantelpiece. Adjoining it was a small boudoir, carpeted and curtained in rose velvet like the bedchamber, furnished with a chaise longue, several armchairs, and a delicate Queen Anne *secrétaire*. Here, too, a fire burned in the grate.

A door in the far wall connected the boudoir with his lordship's apartments. Had these been Helen's rooms? On one hand, it seemed obvious that they had been, but on the other, Gabrielle couldn't believe that Nathaniel would have installed his mistress-of-the-moment in the apartment of his late, beloved wife. He was a forbidding and frequently ill-tempered man, but he had a sensitivity that perhaps truly revealed itself only during his lovemaking. She knew he would not have insulted his wife's memory.

She suppressed any further curiosity about the late Lady Praed. It had no bearing on her reason for being there . . . as did any further interference in Lord Praed's relationship with his son.

She would remain in her apartments until six o'clock, leaving Nathaniel to conduct his daily interview with Jake in private.

Thus resolved, Gabrielle greeted Ellie's arrival and the offer of hot water for a bath with heartfelt enthusiasm. She had no idea how Nathaniel would behave after the afternoon's unpleasantness, but she would leave him to set the tone.

At half past five she was sitting in the bay window of the boudoir, watching the dusk roll in from the river, listening to the loud cawing of a flock of rooks settling for the night in a stand of conifers at the end of the garden. Nathaniel's family estate was beautiful, flanked on one side by the Beaulieu River meandering through tidal marshes to the Solent, the wide body of water be-

tween the mainland and the Isle of Wight, and on the
other by the primeval majesty of the New Forest.

They'd ridden that afternoon in the Forest, crossing
the gorse- and heather-strewn common land into the
broad rides beneath the centuries-old oaks and beeches.
It was not a part of the country Gabrielle knew, but she
felt its tug and had seen in Nathaniel's relaxed, peaceful expression that this distinctive contrast of sea and
forest ran in his blood.

A soft tap on the door disturbed her reverie. Un-
sure whether she'd really heard it, she turned her head
toward the door. The tap came again, more of a
scratching than a definite signal.

"Come in."

The door opened slowly. Jake stood there, his hand
still on the knob, a serious expression on his face, his
round brown eyes solemn. He was very clean and tidy,
his starched white shirt with ruffled collar buttoned
onto his nankeen trousers and his hair glistening
damply from judicious wetting to keep it lying neatly
on his forehead.

"Jake?" Gabrielle rose and crossed the room. "This
is a surprise." She smiled down at him. "Come in."

Jake shook his head. "I have to go to the library."
But he still stood there, holding the door, staring down
at his feet in their buttoned boots.

"Your papa will be waiting for you," Gabrielle
agreed, glancing at the clock.

"You coming too?" He raised his eyes from the
floor. "To see Papa?"

Nathaniel had forbidden Miss Primmer to bring the
child to him, Gabrielle remembered. Was Jake really so
shy of his father that he couldn't face him alone? It was
ridiculous. And yet, perhaps not. Children could be intimidated by many things, and Nathaniel, except in
certain very specific instances, was not an inviting person.

"If you like." She made up her mind. She'd accompany the child, but she'd take no part in the conversation.

Taking the child's hand, she walked down the stairs with him. "How was Black Rob, Jake? Did you trot with him?"

"No," Jake said solemnly. "But I rode him without Milner holding the bridle. Tomorrow I'll trot ... but just in the paddock," he added. "Until I feel braver, Milner says."

"That's very sensible," Gabrielle agreed. "How did you know where to find me?"

"Primmy said you were staying in the Queen's Suite. It's called that 'cause a queen stayed there once."

"Oh, which queen?"

"I don't know."

They'd reached the library and Jake paused, raising his hand to knock on the paneled door.

Gabrielle felt the stiffness in the small frame and smiled down at him. She opened the door before he could knock.

"Jake says a queen once slept in my bedroom, Nathaniel. Which one?"

Nathaniel was reading papers at the big desk. He raised his head and looked at her and was struck anew by the unerring flair that determined her clothes. Her gown of soft, clinging crepe was the color of slate and heather with long, tight sleeves buttoned at the wrist. A triple tier of black lace ruffles at her throat formed the high neck appropriate for an afternoon gown. Her hair was piled in a knot on top of her head, with a cluster of ringlets falling over her ears.

The image of her naked body on the seat of the carriage that morning suddenly obtruded on this vision of understated elegance and it took his breath away, banishing all the lingering resentments of the afternoon and the cold detachment with which he'd set his trap. "I like that gown," he declared abruptly.

"I apologize for the informality," she said with a

gravity belied by the mocking glimmer of laughter in her eyes. "I'm afraid I didn't bring any evening wear . . . not being certain of my destination."

"We don't stand on ceremony in the country," he assured her with matching solemnity, indicating his own unassuming morning dress of buff pantaloons and coat of brown superfine.

"I prefer it that way," she said, her tongue touching her lips, and they both knew she was not referring to evening dress.

Jake's hand moved in hers, and she shook herself free of the gossamer strands of arousal. "Which queen?" she asked again, as if the previous exchange had not interrupted the preceding train of thought.

"Queen Caroline, George the Second's wife," he said. "She spent a night here on her way from Southampton to London." He rose to his feet. "May I pour you a glass of sherry? Or would you prefer madeira?"

"Sherry, thank you." She took the glass he handed her and sat down on the window seat, picking up a periodical from the side table. It was a copy of the *Farmer's Almanac*, hardly stimulating reading for a nonfarmer, but it was all that came immediately to hand and would serve to indicate to Nathaniel that she had withdrawn her attention from himself and Jake.

Nathaniel perched on the edge of the desk, stretching his legs out in front of him as he sipped his own sherry. Jake shifted his feet on the carpet and waited for the inevitable questions about his schoolroom progress in his father's absence.

Gabrielle idly turned the pages of the almanac and listened to the stilted question-and-answer session. It was excruciatingly painful to listen to Nathaniel's careful questions and the child's monosyllabic replies, and she had to bite her tongue to keep from interrupting. There seemed no connection, either physical or emotional, between the man and the child. She had an almost overpowering urge to fling her arms around the two of them and push them together.

What was it that made Nathaniel so distant, so chilly with his son? It surely couldn't just be that he was trying to toughen him up. He'd obviously had a troubled relationship with his own father, but he said he had no intention of following that example. Didn't he realize that his manner could be as hurtful to the child as any crude physical discipline?

Obviously not. Nathaniel was dismissing the child, sending him back to the nursery with a handshake. It was absurd, Gabrielle thought, watching covertly as Jake's tiny, dimpled hand disappeared into his father's large one and the child bobbed his head in a half-bow of formal farewell.

"Say good night to her ladyship," Nathaniel instructed Jake, reaching to refill his glass, relief clear in every line of his body now that his parenting session was over for the day.

"Good night, Jake." Gabrielle reached for the child as he approached, put her arms around him and kissed him. "Is Primmy going to read you a story?"

"She might," Jake said. He stayed for a moment in the circle of her arm, his body leaning against her with a slight ambivalent awkwardness as if he wanted to stay but didn't know whether he should.

Gabrielle kissed him again. "Tomorrow, I'll tell you one of my stories," she promised.

"Do you know lots?"

Something had happened to the room, Nathaniel thought in vague bemusement. The light seemed to have softened, the crackling of the fire to have intensified, imbuing his customarily austere library with a domestic, hospitable warmth and comfort. And it was emanating from Gabrielle. The curtains were still open behind her, and the rising moon hung low over the dark curve of the river, a silver and black background for the vibrant head and pale skin.

"Oh, I know lots of stories," she answered Jake, gently putting him from her as she became aware of Nathaniel's silent frowning observation. "Good night, Jake."

The door closed on the child's departure and there was an uncomfortable silence until Nathaniel said, "I'd prefer it if you didn't make promises to my son, particularly ones that will interfere in his routine."

"Nathaniel, I just offered to tell him a bedtime story," she exclaimed in soft-voiced exasperation. "If you don't want me to do it, why don't *you* tell him one?"

"I don't know any," Nathaniel said crossly.

"Oh, you must remember some from your childhood." She regarded him in disbelief over the rim of her glass.

He shook his head. "I was never told any to remember."

"Poor little boy," she said softly. "What a horrible childhood you had."

"It was not horrible in the least." He scowled into the fireplace.

"Were you an only child?"

"Yes, like you."

"How did you know that?"

"Miles said something." He shrugged and drained his glass before standing up. "If you're ready, we should go in to dinner. I don't like to upset the cook. She's inclined to fret if her dinner spoils."

"I can't say I blame her." Gabrielle rose and took his formally proffered arm. "Of course I was just eight when I went to live with Georgie's family and stayed with them until I was eighteen. So I don't feel like an only child."

Nathaniel made no response as he held the door to the dining room for her. It was a massive room with heavy oak furniture and dark paneling. The long table had two place settings, one at each end. Candles in ornate silver holders marched down the middle of the expanse, the yellow pools of light merely accentuating the vast distance between the two diners.

Gabrielle opened her mouth to suggest a more friendly arrangement that would be easier on the serving staff, and then closed it firmly. She'd spoken out of turn quite enough for one day. She was still a guest in Nathaniel's house, however unorthodox the arrangement.

She took the seat Nathaniel pulled out for her and then gazed down the table at him with what she hoped was an expression of intelligent, courteous companionship.

"Do you know Georgie's family?"

"Not really," Nathaniel said, taking the scent of his wine before gesturing to the footman to fill Gabrielle's glass. The man's footsteps sounded very loud on the waxed oak floor as they progressed the length of the table.

"Georgie's the eldest of six," Gabrielle persevered, feeling in some way as if she had to explain her own ease with children to a man who clearly didn't know the first thing about them.

She smiled slightly. The DeVanes were a large, erratic family, generally happy, tumbling in and out of scrapes that Lady DeVane regarded with vague dismay on the rare occasions she noticed and her husband responded to with indiscriminate clouts and caresses. None of the children were ever much perturbed at finding themselves on the receiving end of one rather than the other for whatever reason. Justice was a movable feast in the DeVane household and accepted as such with cheerful pragmatism.

Gabrielle helped herself from a dish of artichokes presented by the peripatetic footman and began to describe life in the DeVane household to her companion. She generally considered herself a lively conversationalist; however, Nathaniel responded to her remarks and stories with at best a noncommittal murmur, at worst, a frown and a vague grunt.

After a while she decided to leave the conversation to Nathaniel, and fell silent. The silence was disturbed only by the footman's movements and quiet queries.

"I'll leave you to your port," she said when the covers had finally been removed, the footman had left, and the silence had remained unbroken through the entire second course.

"That seems unnecessary," Nathaniel said, filling his glass from the decanter at his elbow. "With just the two of us . . . unless, of course, you'd rather withdraw."

"I don't think it'll make much difference," she commented, leaning back in her chair. "Since your dislike of conversation at mealtimes is so profound, I can hardly see that my company could matter one way or the other. My poor efforts at conversation have certainly failed to entertain you."

Nathaniel glared in the candlelight. "This is a damn stupid way to dine," he stated. "Who the hell decided to set the table like this? I can barely see you, let alone converse."

Gabrielle pushed back her chair. "If you're prepared to share the port, I'll join you down at that end."

"I wish you would." He rose as she came the length of the table and took the chair next to him. "I suppose you're going to accuse me of being ill-tempered and surly again."

"Deny it," she challenged him.

He made a rueful grimace and cracked a walnut between finger and thumb. "I can't, damn you." He peeled the nut and placed it on her plate.

"Well, I don't suppose my conversation was all that stimulating," she said cheerfully, popping the nut into her mouth. "Shall we try again? What topic would be most suitable? Children and childhoods are clearly forbidden." She cast him a sideways glance to gauge his reaction to this frank statement.

His expression was dark, then he shrugged. "It's not a subject that inspires me, I grant you. And I don't care to talk about Jake, so if you don't mind, from now on we'll leave him out of our conversations."

"If you say so."

She took a sip of port, her eyes, bright with sensual suggestion, smiling at him over the lip of the glass.

8

Charles-Maurice de Talleyrand-Perigord leaned over the railed gallery overlooking the ballroom of the elegant eighteenth-century palace on Miodowa Street in Warsaw, surveying his guests below. It was a sight to satisfy the most ambitious statesman. The flower of Poland's nobility and the Emperor Napoleon's triumphant court were gathered together for the opening of the carnival season as guests of the emperor's Minister for Foreign Affairs, recently given the title of Prince of Benevento by his grateful emperor. The ball, as Talleyrand had intended, was turning out to be the most brilliant function Warsaw had seen since the glorious days of Poland's monarchy—before Russia, Austria, and Prussia had partitioned the country, each taking her share.

In this frozen winter of 1807, the Poles had welcomed Napoleon, his army, and his court with fervent adulation, hoping as always for the emperor's protection and support in their bid for the restoration of Polish independence. Napoleon received their adulation as readily as he received their soldiers and the contents of their coffers, but he promised nothing in return.

The Prince of Benevento watched the swirling bejeweled throng below and wondered how many of them understood that their savior was no savior. They had welcomed his entrance into snow-covered Warsaw with two triumphal arches, brilliantly lit and inscribed with the legend: LONG LIVE NAPOLEON, THE SAVIOR OF POLAND. HE WAS SENT TO US STRAIGHT FROM HEAVEN. There had been torch parades through the city and bonfires lit around the old royal palace high on a cliff over the Vistula, where the emperor was to reside, and every house and shop sported a gold Napoleonic eagle.

But their *liberator* would bleed them white and then abandon them as a sop to his own defeated enemies, the Austrians, the Prussians, and the Russians. The Partition of Poland would not be ending any time soon.

There were some areas in which his master was very shortsighted, Talleyrand reflected, tapping his long fingers on the gilded railing. A strong Poland was essential to the stability of the Continent. A northern barrier, it would act as a vital buffer state between Russia and the West. But left partitioned, it was as helpless as a wounded bird facing the cat.

"There is at least some compensation for this dismal country's terrible climate."

Talleyrand turned at the voice of his son. Charles de Flahaut leaned over the railing at his father's side, inspecting the scene. Although the Comte de Flahaut had officially recognized the child as his own, Talleyrand's paternity had always been privately acknowledged both by his son and the world, and his natural father's influence ran through every aspect of the young man's career.

"The women, you mean." Talleyrand smiled. "They're unusually attractive, I agree."

"And one in particular," Charles mused. "The emperor seems much struck by Madame Walewska." He glanced sideways at the older man, his eyes shrewd.

"Indeed," Talleyrand agreed with another bland smile. "But are you surprised? She's a charming combination of beauty and intelligence, with such a sweetly shy manner. The emperor finds her most refreshing after Josephine . . . and the others. You know how cynical he's become about women these days."

"And the lovely Marie might well exert a beneficial influence . . . ?" suggested Charles with the same shrewd gleam in his eye.

"Perhaps so, *mon fils*, perhaps so."

The old fox wasn't giving anything away, as usual, Charles reflected with an inner chuckle. But he'd been watching his father's skillful maneuvers with the entrancing young wife of the elderly Chamberlain Anastase Walewski. If Marie Walewska became Napoleon's mistress, she might well influence him in Poland's favor where all the blandishments and pleas of the country's nobility and politicians had failed.

He moved away, leaving his father to continue his observation. The exquisite Madame Walewska, in a delicate gown of white satin over a pale gold and pink underskirt, a simple laurel wreath on her fair curls, was partnering the emperor in a quadrille. The contrast between the lady's exquisite grace and her partner's clumsiness was laughable, but Napoleon wouldn't give a fig for his awkward performance, as Talleyrand knew well. In the emperor's opinion, a man at home on a battlefield had no right to be at home on the dance floor.

The emperor, however, was making no secret of the fact that he found Madame Walewska enchanting. However, could the lady be persuaded to sacrifice her honor for her country? Talleyrand had discovered that Marie was passionately devoted to the cause of Polish liberation. He knew she would give everything she had, maybe even her life, in the cause, as, indeed, so many of her countrymen were doing. But she was young, innocent, delicately bred. Would she give Napoleon the one thing he wanted?

His eyes flickered to a deep window embrasure, where Anastase Walewski stood preening himself as he watched his wife. There would be no trouble from the old man, Talleyrand thought with cynical knowledge. He'd give his wife to Napoleon without a qualm for the sake of the reflected glory.

However, to be on the safe side, Napoleon's Minister for Foreign Affairs would devote some flattering attention to the self-important chancellor.

The prince moved away from the railing and limped to the sweeping curve of staircase leading down to the ballroom. Pimping for his emperor was a new experience, but Talleyrand used what tools were at hand in his diplomacy. If the way to the liberation of Poland lay through the emperor's bed, then so be it.

It might be useful to inform Gabrielle of Napoleon's new love interest. He would send a letter by express messenger to the contact in London, who would send it on to the Vanbrughs' house in Kent—the seemingly chatty, innocuous letter of a godfather to his dearly loved godchild. Gabrielle would pass the nugget on to her spymaster as a token of good faith and further proof of her access to the private ears of the emperor's inner circle. Disseminating the information would do France and Talleyrand's own plans no harm. The English were only observers in the fate of Poland.

Smiling benignly, he crossed the room toward Chancellor Anastase Walewski, preparing to congratulate him on his wife's success and the possibility of his imminent cuckledom.

The faces crowded closer. Sweating, red, eyes bloodshot, the mob pressed forward. Their mouths were open, gaping holes in the grotesque faces as they yelled their obscenities at the man and woman standing at bay behind a long table against the salon wall.

A cudgel smashed against the polished tabletop, gouging

a great wound in the rosewood. The woman shrank back against the silk-covered wall and her husband tried to speak above the tumult. His tones were measured, reasonable, and they were drowned under screeching, mocking laughter and more obscenities.

A citoyenne in the red bonnet of the Revolution spat across the table, and from somewhere came the sound of smashing glass as a window broke beneath the assault of a cudgel.

A man in the bloodstained apron of a butcher struggled to lift the edge of the table. Another heaved with him, the veins in his forearms great blue ropes beneath the weather-beaten skin. The table fell onto its side with an almighty crash. The couple behind were now exposed to the mob, their fragile barrier demolished. Hands reached for them, hauled them out, and they were lost in the throng, pushed and jostled to the great double doors of the salon. The sounds of breaking glass continued and the child, lying rigid along the beams of the ceiling, smelled smoke as someone fired the tapestries in the long gallery upstairs and the orgy of destruction reached new levels of enthusiasm. . . .

The narrow cobbled street was thronged, the stench of un-washed humanity heavy in the sultry summer air. The open tumbrils clattered over the cobbles in an endless stream, their passengers standing cheek by jowl, hands bound in front of them, hair scraped back from their faces, white faces staring unseeing into the jeering crowd running beside the carts, pelting them with rock-hard dried mud and rub-bish from the kennels.

The child now stood at a gabled window under the eaves of a wine shop. She hugged the shadows as she looked out on the scene below. It was the same scene every day, from dawn to dusk when Madame Guillotine closed her eyes for the night.

The face of a woman among the condemned in the sec-ond cart became suddenly sharply defined amid the sea of *desperation. The child pressed her hand to her mouth to keep from crying out as she watched the cart pass below the window and out of sight around the corner of the Rue de Seine. . . .*

The low, heartbroken sobbing jerked Nathaniel into full awareness before he realized what it was. The bedroom was filled with moonlight, the ruddy glow of the dying embers in the grate a counterpoint to the cold silver clarity of the light.

Gabrielle was sitting up beside him, tears sliding out from her closed lids to track down her cheeks. The sobs were in her throat, and she rocked her body as she hunched pitifully over her drawn-up knees.

"Gabrielle," he whispered, shocked to his core. She made no response, and he touched her bare back. Her skin was slick with sweat and cold as the grave.

"Gabrielle," he said again, louder this time, his warm palm cupping the damp curve of her shoulder. When her eyes remained shut and the sobs continued, he realized she was still asleep. Fast asleep, she sat hunched over her knees, racked with some devastating inner anguish. What nightmare world was she inhabiting?

"Gabrielle! Wake up!" He spoke with a calm authority, swiveling to take her shoulders from the front and shake her awake. "Wake up, you're having a bad dream."

Her eyes opened and the sadness in them struck to his heart. The dark red ringlets clustering around her face clung to her cheeks, damp with tears and sweat, and she stared at him for a minute, unrecognizing. The sobs gathered in her throat, but as he watched in impotent compassion, she swallowed vigorously, wiped the back of her arm over her eyes, and loosened her hair with her fingers, tossing it back over her shoulders.

"I'm sorry," she said, her voice thick with the residue of tears. "Did I wake you?"

"What was it?" he asked gently. "What were you dreaming?"

Her shoulders lifted in an infinitesimal shrug and she shook her head. "Nothing . . . nothing at all." She lay down again, closing her eyes firmly. "Go back to sleep, Nathaniel. I'm sorry I woke you."

"That won't do," he said sharply, gazing down at her.

"What won't?" She rolled onto her side in the fetal position. "I'm sleepy."

He could feel the jagged edges of her pain as an almost palpable aura around the curled figure, and he knew she was as wide awake as he was.

"It won't do," he repeated, swinging out of bed. "And don't pretend you're sleepy, because I know damn well you're as far from sleep as you could possibly be."

He went over to the fireplace and bent to rake through the embers, stirring them into flickering life. He tossed kindling onto the flicker and waited until the dry wood caught. Then he turned back to the bed.

Gabrielle was lying on her back now, her eyes still resolutely closed. Tears stained the translucent pallor of her cheeks, and there was a bead of blood on her lower lip where she'd bitten it.

A few hours earlier he'd fallen into a satiated sleep beside a bold, imperious, exciting woman of inventive and ingenious passion. And he'd woken beside a vulnerable, deeply hurt woman who looked both much younger than her years and yet paradoxically older.

"Gabrielle." He came and sat on the bed beside her, laying a hand on her stomach, feeling the muscles jump in instant reflex against his cool palm. "I want to know what you were dreaming."

Her eyes opened and he saw the residue of stark pain in their charcoal depths.

"It was nothing, I told you. Nothing important. I'm sorry I woke you."

"Don't keep saying that." Impatience, never far below the surface, broke through his compassion. "You were dreaming something terrible."

Sighing, Gabrielle sat up. "And what if I was? We're all entitled to our privacy, Nathaniel. You have no rights over my soul."

Nathaniel stood up abruptly. "Now, just listen to me. We make the most wonderful, transcendent love for hours and I fall asleep holding you in my arms, feeling your breathing, smelling your skin and your hair, aware of every millimeter of your skin touching mine. And then I wake in the middle of the night to find you soaked in sweat, sobbing in utter desolation, and you tell me I'm not entitled to know what's the matter. Well, it won't do, Gabrielle. Passion can't exist in a vacuum." He glared at her.

"Biting my head off isn't going to encourage me to bare my soul," she observed. A shiver ran through her as the sweat cooled in the cold night air and goose bumps rose on her skin.

Nathaniel heard the beginning of resignation in her voice. He turned to the armoire and drew out a heavy velvet robe. "Put this on and come to the fire," he said, his voice calm and gentle now. Kindness on the heels of exasperation could be a potent persuader, as any skilled interrogator knew. Throwing another robe around his own shoulders, he went to the door. "I'll bring up some cognac."

"I'd love some warm milk," Gabrielle murmured, huddling into the warm folds of the robe. "If you're going downstairs."

Nathaniel scratched his head. He rarely ventured into the back regions of his house and wasn't at all certain that he'd know how to produce such a commodity.

Gabrielle was smiling at him in perfect comprehension, just a tinge of her customary mockery in her eyes. "I'll come with you," she said. "I'm sure the kitchen fire's well banked for the night. It'll be warmer than here."

"And then I'll hear the story," he asserted.

Gabrielle had shared the nightmare with only two others: Georgie and Guillaume. They were the only people until then with whom she'd shared a bed throughout the long, dark hours of the night when the memories of terror awoke. But to tell Nathaniel was to reveal a weakness—a corner of her soul—to the enemy. Then again, the pragmatic voice of reason said, it would substantiate her hostility to her father's nation.

Reason won over instinctive reluctance. "Yes, I'll tell you," she said. "It'll probably happen again, so it's only reasonable that you should know."

Nathaniel held out his hand. They went down to the kitchen, the skirts of his velvet robe brushing Gabrielle's bare toes. She set a pan of milk on the range and sat down, propping her feet on the shiny brass fender before the fire, while Nathaniel fetched the decanter of cognac from the library.

"So?" he said quietly when they were both sitting in the hushed kitchen, only the loud ticking of the longcase clock disturbing the somnolent peace.

Gabrielle cupped her hands around the mug of hot milk, inhaling the brandy-rich steam. "At the beginning of the Revolution, my father voted with the Third Estate at the Estates General, with the Duc d'Orléans and Mirabeau and Talleyrand. They all believed in reform. When matters ran out of hand, Talleyrand went into exile." She shrugged and allowed a flicker of distaste to tinge her words. Nathaniel must believe that she held no brief for her godfather.

"He's a wily bird . . . wilier than my father ever was. Talleyrand knew the fickleness of the wind and the populace when anarchy reigns, and he always knows where his best interests lie. My father, I think, believed that the people would always know him for what he was. He truly believed that he could not be harmed by those whom he'd sworn to support."

"But the Terror didn't distinguish," Nathaniel said.

"No," she agreed with a somber headshake. "It swallowed its own most fanatical supporters as eagerly as it swallowed the *aristos*. Anyway, my parents were taken one afternoon by the mob. They were taken directly to the Tribunal, condemned, and executed the next day ... at least," she added, "my mother was. I saw her in the tumbril. I don't know exactly what happened to my father. He disappeared into the prisons and was never heard of again."

"And where were you?" Nathaniel prompted.

"When they realized the mob was coming, my father hid me in the rafters of the salon. They were broad oak beams, quite wide enough for a small child to lie on, hidden from below." She raised her eyes to him over the lip of her mug. "In the nightmare I relive that afternoon. It's not really a nightmare in that it's not all jumbled and symbolic the way dreams usually are. It's always just a very straight repicturing ... reliving ... of what happened. And then afterward, always, I relive seeing my mother in the tumbril on her way to the guillotine."

She drank deeply and fell silent. The bare bones of the story were all she was prepared to reveal.

"How did you escape France?"

"Talleyrand," she said. "He kept contacts in Paris throughout the Terror, although don't ask me how. He's an expert opportunist, a master at keeping a foot in every camp."

She stared into the fire. "He probably could have saved my parents ... oh, I don't know. I just sometimes think that his attentions to me have been out of guilt." She shook her head impatiently. "Although I can't imagine His Highness of Benevento feeling guilt for anything. He's far too pragmatic."

Nathaniel absorbed this and tucked it away for future reflection. "So what happened next?"

"Talleyrand's contacts smuggled me out of Paris and onto a fishing boat in Brittany. I was deposited on the doorstep of the DeVanes' London house early one morning by a French refugee who'd been told where to take me. The DeVanes took in an almost mute, terrified, grieving child and left her alone to come to herself in her own time. They put up with my silences, my grief, my moods, automatically assumed I would join them in their pursuits and accepted it when I didn't. And one day I came out of it. I stayed with them until I was eighteen. They're my family, and their loyalties are mine."

She smiled slightly over the lip of her cup. "I don't have enough words to describe what they did for me. I tried to describe at dinner what a large, loving, and chaotic family they are."

"Yes," Nathaniel said, uncomfortably remembering his own surly, monosyllabic response to those attempts at conversation. "I wasn't too receptive, was I?"

"You could say that." Her smile broadened. "But you recovered your good humor . . . what there is of it," she added with the customary mocking glimmer in her eye.

Nathaniel shook his head in rueful acceptance. "Miles and Simon are always telling me what an illtempered bastard I am."

"Why are you?" Gabrielle asked, putting her empty cup on the floor beside her chair. "I think a little reciprocation is in order. Tell me something about yourself." Even as she made the demand, she regretted it. She didn't want to know any secrets about Nathaniel Praed. But it was too late to withdraw the question.

Nathaniel shook his head, throwing his hand wide in a comprehensive gesture. "You're in my house, sharing my life. The story's there to be read."

"But perhaps I don't read the language," she said, unsmiling now.

Again he shook his head in brusque dismissal. "I doubt that, madame. I have the unshakable conviction that you're multilingual. Let's go back to bed." He turned to the door.

Gabrielle concealed her relief at this escape.

"You go on up," she said. "I'm not sleepy yet. I'll stay by the fire for a while. I'll sleep in my own bed, so I don't disturb you when I come up."

Nathaniel, holding the door latch, turned back to her. His eyes raked her face. Her expression was calm, the dark eyes returning his scrutiny with candor. "If you're sure that's what you want," he said.

"Quite sure. I'm perfectly calm now. It won't happen again tonight."

He continued to regard her for a moment, then nodded as if satisfied. "Don't stay up too long, then."

"Good night, Nathaniel."

"Good night, Gabrielle." The door closed softly on his departure.

Gabrielle gazed into the vermilion glow of the fire, flexing her toes against the fender in the warmth. The longcase clock struck three. The household was asleep and would remain so for at least another two hours. Nathaniel would be asleep soon. She'd intended to explore the safe tonight, but an excess of tumultuous passion had somehow knocked her out. It seemed the nightmare had given her a second chance.

Without further thought she rose and went to the door, her bare feet soundless on the stone flags of the kitchen floor. She stood in the narrow corridor leading to the main hall, ears pricked for the slightest sound of movement. A kitchen cat brushed against her legs as it slithered by on a mouse hunt, nose twitching, ears flattened, tail erect.

To Gabrielle's ears, the sleeping house seemed filled with little sounds—creaks and whispers and rustles. She could hear her own heart and the rush of her blood. Scaling walls and setting a hunter to an outrageous fence required a different kind of courage from this creeping around illicitly, prying into someone else's privacy.

But she'd never lacked the courage when working with Guillaume, and she wasn't about to let his memory down.

She ran on tiptoe down the corridor and entered the great square hall. The double doors to the library were on her right. Inside, she closed the doors softly and stood, accustoming her eyes to the moonlit room. The servants must have pulled back the curtains before retiring, and the long windows were filled with silver light. The heavy furniture formed massive hunched shapes on the Aubusson carpet.

Gabrielle slid out the volumes of Locke's *Treatise on Government*, placing them soundlessly on the table behind her. She stood and looked without moving at the gray metal safe set into the paneled wall, trying to picture the tumblers within the lock, to project her mind into them. It was a powerful way to concentrate.

She placed her ear against the lock and began delicately to turn the knob. The clicks sounded like crashing cymbals in the silence, but experience told her that only she could hear them. Her fingers were slippery with sweat and her shoulders cramped abruptly with the tension.

She straightened, rolling her shoulders, and dried her sweating fingers on the skirt of the robe. Then she bent again to her task, listening for the sweet connection when the tumblers meshed. The night stretched into eternity in the silent, silver-washed room. The winter-bare branch of a tree scraped against the window and her heart jumped into her throat. She took a deep breath and continued with the delicate manipulation.

"Got it!" she breathed in soft satisfaction as she felt the tumblers connect. Gently, she eased open the door of the safe and surveyed its contents—the spymaster's secrets laid bare.

Wiping her hands again, she took out the sheaf of

papers. She hadn't known what she'd find, but this series of neat accounting documents, columns of figures, prices of wheat, lists of repairs to tenant housing, was not what she'd expected.

Disappointed, she replaced the papers and closed the safe. Back to square one. She turned to pick up the volumes from the side table. Something caught her eye. A shaft of moonlight set something aglimmer on the carpet at the bottom of the bookcase.

She bent to look more closely. A fine strand of silvery hair lay on the carpet. Her body went very still as her mind raced. It was easily explained. Nathaniel had been at the safe earlier, she'd seen him. He could have brushed a fallen hair from his shoulder.

But supposing he hadn't? The hair was an old trick to test for intruders. Could Nathaniel be testing her?

Of course he could. He was a spymaster. The cleverest the English had ever had, according to Talleyrand and Fouché. Why else would he so nonchalantly reveal the location of his safe?

Damn the man! He was a crafty, devious, bloody-minded, oversuspicious snake! And now she'd have to put it back.

The whole tedious business of manipulating the knob began again. She refused to wonder how long she'd been down here ... to speculate on whether Nathaniel was asleep ... to consider for one minute the possibility of discovery.

The safe door finally opened again. Gabrielle held the hair between finger and thumb. Where had he placed it? At the top, or at the side?

Merde! She couldn't possibly know. But then again, perhaps it wouldn't matter. As soon as he opened the door, the hair would surely fall out just as it had when she'd opened it. And he'd never see where it came from. But he might be looking for it.

She had no choice. Swiftly yet delicately she inserted the hair between the upper edges of the safe and its door and closed the door again. She wiped the surface of the safe with the full sleeve of the robe so there were no smudges or fingerprints. Then her heart sank again. Could he have used a film of dusting powder as well? If so, she was lost.

There was no sign of powder now and no use in worrying about it, she told herself briskly, replacing the volumes of Locke. She looked around the room again.

To her astonishment, she saw from the clock that the entire futile operation had lasted less than half an hour.

Her spirit rebelled at retiring empty-handed. There was still the locked drawer in the desk. A much easier proposition, and it might yield something of interest.

She flitted to the desk. The paper knife was where it had been that morning. She sat in Nathaniel's big leather chair and gently slid the blade of the knife between the top of the drawer and the desk, feeling for the hinge of the lock. Once located, it was simplicity itself to press the hinge down with the tip of the knife, springing the lock. The drawer contained a roll of parchment tied with a black ribbon.

Gabrielle looked at it, chewing her lip. Surely a spymaster wouldn't keep precious secrets tied up with a ribbon. They must be private documents.

Just to be sure, she lifted the roll of papers from the drawer, untied the ribbon, and unrolled them.

They were letters, very private letters. Love letters. They were a courtship correspondence between Nathaniel Praed and his then fiancée, Helen. Gabrielle stared at the signatures, hardly taking in the contents. She hadn't bargained for anything quite so intimate.

Suddenly, the fine hairs on the nape of her neck rose and her scalp crawled. She couldn't hear anything, but the knowledge that someone was approaching ran in her veins, turning her blood as cold and thin as a mountain stream. She dropped the letters into the drawer, the ribbon on top of them, and softly closed the drawer just as the doorknob turned.

"I've been looking all over for you. I can't go to sleep when you're staying up on your own. What are you doing in here? It's as cold as charity."

Nathaniel, still in his robe, stood in the doorway, squinting into the silvered dimness.

Gabrielle's heart hammered. How long had he been looking all over for her? How had she not heard his steps in the house? What if he'd walked in a minute earlier?

"I was looking for something to read," she said, rising casually from the chair, turning to lean against the desk with the appearance of complete relaxation while covering the violated drawer with the skirts of Nathaniel's robe. Not that there was anything to see, but for the moment she was so unnerved, she could almost imagine her guilt gleaming behind her.

"In the dark?" Nathaniel stepped farther into the room.

"I was looking for flint and tinder." Both commodities were in full view on the mantelshelf, and she averted her eyes.

"I'll light the candle for you." Nathaniel strolled over to the fireplace. Flint scraped and a pool of golden light fell from the candle on the mantelpiece.

"What do you feel like reading?" Taking the candlestick, he held it high and walked over to the bookshelves.

Gabrielle pushed herself away from the desk. Somehow, she'd have to reopen the drawer and retie the letters with the black ribbon. Surely he wouldn't want to look at them tonight. *Oh, please don't let him want to revisit the correspondence tonight!*

"I don't really know. I was feeling restless." She came up beside him, brushing against him as she examined the spines of the books under the candlelight.

Nathaniel glanced down at her. Her pallor in the

golden glow seemed more pronounced than usual. "I don't know about restless," he commented. "You look drained. Why don't you try to sleep instead?"

"Yes, perhaps I will." She pushed back her hair and offered him what she hoped was a natural smile. Lightly, she blew out the candle he held. "Let's go up-stairs."

Nathaniel made no attempt to persuade her to join him in his bed when she turned toward her own apartments. He said only, "If you need me, you know where to find me."

"Yes," she replied. "Thank you."

She stood by the connecting door between her boudoir and Nathaniel's apartments for ten minutes, listening for the silence that would tell her he was asleep again. When she could no longer hear the creak of the bedropes as he settled himself for sleep, she sped down to the library, once again blocking her mind to all thoughts of discovery, worked her trick with the paper knife again, retied the letters, and replaced them in as near to their original position as she could remember.

It had been an unproductive night's work ... except that she now knew that the spymaster did not trust her.

9

"How long will it take us to journey to Burley Manor, Simon?"

"Burley Manor?" Lord Vanbrugh looked up from his platter of sirloin, regarding his wife with some surprise as she entered the breakfast parlor.

"Yes. I've just had a letter from Gabby." Georgiana flourished a sheet of paper that had arrived with her morning chocolate. "She wants us to send on all her belongings. She's staying with Lord Praed for—let me see, how did she put it—ah, yes, here it is, *an indefinite period*, she says."

Georgie looked up, a glimmer of mischievous amusement in her blue eyes. "Isn't it scandalous?"

"It sounds just like Gabby," Miles Bennet observed, taking a draft of ale from his pewter tankard. "Although not at all like Nathaniel."

"Well, it's clearly our bounden duty to go there and save her reputation," Georgie declared, reaching across her husband's shoulder to take a mushroom from his plate.

"*Go there?*" Simon and Miles declared in unison, looking appalled.

"Descend on a man without warning when he's involved in . . . in . . . intimate, private business?" Miles continued, shaking his head in horror.

Georgie swallowed her mushroom and stole another. "Gabby's as much a sister to me as my own," she said. "Mama would insist it was my family duty to rescue her from social disaster." She gave a smug little nod of her head.

"You crafty minx." Her husband slapped her hand aside as it began a renewed forage of his plate. "You're not fooling me for one minute. You're just nosy!"

"Not at all," Georgie declared with an air of injured innocence. "If it gets out that Gabby's staying unchaperoned under a bachelor roof, she'll be ruined. Papa would say it was as much your duty as mine to offer our protection. In fact," she added thoughtfully, "he'd probably expect you to call Lord Praed out."

"Good God! What a hideous prospect. No man in his right mind would attempt a duel of any kind with Nathaniel Praed."

"Not if he intended to come out of it alive," Miles agreed, chuckling. "Georgie my dear, a man does not interfere in the private concerns of his friends."

"What a pair of lily-livers you are," Georgie said in disgust. "Well, I am going if you're not! Gabby needs me." She turned and swept from the breakfast parlor.

Simon groaned.

"You could always forbid it," Miles suggested tentatively, regarding his friend with some compassion.

"It wouldn't work," Simon said with conviction. "Georgie may act the demure helpmeet and look as if butter wouldn't melt in her mouth, but she's a DeVane, remember."

"Ah, yes."

Gloomy silence fell over the breakfast table as the two men contemplated the obdurate personality of the DeVanes.

"Of course, she could be right," Miles said finally. "If it ever did get out . . ."

"That's not what interests my inquisitive wife in the least," Simon said forcibly. "She wants to gossip with Gabby and find out exactly what's going on. Can you imagine how Nathaniel's going to view such an imposition . . . the three of us descending—"

"Hey! Who said anything about *three?*" Miles exclaimed hastily.

"You don't think I'd go without you!" his friend demanded. "Oh, no, dear boy, we're in this one together."

"*I'm* not married to a DeVane," Miles pointed out.

"Nathaniel's as much your friend as he is mine."

"But this isn't about Nathaniel, it's about Gabby's reputation. And she's your kin, not mine."

"And you're my cousin and therefore connected to that *enfant terrible* too."

"Oh, that's outrageous! Of all the spurious, tenuous threads of connection . . ."

"Nevertheless, my dear fellow, you're coming with us." Simon pushed back his chair and rose from the table. "I can't permit Georgie to go alone. Two women under a bachelor roof is simply doubly scandalous. Her father would visit me with a horsewhip!"

"And you're unable to rule your wife," Miles observed.

" 'Fraid so," Simon agreed with an accepting shrug, his hand on the doorknob. "We'll say we're passing through and thought we'd ask for a night's hospitality. With any luck, one evening with Gabby should satisfy Georgie's inveterate curiosity."

"And you think that'll fool Nathaniel?"

"No, of course it won't. But he'll not turn us away even if he refuses to speak two words all evening. It wouldn't be the first time, would it?"

"No," murmured Miles moodily as the door closed behind Lord Vanbrugh. "Far from it." He put up his eye glass and examined the chafing dishes on the sideboard, but for some reason his appetite for breakfast had diminished.

"Oh, it looks as if you have a stack of work to do," Gabrielle observed, entering the library in the bright sun of relatively early morning.

Nathaniel looked up from the desk and ran a hand through his crisp dark thatch of hair. "Yes, dispatches," he agreed. "You'll have to amuse yourself, I'm afraid."

"I'm perfectly capable of doing so, sir."

Nathaniel nodded, then abruptly pushed back his chair. He took a sheaf of papers off the desk and strolled casually to the bookshelves.

Gabrielle wandered over to the window, looking with apparent idle interest across the stone-flagged terrace to the frost-tipped lawn beyond.

The fine hairs on the nape of her neck were prickling as she heard his movements and visualized his hands removing the volumes of Locke, his fingers manipulating the lock of the safe, his eyes searching for the telltale hair.

Nathaniel glanced over his shoulder at Gabrielle's averted back. He'd waited for her to be in the room before he checked the safe for signs of tampering.

Turning back to the safe, he began to manipulate the lock. Before opening the door, he looked behind him again and swore loudly. "Hell and damnation!"

"What's the matter?" Gabrielle said calmly, turning from her contemplation of the garden. Her eyes were calm, her ivory complexion as translucent as ever. "Have you forgotten the combination, Sir Spymaster?" One of her crooked little smiles accompanied the teasing question.

No revealing reaction there, Nathaniel decided. Not a flicker of anxiety in her gaze. "No, but I caught my fingernail in the lock," he said, sucking his index finger for the sake of verisimilitude, before gently easing open the door of the safe.

"Oh, there's Jake," Gabrielle said loudly, flinging open the window and calling the child's name in echoing tones.

Startled, Nathaniel looked back at her for the barest instant, the door of the safe in his hand. He returned his attention to the safe in time to see the hair fluttering to the floor.

Gabrielle was talking to Jake through the window, apparently oblivious of Nathaniel as he bent to pick up the hair.

"What are you up to this morning, Jake?" She pinched the child's nose.

"Primmy and me are going for a nature walk," he said solemnly, peering around her with an anxious twitch of his mouth at the dark shape of his father in the back of the room.

The governess stood behind him, smiling nervously, twisting her gloved hands. "Now, don't disturb her ladyship, Jake."

"He's not disturbing me," Gabrielle reassured. "What do you collect on your walks?"

"We don't collect things," Jake said. "We only look."

"Oh." Gabrielle could think of no response to this. The DeVane children had taken the business of collecting very seriously and competitively—insects, tadpoles, flowers, butterflies—and she'd discovered its appeal soon enough herself. Just looking at things seemed rather dull work for a six-year-old.

"We don't like to bring dirty things into the schoolroom," Miss Primmer explained.

"No, I suppose not," Gabrielle agreed.

"An' Nurse doesn't like anything in the nursery." Jake added his mite. "She says it's bad enough with all the flies and things that come in on their own."

"Come along now, Jake." The governess took the

child's hand. "We have to be back by eleven o'clock for your lesson with the globes. His lordship will want to know this evening how well you've learned about the oceans."

Jake's expression lost some of its liveliness and his eyes darted anxiously beneath Gabrielle's arm as she held open the window. There was no reaction from his father, so he dutifully took his governess's outstretched hand and bade Gabrielle good-bye.

She closed the window again, watching the woman and child walk briskly across the grass to the driveway. They wouldn't see much of interest if they kept up that pace, Gabrielle reflected.

She turned back to the room, the cheerful smile still on her lips, no sign of the violent turmoil in her head.

Nathaniel closed the safe with a snap. For a second his eyes rested on her, brown and unreadable.

"How very fierce you look," she said lightly, her pulses racing. "Is something troubling you? Did you object to my talking to Jake?"

"No," he said, and sat down again behind his desk, pointedly sorting through the papers.

"Don't let me disturb you," Gabrielle said. "I realize you have work to do." *Had she given herself away?* It was impossible to tell from his demeanor.

Nathaniel merely grunted and dipped his pen in the inkstand.

"I was wondering . . ." Gabrielle began. "Oh, but I'm sorry, I didn't mean to disturb you." She moved around the room, straightening cushions, tidying the periodicals on the side table, humming to herself, trying to decide how best to resolve her uncertainty. Maybe if she broached the subject of espionage directly, he'd give her some clue.

"I was wondering if you have agents in every city on the Continent?"

"Most." He didn't raise his eyes and answered with brusque impatience.

Gabrielle ignored the tone. "I suppose you must have people placed strategically in all the royal courts too. I wonder if you have anyone close to Talleyrand? Or in Madame de Staël's salon in Paris, perhaps?"

Nathaniel's lips thinned. "Have you had breakfast?"

"Not yet. Have you?"

"Yes."

"Mmm. It doesn't seem to have improved your conversational skills. I thought you were averse to conversation only at the table."

"I am never averse to conversation, only to prattle."

Gabrielle whistled appreciatively. "Now, that's a home hit, sir."

"I doubt that, ma'am," he said aridly.

Gabrielle persevered in the same musing fashion. "Do you ever go to work in the field yourself, I wonder? Or does a spymaster just sit in the middle of the web, masterminding machinations? I wonder what it must feel like to send people into danger without exposing oneself occasionally."

"It seems to me you do all too much wondering, madame. Go and have your breakfast." Nathaniel kept his eyes resolutely on his papers.

"It really is very difficult to find an acceptable topic of conversation," Gabrielle observed, shaking her head. "Children and childhoods are taboo. Your work is absolutely forbidden. Any speculation as to why you're such an irritable bastard is equally prohibited. It really makes a body wonder how to fulfill the social duties of a polite guest."

For a moment there was no response, then Nathaniel raised his head. He seemed to be considering something, and then one of his rare smiles spread slowly from his eyes to his mouth. "There's one perfectly acceptable topic, Gabrielle. I'm surprised you haven't come up with it."

"Oh?" She had the sudden absolute conviction that all was well. She had escaped his trap. She could feel her own smile responding involuntarily to his, even as she wondered if he knew the power of a smile that he hoarded with such care.

"Sex," he said succinctly. His eyes narrowed but the smile remained. "Did you know that you have a delicious little cluster of freckles under your right breast, shaped rather like a daisy . . . and what's really delicious is that you have almost the identical configuration on the curve of your backside? Definitely worth closer inspection, I think . . ."

"Nathaniel!" she said, the soft protest belied by her chuckle and the gleam in her eye.

"I wish it were strawberry season," he continued.

"I'm sure I shouldn't ask—at least not before breakfast—but why?" Her knees were unaccountably quivery and she hastily perched on the sofa arm.

"Oh, I have a fantasy," he said in the same matter-of-fact tones. "I want to fill your navel with champagne and dip strawberries into it."

Gabrielle's limbs turned to melted butter and her loins throbbed.

"Will you be working all day?"

"Not if you leave me alone now."

"Is that a promise?"

"It could be . . . now, *go!*"

"Yes, sir." She wrestled with her tumultuous body for a minute and then managed to offer him a mock salute as she went to the door.

"Gabrielle?"

"Sir?"

"See if you can think of a January substitute for strawberries before this afternoon."

"And the champagne?"

"I've several cases of a very fine vintage in the cellar."

Gabrielle smiled at the crisp dark head still bent over his papers as if they were discussing the menu for din ner. A difficult, irascible, reclusive man was Nathaniel Praed, but it didn't seem to diminish his sensuality one iota.

"Until later, then, my lord."

"Until later, countess."

She closed the door behind her and, still smiling, went toward the small breakfast parlor behind the stairs. At the foot of the stairs she paused, and then, without forethought, went up until she was on a level with the portrait of Helen, Lady Praed.

The sweetly smiling eyes looked across at her, the gentle mouth curving softly. What had Helen known of her husband's vibrant sensuality? Of his unerring touch and instinct? Of his arousing hand?

Gabrielle inhaled sharply as desire again jolted her belly with the force of a lightning bolt. There had been no words of earthy passion in the letters she'd seen last night. Nathaniel had written tender, loving words describing Helen's smile, the sweetness of her eyes, of how he could barely endure the waiting until they should be together. They were the thoughtful words of a man deeply in love, careful not to say or do anything that would frighten or injure his beloved.

And Helen's responses ... but Gabrielle hadn't read those. It was bad enough that she'd been unable to tear her eyes from Nathaniel's writing, let alone that she would dig into the private feelings of a woman long dead whom she'd never met.

She turned abruptly from the portrait and went back downstairs to the breakfast parlor. Nathaniel's relationship with Helen was dangerous territory best left well alone. And the same applied to his relationship with his son.

It became hard to keep to that resolution later that

day when Miss Primmer came out of the library just before nuncheon, her face screwed tight, lower lip trembling, a handkerchief held to her mouth.

Gabrielle, coming in from a walk around the shrubbery spent contemplating a substitute for strawberries, stopped in concern. "Why, Miss Primmer, what is it? Something's upset you." Her eyes flicked to the closed library door. Presumably the governess had just had an interview with her employer.

"Oh, dear, countess ... too kind of you ... it's just ... I knew it had to happen, of course ... and his lordship is being most generous ... excellent character and a month's wages ... but, oh, dear, I can't help worrying ..."

She pulled herself up short, dabbed at her eyes, and straightened her bowed shoulders. "Goodness me, how I do run on," she said with pathetic dignity. "Take no notice of me, my dear countess. It's just such a shock, coming so soon ... I had thought maybe another two years ... but his lordship knows best, of course."

"I wonder," Gabrielle murmured. Not when it came to his son. "Come up to my sitting room, Miss Primmer, and take a glass of sherry with me. Then you can tell me all about it." She linked her arm with the governess's and urged her upstairs, ignoring the feeble protests.

Miss Primmer allowed herself to be put in an armchair, a glass of sherry pressed into her hand even while she demurred faintly.

"His lordship told me he was considering employing a tutor for Jake," Gabrielle said directly, sitting on the broad window seat.

"Yes ... and, of course, I know it has to happen ... but I did think it wouldn't be so sudden. Jake is such a shy little boy ... it would be so much better if I could stay with him for a little while until he becomes accustomed to someone else."

"You mean Lord Praed is turning you out as soon as

the tutor arrives?" Gabrielle couldn't keep the shocked disapproval from her voice even though she'd told herself it was none of her business.

Miss Primmer nodded, sniffed, dabbed at her nose with her handkerchief, and took a rather large gulp of sherry. "His lordship is all generosity, I mustn't complain, countess, but I do think Jake needs some time."

"Yes." Gabrielle leaned back against the wall of the window embrasure, turning her head slightly to look out over the river. Miss Primmer might not dwell upon her own misfortunes, but it was no pleasant matter to be turned out in middle years after long service, an excellent reference and a month's wages notwithstanding. A governess's life was not to be envied.

"I have a married sister," Miss Primmer was continuing, as if divining her companion's thoughts. "I'll be able to stay with her for a little while until I find another situation. I can be useful around the house and with the children. It gives Nurse a rest, you understand."

"Perfectly," Gabrielle said. An indigent relative offered house room could certainly be put to good use.

"But it's Jake I worry about," Miss Primmer reiterated. "I don't know how to tell him."

"I think that task should be left to Lord Praed," Gabrielle stated firmly.

"Oh, but I'm sure he expects me to break it . . . oh, dear, that's not what I mean . . . to prepare the child."

"Nevertheless, I don't think you should say anything—if you would take my advice, of course." She reached for the decanter, offering to refill her visitor's glass.

"Oh, too kind . . . no . . . no, thank you, it makes me quite giddy . . . not used to it, you understand."

Indeed the lady's cheek was somewhat flushed, her eyes rather bright.

"I must go back to the schoolroom. Jake will have finished his nuncheon now." Miss Primmer rose slightly unsteadily to her feet. "Oh, dear," she murmured, taking hold of the back of the chair. "You've been very kind, countess."

Gabrielle shook her head. "Not at all." She escorted her visitor to the door. "Don't say anything to Jake just yet."

Miss Primmer looked at her with a gleam of hope in her eye. "Do you think it's possible his lordship might change his mind?"

"I don't know," Gabrielle said with perfect truth. "But perhaps he might reconsider the timing of your departure."

The governess bustled off looking a little less forlorn, and Gabrielle returned to the window seat. There was something about little Jake that tugged at her. Maybe it was the memory of herself as a child, so alone and frightened and confused. Jake was no orphan, but he was motherless and his relationship with his father was fractured, to say the least. And one of the loving and reliable pillars of his short existence was about to be snatched from him. And there'd be no chaotic and loving DeVanes to take her place, only a tutor and the harsh realities of school.

Gabrielle had heard enough about these realities from the DeVane boys to know the child Jake was now would barely survive physically, let alone emotionally. Why didn't Nathaniel realize it? But of course that was what lay behind this banishment of the governess. It was preparation. It would certainly prepare Jake for random severity. . . .

"I hope your imagination's been working overtime this morning."

It was Nathaniel's voice, his other voice, the one that accompanied the lingering hand of arousal. Gabrielle turned her head to the connecting door, where he lounged against the doorjamb in his shirt-sleeves, deliberately unbuttoning the cuffs.

"Comfits," she said, suddenly breathless, all thoughts of troubled children flown from her mind.

"Comfits?" His eyebrows rose. He rolled back the cuffs of his shirt.

"Sugar plums and sugared almonds," she explained. "A perfect accompaniment to champagne."

He nodded slowly. "Yes, I believe that will do nicely." He gestured past him to his own room. "Will you walk into my parlor, madame?" The brown eyes were aglow, his mouth curved with promise.

"With pleasure, sir." Gabrielle walked past him, and he closed the door.

"My, you have been busy," she observed, taking in the table set for nuncheon in the window. "Two bottles of champagne, no less!"

"I'm planning a long afternoon."

"But we have no comfits," she pointed out. "Ham and cold chicken, but no sugar plums."

"Hothouse grapes, however," he said, plucking a succulent black grape from the bunch sitting on a chased silver salver.

"It seems you had no need of my imagination, Lord Praed," she murmured, watching fascinated as he peeled the grape with his teeth.

"Two imaginations are twice as good as one," he said. "I shall ring for sugar plums in a minute." He placed the grape against her lips. "Open."

His fingertips inserted the peeled grape between her lips and he smiled as she curled her tongue around the fruit, savoring its coolness and the texture of the flesh before biting into it.

"A promise," he said softly.

"I think sugared almonds are the best," Gabrielle declared, dipping one of the comfits in her personal champagne thimble. "There's something about the crunchiness of the nut with the silkiness of the champagne. What's your opinion?"

"I don't think I'm capable of one," Nathaniel murmured, stretching his body beneath the butterfly flickers of her tongue sipping nectar from his navel. He drew a sharp breath as cold drops trickled over his skin when she carefully refilled the thimble.

"Keep still," she commanded. "You'll spill it."

A quiver of laughter ran through him as he struggled to hold himself immobile.

"I'll try a grape this time," Gabrielle said consideringly, reaching sideways to select one from the depleted bunch. "Just to refresh my memory." She popped the grape between her lips, and her laughing eyes held his for a moment before she bent her head.

He could feel her weight resting lightly across his thighs, her breath on his skin, the tickling brush of the dark red ringlets across his belly as she dipped the grape into the champagne well. Holding the succulent dripping fruit between her lips, she moved up his body until her face hung over his.

Nathaniel opened his mouth, closing his eyes, and she lowered her mouth to his, delicately pushing the grape between his lips with her tongue.

"Sugar plum now?" She ran her flat thumb over his mouth, the lingering embers of satisfied desire glowing in her eyes.

"If you're trying to rekindle my flagging energies, ma'am, I'm very much afraid it's not going to work," he said, smiling as he ran his hands through the cascading ringlets, lifting them away from her face. "You have unmanned me, love."

Gabrielle chuckled and pushed herself upright so that she was sitting astride his thighs again. "I don't think I'm prepared to admit defeat quite so soon."

"Mercy!" he cried, reaching down to seize her

hands as they set to work with wicked, dexterous skill. "Come cuddle for a minute."

"If you'd prefer," Gabrielle acquiesced equably, lying down beside him. "Just remember I wasn't the first to cry quits."

"*You* don't have to work as hard," Nathaniel pointed out, running a lazy hand down her spine as she curled against his side.

Gabrielle smiled and kissed the hollow of his shoulder, savoring the salt tang of his skin. "Don't you think it might be easier for Jake to become accustomed to a tutor if Miss Primmer stays around for a while." She kept her tone lightly conversational, tracing the shape of his ear with her little finger.

"I thought we'd agreed that Jake was not a suitable topic for conversation." Nathaniel spoke with constraint, but it was clear he was making an effort to restrain his rising annoyance. The stroking hand lifted from her back, leaving a cold space.

Against her better judgment, Gabrielle persevered. She hadn't intended to say anything at all yet, but somehow the long intimacy of the afternoon had blunted her natural caution and the words had formed themselves and spoken themselves.

"I just wonder if you've considered all the aspects," she said, kissing his ear.

"Don't do that, Gabrielle." Nathaniel jerked his head sideways. "I don't like it."

"You don't like my kissing your ear, or talking about Jake?" *In for a penny, in for a pound.*

"The latter," he said. "It's not your business, and you have no right to presume on the basis of what . . . of what we've been doing all afternoon."

"It's called making love, I believe." Gabrielle sat up. "And I don't mean to presume. But there are other ways of looking at things and maybe you're being a bit shortsighted."

Nathaniel sighed. "I would really appreciate it if you didn't spend time discussing my private affairs with my staff while you're here."

Gabrielle gulped. Was that what she'd been doing? "Miss Primmer was very upset. I just asked her what the matter was." She could hear the defensive note in her voice.

"And she poured out her woes and her opinions into your receptive ear, presumably hoping that you would use your influence while my guard was down."

Gabrielle winced. "I don't believe that was the case. She doesn't strike me as manipulative, poor woman."

"Oh, for God's sake!" Nathaniel gave up the attempt at restraint. "Poor woman, indeed. You've been listening to her wailing and now I'm some harsh and exploitative employer turning out a pathetic, homeless crone—"

"Oh, stop it!" Gabrielle lost her own temper. "That's not it at all, and you know it. She was very insistent about your generosity, but she was concerned for Jake—as we all are, presumably even his father!" She glared at him through a veil of unruly dark red curls.

Nathaniel swung out of bed. "Yes, *even* his father. I think you've said enough, Gabrielle. If we're to salvage anything of this afternoon, I suggest we part company and cool off."

Dismissals didn't come much clearer than that. If she wasn't careful, he'd be calling a halt to their interlude long before the two weeks were up, and she'd have failed.

Without a word Gabrielle slipped from the bed, gathered up her discarded garments, and went naked to the connecting door.

"Don't forget that *you* were the one who pointed out that passion can't exist in a vacuum," she said as she left. She closed the door behind her with deliberate softness.

Nathaniel swore under his breath as he looked around the room at the tumbled covers and the remains of their lascivious picnic. Lustful interludes with no strings to the future and no connections with the past. Who on earth had they been trying to fool?

10

The memorandum was clear and precise: *Le lièvre noir removed June 6, 1806. Agent six disappeared during assignment, presumed dead. No repercussions—death before capture is presumed.*

Gabrielle stared down at the paper in her hand, stared down at Nathaniel's elegant script. A jet of fury leaped through her veins with all the vigor and crystal clarity of the fountains in the gardens of Versailles.

She'd known it, but the confirmation, here in her hand, burning into her eyes, shook her more deeply than she could ever have believed it would.

The document belonged in a file of private memoranda—notations, emotionless statements of the success or failure of various enterprises under Lord Praed's direction. It was the spymaster's personal, professional diary. And it contained the confirmation of Guillaume's death as it was ordered by Nathaniel Praed.

Gabrielle took a deep, slow breath and looked around Nathaniel's bedchamber. Late afternoon shadows gathered in the corners of the meticulously tidy apartment. There were very few personal touches in the room, which was furnished with an almost spartan simplicity.

The house was very silent and there was a curious suspended quality to the quiet. The ormolu clock on the mantel chimed four o'clock. Nathaniel wasn't expected to return from his ride around the estate with the bailiff until close to dusk, but there was no point taking chances. There was still much to be learned from the file, but the search of Nathaniel's chamber had taken the best part of two hours and it was all too easy to make mistakes at the end if one cut things too fine.

Gabrielle slipped the folder back into the cavity beneath the false bottom of the top drawer of the armoire. She stared down into the space, concentrating as she pictured the position of the folder when she'd first lifted the false bottom. Satisfied that the folder was replaced at exactly the same angle, she dropped the bottom of the drawer into place and meticulously replaced the linen cravats that had covered it. She had removed each one separately to be sure there were no booby traps between the folds, but had found no strategically positioned pieces of cotton or fluff.

Again she stared down into the drawer, picturing it as it had been before her disturbance. It looked the same. She slid the drawer closed and drew from her skirt pocket a small envelope containing a fine white powder.

Her tongue dampened her lips, and a deep, intense frown drew her eyebrows together as she sprinkled a film of the powder over the top of the armoire to reproduce the undisturbed surface she'd found.

It was the dust that had alerted her to the hiding place, although she was willing to admit that she might not have noticed it if she hadn't had such a scare over possibly missing something like it with the safe. But she had her own supply of the spy's tricks of his trade, and substitution was no problem.

She backed toward the door that connected with her boudoir and then stood very still, examining the room, mentally checking everything over. It all looked the same, and she was willing to lay odds that not even someone as experienced as Nathaniel would be able to tell there'd been an intruder.

Gabrielle slipped through the door and back into the safety of her own apartments. Only then did she allow the grief to resurface. It welled up from deep within her, great racking gobbets of sorrow filling her throat so she could barely breathe, tears pouring heedlessly from her eyes, soaking the front of her gown, her face contorted with the raw brutality of her emotion.

She stood quite still and silent under the violent buffeting of indescribable sorrow, and then as it ebbed she waited for the cleansing fire of anger to sweep through her, hardening her with the compelling power of vengeance.

She would be revenged upon Nathaniel Praed and his secret service. And it would be the subtlest revenge and all the more satisfying for it. She would use and manipulate the man who had ordered her lover's murder. And he'd never know what a dupe she'd made of him. Not unless she decided to tell him, of course. And maybe one day she would . . . and how she'd enjoy the telling.

Calm again, she washed her face, bathing her eyes with cold water until the swollen lids subsided and the translucent pallor of her complexion was restored.

Then she sat down in her favorite spot on the window seat to collect her thoughts. After her disappointment with the library safe, she'd decided that Nathaniel must have removed his vital documents and it stood to reason that he wouldn't have left them lying casually around. Yesterday, when he'd ridden into Southampton on business, she'd conducted a thorough search of the small office where he dealt with estate business and met with his bailiff.

It had turned up nothing, although she was the first to admit that didn't mean there *was* nothing; it was always possible to conceal things from the most experienced spy. But that afternoon she'd attacked the next most obvious place and had turned up gold. It was ironic that Nathaniel's precautions had given away the hiding place. But then, she'd profited from the lesson of the library.

A tap on the door heralded Jake's now-customary evening arrival. He was looking remarkably cheerful, the reason obvious in his first bubbling announcement.

"Papa doesn't want to see me in the library today 'cause he's still doing business with the bailiff. So we can have a really *long* story." There was utter confidence in his assertion as he clambered onto the window seat beside her and beamed up at her.

Gabrielle smiled and encircled him with one arm. "Which story?"

Jake tilted his head, a little frown on his brow as he considered the question. He resembled the portrait of Helen much more nearly than he did his father, but there were moments like this one when an expression, the tilt of his head, or some tiny gesture would remind Gabrielle of Nathaniel with an almost heart-stopping accuracy.

"The one about when you and Georgie an' Kip rode the ram with the curly horns and he chased you out of the field and you got stuck in a bramble hedge."

"You know it already," Gabrielle laughed.

"Yes, but I want to hear it again." He stuck his thumb in his mouth and snuggled against her.

Children were always immensely comforted by the familiar, Gabrielle reflected as she began the tale, searching for some interesting and hitherto unrevealed embellishments to enliven the narrative.

She heard the door to Nathaniel's bedchamber open and close. Heard his footsteps on the bare polished floor. Heard the sound of a drawer being opened, a cupboard door unlatched. Her heart began to speed but her voice didn't falter as she continued with the story. She felt the child stiffen against her for a minute as he, too, heard the sounds of his father's proximity, then Jake relaxed again.

Nathaniel opened the connecting door and stood leaning against the jamb in his shirt-sleeves, one-handedly loosening his cravat as he took in the cozy scene.

Gabrielle's skin prickled as her eyes absorbed the long-fingered hand against the white lawn of his cravat, the lean, athletic frame, and her body shot off on one of its unilateral journeys into the world of throbbing arousal as she felt as vividly as if it were real his hand and his body on hers. Ten minutes earlier she'd been filled with lethal hatred for this man, and now she could think only of what his body did to hers.

"Nathaniel." Somehow, despite the swirling turmoil as her physical responses warred with her emotions, she managed to greet him with a serene smile, her arm tightening around the child as she felt the currents of unease flowing through the small body. "We're just finishing a story. Did you have a successful afternoon?"

"Tedious, but I achieved what I had to," he said. "Isn't it time you were in bed, Jake?"

"I can't tell the time yet," Jake confessed in a tiny voice, his solemn, liquid brown eyes regarding his father anxiously.

Nathaniel made no immediate response. He was struck by the comfortable intimacy of the woman and child and the softness that surrounded Gabrielle like an aura. It was feminine and loving and it seemed to flow over Jake. How had he ever thought she lacked womanly tenderness? The more he learned of her, the less it seemed he knew.

"Hasn't Miss Primmer tried to teach you?" he asked after a minute.

"I'm not very good at it," Jake confessed, wriggling uncomfortably. As always, the atmosphere in the room had changed with his father's arrival, and he could feel something different in Gabby, almost as if she were angry about something. He hated it when people were angry. When Cook shouted at Hetty, the scullery maid, and Hetty cried, he always felt like crying himself and his tummy went into a hard knot. But even though he could feel something was wrong, Gabby was smiling. His father wasn't, but then, Jake didn't think his father ever smiled.

"Well, I think it's time you became good at it," Nathaniel said, glancing at the Chippendale clock on the wall above the chaise longue. "It's almost six."

"Yes, sir," Jake murmured with downcast eyes. He squirmed out of Gabrielle's hold and slid off the window seat.

"Don't you want to hear the end of the story?" Gabrielle asked, laying a hand on his arm.

Jake glanced at his father and then stared down at his feet again, mumbling something inaudible.

"Finish the story," Nathaniel said abruptly, feeling like an ogre from a fairy tale casting gloom and despondency wherever he went. Anyone would think he took pleasure in making the child unhappy, but for some reason everything he said to the boy came out wrong. And Jake looked at him all the time as if he was expecting harshness. Had *he* looked at his father with the same apprehension? If so, he'd certainly had a good deal more cause than Jake.

He shook his head with an impatient gesture. "I have to get out of my dirt before dinner, Gabrielle. I'll see you in the library in half an hour."

She inclined her head in acknowledgment and lifted Jake back onto the window seat. The child's eyes darted toward his father, and on impulse Nathaniel stepped forward and awkwardly patted his head.

"Good night, Jake."

The salute so startled the boy that he stared dumbly at Nathaniel, who, without waiting for a response, turned and went into his own room, closing the door behind him.

Now, that had been quite promising, Gabrielle thought as she resumed the story. Whatever ill she might wish Nathaniel, it belonged in the dark world of espionage and bore no relevance to his relationship with his child. If she could effect some changes there, inject a ray of warmth, then she would do it.

Nathaniel stood frowning, stroking his chin thoughtfully behind the closed door of his own chamber. His eyes darted to the armoire. He'd checked it as soon as he'd first entered the room. The film of powder remained undisturbed. And the second safe he kept concealed beneath a loose floorboard under his bed also bore no signs of intrusion. Not that he would expect anyone to find it without a wholesale search that would involve tipping up the massive poster bed. Gabrielle certainly couldn't move it alone.

He glanced over his shoulder at the closed door and nodded thoughtfully. So far, it appeared that Gabrielle was what she seemed. One more thing remained before he would be completely satisfied, however. He must search her possessions. As soon as the Vanbrughs sent on the rest of her luggage, he would conduct that search and then, so long as it turned up nothing even remotely out of place, he would reconsider employing Gabrielle in the network.

That evening Gabrielle's particular brand of sensual challenge seemed even more pointedly mischievous than usual, and once or twice Nathaniel, even as he responded, felt a stirring of unease. There was a brittleness to her, almost a hint of desperation. He told himself he was being fanciful, that his mistress was just in one of her more intensely passionate moods, and as they soared to the heights of ecstasy during the glorious hours of the night, he forgot his earlier misgivings in the kaleidoscopic wonders of their fusion.

Gabrielle sought to vanquish turmoil in the clean responses of passion. She told herself that the afternoon's discovery altered nothing, since it merely confirmed what she had already known. But whoever Nathaniel Praed was ... whatever he had done ... nothing could diminish the power of their mutual obsession, an obsession that would facilitate her revenge.

She awoke the next morning lying on her stomach, her body pressed into the mattress with Nathaniel's length measured along her back.

"Is it morning?" she murmured, stretching her arms over her head, her toes reaching to the foot of the bed in a bone-cracking stretch beneath his weight.

"Mmmm."

"What are you doing?" She wriggled beneath him, tightening her thighs in playful resistance.

"Guess." He nipped her earlobe, inserting a knee firmly between her closed thighs.

"Supposing I hadn't woken up."

"I'd have been mortally offended."

Gabrielle chuckled lazily, yielding to the insistent pressure of his probing flesh.

Winter sun filled the room half an hour later when Nathaniel reluctantly pushed aside the sheet and stood up, stretching and yawning. He smiled down at Gabrielle's prone figure, her nose still buried in the pillow. Leaning over, he scribbled a fingernail along her spine and smoothed a flat palm over the peach roundness of her bottom.

"It looks like a beautiful day. If it's not too cold and the wind and tide are right, would you like to go for a sail on the river?"

"I should love to," she said sincerely. "Will you teach me how to sail?"

"If you like." Something remarkably like a grin

curved the corners of his mouth. "Are you a patient pupil?"

"That depends on the instructor, sir." She rolled onto her back and squinted up at him with a quizzical smile. "I'd guess patience is not your long suit ... so, perhaps it would be a bad idea."

"Oh, I might surprise you," he said blandly. "I'm not totally predictable."

"Then surprise me."

"With pleasure, ma'am." Bending over her, he ran a fingertip over her nipples until they rose beneath the caress, then, with a smug nod of satisfaction he left her, smiling in languid satiation.

For the remainder of that day Gabrielle saw a different side to Nathaniel. He was a humorous, relaxed companion concerned with her welfare and her pleasure, exhibiting an extraordinary amount of patience as he taught her how to rig the sails, how to catch the wind, how to gauge the exact moment to tack across the broad river.

They kept to the river and the tidal cuts in the marshes, not venturing into the choppy winter Solent. It was cold and exhilarating, and for these few hours the dark inner worlds ruled by suspicion, calculation, betrayal, and vengeance were held at bay.

At noon they tied the twelve-foot dinghy to an isolated jetty and tramped across the marshy grass to a thatched inn. Nathaniel was greeted with an easy warmth by the fishermen in the taproom. There was an equality to the conversation that fascinated Gabrielle, given that Lord Praed was the lord of the manor and these his tenants. She herself was virtually ignored, and she assumed that women didn't frequent the village tavern.

She sat contentedly by the fire, drank porter, and ate a succulent meat pie and a large wedge of cheddar with pickled onions. Nathaniel meanwhile sat up at the bar in his shirt-sleeves, one leg propped on the rung of a stool, his hand curled around a tankard of ale as he talked tides and winds and fishing with his fellow drinkers.

Gabrielle suddenly wondered what Jake would think if he could see his father like this. It was Jake Nathaniel should be teaching to sail and fish. He should be introducing his son to the locals with whom he was on such easy terms.

She stretched her toes to the fire and closed her eyes.

"Come on, sleepy. The tide will turn in half an hour and we're on a lee shore." Nathaniel stood between her and the fire, blocking the warmth as he put on his coat again.

"What's a lee shore?" Gabrielle said, yawning.

"One that's windbound," he responded, holding down a hand to pull her to her feet. "Not easy to sail off, and if the tide's running out, we could find ourselves hauling the boat down the channel by hand, up to our knees in mud."

"That does not sound like an appealing prospect." Gabrielle followed him out in the chilly afternoon and back to the dinghy.

"That was a lovely day," Gabrielle said truthfully as they walked back from the boathouse to the house at the end of the afternoon. She gave him her crooked smile, linking her arm through his.

Nathaniel leaned over and kissed the tip of her nose. "You've been the most amazingly docile companion for once."

"Docile? Me?"

"Yes, you," he said. "And you shall have your reward when— Who the hell is here?"

He stopped on the path leading to the side of the house and the gun room door that Nathaniel always used when entering the house from the grounds. From there they could see the gravel sweep before the front door. A chaise stood at the bottom of the steps, the team snorting, their breath steaming in the late afternoon air. Servants were unloading baggage from the roof of the carriage under the direction of Bartram, and Mrs. Bailey could be seen on the front step, ushering someone within doors.

Gabrielle strained her eyes in the gathering dusk, trying to make out the emblazoned panels of the coach, then she said with a joyous laugh, "Oh, it's Georgie. She must have brought my things herself. And she must have come with Simon—she couldn't possibly pay an overnight visit to a bachelor's establishment without him."

"You did," Nathaniel pointed out glumly.

"Oh, but I'm different," Gabrielle declared with perfect truth. Gathering up her skirts, she ran toward the front of the house.

Rather more slowly and with a distinct downturn to his mouth, Nathaniel entered the house through the gun room door. He was not yet ready to greet his guests with Gabrielle's enthusiasm.

11

_____

"Georgie, how wonderful to see you!" Gabrielle flew up the steps and into the hall, arms flung wide to embrace her cousin. "What a wonderful surprise."

"I couldn't resist it," Georgie murmured into her ear as she hugged her. "Simon and Miles are as cross as two sticks."

Gabrielle gave her a conspiratorial squeeze, then drew back to greet the two men standing behind Georgie, her crooked smile faintly mocking as she saw their clear discomfort. "Simon . . . and Miles too. How kind of you to escort my luggage."

"We were just passing," Simon said, kissing her cheek.

"Yes, just passing," Miles agreed, taking her proffered hand and raising it to his lips. "You're looking very . . . um . . . very well," he finished somewhat lamely.

"Positively windblown," Georgie declared, removing her velvet bonnet and shaking loose her golden ringlets. "What have you been doing?"

"Sailing on the river," Gabby replied. "Nathaniel was teaching me . . . where _is_ Nathaniel?" She looked around, puzzled, having assumed he would have followed her up the steps. "He must have come in through the gun room. But why would he do that when he knew he had visitors?"

Miles and Simon exchanged a dourly comprehending look just as Nathaniel entered the hall from the side corridor.

"Well, well," he drawled. "This is an unexpected pleasure. To what do I owe it? Or shouldn't I ask?"

"We were just passing," Simon repeated as awkwardly as before. "Just passing and we thought we'd drop in on our way and leave Gabby's luggage." He cast a fierce glance for support toward Miles, who was trying to be invisible.

"Yes . . . yes, just passing," Miles reiterated, clearing his throat.

"Passing from whence to where?" demanded Nathaniel. "As far as I know, Burley Manor isn't en route to anywhere that would entice Lord and Lady Vanbrugh *or* Mr. Miles Bennet in the middle of the Season. Far too countrified."

A dull flush appeared on Miles's cheekbones at this caustic statement, and he shot an I-told-you-so glare toward Simon, who pursed his lips but said nothing. Even Georgie appeared to lose some of the assurance that had so far swept all opposition aside.

"For heaven's sake, Nathaniel!" Gabrielle exclaimed. "Don't be such a miserable grouch! They're your friends and they've come all this way to visit you, the least you can do is offer them some refreshment. Besides, they were doing me a favor, bringing my luggage so quickly."

"I stand corrected, ma'am," Nathaniel said as sardonically as before. "I was forgetting your own claims on my hospitality. Of course they must extend to your friends."

Gabrielle drew in a sharp breath, but before she

could come up with anything suitably cutting, Nathaniel gestured toward the library.

"I'm afraid there's no fire in the drawing room, gentlemen, since I wasn't expecting guests, but come into the library. I'm sure I can produce a bottle of decent claret. Gabrielle, I will leave you to entertain Lady Vanbrugh."

"He is *so* rude," Georgie declared in a fierce undertone. "How can you stand him, Gabby?"

"All in good time," Gabrielle said with a grin. "I know perfectly well that's why you're here. Let's go up to my boudoir and we can have a comfortable coze."

"I beg your pardon, my lady . . ." Mrs. Bailey, who'd been standing in the shadows, a silent observer of the last minutes, stepped forward. "Should I prepare bedchambers for his lordship's guests?"

"Yes, if you please." Gabrielle smiled warmly. "Lord and Lady Vanbrugh and Mr. Bennet will be staying overnight, of course. You'll know how best to accommodate them."

"So I'll tell cook there'll be five for dinner?" Mrs. Bailey still sounded a trifle hesitant.

"Yes," Gabrielle said. "And could you send Ellie up to my boudoir with some tea, please. I'm sure Lady Vanbrugh will be glad of a cup after her journey."

She swept Georgie upstairs to the Queen's Suite, closing the door firmly behind them.

"What a pleasant room." Georgie looked around the apartment with a shrewdly appreciative eye, assessing the elegance of its furnishings, the richness of the carpet and draperies.

"It's a very pleasant house altogether," Gabrielle agreed, drawing the curtains across the window, closing out the encroaching dusk. "Take off your pelisse and sit by the fire, Georgie. I know how you detest exertion of any kind, and traveling in particular, so only overriding curiosity could have brought you here. I'm deeply complimented, I assure you."

Georgie was not a whit put out by this teasing, she was far too accustomed to it. Her cousin had always been three times as energetic as herself, and the contrast between them was something of a family joke.

"Well, you really are behaving scandalously," she declared, tossing her pelisse over a chair and bending to warm her hands at the fire. "If word of this gets out, I dread to think how you'll be received in London. Why, you might be denied vouchers for Almacks." Georgie's tone invested this last hideous possibility with suitable solemnity, but her eyes, burning with curiosity and excitement, belied the tone.

"Stuff," Gabrielle scoffed. "It's not going to get out unless you or Simon or Miles blabs about it . . . and I know you won't. I shall simply let it be known that I returned to France for a couple of months."

She regarded her cousin through narrowed eyes. "Come clean, Georgie. You don't have a prudish bone in your body and you're certainly not here as chaperone to safeguard my precious reputation. You're here because you want to see for yourself what's going on."

Georgie laughed and sat down by the fire. "Yes, I do. So tell all, and start from the beginning."

"Listen closely," Gabrielle said in the hushed tones of one about to tell a scandalous *on dit* in the greatest secrecy. Georgie's benign thirst for gossip would be easily quenched with the surface truth—the actual facts were so far from her experience, she wouldn't be able to credit them anyway. Gabrielle was a past master at entertaining her cousin and knew exactly what details of her liaison with the misanthropic and utterly discourteous Lord Praed would amuse Georgie.

Downstairs, Simon took a glass of wine from his still-unbending host and coughed. "I suppose you've a right to resent the intrusion, Nathaniel. But Georgie insisted on checking up on Gabby."

"Insisted?" Nathaniel's eyebrows lifted incredulously as he took the scent of his wine.

"Insisted," Miles put in. "She's a DeVane," he added, as if this were sufficient explanation for all but the village idiot.

"You have my sympathies, Vanbrugh," Nathaniel said coolly. "And how long do you imagine it will take your wife to complete her ... her checking up? An hour, maybe, two at the outside?"

"For God's sake, Praed!" Miles exploded. "You're not going to throw us out tonight, surely!"

"There's bound to be an inn in Lymington," Simon said stiffly. He stood up, placing his half-empty glass on the side table. "Forgive us for the intrusion. Perhaps you'd ask a servant to summon my wife and have the horses put to the carriage again."

Nathaniel's lips twitched and bright laughter sprang suddenly into his eyes. "If you leave in high dudgeon, Simon, that *enfant terrible* you foisted on me will probably string me up by my thumbs. You may be married to a DeVane, but I tell you, only those who hold their lives cheap would go in the ring with Gabrielle de Beaucaire."

There was a stunned silence as Nathaniel's visitors struggled with this abrupt volte-face. Then Simon's rigid features dissolved into their customary warm geniality.

"You bastard," he said, punching Nathaniel with some force on the shoulder. "You knew how much at a disadvantage we were, and you took shameless advantage of it."

"Habit," Nathaniel confessed with a half-smile. "I hadn't expected to be pleased to see you, but curiously, I find that I am."

Miles gave a guffaw of laughter. "Gabby's clearly a miracle worker."

"She has some small talent," Nathaniel agreed, refilling their glasses.

It occurred to him that this unexpected visit might well prove fortuitous. At some point, when he could separate the two men, he'd sit down with Simon and go over Gabrielle's qualifications for the service with him again. Now that he was no longer against the idea in principle, he'd be a little more searching in his questions.

Jake was full of curiosity when he tapped on Gabrielle's door just before six. He'd heard the arrival of the visitors, and Miss Primmer and Nurse had been discussing them while he had his supper. His godfather was here, but there was another lady too, something that intrigued Jake mightily.

He entered at Gabrielle's bidding and gazed wide-eyed with frank curiosity at the pretty woman sitting by the fire. She wore a driving dress of soft beige and the blouse beneath had high ruffles that brushed under her chin. She struck him as soft and curvy and smiling, and her hair gleamed gold in the firelight. Gabby wasn't soft and curvy and golden, he realized, but with a rush of fierce loyalty he decided that she was much more beautiful than the other lady.

"Jake, come and meet Lady Vanbrugh." Gabby held out her hand to him and he stepped forward, bowing with jerky formality to her guest.

"This is Jake, Georgie," Gabby said, drawing him against her with an encircling arm. "Nathaniel likes to see him in the library before he goes to bed, so we usually go down together."

Georgie smiled at Jake. "I have a little boy too, but he's much smaller than you."

"What's his name?"

"Edward . . . we call him Ned."

"Oh . . . are you going to tell me a story tonight, Gabby?" Jake dismissed the unknown Ned in favor of his own pressing concerns.

"Perhaps not tonight," Gabrielle said. "Since Papa has visitors. And your godfather is here too. Let's go down to the library."

Jake hung back, chewing his lip, then said, "Papa doesn't let me go to the library when he has visitors."

"Oh, but this is your godfather," Gabrielle said. "And these visitors are my special friends, so I'm sure he'll want you to be introduced. Are you coming, Georgie? Or would you like to go to your own bedchamber and dress for dinner?"

"Oh, I'm coming," Georgie said readily, rising to her feet.

Gabrielle chuckled. She hadn't expected anything different.

If Nathaniel was put out by the interruption, he gave no sign. Gabrielle seemed to have taken charge of the situation anyway, he reflected, watching as she presented Jake to Simon and eased the meeting of the shy child with his awkwardly hearty godparent. Miles had had little to do with his godson hitherto, and little experience of children in general, so his attempts to put Jake at his ease tended to create the opposite effect.

Despite Gabrielle's efforts, however, Jake showed little reluctance when Nathaniel sent him back to the nursery after fifteen minutes. He bade a formal good night with his stiff, jerky little bows to all except Gabby.

"Won't you tell me a story?" His voice was barely above a whisper as he approached her.

"Not tonight, love. I have to dress for dinner, but I'll come and kiss you when you're in bed and sing you one of my funny songs. Actually, there's one that Georgie and I used to sing together. Do you remember it, Georgie? The one about the man with the beard that the birds nested in?"

Nathaniel listened to the women's laughter, recognizing the intimacy of shared childhood. Simon shared it too, to a lesser extent, he realized. He certainly had an almost brotherly ease with Gabrielle. The three of them were trying to remember the words of the silly schoolroom songs they'd sung together, and their laughter was so infectious that even the timorous child was smiling, clinging to Gabrielle's skirts, watching the adults' faces with his round brown eyes.

A wash of loneliness surprised Nathaniel as he suddenly saw himself at Jake's age. A lonely little boy living on the periphery of adult lives. He couldn't remember being touched, not in the way Gabrielle was always touching Jake. He'd been touched by nursemaids in the general day-to-day business of caring for a child. His father had laid a hand on him only in punishment. He didn't think his mother had ever touched him.

"I hate to interrupt this merriment, but we should change for dinner," he said, rising to his feet. "Jake, it's past time you were upstairs. Nurse will be looking for you." He hadn't meant to say anything like that. He'd wanted somehow to join the laughing group, to be acknowledged by them and to have a part in the union Gabrielle so obviously shared with his son. But he heard his voice, sharp and disapproving, speaking narrow, mean words.

The laughter left the child's eyes and he went with instant obedience to the door. Nathaniel felt a sudden ache beneath his breastbone, as if something had been twisted there. It wasn't physical, yet it felt as powerful as if it were. As the boy passed him, he put his hand out and ruffled his hair as he had done the other night. And as it had done then, the gesture startled them both.

"I don't fully understand." Later that night Simon paced the library, a perturbed frown disturbing his usually equable expression. "What is it that you suspect Gabrielle of?"

"Nothing at this point," Nathaniel said with more patience than usual. He was leaning against the mantelshelf, comprehension in the brown eyes as he regarded his guest's agitation. It was never comfortable to have one's judgment questioned, particularly when it related to a close friend.

"But I've a suspicious mind, Simon. I have to have in my business."

"Yes, I understand that," Simon said with a brusque gesture that set the amber liquid in his brandy goblet slopping against the crystal. "But I told you what information Gabrielle brought to us. I've explained her history . . . for God's sake, man, I've known her since she was a scrubby brat with pigtails!"

Nathaniel sighed. "Yes, I know that, Simon. But I have to be cautious. *Timeo Danaos et dona ferentes.*" He raised an eyebrow. "The Trojan horse was a powerful weapon, my friend."

Simon stared, incredulous. "You think Gabrielle could be planted by the French? Don't be ridiculous!" He drained his glass in one gulp and thumped it on the table, reaching into his pocket for his snuffbox.

Nathaniel said nothing, watching as Simon took a hefty pinch of snuff and succumbed to a fit of sneezing as violent as his distress at Nathaniel's inquisition.

When the spasms had subsided, Nathaniel said evenly, "I don't suspect anything, Simon. I'm just being cautious. Her credentials are almost too perfect, her contacts are a spymaster's dream. I *have* to satisfy myself that Gabrielle is what she seems. Once I'm satisfied, I'll gladly employ her in the service."

Simon blew his nose vigorously. "You said she was undisciplined."

"So she is," Nathaniel agreed calmly. "But she's also resourceful and courageous, and I can keep my own rein on her if I decide to employ her."

Simon flung himself down in a deep wing chair by the fire. "So what do you want to know?"

"I just want to go through the whole story again from the beginning. Just bear with my questions."

Simon nodded with a sigh. "Very well. But it does seem to me that living together in such . . . such close quarters ought to give you ample opportunity to form your own judgments."

Nathaniel's lips thinned. "I don't believe that's any of your business."

"Oh, don't you?" Simon demanded morosely. "According to Georgie, Lord DeVane would expect me to call you out for debauching his honorary daughter."

Nathaniel threw back his head and roared with laughter. "Is that what I've done, indeed? If you ask me, the boot is definitely on the other foot. It was my honor that was suborned by that shameless wild woman . . . and at your instigation, my friend."

Simon grinned reluctantly. "Well, I didn't suggest she seduce you, but I did imply that she'd have to employ unorthodox measures to gain your attention."

"She certainly did that! Now, can we get on with these questions?"

"Go ahead." Simon leaned over to refill his glass from the decanter on the side table and then sat back cradling the goblet between his hands. Of course Nathaniel was right. Every caution was essential, even where Gabrielle was concerned.

It was an exhaustive and exhausting session, but when the two men parted in the early hours of the morning, Nathaniel had failed to find any holes or even weak spots in Simon's narrative. It would appear that Gabrielle was everything she seemed to be.

He had one last test for Gabrielle. But first he needed to ensure her absence for an hour or two.

"Oh, Gabby, I forgot to give you this letter. It arrived for you just before we left Vanbrugh Court." Georgie entered the breakfast parlor the next morning, flourishing an envelope. She dropped it beside Gabrielle's plate and smiled around the table.

"Good morning, everyone. I slept like a baby. I think the air in Hampshire must be more restful than in Kent." She leaned over to kiss her husband. "You were up betimes this morning."

"Some of us have been up for hours," Gabrielle said, picking up the letter. The envelope bore Talleyrand's elegant script. "Some of us have already had a two-hour ride."

"And thus feel we deserve our breakfast," Simon added, pinching his wife's cheek. "Unlike lazy ladies who don't bestir themselves until past mid-morning."

Georgie merely smiled at this good-natured raillery and turned to examine the chafing dishes on the sideboard.

Nathaniel leaned back in his chair, one booted ankle resting on his thigh, his hand circling a tankard of ale on the table. His eyes rested on Gabrielle, watching her face as she slit the envelope with her butter knife. The handwriting on the envelope was almost as familiar to him as his own.

Gabrielle had been expecting a letter from Talleyrand relatively early in her assignment, and it had been agreed initially that she would use the Vanbrughs' address as a poste restante. Once she'd established herself in the network, she would inform her godfather and they would use a more efficient channel.

Gabrielle wondered if Nathaniel recognized the handwriting. It was highly likely he'd seen examples of it in his work. Some of Talleyrand's correspondence would have surely fallen into English hands at some point.

"It's from Talleyrand," she said calmly, glancing across the table at Nathaniel. He inclined his head in a gesture of acknowledgment and raised his tankard to his lips.

Gabrielle decided he *had* recognized the handwriting and she'd probably just passed another test.

"Quite an honor to have such a notable correspondent," Miles observed innocently, frowning with concentration as he filleted a kipper.

"Oh, I'm fully sensible of the honor," Gabrielle said with a tinge of irony that neither Simon nor Nathaniel could miss. "My godfather is a regular and most interesting correspondent."

"And a consummate politician," Miles said comfortably.

"Indubitably," Gabrielle agreed. "He's the cleverest man in Europe, not excluding the emperor. And his cleverness is exceeded only by his ambition. I defy anyone to untangle the personal motives behind his allegiances. If it suited him to abandon Napoleon, he would do so without a qualm."

"A pragmatic gentleman," Nathaniel commented with a shrug. "Lady Vanbrugh, may I pass you the marmalade?"

"There's no need to be so formal, Nathaniel," Gabrielle said, unfolding the sheets of paper in leisurely fashion.

"No, indeed not," Georgie agreed, slightly flustered because she still could not like Nathaniel Praed, despite the magic he so clearly weaved around Gabby.

"You do me too much honor, ma'am," Nathaniel said, confirming Georgie in her dislike.

"Pompous ass. Take no notice of him, Georgie." Gabrielle picked up a roll from the basket on the table in front of her and threw it across the table. It landed in Nathaniel's tankard, splattering ale over his shirt.

"Why you . . . !" He pushed back his chair, half rising to his feet. Gabrielle's chin lifted and she met his indignant glare with challenging eyes and her mocking, crooked smile.

"What am I?"

"Devil's spawn," he said with a reluctant grin, resuming his seat, dabbing at the mess on his shirt with his napkin.

Simon and Miles exchanged a look of total incredulity and Georgie stared in unabashed amazement at her cousin who, with a complacent smile, had turned to her letter.

It was clear at first glance that she was supposed to share its contents with the English spymaster. It was a cheerful, chatty letter describing the social scene at Warsaw, Napoleon's reception by the Poles, and the emperor's fascination with Marie Walewksa.

Presumably that was the nugget she was to pass on. It was a piece of information that would be of general interest to the English government, and at this point it was something known only to Napoleon's intimates. If Gabrielle passed on the information, it would add credence to her claims of intimate connections within the court surrounding the emperor.

"Well, it seems Napoleon has found himself another Josephine," she said, looking up, realizing that Nathaniel had been watching her carefully as she'd read the letter. What had he been watching for? Signs of evasion or calculation, perhaps. Well, he wouldn't see them. All the years with Guillaume had taught her to show on her face only what she chose.

"In Poland?" Nathaniel inquired casually.

"The wife of a Polish chancellor," she said. "I'll read the letter to you. It's quite entertaining."

It was the civilized letter of a civilized man, full of observations and impressions, descriptions that were pointed and witty, Nathaniel reflected. The significance of a liaison between Napoleon and the Polish noblewoman was not elaborated upon, but it would be obvious to any intelligent observer of the world's affairs.

It would be interesting to read Gabrielle's reply. That would tell him much more about the relationship between the diplomat and his goddaughter than this seemingly innocuous communication. Did she conceal her hostility from Talleyrand under a dutiful filial response? From what he knew of Gabrielle, he'd find that hard to believe. And yet as he'd already observed, the more he learned about her, the less he truly knew her.

"Interesting," he said noncommittally when she refolded the letter and slipped it back in its envelope. "I wonder how Josephine will react."

"She's an extremely jealous woman," Gabrielle observed, pouring coffee into her cup. "For some reason she doesn't consider her own infidelities to be of the least importance compared with Napoleon's. She writes him outraged letters whenever rumors reach her of some possible liaison. He describes her as a tigress when she's jealous, but all she has to do is weep and he comes running again. He's very susceptible to women's tears."

"Then it's to be hoped Madame Walewska learns that rapidly," Simon commented. "Since I'm sure she has an ulterior motive in becoming his mistress."

"Power is a powerful aphrodisiac," Gabrielle said lightly. "Talleyrand told me that Napoleon is actually very sensitive about the smallness of his . . . his . . . private parts."

"Gabrielle!" Georgie protested, although her eyes shone with interest.

"Not a suitable topic for the breakfast table? Or is it the mixed company that troubles you?" her cousin inquired impishly.

"Both, I imagine," Nathaniel said, pushing back his chair. "Spare our blushes, you outrageous woman."

Gabrielle laughed. "Very well, I'll change the subject. What are we going to do today?"

"We should be on our way," Simon said.

"Oh, must you?" Gabrielle looked disappointed.

"Yes," Miles said firmly. "We've intruded sufficiently."

"If you leave within the hour, you could probably make it back to London in time for a late dinner," Nathaniel said readily.

Even Georgie recognized that Nathaniel this time was making fun of himself and joined in the laughter, but no one attempted to alter the plan, and an hour later Gabrielle waved the chaise away from the house.

"Are you tired of being alone with me?" Nathaniel inquired as they turned back into the hall.

"No." She shook her head. "Far from it. But that said, I imagine I'm a more sociable being than you."

"That wouldn't be difficult," he agreed with a wry smile. "I'm afraid I'm going to be very boring and shut myself up with some work."

Gabrielle shrugged. "I wouldn't mind going into town to do some shopping."

"I'll tell Milner to bring the brougham round from the stables."

"I'd rather take your curricle and your grays."

Nathaniel regarded her quizzically. "I don't wish to offend you, ma'am, but they'll be very fresh."

"I can handle them."

"Yes, I'm sure you can." He shook his head with a resigned chuckle. "Very well. But Milner had better go with you." He turned aside toward the library.

"Could I take Jake?"

The question arrested him with his hand on the library door. "He has lessons."

"A surprise holiday never did anyone any harm."

"You don't want a child hanging on to your skirts while you're shopping."

"If I didn't, I wouldn't have suggested it," she pointed out.

To his surprise, Nathaniel heard himself saying, "If you really want to, I see no objection."

"Thank you," Gabrielle said with quiet satisfaction. One made progress little by little.

Nathaniel watched the departure of the curricle from the library window an hour later. Jake was bouncing on the gravel like an india rubber ball, apparently chattering nineteen to the dozen to the patient Milner and the smiling Gabrielle, who swung herself gracefully into the curricle and took up the reins. Milner lifted Jake onto the seat beside her and then jumped up behind.

Nathaniel watched critically as Gabrielle felt the grays' mouths with a delicate pull on the reins. They were very fresh, stamping the gravel, lifting their heads to the brisk wind blowing in from the river, their breath steaming in the cold air. He wondered uneasily if he'd been wise to allow her to drive them. She gave the order to the groom to release their heads, and the horses plunged forward.

Nathaniel drew breath sharply, then relaxed as he saw her draw on the reins, asserting her mastery, bringing the grays round on the gravel and trotting them sedately down the drive. Gabrielle was clearly a capital whip—as he'd expected.

He went upstairs to the Queen's Suite. He had a good two hours in hand to conduct his search.

12

Jake was in seventh heaven at this unexpected holiday. He chattered throughout the short drive, too excited to take much notice of what they passed on the way, demanding to know what shops they would go to and what Gabrielle wanted to buy, and whether they could buy an ice from the tea shop on the quay. Primmy had once bought him an ice there a long time ago when he'd had to go to the dentist and he'd been very brave. The afternoon stretched magically ahead for the child, an uncharted landscape with no limits.

Gabrielle listened attentively to the boy's seemingly irrelevant prattle as they drove along the country lanes between hedgerows bright with holly berries. It was almost as if someone had taken the lid off a bubbling well, she thought. Jake talked as if he could talk forever. Was he not used to an audience? she wondered as he embarked on a convoluted description of some fantasy game he liked to play. It was an elaborate and imaginative scenario, the details lovingly and carefully described to his attentive listener. This was clearly a child who lived in his head, she concluded, as the rich inner landscape took shape for her. And Nathaniel presumably had no idea.

What kind of child had he been? As lonely as Jake, certainly, but tougher, she suspected. The son of the daunting-looking sixth Lady Praed, rather than the sweetfaced, gentle-natured Helen, seventh Lady Praed.

As she thought these thoughts and lent an attentive ear to the child's chatter, the seventh Lord Praed was conducting a systematic search of her possessions.

Nathaniel had conducted many such searches in his career, more often than not under conditions of secrecy and the threat of imminent exposure. That afternoon he was in his own house, secure in the knowledge that Gabrielle was well out of the way and that no one would either question his presence in this room or interrupt him.

It gave him the leisure to proceed with excessive thoroughness. Coldly, he blocked out all thought of the personality behind the possessions as he examined the gowns in the wardrobe, checking seams and hems. She had an enormous number of shoes, he registered distantly as he examined the soles of each one, testing for the hollow sound that would indicate a cavity in the heel.

He went through the lacy undergarments in the drawers of the armoire, looking for concealed pockets, loose seams. He had the advantage of Gabrielle in that he knew the room itself contained no secret hiding places. If she did have anything compromising, it would be in her possessions, unless she'd made her own hiding place in the furniture or draperies.

He went through her jewel case, raising his eyebrows slightly at the priceless gems, realizing that so far he'd seen Gabrielle wear barely half of the treasure of the Hawksworths.

He went through the contents of the *secrétaire*, running his eye over the letter from Talleyrand that she'd read at breakfast. She'd left nothing out in her reading. There was no other correspondence, no journal even.

He stripped the bed and examined the mattress. There were no suspicious cuts or lumps. He ran his hands along the curtains at the windows and around the bed. He looked under the carpets, turned the chairs upside down, and lifted the cushions.

There was nothing to be found. He wondered if he'd expected to find anything. And only then did he realize how relieved he was.

He stretched in the shaft of weak sunlight falling from the window and ran his fingers through the silver swatches at his temples. Then his eye fell on the books on the floor beside the window seat. For some reason, he'd missed them.

He bent to pick them up. There was a copy of *Delphine* by Madame de Staël and a copy of Voltaire's *Lettres philosophiques*. He opened the latter, shaking out the pages. Nothing fluttered loose. He did the same for *Delphine* with the same results. Idly, he picked up the Voltaire again. It had been a long time since he'd read this critique of prerevolutionary French institutions. The inflammatory book had sent the author into exile and was generally considered an incitement to the revolution that had followed its publication.

He flipped through the pages, his eye running over the text. Suddenly he went cold, the hairs on his forearms rising.

He stared down at a long paragraph where certain letters were marked faintly with lead pencil. There were numerical annotations in the margin.

With a heart of stone he took the book into his own room next door and copied out the passage, including the annotations. He would master the code at his leisure. Then he replaced the book and checked the room to make sure that everything was as he'd found it. The bed looked a little less neat than it had, but no one would notice. He smoothed the coverlet and then went down to the library to await the return of Gabrielle and his son.

He'd used such codes himself many times, he reflected distantly as he poured himself a glass of cognac. Books were the ideal medium. They were such a natural component of one's personal possessions, easy to carry around, and only those fluent in the language of spies would notice on a casual glance anything remarkable about faint markings on the text.

Fluent in the language of spies . . . Dear God in heaven! Of all the treacherous, duplicitous *whores*—peddling the glorious wares of her body while she betrayed . . .

He hurled the glass into the fireplace. The delicate crystal shattered and the fire spurted blue flame as drops of brandy splattered on the logs.

How close he'd been to believing her! A hairbreadth away from entrusting her with the most sensitive political intelligence and the lives of half a dozen agents in France. A hairbreadth away from entrusting her with his own soul . . .

What a fool! How could he have been such a fool? With her laughter and her challenges and exuberance . . . with the glorious wildness of her passion and her deeply erotic sensuality . . . she'd wormed her way under his skin, nibbling away at his defenses like some internal parasite, destroying the protective shield he'd erected since Helen's death.

She'd entranced him and captivated his son in order to betray him.

Icy sweat broke out on his brow as a wave of revulsion swept through him. Jake—she'd used the child, Helen's child, to weave her damnable spells around her quarry, to learn his secrets, to exploit his weaknesses. And he'd let it happen.

And her friends. He saw her laughing with Simon and Georgie, singing that silly song, joined in the deepest intimacies of a shared past. A shared past to be exploited, without conscience and without loyalty. She had duped Simon as neatly as she'd almost duped himself.

He stared into the fire and in the wreathing flames he could see Gabrielle's body contorted with joy, her hair flowing on the white pillow, her limbs twisting around his, drawing him ever closer to her center, to be engulfed in the glorious conflagration of their fusion.

With a violent oath he swung away from the fire and its mesmerizing images. He strode out of the library and left the house, almost running down to the river, heedless of the sharp edge to the wind gusting off the water, ruffling the feathers of the mallards as they clustered among the reeds on the far bank. A flock of geese rose from the water at his approach, and the vigorous flapping of their wings and their mournful cry of warning echoed his bleak fury.

As he strode along the bank he fought to defeat the images, to banish emotion, to rediscover the cold pragmatism of the spymaster. He'd unmasked a double agent. Gabrielle de Beaucaire was a French spy as intent on betraying Nathaniel Praed's country as he was on betraying hers. He must see just that simple fact. There was only one issue: What was he to do with her?

He could hand her over to the people who knew how to extract information. They would wring every last scrap of knowledge from her and then they would hang her. Spying was unprotected by the civilized laws governing the treatment of prisoners of war. Gabrielle knew that. She knew what she risked in this venture.

Or . . . or he could use her as she had tried to use him.

There would be little personal satisfaction in condemning her to the dungeons and instruments of the interrogators and the hangman's rope. It would relieve none of his own wounds and would do nothing to salvage his shattered pride. But to turn the tables . . . to outwit Talleyrand and Fouché with their own tool!

Now, that was a plan that carried the deepest satisfaction. He would spin his own web. Gabrielle would carry false information to her masters in Paris, and that information would entrap the French network.

The evening mist rolled in over the river and Nathaniel paused under a willow tree. He bent to pick up a smooth round stone and sent it skimming over the wind-ruffled water. His features were etched in granite, his eyes hard and flat as he stared sightlessly across to the mud-furrowed fields along the opposite bank. Somehow, he would have to behave with Gabrielle as if nothing had changed. In fact, he must deepen their intimacy, allow her to feel that he had relaxed completely with her. When he told her he had changed his mind and was prepared to bring her into the service, she must believe her seduction had succeeded.

As it so nearly had. By God, she'd made a fool of him with her charcoal eyes and the rich curves of her body and the uninhibited glories of her sexuality.

Enough! He spoke the word aloud, a fierce and desperate attempt to halt the swiftly spiraling fury and self-disgust that threatened to engulf him again.

Slowly, cold pragmatism overcame futile passion. He shivered under the blast of bitter wind racing across the tidal marshes from the sea. It seemed to penetrate his skin, lodging deep in the marrow of his bones, an icy shaft stabbing his heart.

It was time to go back, to face what had to be faced. He returned to the house, arriving just as the curricle drew up before the house. He stood in the hall and waited for them to enter.

His son's eyes were shining and he had a smear of something sticky around his mouth. He was talking to Bartram, who'd opened the door for them, and instantly included the hovering Mrs. Bailey in a convoluted account of his excursion. His eyes darted toward his father, and he offered a timid smile as if to include him in the telling.

"I had two pink ices and Gabby bought some new gloves, and there were these puppies in a basket that some little girl was trying to sell, an' some men got into a fight on the quay an' Gabby said we'd better keep out of the way because they were rough sailors. . . ."

Gabrielle was smiling down at him as she drew off her gloves. She cast a glance toward Nathaniel, her eyes warm as she invited him to share in Jake's delight. *She was using his son.* Bitter bile filled his mouth and his fingers flexed. He could feel the slender column of her throat between his hands, the pulse beating in frantic fear as his fingers tightened . . . squeezed. . . .

Again he fought the crimson tide of passion until his head was a cold, clear space.

"That'll do, Jake," he said curtly. "It's almost your suppertime. It's to be hoped you can eat something after stuffing yourself with ices all afternoon. Go up to the schoolroom."

Jake's face fell and the bubbling words died on his lips, the light faded from his eyes. Without another word he ran to the stairs and scampered up them.

Gabrielle frowned slightly and Mrs. Bailey with a murmur of excuse returned to the kitchen.

"That was a little harsh, wasn't it?" Gabrielle said quietly, going ahead of Nathaniel into the library. "He wasn't doing any harm."

"You kept him out far too late, and I certainly don't want him witnessing sailors' brawls on the quay. I'd have thought you'd have had more sense."

"I'm sorry," she said simply. The Nathaniel of the breakfast table raillery seemed to have disappeared. She couldn't imagine throwing a roll at the man who stood before her now, but then, she was becoming accustomed to his changes of mood. It was hard for little Jake, though. One minute his father unbent toward him and the next reverted to his old manner. However, she knew enough about Nathaniel now to realize that she'd achieve nothing by pursuing the issue at this point.

"I'll go and dress for dinner."

Nathaniel pulled himself up sharply. He offered a conciliatory smile. "Sorry, I didn't mean to snap. I was a little worried because you were out so long. Would you like a glass of sherry before you go upstairs?"

"Thank you." Gabrielle took the glass with a smile that she felt could have been more animated. Nathaniel's greeting had certainly doused the pleasantness of her afternoon with Jake, and there was a strange atmosphere in the house. Rather empty and bleak, but that was probably because Georgie's vibrant presence had departed.

The anticlimax of their visitors' departure seemed the only logical explanation for the slight constraint throughout the evening. Gabrielle tried to shake off the tendrils of depression that clung to them both, but Nathaniel was abstracted and failed to respond to her various sallies.

"Is something troubling you?" she asked as they got up from the dinner table.

"I have a problem with one of my agents in Toulouse," he said. "It's distracting me, I'm afraid."

"Oh," she said casually. "Not a problem you'd care to share, I presume."

"No," he said. "At least not at the moment."

Gabrielle raised an eyebrow at this. Could she be making headway at last? She'd originally given herself two weeks to persuade him to change his mind, but was beginning to accept that the way things were going, she was going to need more time before the English spymaster threw in the towel and accepted her in his network.

"Well, I'll leave you to your cogitations," she said. "I should reply to my godfather's letter." She turned to the stairs and then paused, one hand on the newel post. "Anything you'd like me to tell him?"

Treacherous whore! "Not at the moment," he repeated, smiling. "I'll frank the letter for you when it's written." *And read it too, with the aid of the code, once I've broken it.*

Gabrielle composed her response to Talleyrand with great care. Hidden within the chatty, innocuous text was a brief factual account of her activities so far; what she had learned from the spymaster's diary; and her belief that if she persevered, he would eventually accept her in the network.

She sanded the paper, folded it, and sealed the envelope with a wafer before taking it downstairs and leaving it on the hall table for Nathaniel to frank before the carrier collected the mail.

Five minutes after she'd returned upstairs, Nathaniel came out of the library, picked up the envelope, and dropped it in his pocket. He would decipher its real message in the privacy of his bedchamber later.

Gabrielle stood for a minute in her boudoir, looking out the uncurtained window into the night. Rain lashed against the panes, dreary English rain that crept into one's bones. She drew the curtains tightly, then threw another log on the fire. Hugging her breasts with her crossed arms, she stared into the fire. For the first time in this crusade of vengeance, serpents of doubt raised their heads and hissed softly in her mind and in her heart.

If Nathaniel had not been responsible for Guillaume's murder, would she still be willing to betray him? She'd been involved in French intelligence for five years. But a courier's work hadn't involved direct contact and her adversaries had been nameless and faceless. This was very different.

She closed her eyes, seeing Guillaume's face in the red glow behind her eyelids. She could hear his voice, quiet and level, telling her that the end justified the means. That in the land of shadows where they worked, ordinary ethical considerations didn't apply.

Nathaniel Praed didn't operate by those considerations, and one must meet fire with fire. She was carrying on Guillaume's work because her loyalties lay first and foremost with his memory.

When she returned to France at Talleyrand's bidding six years earlier, she'd left England and the DeVanes with deep reluctance, but her godfather had insisted that her father would have wanted her to take her place in French society, reconstituted after the chaos of revolution. England and France had just signed the Peace of Amiens, but the peace had not lasted long and soon Gabrielle had found herself with an emotional foot in both camps. Then she'd met Guillaume, and had buried her English loyalties deep, even the abiding friendship and gratitude she owed the DeVanes.

When Nathaniel joined her in bed that night, she welcomed him with a fierce eagerness for their fusion, desperate to blind herself to all but the physical contact, the explosive satisfaction of the lust that nothing could blunt between them.

Nathaniel awoke first the next morning. He lay in the dim light of dawn, preparing himself for what he was about to do. He turned his head toward the dark one on the pillow beside him. Paper-thin, blue-veined eyelids shielded the sometimes passionate, sometimes mocking, frequently challenging charcoal eyes. Black lashes formed dark crescents against the white skin, where just the faintest bloom of sleep tinged the high cheekbones. The retroussé nose wrinkled slightly, and her mouth tightened suddenly as if her sleeping thoughts disturbed her in some way.

And so they should, he thought bitterly, such an accomplished spy, she was. The concealed message in the letter to her godfather had been a masterpiece.

He wondered how best to wake her. She preferred a slow awakening, so . . .

He drew his knees up, catching the sheet and blanket on his feet, and then thrust out his legs, kicking the covers to the foot of the bed, baring Gabrielle's naked body to the chill morning air and his own gaze.

Gabrielle was so deeply asleep that the abrupt change in temperature caused only an instinctive response. She rolled onto her side, curling her body as she reached blindly for the covers, searching with innate animal impulse for the lost warmth.

Nathaniel tapped the curve of her buttocks thus presented to him. "Wake up, Gabrielle."

Gabrielle rolled onto her back and her eyes flew open. She covered her breasts with her arms. "I'm cold! What's happened to the blanket?"

"I kicked it off."

"Brute!" She sat up, reaching down for the covers, still too muzzy to question what he'd said. "Oh . . . that's better." With a sigh of relief she fell back on the pillows, dragging the blanket up to her neck and closing her eyes again.

"I said wake up!" Firmly, he unhooked her fingers and again stripped off the blanket. "You have a debt of honor to pay." He raised an eyebrow as Gabrielle blinked in bemusement.

"Today's the day I have a handmaiden for twenty-four hours," Nathaniel announced. "I believe I win the wager."

Gabrielle closed her eyes to hide the rush of speculation at these words. Curiously, she'd forgotten the wager, she'd been too busy concentrating on discovering his secrets and winning his confidence. But it didn't surprise her that Nathaniel had remembered. It was the kind of thing he would remember. And if today was Sunday, and, judging from the pealing church bells outside, it seemed that it was, then the two weeks were up and Nathaniel Praed had not recruited her into his spy network.

Maybe a day of passionate lust would chase off the demons of depression that dogged her at the moment.

"Well, now," she drawled, still keeping her eyes closed. "As I recall, we agreed it was a wager as well to be lost as won."

"You'll have to tell me about that this time tomorrow," he murmured. "For now I can concentrate only on the privileges of the winner."

Her eyes opened. "So, make your wishes known, my lord."

"Well, first, I'd like you to understand that for twenty-four hours every inch and every cell of your body is at my disposal—and that includes your tongue, madame, which I wish you for once to keep under control."

Reaching out, he ran his flat thumb over her mouth. "And since I don't want to put too great a strain on your powers of compliance, I'll help you by imposing a rule of silence. As of now."

Gabrielle's eyes spoke volumes as she absorbed this statement. Surprise and a shade of resistance leaped out at him from the deep gray pools. Automatically, she opened her mouth to demand further explanation and Nathaniel's thumb pressed firmly against her lips.

"Now," he said softly. "You had better disappear next door while I arrange matters here. I'll call you when I'm ready."

Something didn't feel right. But it was a game they'd both agreed to play. Gabrielle slipped off the bed and went toward the connecting door.

"Oh . . . and Gabrielle . . ." His voice arrested her as she turned the knob. "Don't get dressed."

Now, what did he have in mind? His instructions so far indicated he intended to hold her to the very letter of the wager as well as its spirit, and she couldn't help her initial response, that little spurt of annoyed resistance coming on the heels of a vague stirring of unease.

Gabrielle wrapped herself in a cashmere shawl against the morning cold and sat on her accustomed seat in the window to await his summons. As she relaxed, little prickles of excitement began to stir the downy hairs on the nape of her neck and flutter in the pit of her stomach. Twenty-four hours was a long time . . . and Nathaniel was an inspired lover with an extravagant sense of fantasy.

Silence, she was to discover as the long morning moved into afternoon, had the most powerful effect on the senses. It facilitated an extraordinary concentration on touch and feel, on taste and sight and smell. She imagined it was like moving in the womb, as Nathaniel rolled her beneath him with a fluid maneuver of her body that didn't disturb the union of their loins, and she felt the coolness of the sheets against her back, where before there had been the softness of the fire-warmed air of the bedchamber, and his body pressed into hers, molding the planes and concavities of his torso to the softer curves and indentations beneath him.

And in this closed world of silent concentration, she found herself focusing intensely on Nathaniel, and she could feel currents in his body that disturbed the smooth rhythms of their lovemaking. Sometimes, she detected a distance in him, as if, while his body played on hers, he himself was absent, was looking down upon their twisting, sinuous forms with a cool objectivity. The realization would chill her and then he would move over her again, would make some quiet demand that intensified their mutual pleasure, and the disturbance would pass.

Passive compliance, she also discovered throughout those long hours, had the same effect as the silence, or perhaps the one facilitated the other. She had only to *be* in this coupling. Her self didn't have to inhabit her body; indeed, her self was only an ever-shifting pool of sensations. She obeyed the authoritative touch, the soft-voiced command, and only once or twice did an uneasy resistance rustle through her, a tiny disturbance like a light breeze in autumnal leaves, when the body on hers felt as if it belonged to a stranger.

It was dusk before Nathaniel broke the spell. He was sprawled on the long couch beneath the windows, Gabrielle's bright head resting on his belly as she knelt on the floor beside the sofa, one languid hand stroking intimately between his thighs.

His gaze fell on the Chippendale clock on the wall above the fireplace. It was six o'clock. He moved his hand down, twisting his fingers in the dark red curls, turning her head on his belly so that she was looking toward him. Her eyes were heavy with fulfillment, her features somehow smudged, no longer sharply delineated on the pale, translucent skin.

"Enough, now," he said quietly, and yet his voice sounded shockingly loud after the long hours of silence in the firelit intimacy of their love chamber.

Gabrielle smiled dreamily, her eyes asking a question.

"You may speak," Nathaniel pronounced.

"I think I've forgotten how to. Perhaps it's tomorrow rather than today."

Nathaniel shook his head and said nothing.

Again Gabrielle felt that dart of unease. His eyes were unreadable as they looked down into her face, and she was used to seeing warm tenderness, a languid glow of satiation in their brown depths after such an excess of sensual joy.

But perhaps she was imagining it. They had been strange hours, eliciting new responses. Nathaniel had led them into uncharted territory, and unfamiliar emotions were to be discovered in such a landscape.

Without moving her position or ceasing her strok-

ing attentions, she attempted to reassert the comforting
realities of every day. "I seem to be hungry."

To her relief, Nathaniel responded in the same
tone, and the ordinary contours of the room reappeared
and she was conscious of the prickle of the carpet beneath her knees and the dampness of his skin under her
cheek.

"Me too," he said briskly. He caught her busy hand
and put it away from him. "Now move your head,
woman." He heaved himself upright and swung his legs
off the sofa, looking around the disheveled room, where
a bathtub of long-cold water still stood before the fire,
and a table bore the remains of a cold chicken and a
bowl of fruit.

Bending, he caught Gabrielle beneath the arms and
hauled her upright. She swayed and leaned against him,
nudging at his thighs with one knee.

"That'll do," Nathaniel instructed, taking her waist
and moving her aside. He filled two glasses from a depleted wine bottle and handed one to her. "Drink this."

Gabrielle sipped and regarded him with a quizzically raised eyebrow. "So what now, Sir Spymaster?
You've another twelve hours to enjoy your prize."

"No," Nathaniel said. "I'm declaring a morato-
rium."

"Oh? Why so?" She was puzzled and taken aback.

"Because it doesn't seem entirely fair," he said,
reaching for a dressing gown and shrugging into it. "I
won the wager under false pretenses."

"What?" Gabrielle became suddenly conscious of
her own nakedness as Nathaniel wrapped the robe
around himself, tying the girdle securely. The atmosphere in the room was fractured in some way, and she
felt an overwhelming sense of vulnerability.

"I've decided to take you into the network," he
stated calmly. "So, one could say that I cheated you out
of your winnings."

Gabrielle stood very still, trying to make sense of

this. "Then you didn't play fair," she said finally in tones of hurt confusion.

"Fair play, my dear, is not to be expected in the world of espionage," he pointed out in a voice like sere leaves. His eyes raked her face, looking for a conscious flash in her eyes, a hint of color in her cheeks, but there was nothing. Gabrielle de Beaucaire knew the underworld and the many dark faces of man, and she wore the velvet cloak of deceit as easily as he wore it himself.

"No, I suppose it's not," she said, suddenly matter-of-fact, going toward her own door. She paused, her hand on the latch as an explanation occurred to her for the strange, disturbing moments. "Was there some kind of test embodied in the last hours, Nathaniel?"

"I wanted to see whether I could trust you to play with the team," he said casually. "Whether you could control your own vigorous responses and follow the direction of a leader." He smiled. "It seems you can . . . in bed, at least. I'm willing to assume you'll be able to do it in other situations."

Gabrielle went into her own room. Distaste nibbled at her soul at the thought that all the while he'd been watching her, assessing her, as she lay open to him, her defenses down, utterly trusting in the loving congress that had always been inviolate, untouched by her own muddled emotions. He'd used sex to discover something about her. Surely he could have chosen some other arena.

But she'd succeeded. That was the important thing. Coldly, she concentrated on that fact. From now on she'd have access to the spymaster's world.

Nathaniel found himself staring at the closed door. Despite the ruthless pragmatism that had lain behind the scenario he had engineered that day, he was as stirred by her as ever. She had been more exciting in the role she'd played at his direction than he could ever have believed possible. Absorbing herself into the fantasy with her own brand of erotic magic.

Gabrielle de Beaucaire was a woman unlike any other. She could meet him and match him on every level—from hasty, lustful tumbling to exquisite love games; from angry challenge to witty retort; from analytic discourse to novel opinion. And on the back of a hunter, honesty obliged him to admit that Gabrielle probably had the edge.

His eye fell on the rumpled bed, the piled cushions on the floor where their game had led them at one point, the straight-backed chair where Gabrielle had—

Helen hadn't cared for hunting. The thought burst through his lascivious reverie. She'd been like Jake, timid on horseback. She'd not been playful either. A quietly smiling, grave woman of sweet disposition, she'd lent herself to him willingly, but he remembered now how once or twice he'd had the nagging suspicion that she'd found the sweaty antics of entwined naked bodies faintly ridiculous at best, distasteful at worst. He hadn't dwelt upon the suspicion, of course . . . had dismissed it as silly. Helen was too sweet and compliant to make such feelings overt, and what man wanted to see himself as ridiculous in the eyes of an adoring wife?

Gabrielle mocked him, challenged him, laughed at him, but nothing they did together, however outrageous, undignified, and sometimes downright silly, made him feel ridiculous. He did things with Gabrielle that he couldn't have imagined doing with Helen. Could never reveal to anyone else without being covered with embarrassment.

But they were alike, he and Gabrielle. They played in the same dark world . . . but on opposite sides. They understood risks and took them boldly. It was hardly surprising that they should be so well matched . . . in challenge as well as in treachery.

13

Several days later, a day filled with the intimations of spring, when crocuses and daffodils pushed through the lawn under the ancient oak trees and the weak sun brought a sparkle to the wide gray river, Gabrielle came into the house with a nosegay of snowdrops she'd picked in the orchard. She was smiling unconsciously as she inhaled their delicate fragrance.

Jake suddenly raced past her. His head was down and he bumped against her as he ran for the open front door behind her. He didn't stop to greet her, or even apologize for knocking into her, but flew down the steps of the house.

"Jake!" Gabrielle dropped the snowdrops on the console table and ran to the door, calling the child. But Jake's pace didn't decrease as he headed down the driveway. He was hatless and coatless, a condition not ordinarily permitted by his oversolicitous nurse or the zealous Miss Primmer.

"Jake!" Nathaniel came out of the library, scowling ferociously. "Where the devil has he gone? He has absolutely no manners! What has that ineffectual governess been teaching him?"

"He ran outside," Gabrielle said, turning back to the hall. "He seemed distraught. What have you said to him?"

The accusatory note in her voice was clear for both of them to hear, and Nathaniel's scowl deepened. A man appeared in the doorway behind him, a thin man with a lorgnette and lank, greasy hair, wearing dusty topboots and a morning coat of olive drab that had clearly seen better days.

"He'll become accustomed to the idea, Lord Praed," the man said with an unctuous smile.

Gabrielle took an instant and limitless dislike to the stranger. She stared at him with undisguised hauteur and raised an inquiring eyebrow at Nathaniel.

Nathaniel looked slightly and most unusually discomfited. "I beg your pardon, countess," he said stiffly. "Mr. Jeffrys is to be Jake's tutor. He comes most highly recommended."

"How comforting," Gabrielle said. "When did you arrive, Mr. Jeffrys?"

"This morning, my lady." The tutor-to-be inclined his angular frame from the waist in an inelegant and unpracticed bow. "Lord Praed's request for a recommendation for a tutor reached Harrow on Monday, and I came immediately. I am always the master's first choice when such requests are made. I pride myself on being able to prepare the sons of the nobility for entrance into our hallowed portals." His obsequious smile revealed yellow teeth.

Like moldering tombstones, Gabrielle thought. "How gratifying for you, Mr. Jeffrys," she said. "I trust you're well qualified to prepare mere babes for the rigors of such an establishment. They must perforce learn to withstand the severity and privations of such a life."

Mr. Jeffrys looked at her uneasily. What she'd said was nothing but the truth, of course. It was what he did best. But something about her tone and manner confused him. He tried another smile. "I pride myself on

my successes, my lady ... some of the noblest families
in the land ..." The smile hung in the air, as if it
couldn't find a home.

"If you'll excuse us, countess. We have some further business to discuss," Nathaniel said frigidly. He
turned back to the library. "Jeffrys ..."

"Oh, yes, my lord ... the details ... of course, my
lord."

And where the hell did Primmy fit into all this?
Gabrielle thought furiously. Nathaniel had said nothing
about the progress of his plans for a tutor, not to
Gabrielle and she presumed not to Primmy, who treated
her as a confidante and would most certainly have told
her. Indeed, the governess had been cherishing hopes
that his lordship had changed his mind, since he'd
never mentioned the matter again. And now this. Jake
presented to his new mentor without preparation, and
Miss Primmer out on her ear.

"Just one minute, my lord." She put out an imperative hand. "I'd like a private word. I'm sure Mr. Jeffrys
will excuse us." She turned toward the dining room
without waiting for a response from Nathaniel, who
hesitated for a second before waving the tutor curtly
back to the library and following her.

He slammed the door behind him. "Well?"

Gabrielle was trembling with rage. What did the
man have for empathy and insight? Cloth, presumably.
As dark and impenetrable a material as could be found.

"Forgive me if I'm mistaken," she said in tones of
icy incredulity, "but did you just spring that—that ...
odious creepy creature on Jake? Of course you didn't!
Of course you explained what was going to happen a
long time ago, didn't you? It's just that he hasn't mentioned it to me. But children do have short memories
and—"

"Hold your tongue!" Nathaniel ordered with low-
voiced ferocity, a dull flush spreading to his forehead.
"This is no concern of yours, as I've told you a dozen

times. Jake is *my* son, and how I handle him is *my* business."

"So you just summon him one morning, inform him that that odious man is going to rule his life from now until he's sent away to school, and that Primmy is going. Oh, when is she to leave, by the way? Is she packing her bags now?"

"Don't talk to me in this fashion—"

"I'll talk to you any way I like, Lord Praed," she interrupted, her pale complexion now whiter than milk, her eyes dark pools of molten lava, the skin around her mouth blue-tinged with fury. "Of all the crass—"

"Stop this at once!" Beside himself, he seized her upper arms and in unthinking reaction Gabrielle swung her flat palm against his cheek. The ugly crack hung for the barest instant in the air before it was repeated and Gabrielle spun away from him, her hand pressed to her own flaming cheek.

There was a terrible silence. She gazed sightlessly out the window, tears as much of shock as pain filming her eyes.

Nathaniel drew a deep shuddering breath. "I'm sorry."

"So am I," she said, her voice shaking. "How ugly . . . I don't know how it happened."

"I think we have to learn to be very careful," Nathaniel said wearily.

"Yes," Gabrielle agreed. She still couldn't turn to look at him, and he made no move toward her.

The silence elongated, grew leaden, and then Nathaniel turned and left the dining room, closing the door quietly behind him.

The raw violence of the encounter left Gabrielle feeling drained and sick. She sat down at the table, resting her still-stinging cheek on her palm, and waited until the shock had dissipated somewhat and she could think clearly.

Nathaniel was wrong-headed in his dealings with

Jake. But that didn't give her the right to speak to him as she had. She could have said the same things reasonably, without hurling insults and sarcasm at him. A few days ago she'd thought she'd been making some headway, but matters between father and son seemed to have reverted to the old bad ways, and somehow she'd lost the patience for subtle teaching by example.

Perhaps it wasn't the patience she'd lost but Nathaniel's attention. Since he'd agreed to employ her in the network, his attitude had changed toward her. They spent hours in his office constructing a code she would use to pass on her intelligence, and she had to pretend the incompetence of a tyro while her mind leaped three steps ahead of his painstaking tutorial. They studied maps of Europe and discussed the kind of intelligence that the English spymaster would find invaluable, and she offered suggestions as to how she could acquire it.

They made love every night with the same wild passion and slept until morning in each other's arms, but a different dimension had entered their relationship. The natural equality had vanished. Nathaniel was instructor, director, employer. He wasn't cold in these roles, but he was businesslike and distant and Gabrielle followed his lead because it was what she was there to do.

But all the rational thought in the world didn't diminish the sense of loss over the days when they'd sparred and loved as if nothing else could ever concern them.

And how on earth were they to recover from that vile encounter?

A cloud of depression settled over her as she stood up and left the dining room to go in search of Jake.

She ran the child to earth behind the boathouse. He was huddled on the narrow jetty, shoulders hunched, chin pressed into his chest.

Gabrielle dropped a coat around his shoulders and

sat down beside him, drawing him into the curve of her arm. He snuffled and swallowed a sob.

"I want Primmy. I don't want her to go away."

Gabrielle let him cry, offering soothing murmurs and the warm comfort of her body until he'd exhausted his tears. Then she tried to explain why his father had decided this was best for him. It was hard to be convincing when she was so far from convinced herself. But Nathaniel was such a distant authoritarian figure in the child's life that she felt she could at least impress upon Jake that his father had only his best interests at heart. And she did believe that. Nathaniel simply didn't know what those best interests were.

Jake was not to be persuaded, and he trailed dolefully after her as they returned to the house.

She accompanied him to the nursery, where a resolutely dry-eyed Miss Primmer told her she'd been given two weeks notice by his lordship and a most generous settlement. His lordship was all kindness, all consideration. But the governess hugged her wan charge convulsively as she made these vigorous protestations, and Jake's tears began to flow again.

There seemed nothing useful she could do, nothing comforting to be said at this point, and Gabrielle left them together.

Mr. Jeffrys passed her on the stairs. He was fussily directing the footman to be careful with his trunk of books and globes. He gave Gabrielle yet another ingratiating smile that she ignored, even as she wondered what interpretation he'd put on her presence. Nathaniel hadn't introduced her, although he'd referred to her as "countess." Presumably, he expected the same discreet acceptance from the tutor that he did from the rest of his staff.

Mrs. Bailey came out of the drawing room, feather duster in hand, as Gabrielle reached the hall. She bore the air of one attending at a deathbed.

"Did you wish me to put the snowdrops in your

boudoir, ma'am?" The housekeeper gestured to the bunch of delicate flowers that Gabrielle had abandoned on the console table in the earlier flurry.

"Oh, yes, thank you."

"Miss Primmer will be sadly missed," the housekeeper observed, picking up the flowers. "And I don't know what to make of that tutor. All smarm and smiles, he is, but you mark my words, once he gets his feet under the table, he'll be giving orders left, right, and center. I know the type."

It was an extraordinary speech from the discreet Mrs. Bailey. Gabrielle was hard pressed to know how to respond. She wanted to agree, but couldn't without seeming to criticize Nathaniel to his staff. She offered a vague smile and satisfied herself with agreeing that Miss Primmer would indeed be missed, then she made her escape into the garden in search of privacy and tranquil surroundings.

There was a stone sundial and bench in the middle of the shrubbery, and she made her way there, knowing she would be invisible from the house.

She leaned back against the seat and raised her face to the pale sun, closing her eyes, allowing the feeble warmth to caress her eyelids. A fresh breeze carried the scents of the river and marshes and a chaffinch chirped busily from a bay tree.

She was so deeply immersed in her meditation that she didn't hear the footsteps on the gravel path behind her. When the hand fell on her head, she jumped with a startled cry.

"Penny for them," Nathaniel said quietly, keeping his hand where it was.

Gabrielle shrugged. "I was just musing."

His hand slipped to clasp the back of her neck. "May I share the muse?"

She arched her neck against the warm, firm pressure of his hand. "How did that happen, Nathaniel? Civilized people don't get into those kinds of fights."

"No, only excessively passionate people who both know they deserve to be flogged for such disgraceful lack of control," he agreed with a wry, self-mocking smile. Still holding her neck, he moved around the bench and sat down beside her.

"How about a pact of mutual forgiveness?" His fingers tightened around the slim column of her neck.

"Done," she said.

They sat in silence for a while. It was a companionable silence. Gabrielle was acutely conscious of his hand on her neck, of the moving blood beneath his skin, of his even breathing, of the warm proximity of his body. She realized suddenly that she'd become accustomed to such moments, and they'd been absent in the last days. Only now did she realize how much she'd missed these periods of silent and effortless communion in the turbulent seas of passion.

"I want you to go to Paris." Nathaniel's startling announcement broke the silence.

"When?" She turned on the bench to look at him.

"In three days time." He let his hands fall from her and leaned forward, his elbows resting on his knees. "I need a courier to take a vital message to my agents in Paris. I told you I was having problems with the network in Toulouse?"

"Yes?" Her mind was in a ferment. It was what she'd been working toward, but she hadn't expected him to send her into the field so soon—or so abruptly.

"I'll give you your instructions just before you leave. Your papers are in order, I assume?"

"Yes, I have a *laissez passer* signed by Fouché, no less."

"Good." He stood up. "There'll be a fishing boat sailing from Lymington to Cherbourg in three days. You'll sail on her and be put ashore in a small village just along the coast. From there you'll be able to make your own arrangements."

"I see."

A silver eyebrow rose quizzically as he regarded her. "For some reason I'd expected a little more enthusiasm. It's what you've been wanting, after all."

She summoned a smile. "You just took me by surprise, that's all."

"Well, having made the decision, I can see little point in waiting."

"No, neither can I," she agreed, injecting firm confidence into the statement. "But you will tell me exactly what to do?"

"To the letter," he said. "Now, if you'll excuse me, I have to meet with the bailiff. I'll see you at nuncheon."

Gabrielle nodded and watched him stride off down the gravel path toward the house. So it was the end of the passionate interlude. Once she was working in the field, there'd be few opportunities for lustful encounters between the spymaster and his agent. In fact, Nathaniel would probably consider them dangerously out of bounds in a working relationship. Perhaps that lay behind the distancing of the past few days. He was preparing them both for the inevitable separation.

Well, in many ways it would be a relief. Vengeance would become relatively simple again. Apart from him, she would manage to overcome her addiction to Nathaniel Praed's lovemaking. She'd have to, wouldn't she?

The courier bearing Gabrielle's letter caught up with Charles-Maurice de Talleyrand-Perigord in an inn in a small village in East Prussia, where he'd stopped for the night on his way back to Paris. He was in no cheerful frame of mind. His crippled leg ached unmercifully from the cold and the violent jolting of the carriage along the broken, ice-covered roads of a part of the world he was rapidly considering totally benighted, and not even the prospect of his comfortable house in the rue d'Anjou could truly compensate for the miseries of the journey.

Napoleon's victory over the Russians at Eylau on February eighth had finally given his Minister for Foreign Affairs the opportunity to leave the emperor's side. Napoleon had correctly described Eylau as "not a battle but a slaughter," in which the Russians lost nearly twenty-six thousand men, and the French casualties were almost as disastrous. It was moot which side could truly claim victory. Alexander had congratulated his own General Bennigsen on defeating "the one who has never yet known defeat." However, since Bennigsen ordered his troops to fall back on Kaliningrad, technically Napoleon remained master of the field.

Poor consolation for the widows and orphans on either side! Talleyrand reflected, gazing morosely into the clear liquid in his rather smeared vodka glass. But now the emperor was marching the army to Osterode to make winter quarters, and Talleyrand was free to shake the dust of Eastern Prussia from his boots. With luck he'd reach Paris by the end of the week.

He stared into the meager fire and sipped his vodka, nothing more civilized being offered in this wayside halt. Absently he rubbed his aching leg and reexamined the decoded message within the letter. Gabrielle had become an expert at this means of communication during her work as a courier, and she had the kind of mind that lent itself to the construction of cryptic yet nonetheless informative messages.

But something niggled at him. Not in the coded message but in the letter that enclosed it. It was a somewhat formal communication, as her role demanded. For public consumption, she held no brief for her godfather and wouldn't therefore engage in anything other than dutifully courteous correspondence. Should anyone happen to look over her shoulder while she was writing the letter, they would read only the tone they would expect.

But Talleyrand was sensing something awry in the relationship between the spymaster and Gabrielle. The vengeful seduction had gone exactly according to plan, and she expected to gain the spymaster's total confidence very shortly, but she was withholding something . . . there was a sense of uncertainty, a slight ambiguity in her expressions that caused her godfather considerable speculation. Only someone who knew her as well as he did would have been aware of it, and Gabrielle probably hadn't been aware of it herself. But something had occurred that might well muddy the waters of the minister's perfect plan.

Talleyrand kicked at a slipping log in the grate. Gabrielle knew that his goal was not the destruction of Nathaniel Praed, but quite the opposite. The spymaster was to be the recipient of selected information that he would pass on to his government, and thus Talleyrand would be in a position to manipulate the war to his own desired end: the defeat of Napoleon. Only thus would peace and stability return to Europe without the destruction of France. Napoleon had served his purpose in stabilizing the country after the postrevolution chaos, but now he no longer spoke for France. He was a megalomaniac and he had to be stopped before his territorial ambitions ruined his country by creating a coalition of vengeful powers headed by England that France would be unable to withstand.

But Gabrielle had her own overriding personal motive for manipulating Nathaniel Praed. It was that that made her a perfect partner in her godfather's scheme. If something was going on that would eradicate Gabrielle's own motivation, how would that affect her willingness to play Talleyrand's deep game?

Talleyrand sighed and examined a plate of pickled cabbage and fat sausage with a disgusted twitch of his thin, aristocratic mouth. Peasant food! It was a far cry from the gourmet chefs in Warsaw, let alone Paris. But he had to endure only a few more days.

14

Jake lay in the nursery, staring at the black square of the window at the end of his bed. The springlike day had given way to a violent, blustery night and the bare branches of the oak tree outside scratched against the panes. He could hear the slapping of the river against the jetty and the scream of a benighted sea gull fleeing inland from the choppy waters of the Solent.

His stomach hurt and felt empty, as if he'd had no supper. But he'd had an egg and toast and Nurse had made him hot chocolate and Primmy had read him a story. Gabby had come to kiss him good night. He could still smell her hair as she'd bent over him. It smelled like the flowers she had in her boudoir.

He wanted to cry, but he felt all dried up. Whenever he thought about being left alone by Primmy and Gabby, he wanted to scream and shout and throw something. He wanted to hurt someone. It was Papa's fault ... everything was Papa's fault. He'd brought that horrible man who smelled like sour milk and wore a black gown and flapped around the schoolroom like the gigantic crow that lived in the elm tree behind the orchard. Papa had told Primmy she had to leave, and now he was sending Gabby away. Why couldn't Papa go away and never come back . . . never!

Jake sniffed and stared dry-eyed at the window. It was wicked to think something like that, but he couldn't help it, and he didn't care if God did strike him dead. It would be better than staying here alone with that nasty man and his swishy stick and his Latin verbs.

Why wouldn't Gabby let him go with her? He'd asked and asked but she'd said no, it was too far and Papa wouldn't like it and he had to go to school. . . .

Well, he wasn't going to school, and he didn't care about Papa. He was going with Gabby.

Jake tossed onto his side and curled up, feeling for the knitted donkey that Nurse had made him when he was a baby. It had slipped to the bottom of his bed, and he pulled it up with his feet, wrapping his body around it, smelling its familiar woolly smell. His thumb took the forbidden path into his mouth and his eyes closed. He wasn't staying here. He was going to run away with Gabby.

For the next two days Jake listened. He listened to the servants, to Primmy when she talked to Nurse, to Milner in the stables when he went for his riding lessons. The only person he didn't listen to was Mr. Jeffrys, but then, the tutor didn't talk about Gabby and when she was leaving Burley Manor. The swishy stick stung his knuckles when he was inattentive, but Jake didn't care. His whole body seemed centered on his glowing purpose, and he could think of nothing else.

From Milner he discovered that Gabby was driving to Lymington in the chaise on Thursday evening. Gabby told him she was taking a fishing boat to France from Lymington quay. Jake knew that fishing boats had decks with coils of rope and nets, and usually they had a cabin. He would find somewhere to hide, he was sure.

The chaise had a narrow ledge at the back and a strap for a spare groom to hang on to, but there wouldn't be a groom on the short journey to Lymington. The prospect of clinging up there himself made him feel rather sick, but it didn't dent his purpose in the least.

From Primmy and Nurse, he learned that his father was leaving on the same day and expected to be away for several weeks. If his father was away, Jake couldn't see how he'd discover that Jake had gone until he came back, so there'd be nobody to chase him even when his disappearance was discovered. And that wouldn't be until the morning, when Nurse came to wake him up. And once they reached France, Gabby would look after him. His mind couldn't stretch beyond that immediate goal, and he was untroubled by speculation on the future.

Gabrielle was puzzled by the suppressed excitement she felt in the child. She'd expected him to be unhappy, cross even, blaming her for leaving him. But instead his eyes were unnaturally bright and he giggled in a most unJakelike fashion, and he seemed hard pressed to put a coherent sentence together. Primmy commented on it too, and Mr. Jeffrys complained at length to his employer about his pupil's general inattentiveness.

Nathaniel heard the complaint in frowning silence, then delivered the acerbic comment that he'd assumed a tutor to whom he paid the princely sum of one hundred pounds a quarter would know how to command the attention of a six-year-old.

A chagrined Mr. Jeffrys left the library, and Gabrielle observed from her secluded fireside corner, "Much as I enjoy his discomfiture, I hope he doesn't take his mortification out on Jake in the interests of gaining his attention."

"Jeffrys knows exactly what I will and will not permit," Nathaniel said shortly.

"And how are you to know if he doesn't keep

within those boundaries?" she inquired. "I don't see Jake telling you, do you?"

Nathaniel ran his hands through his hair in a gesture of frustration. "I don't know why he wouldn't. I give him plenty of opportunity to talk to me."

Gabrielle shook her head but said nothing. It was too late now for her opinions. They hadn't been accepted before, and there was no reason to believe that a flash of insight would illuminate the eve of departure and bring forth a change of heart.

Nathaniel had made all the arrangements for her journey and given her the details calmly and efficiently, as if he weren't describing the way she would walk out of his life forever. Gabrielle had responded in the same fashion. They were pleasant and polite to each other; they made love, but the spark was missing. Gabrielle supposed it eased the prospect of parting. One withdrew from addiction by slow steps. But it also felt soulless, almost as if they were determined now to negate the strength of what they'd shared.

They dined early on the Thursday evening and Gabrielle went up to say good-bye to Jake. The little boy was sitting up in bed, unusually pale, but his brown eyes had an almost febrile glitter to them. Gabrielle felt his forehead as she kissed him. He was warm but not feverish. Most unusually, he didn't seem to want her to stay. Instead of prolonging the visit in his customary fashion with questions, requests for another story, or endless narratives with neither beginning nor end, he docilely accepted her good-bye kiss and said good night, snuggling down almost before she'd left the nursery.

It was a relief, of course. She'd been dreading tears and recriminations. But it was still a little hurtful to think how quickly one could be dismissed by both father and son.

"Are you ready?" Nathaniel came into her apartments just before nine o'clock. "The tide's full at eleven o'clock and you have to catch it."

"Yes, I'm ready." She looked up from the jewel casket she was closing and blinked in surprise. Nathaniel was wearing boots and britches, a plain white linen shirt open at the neck with a scarf knotted carelessly at his throat. He had a cloak slung over one arm and leather gauntlets held in one hand.

"That's a very serviceable dress," she commented. "Are you intending to travel all night?"

"It might be necessary," he replied in the tone that she'd learned prohibited further inquiry. "Has Bartram taken your traps to the chaise?"

"Yes, and I've said good-bye to Ellie and Mrs. Bailey."

"Then let's go."

There was a lump in Gabrielle's throat as she followed him downstairs. She couldn't understand why she wasn't excited, triumphant at the success of her plan. She had the spymaster where she wanted him. But she was aware only of a bleak depression and a deep and irrational hurt. She wanted Nathaniel to be as regretful at their parting as she was, and he patently wasn't.

Nathaniel handed her into the chaise waiting at the door and climbed in after her, first checking that the luggage was properly stowed on the roof. He knocked on the panel, the coachman clicked his whip, and the carriage moved down the long drive.

At the bottom of the drive they stopped while the gatekeeper opened the gate for them. A small figure crept out of the bushes and clambered onto the narrow ledge, standing on tiptoe to seize the leather strap, pressing his slight body against the back of the coach as it rattled through the gate and down the lane. The gatekeeper closed the gate after them, muttering to himself as his rheumaticky hands fumbled with the heavy iron bar. He was shortsighted and it was a dark

night. If he discerned a darker shadow against the rear
panels of the coach as it swayed down the road, he
thought nothing of it.

Gabrielle tried to think of some topic of conversation, something to break the silence. But there'd only
ever been one acceptable topic of conversation, and it
was hardly appropriate at this juncture. Although the
last time they'd traveled in the coach, on the way from
Vanbrugh Court, it had been more than appropriate. . . .

Nathaniel sat back against the squabs, his arms
folded across his chest, his eyes hooded as he watched
her face in the shifting shadows of the coach. She
wasn't happy about this mission; in fact, if asked, he
would have said she was downright depressed. As indeed he would be if he believed they were about to part
ways. Not even her treachery, it seemed, could destroy
his passion for her. There was some level on which they
were totally compatible, and in his more detached moments it struck him as the most damnable twist of fate
that they should find themselves on opposite sides in
the dirty war they fought. They would have made the
most amazing partners if they shared the same goals and
the same loyalties.

Instead, they were bitterest enemies, each out to
manipulate and betray the other. And in his heart he
knew that even if he won, as he intended to, they
would still both be losers.

In half an hour the chaise clattered across the cobbles at the Lymington quay. Lamplight poured out from
the Black Swan Inn as inebriated fishermen staggered
out, yelling, cursing, and singing. Most made their way
to the fleet of boats tied up at the quay, leaping on
decks with a dexterity that belied the effects of carous-
ing. But time and tide made no concessions when a
man's livelihood came from the sea.

Jake slipped to the cobbles and darted behind a coil
of tarred rope. In the general melee no one noticed a

small boy in nankeen britches and a knitted blue jersey.
He watched as the coachman snapped his fingers at one
of the inn's ostlers lounging against the timbered wall
of the inn with a pipe in his hand. The man shook out
the pipe and sauntered across. Money changed hands,
and between them the ostler and coachman unloaded
the bags from the roof of the chaise. They took them to
a relatively large fishing boat at the far end of the quay.
A man standing in the stern greeted them with a hail
and gestured that they should come aboard.

Jake slipped from his hiding place and darted forward. His father and Gabby were still standing by the
coach, talking to each other. No one was looking in his
direction. Around him people were running, shouting,
leaping from the quay to the boat decks and back
again. Ropes were being untied, sheets loosened, and
sails unfurled. Lymington estuary was in full flood, the
tide flowing strongly toward the Solent at its mouth,
and there was a night of fishing and crabbing to be
done. Some would trawl their nets in the deep waters
off the Brittany coast, on the lookout for hostile French
shipping, and one craft at least, like the *Curlew*, would
ferry and offload those who sailed by night about
clandestine business.

The three men had their backs turned to the gang-
way. Jake leaped across it in four steps and dived behind a roll of canvas sailcloth in the bow of the boat.
He crouched there, his heart beating fast, but too excited for fear. In a minute Gabby would come aboard
and his father would drive off and the boat would sail
out of the river. He wouldn't tell anyone he was there
until they got to France. How long did it take to sail to
France? Perhaps all night?

"Let's get you aboard," Nathaniel said, putting an
arm lightly around Gabrielle's shoulders, shepherding
her toward the craft riding easily on the swelling tide.
"I'll give you your detailed instructions in the cabin."

He went ahead of her across the gangplank,

jumped down to the deck, and, turning, held out his hand to her. He was smiling, and there was something raffish about him, Gabrielle realized as he stood there in the torchlit night, the carelessly knotted kerchief at his throat, one booted foot on the gangplank, his other hand resting on his knee, the cloak falling back from his shoulders revealing the slender, tensile frame.

She didn't think she'd ever seen him like this, radiating some secret pleasure . . . just like Jake, she thought, recognizing one of those flashes of similarity between parent and child.

Nathaniel was obviously relishing the prospect of whatever adventure awaited him once she'd left. Not to be outdone, Gabrielle forced a smile of her own and sprang lightly across the gangplank, disdaining his helping hand with an airy wave.

"There's a cabin of sorts below," Nathaniel said, ushering her toward the hatchway. "Primitive, I'm afraid, but hopefully not too fishy." His voice was bright and his eyes had the wicked gleam in their depths that Gabrielle associated with their most imaginative playtimes.

Obviously the prospect of a dangerous piece of espionage, or whatever he was about to engage upon, gave him as much of a sexual thrill as lovemaking, she decided morosely, following him down the narrow companionway.

There was a strong smell of fish, and the oil lantern hanging from the low ceiling gave off noxious smoky fumes, its flickering light casting grotesque shadows on the planked bulkhead. A skinny bunk was set into the bulkhead with a coarse blanket over a straw pallet. It was airless and yet dank and chill. However, Gabrielle told herself, the journey shouldn't take more than twelve or thirteen hours, and she could always go up on deck.

She turned to her companion. "So, perhaps you'd better give me my instructions."

Nathaniel leaned back against the stained planking of the bolted-down central table, arms folded, his eyes hooded.

"No, I think I'll wait a bit."

"Wait? But for heaven's sake, Nathaniel, the boat's about to sail."

"I know."

"Just what are you getting at?" Gabrielle glared at him in infuriated bewilderment.

Nathaniel remained unmoved. "Simply that you're not going alone."

Gabrielle felt as if she'd lost touch with her own moorings just as the boat lurched beneath her and a voice yelled an instruction accompanying the squeak of a sail running up the masthead. She grabbed the edge of the table as the boat swung slowly away from the quayside and the wind filled the mainsail.

"You're coming to France?" she asked carefully.

"Just so."

"But why?"

"My dear girl, I never send an agent into the field alone on a first mission," he informed her coolly. "They always have a mentor, someone who knows the area and the setup. I'm going to act as your mentor on this mission, and if all goes well, then I daresay future ones you may conduct alone."

"Well, why didn't you tell me?" she demanded, her eyes blazing.

"I wanted to see how you would behave when faced with the prospect of going alone into danger."

The authoritarian, matter-of-fact statement was the last straw. What the devil did he know about how she faced danger?

"I am sick to death of your damn tests," Gabrielle declared, jabbing at his chest with a forefinger. "Who the hell do you think you are?"

"Your spymaster," he said, catching the jabbing finger and holding it away from him. "And you will submit to any test I decide to set—unless you wish to abandon this plan?"

Gabrielle drew breath deep into her lungs. He was still holding her finger, and there was a sudden intensity in the eyes resting on her face.

Tell me you'll give it up. Go on, Gabrielle, say it. It's not too late. The fervency of his unspoken thoughts shocked him. He'd believed he was resigned, accepting of her treachery, but he wasn't. He didn't know if he could forgive, if they could make some new start. But perhaps if Gabrielle pulled back now . . .

Their eyes held for a minute, then Gabrielle laughed and pulled her finger out of his grip. "Don't be silly. Of course I don't want to."

"No, of course not," he said.

Gabrielle sat down on the narrow bunk, frowning. At least it offered a satisfactory explanation for why Nathaniel hadn't appeared unduly depressed at the prospect of their parting. But she wasn't accustomed to having the ground cut from beneath her feet, and just recently Nathaniel had been doing that with tiresome regularity.

Yet, despite her annoyance, she couldn't deny the little prickles of pleasure and excitement at the prospect of extending their time together despite the complications that were bound to result.

"So you're traveling to Paris?" she said after a minute.

"Yes, under your protection," he informed her without batting an eyelid. "Your *laissez passer* I assume will cover a servant."

Gabrielle gazed at him, for a moment speechless. Of all the effrontery! But it was still a brilliant strategy, one she would have come up with herself.

"Nathaniel Praed, you are . . . you are . . . oh, there isn't a word strong enough to describe you."

Nathaniel reached for her, hauling her to her feet

and pulling her between his knees. Her eyes were on a level with his.

"Would you rather travel alone, Gabrielle?"

She shook her head ruefully. "No. You know I wouldn't. I didn't want us to part."

"I know you didn't. And neither did I. We seem to be intertwined, you and I," he said with a dry smile.

"Yes," Gabrielle agreed quietly. A chill ran down her spine as someone walked over her grave. Intertwined enemies. Deadly enemies. She hated Nathaniel for what he had done to Guillaume and to her, and yet she could barely contemplate being away from him.

She looked into his eyes and saw her own reflection in the dark irises. There was something in the brown depths that she couldn't read, something of a most powerful intensity that sent renewed chills over her skin. It was more than simple passion, it was almost menacing. And then he caught her head between his hands and brought his mouth to hers and reason and unease yielded to the familiar heady rush of desire.

On deck, Jake shivered in his hiding place as the fishing boat ran before the wind up the estuary. Papa had gone into the cabin with Gabby and hadn't come out. He was still on the boat, and now they were going to France.

Voices reached him from the other side of his hiding place, the rough male voices of the skipper and his crew. Jake shivered with terror and the tears tracked soundlessly down his cheeks. He inched closer to the deck rail and the surging cold black water beneath. He couldn't swim. If he jumped, he'd drown. But if he stayed, they'd find him. And Papa would find him . . . and . . .

He couldn't imagine what his father would do when he found him. He shrank down as far as he could behind the sailcloth and closed his eyes tightly, trying to believe as he had when he was very little that if he couldn't see people, they couldn't see him.

"Oh, that's better." Gabby's voice penetrated his terrified trance. "It's so stuffy in there."

"It'll be very cold once we round the Needles and reach the open sea," Nathaniel replied. "You'll be glad enough of the shelter then."

"Maybe." Gabrielle held the deck rail and threw back her head, looking up into the overcast sky, where the misty shadow of the moon hung over them. The spray stung her face and she breathed deeply of the salt-tanged air. It felt good deep in her lungs. She looked back to the diminishing lights of Lymington quay. "I hope it stays calm. I'm not the world's best sailor."

"Goodness me," Nathaniel said in tones of feigned amazement. "Don't tell me you have a weakness."

"Unkind," she protested with a soft laugh. "I have many weaknesses." *Being here with you is one of them.* But for the moment there was nothing to be gained by fighting that weakness.

"I'm hungry," she said. "It seems ages since dinner. It must be the sea air."

"You've been sailing for only half an hour," Nathaniel pointed out. "However, I had the fore-thought to bring some provisions. Shall we go below?"

"No, let's have a picnic up here."

The voices were so close to Jake, he could almost imagine touching Gabrielle. He wanted to jump up and run to her, bury his head in her skirt, feel her warmth and her arms around him, her lips brushing his cheek when she kissed him, her hand ruffling his hair. But then his father spoke again, and he huddled wretchedly back into his corner.

"So what did you bring?" Gabrielle turned from the rail as Nathaniel reemerged from the companionway. She smiled and the moon broke through a gap in the clouds, throwing her face into silver relief.

Her smile was candid, inviting, as if she had noth-ing to hide, and despite everything he knew, he couldn't prevent his own lips curving in response.

"You'll see. We'll use this as a table." He kicked forward an upturned crate and squatted down before it, feeling into the bag he carried with the air of a magician about to produce a litter of rabbits.

"Cognac, for the warmth," he declared, flourishing the bottle as if it were a prize. "Then one of Cook's special veal and ham pies . . ." This joined the cognac on the makeshift table. "Two chicken drumsticks, a round of cheddar, and some apples. How does that sound?"

"Inspired." Gabrielle sat on the deck, leaning her back against the rail.

"No utensils, I'm afraid. We'll have to drink from the bottle and use my pocket knife for cutting." Nathaniel produced the knife as he handed the cognac to Gabrielle. He cut a V into the golden raised crust of the pie.

Jake listened to the sounds of the picnic. He could smell the food and the nose-tingling aroma of the cognac. He was cold and hungry. His father's voice sounded quite different from normal—gay, lighthearted, full of laughter. Gabby spoke with her mouth full, choked, Papa patted her on the back, and they both laughed. It didn't sound as if they could ever be cross. Jake half rose from his cramped crouch, but his nerve failed him and he shrank back again.

"We're rounding the Needles." Nathaniel stood up and reached a hand down to pull Gabrielle to her feet. "Vicious, aren't they?"

The water boiled around the row of jagged rocks obtruding from the tip of the Isle of Wight. Gabrielle shivered and drew her cloak tighter around her shoulders. The moon had disappeared again and the beacon in the lighthouse glowed strong in the darkness. The mournful clanging of the warning bell carried across the water.

"I've never made this crossing," she said. "I've always crossed from Dover to Calais and vice versa. It seems a lot less wild."

They were leaving the Isle of Wight and the sheltered Solent behind. The wind blew stronger now and the sea had lost its docile quality, stretching ahead and around in a rolling expanse of white-capped surges. The fishing boat seemed to ride the waves with ease, Gabrielle noted with some relief, running a mental check over the state of her stomach. It occurred to her that a greedy supper had perhaps been unwise.

"Let's go below," Nathaniel said. "It's getting chilly and it's late. We should try to snatch a couple of hours sleep."

"That cot's very narrow," Gabrielle demurred, but allowed herself to be urged toward the companionway.

"You can have it, I'll sleep on the floor."

"That'll be horribly uncomfortable."

"I've been more so," he said. "In general, I can sleep anywhere."

Jake listened to their voices fading away as they disappeared below. Despite his fear of discovery, he'd found their proximity comforting. His clothes were damp with the sea spray and he could taste salt on his lips, mingling with the salt of his tears. Unutterable loneliness washed over him between the dark, unfriendly sea and the cloud-thick sky.

In his wretched self-absorption he didn't hear the footsteps until they were upon him. "What the 'ell 'ave we 'ere!"

The violent exclamation brought a cry of terror from the child, who shrank back against the railing. A man towered over him, huge in his britches and sailor's jersey, very like Jake's own. Hands reached down and seized the boy beneath his armpits and hauled him ungently into the air.

"You know what we do wi' stowaways?" the rough voice demanded. "We make 'em swim fer shore."

For a second Jake was held dangling over the railing and his shrill scream split the night air. "*Gabby . . . Gabby!*" He yelled the one name that meant salvation at the top of his lungs.

"What on earth is that racket?" Nathaniel, in the process of helping Gabrielle pull off her boots, dropped her foot abruptly and turned to the companionway. He stuck his head through the hatch. "What's going on?"

"Beggin' yer pardon, sir, but we've got ourselves a stowaway." The sailor held up the kicking, screaming child.

"Gabby!" Jake shrieked again. "I want Gabby."

"Dear God in heaven," Nathaniel whispered. "*Jake!*"

"You know the lad, sir?"

"My son," Nathaniel said quietly. "Give him to me."

"I want Gabby," Jake continued to bellow in pure hysteria, and suddenly she was there, pushing Nathaniel aside as she squeezed through the narrow hatch.

"Jake." She held out her arms and, as the sailor set the boy on his feet, he ran sobbing to her.

"All right," she said, stroking his head. "It's all right. I've got you. It's all right."

Nathaniel stood, watching. It seemed as if this had nothing to do with him, but it was *his* son. Gabrielle had known the child only a few weeks, and it was as if his father didn't exist.

She was curved over the child, her body in a graceful arc of comfort, her hair escaping from its pins, falling forward, blending with his son's fair curls. And it came to him that even if she *had* used the child in her scheming, the warmth and closeness between them was genuine. Gabrielle loved his son.

"I'm right sorry, sir," the sailor was saying, pulling on his earlobe. "I don't know 'ow 'e could 'ave got aboard."

"We'll have to turn back," Nathaniel instructed. "Immediately."

"Can't do that, sir. Tide and wind are runnin' agin us. We'll never make it back round the Needles."

Nathaniel produced a string of barnyard oaths that impressed even the two fishermen. Jake's sobs had faded to heaving gulps, but his head remained buried in Gabrielle's skirts.

"Get below," Nathaniel commanded harshly with a brusque gesture to Gabrielle.

"Come along, Jake." She chivvied the child ahead of her to the companionway, climbed down first, and then lifted him down after her.

Nathaniel jumped the short flight, his face taut with anger. "Come here!" He snapped his fingers at his son, who still clung to Gabrielle's leg, his face buried in her skirt.

Jake's wails increased in volume, but he made no move to obey.

Nathaniel's breath hissed through his teeth as he struggled with his anger. "Gabrielle, let him go. I want you to go on deck, please," he said, his voice now flat and without emotion.

Gabrielle looked down at the fair, curly head pressing against her thigh. She looked up at Nathaniel, then, with calm resolution, bent and picked up Jake.

"You have every right to scold him," she said to Nathaniel. "He needs to understand how much trouble he's caused. But hold him while you do it."

She thrust the child at his father, and Nathaniel in reflex action put out his arms. He found himself holding the boy tightly against his chest. They both looked so astonished at this novel position that, despite the dire circumstances, Gabrielle was hard pressed to keep a straight face as she left them alone.

15

"Hell and the devil," Nathaniel muttered, examining his son's white face held so close to his own. "Just what in the name of goodness did you think you were doing?"

Jake's face crumpled and his mouth opened on a round O in preparation for a fresh wail.

"Don't start bawling again," Nathaniel said sharply. "At this point, my friend, you have nothing to cry about. I can't guarantee that happy state of affairs will continue, but I suggest you reserve your tears for when they might do some good."

Jake's mouth snapped shut, and he held himself rigid in his father's arms, his brown eyes fixed unwaveringly on Nathaniel.

"How did you manage to get here?" Nathaniel demanded after a moment's contemplation of the ramifications of this disastrous arrival. "I want to know exactly how you did it." He shifted the child in his arms and then sat on the cot, holding him somewhat awkwardly on his knee.

Jake stumbled through his narrative, his voice still thick with tears that he effortfully controlled.

"Good God," Nathaniel murmured at story's end. This was the child who chose to draw pictures in the gravel rather than climb trees, who screamed in terror on the back of a pony bigger than a Shetland, who seemed incapable of opening his mouth beyond a monosyllabic answer to a direct question. Jake's courage and ingenuity in this instance astonished his father. That however, didn't alter the seriousness of the situation.

"How do you think Nurse and Miss Primmer are going to feel in the morning, when they go to the nursery and you're not there?"

Jake didn't reply, but the tears now tracked slowly and soundlessly down his cheeks.

"You didn't think about that, did you? They're going to be worried out of their minds wondering what's happened to you."

"You're sending Primmy away," Jake whispered, gulping. "And I want to be with Gabby."

"Yes, well, I can see your point," Nathaniel muttered. "It seems to run in the family." He leaned back against the bulkhead, holding the child lightly, rather surprised at his own sense of humor in the face of this catastrophe.

A shiver suddenly shook the small body and Nathaniel became aware of the child's damp clothing, the hair clinging to his forehead from the sea spray. It was also long past midnight.

"You'd better go to bed," he said, standing up with the child. "There's nothing to be done about this for the moment." He set Jake on his feet and pulled the damp jersey over his head. "You'd better get out of those trousers too."

He stood, frowning, as the child obediently fumbled with the buttons of his nankeen britches. "Here, let me do it." Bending, he swiftly divested the boy of the garment, then wrapped him securely in the blanket from the cot.

"Warmer now?"

Jake nodded, huddling into the coarse wool. He was too shocked and overwhelmed by the events of the night to be aware of the novelty of his father's attentions. Nathaniel picked him up and deposited him on the cot and he curled onto his side, snug in the folds of the blanket.

Nathaniel stood looking down at him for a minute, his frown more one of puzzlement than anger. Then he turned and went back on deck.

Gabrielle stood at the deck rail, wrapped in her cloak against the rising wind. "Well?" she asked as he came to stand beside her.

"I put him to bed. I'm afraid he's usurped the cot."

"That's all right. I'm not tired anyway. Is he all right?"

"Cold and wet and exhausted, I think."

"Hardly surprising." She paused for a minute, then said hesitantly, "Did you punish him?"

Nathaniel shook his head. "It'd be both superfluous and pointless in the circumstances, don't you think?"

"Oh, yes," she agreed. "I just wasn't sure how you would feel."

"I could wish you hadn't bewitched my son," he said, staring moodily over the rail at the dark, heaving mass of the sea.

"That's hardly fair," Gabrielle protested, but without anger. She could well understand Nathaniel's present dismay.

"Isn't it?" He turned to look at her, and that piercing, troubling intensity was in his gaze again.

"I don't know what you mean." She sounded puzzled and uneasy.

Nathaniel pulled himself up sharply. He shook his head, passing a hand wearily over his eyes. "I don't mean anything, really. I was just lashing out. Sorry."

Gabrielle nodded her comprehension. "What are you going to do with him?"

"I don't have much choice," Nathaniel said flatly. "He'll have to come with us."

"Can't you simply turn back with him when we reach Cherbourg?"

Nathaniel shook his head. "The boat's not going back immediately. Dan, the skipper, is an enterprising fellow. He'll potter down the Brittany coast and sail back probably from St. Malo in a week or two, laden to the gunwales with barrels of brandy and any other contraband that comes his way."

"But won't it be dangerous for Jake in Paris?"

"Yes," he said. "But there's a particular safe house where he won't cause any undue remark. On the journey, he can travel with you, protected by your *laissez passer*. No one's going to be interested in a child."

"Maybe we can make it all a game for him," Gabrielle said thoughtfully. "It might not be so alarming for him."

"I don't see what you mean."

"Well, he's very imaginative. He plays games in his head all the time. I think it's common with only children. He creates very elaborate scenarios, too, very detailed and precise. He's described some of them to me. They're very impressive. He's a bright little lad."

Nathaniel didn't look impressed at the thought of his son's fantasy life. "I don't see that it makes much difference whether he sees it as a game or not. The sooner we get to Paris, the sooner I can hide him properly, so we'll be traveling day and night."

The assertion of a spymaster rather than a father, Gabrielle reflected. Nathaniel obviously had no conception of what it would be like to travel bumpy roads without respite in the company of a six-year-old. However, she said only, "Let's go below. The wind's getting up."

There was nothing but the floor to sit on in the bare cabin with its swinging lantern and bolted-down table. Gabrielle noticed with a faint grimace that someone had thoughtfully provided a slop pail in the corner for whatever relief the *Curlew's* passengers might need. There was no possibility of privacy. Not for the first time she reflected that the world had been arranged to suit men.

Nathaniel put his arm around her, and she rested her head on his shoulder as the boat creaked around them and the lantern threw its menacing shadows.

She had been dozing for half an hour, when the motion of the boat changed dramatically. The pail slid across the floor, crashing against the far bulkhead. Her stomach dipped and she groaned.

"I'm going to have to go on deck in the fresh air," she whispered. Jake suddenly wailed, sat up with his eyes still shut, and clutched his stomach.

Gabrielle grabbed the pail and reached him just in time, almost before Nathaniel had grasped what was happening. The child vomited wretchedly, in between moans and wails, and the atmosphere in the confined space grew even more fetid.

Gabrielle held his head over the bucket, murmuring soothing words as she tried to control her own roiling insides. "Can you fetch some cool water?" she asked Nathaniel, who was hovering helplessly. "Just to bathe his face."

"I don't know if there's any fresh on the boat."

"Then salt will do. But surely there's some drinking water?"

"It's only a twelve-hour voyage," he said. It hadn't occurred to him any more than it had to the fishermen to carry a cask of fresh water on board. Nathaniel had made this journey many times, but never with a woman and a child.

He returned in a few minutes with a bucket of seawater. His cloak was wet from both rain and spray, and he lurched against the table as the boat pitched violently, water slopping over the rim of the bucket.

Jake was still vomiting, the violent retching inter-

spersed with his tortured wails and moans of uncomprehending protest at this horrible thing that was happening to him.

Gabrielle took Nathaniel's kerchief soaked in
seawater and bathed the child's hot, sweaty face. Her
expression grew tense as half an hour passed and Jake
continued to vomit, no longer groaning or moaning,
just hanging in her arms over the pail.

"He can't go on like this, poor little mite," she said
worriedly. "He hasn't got anything left inside him. Oh,
God . . ."

She lost the fight with her own nausea and rushed
stumbling to the companionway, her hand over her
mouth. "You'll have to look after him," she managed to
gasp before she clambered up onto the drenched deck
and the blessed fresh night air. Even the rain was a relief. She made it to the railing and gave herself up to
the supreme misery of seasickness, heedless of the gusting wind and soaking spray.

Nathaniel took over at his son's bedside. The
child's agony was wrenching as the spasms racked his
small frame. His face had a waxen, greenish pallor to it,
and in no time at all his eyes had sunk into their sock-
ets, lusterless brown smudges surrounded by black shadows that looked like bruises.

After an hour Nathaniel felt the first stirrings of
alarm. He'd never taken seasickness particularly seriously; it was something some people suffered from and
others didn't. He was feeling mildly queasy himself, but
nothing he couldn't control. The child, however,
seemed to be losing muscle and sinew before his eyes.
He no longer had the strength to sit upright without
support, but if Nathaniel laid him down on the cot, he
instantly began to retch where he lay.

The vivid image of Helen rose in haunting memory
as he stared around at the dancing specters on the bulwark. He'd watched her fade away too, and as quickly.
But she'd bled to death. Jake was just sick.

He told himself this, but he knew Jake was suffering no ordinary sickness. Somehow he had to stop it, give the child some rest. *Why the hell hadn't they brought water?* Something to replace what Jake was losing—at the very least something for him to be sick with—to ease the convulsive heaving of the slight body.

He thought of Gabrielle enduring alone on deck. Savage anger flooded him as he held his son, helpless to relieve his agony, an agony that for the moment seemed to be entirely Gabrielle's responsibility.

His eye fell on the picnic bag and he remembered the brandy. It was a known palliative for seasickness.

What was good for adults might work for children. At least it couldn't make things worse. With grim determination he reached for his bag and took out the brandy bottle. He lifted the child in his arms and felt the fragility of his bones, the clamminess of his skin as he held him against his shoulder.

Gently he coaxed a few drops of liquid into his mouth. Jake protested feebly, choked, retched. With a patience he hadn't known he possessed, Nathaniel persevered. He spoke softly to the child as he held him tightly, holding the bottle to his lips, refusing to allow him to turn his head aside.

Insensibly, Jake's body began to relax. His eyes fluttered open once or twice, but to Nathaniel's alarm there seemed no recognition in them. But the violent spasms decreased in frequency, and after what seemed an eternity Jake seemed to fall asleep in his arms.

Nathaniel held him, unwilling to put him back on the cot in case he woke him and the terrible business began anew. He didn't know how long he sat there with his child, looking down at the small white face, listening in a kind of suspended terror to the shallow breaths coming from the parted lips. He wanted to wipe his face with the kerchief again, but was afraid to wake him.

He thought again of Gabrielle on the windswept,

seaswept deck, locked in her own wretchedness, and he knew that Jake's predicament was not her fault. The child had been running as much away from his father as toward Gabrielle. He could lay much at her door, but not this.

It was a bleak reflection, but honesty obliged him to accept it.

After a long while he felt confident enough to lay the child on the cot again and pull up the blanket. Jake lay on his back, unmoving, but his breathing had deepened and slowed, almost as if he were unconscious. Exhaustion, Nathaniel told himself, but a cold chill of terror lifted his scalp as he felt for the pulse in the fragile wrist. To his relief, it was fast but strong.

Taking the brandy, he crept on tiptoe to the companionway. At first he couldn't see Gabrielle on deck. The wind seemed to have lessened and the pitch and roll was not so pronounced. The light was graying with the approach of the winter dawn, and he discerned the dark, huddled shape by the leeside railing.

"Gabrielle?" He trod over to her.

A groan was her only response.

He squatted beside her, uncorked the brandy, took her shoulders gently, and turned her toward him. "Drink some of this. It'll help."

She gulped and gasped as the fiery liquid scorched her sore throat and warmed her aching belly. "Oh, God," she croaked. "Why are *you* all right?"

"I'm not feeling wonderful, if it's any comfort," he said, half smiling despite everything at this very typical Gabrielle comment even in the face of misery. "Drink some more."

She did so, and a little color returned to her cheeks. "How's Jake?"

"Sleeping, poor little tyke. I've never been so terrified, Gabrielle. Once or twice I thought he was going to give up on me," Nathaniel said, his voice grim.

"There's nothing to him at the moment. He's like a husk."

"He's too small to be sick like that," Gabrielle said. "He needs water."

"We don't have any . . . remember? I gave him brandy instead. I don't know if it was wise, but at least it sent him to sleep."

"Then it was wise," Gabrielle reassured him. She ran her hands through her tangled hair and grimaced. "I think it's over now. The pitch isn't nearly so pronounced, but I'm so cold and wet."

"Come below and change your clothes." Nathaniel stood up, reaching down his hands to help her up. She staggered and fell against him.

"My legs are like jelly. I knew there was a reason why I prefer the Dover to Calais crossing. At least one's misery is short. I should never have let you persuade me into this."

She had amazing powers of recuperation, Nathaniel reflected as he held her against him for a minute. She'd been heaving up her guts for over three hours in the rain and the wind over a violent sea and could still come up with her half-amused, truculent challenges.

Jake stirred and moaned as they reached the cabin, and Nathaniel drew a sharp, anxious breath, crossing swiftly to the cot. The child's eyes fluttered open in the deathly white face.

"Want to go home," he whispered, his voice a fretful thread. "I want to get off this boat. My tummy hurts." Tears slid out of his eyes.

"Hush, now," Nathaniel said gently, kneeling down beside him, smoothing his hair off his damp brow. "Go back to sleep."

"I want Neddy . . . where's Neddy?" Jake's voice began to rise and he tried to sit up. "I want Neddy." He pushed at his father's restraining hands, his voice becoming a sob.

"What's Neddy?" Nathaniel asked softly over his shoulder as Gabrielle came up behind him.

"A knitted donkey," she told him. "He always sleeps with it."

He should have known that, Nathaniel thought with a stab of guilt. He couldn't remember when he'd last visited the nursery.

Jake's feeble protest died and his eyes closed again as exhaustion reclaimed him.

Gabrielle stripped off her wet clothes.

Nathaniel watched her rummaging through one of the portmanteaux in search of dry clothes. She was wearing only her drawers and chemise and, despite his preoccupation, his body stirred. How could she have this effect on him, even in these grim circumstances? Even in this cramped, fetid cabin? How could this heedless and all-consuming passion exist side by side with his savage anger, with his need for vengeance?

If it weren't for that passion, Gabrielle would now be screaming beneath the persuasive hands of the specialists and Jake would be waking up in the nursery at Burley Manor. Instead, driven by lust and pride, he needed to exact his own revenge. And he knew that need was as irrational as the passion, but he couldn't control either.

"I'm going on deck to see what progress we're making," he said abruptly, and left the cabin.

Gabrielle fastened her skirt, frowning in thought. She'd be staying in Talleyrand's house on rue d'Anjou. She didn't know whether her godfather was back from Prussia as yet, but his house was her home in France whether he was there or not. She hoped he would be, since she needed his counsel. Somehow she'd have to ensure that Fouché didn't get wind of the English spymaster's presence in Paris.

Talleyrand wouldn't betray Nathaniel, since he was vital to his own plans, but the brutal police chief would see only the opportunity to break a master spy. He wouldn't hesitate to use an innocent, either, to trap or blackmail. Jake would be in grave danger if Fouché learned the child was with his father. Fouché would certainly interrogate Gabrielle—civilly, of course, or as civilly as that profoundly uncivilized man could manage. He was clever and she'd need all her wits about her if she was to keep to herself those things that she must.

"Well, there are some compensations for your miserable night." Nathaniel jumped down from the hatchway, breaking into her grim reverie. "The wind was strong enough to save us a good hour or so on the crossing. We should pass the Scilly Isles by nine o'clock. We'll land by noon with any luck."

"In broad daylight?"

"There's a secluded cove, protected by a reef that only those who know it can negotiate safely. It's unpatrolled for that reason. The *Curlew* flies the French colors from now on, keeping well out to sea until we make the run for shore."

"You've done this before," she stated.

"Of course. Many times. And Dan's an expert at negotiating the reef." He went to the bunk, looking down at the still-sleeping Jake. "I suppose I can take comfort in knowing he's unlikely ever to run away to sea again."

"Yes," Gabrielle agreed with a half-smile.

"I'll have to buy him some clothes. These are still wet." Nathaniel shook out Jake's discarded britches and jersey.

"How fluent is your French?" Most educated Englishmen spoke it with a degree of ease, but Gabrielle wondered whether the spymaster could pass for native.

"Good enough. Not as good as your English, but it passes. I ensure I'm not garrulous."

"Even at the best of times," Gabrielle agreed with a touch of asperity.

"You're a trifle acerbic this morning, madame."

"I would kill for a cup of coffee," she said in excuse, licking her dry, salty lips.

"Try an apple instead."

"And some cheese. I think it's time for another picnic. I'm famished."

Nathaniel shook his head with the semblance of a grin, reflecting yet again that Gabrielle's powers of recuperation were astonishing. But then, she'd been trained in the same school of endurance he had, so it was hardly surprising. His grin disappeared.

He spread the contents of the bag on the table. They would both have preferred to go on deck, but it didn't occur to either of them to leave Jake alone.

The child slept until they were approaching the telltale greenish ripple of water crossing the opening to the narrow cove. The high cliffs of the Normandy coastline rose on either side, gray and forbidding despite the weak sunlight of a midday in early spring.

Gabrielle was on deck breathing fresh air and regarding the rippling line with some apprehension, when Nathaniel emerged from the cabin, carrying Jake, still wrapped in the blanket.

"He woke up and I thought the air might do him some good."

"Good morning, Jake." Gabrielle greeted the child cheerfully, bending to kiss a cheek that had lost the shiny roundness of health.

Jake turned his head into his father's chest. "I'm cold," he whimpered. "An' I want a drink."

"Have a look at the land." Nathaniel hitched him up in his arms, turning so he could look over his shoulder at the approaching coastline. "Soon we'll be in France."

"Don't want to," Jake said. "I want Nurse an' Primmy. I'm cold."

"I can do something about the cold, but not the rest," his father declared with a valiant effort at patience that was obvious to Gabrielle if not to the pathetic, miserable child.

"I want Neddy and the pot."

"You can do something about the latter but not the former," Gabrielle murmured with a smile. "Shall I take him?"

"If you don't mind." Nathaniel handed his burden over with ill-disguised relief. Jake put his arms around Gabrielle's neck as she carried him back below deck.

Nathaniel leaned against the railing, gazing at the water and the curve of beach ahead. His son's intervention dramatically affected his plans. Until he'd returned Jake to the safety of Burley Manor, he'd have to lie low in Paris. He'd intended to pretend to establish Gabrielle within the network, having alerted his own agents to the impostor, and then feed her false information that would lead to the entrapment of Fouché's agents undercover in London. On this visit he would meet with his own agents in the city and explain the setup to them.

In Paris Gabrielle must be kept well away from himself and Jake. He was certain that she would do nothing deliberately to put Jake in jeopardy, wherever her patriotic loyalties lay, but she was dangerous. Fouché's men could well be watching her. She could let something slip—even the most skillful spies made errors sometimes.

The boat tacked across the mouth of the cove, and he glanced toward the fisherman at the helm. Dan's face was set, beetling brows drawn together as he stared fixedly at the line of green ripples, looking for the break that would grant them safe entrance through the reef.

He swung the helm, glancing up at the sail, gently pulling on the mainsheet to catch the wind at just the right moment. The craft bucked as the wind filled the sail and danced over the line.

Nathaniel held his breath, waiting as always for the

sickening crunch as the keel scraped over the wicked, jagged teeth of rock. But there was nothing. The boat flew gracefully across the one flat patch of water and into the calm safety of the cove.

"All's well, sir," Dan called out, his face breaking into a smile as the tension left him, and his crew laughed and cracked a ribald joke. Dan produced a bottle of brandy, offering it to Nathaniel with unaffected camaraderie.

Nathaniel took a swig and handed back the bottle, offering a jest of his own, flexing his shoulders. They were through once again. One could never be certain, and each time there was the same surge of relief. And this crossing even more so. He had his son—a hostage to fortune—this time.

Gabrielle came up on deck and stood, feet braced on the gently moving deck, the wind whipping back her dark red hair, her face lifted to the sun. In the midday sunlight the lines of fatigue were etched clearly on the white face, but the charcoal eyes were as vibrant as ever and that little crooked smile curved the wide generous mouth. The warm wanting that he was so accustomed to feeling whenever he was with her seeped through his own fatigue.

God damn the woman! Why? Of all the women in the world, why did Gabrielle de Beaucaire have to be treacherous?

16

———

"I don't want this. It's all crust." Jake pushed a piece of bread to the farthest extremity of his plate, his lower lip trembling.

"It'll give you strong teeth," Gabrielle said with determined cheerfulness. "Shall I put some more apricot jam on it?"

"I don't want it!" The child flung out a wild hand to ward her off. "I *hate* crusts."

"It's French bread, Jake," Gabrielle said, still patient. "French bread has a lot of crust."

"I don't like French bread!" Jake picked up the despised bread and hurled it to the floor, tears spilling from his eyes. "I want an egg. I always have an egg for tea ... with soldiers."

"*Soldiers?*" Nathaniel exclaimed, pushing himself away from the door where he'd been leaning in ever-visible irritation.

"Strips of bread and butter," Gabrielle told him. "To dip in the egg. Surely you had soldiers with boiled eggs as a boy."

"I'm very sure I didn't," Nathaniel declared with disgusted vigor. "I've never heard such whimsy!" He came over to the table and hacked another chunk off the baguette. "I've had enough of this, Jake." He plonked the chunk on the child's plate. "Now eat that, at once."

Jake sniffed, but seemed to sense that he'd pushed to the limits of his caretakers' indulgence. "I want some jam."

"*Please*," his father demanded.

Jake snuffled again and produced the required courtesy in a barely audible whisper.

Gabrielle spread jam lavishly on the bread and glanced at Nathaniel's grim features. She jerked her head toward the window at the back of the room, and he nodded and accompanied her away from the table and its disconsolate occupant.

"He's dead tired, Nathaniel," Gabrielle said quietly. "He can't help being like this. Can't we stay overnight here? We could leave at dawn."

Nathaniel scowled, staring through the window down at the inn's stableyard. Since landing at noon, they'd bought an ill-sprung gig and undernourished nag from a local farmer who'd been only too happy to exchange these pathetic commodities for an excessive sum of silver. Any questions he might have asked were stillborn when Gabrielle flashed her *laissez passer* with aristocratic hauteur. The gig had carried them uncomfortably for twenty miles with Jake whimpering in Gabrielle's lap and Nathaniel cursing the scrawny nag along the mud-ridged lanes.

Early evening had brought them into the village of Quineville and Le Lion d'Or, where Nathaniel intended they should dine and exchange the gig for a postchaise that would double the speed of their journey to Paris.

He turned from the window and directed his scowling gaze at the child drooping over his plate at the table. "He can sleep in the chaise, surely."

"He needs a proper bed for a few hours," Gabrielle

said, softly insistent. "He's still dreadfully weak after the crossing."

"The longer we hang around on the roads, the greater the danger." Nathaniel slammed one fist in the palm of his other hand and turned back to the window.

"I don't want this milk," Jake wailed. "It tastes horrid."

"For Christ's sake!" his father muttered.

"It's French milk, love," Gabrielle said, going over to the child, struggling to smile through her own weariness. "It will taste different. The cows eat different grass."

"I hate French milk!" Jake burst into noisy sobs. "I want to go home. I want Nurse an' Primmy."

Gabrielle scooped him off the stool and held him, casting Nathaniel a speaking glance over the curly head.

Nathaniel ran his hands through his hair, disturbing the neat swatches of silver at his temples. "Very well. But we leave at dawn. I'll go and bespeak a bedchamber for you and Jake."

"No, you'd better let me do that. Since I'm here, you might as well spare yourself and take advantage of my native fluency." Her eyebrows rose in a semblance of her old mocking challenge.

Nathaniel failed to respond to this attempt at raillery. "Go and do it, then." He took Jake from her and waved her brusquely to the door.

Gabrielle shrugged and returned to somber reality. "See if you can persuade him to drink some milk. He needs something to line his stomach." The door closed behind her.

"Don't want any milk," Jake whimpered. "It's horrid milk."

"It's perfectly good milk, and you're going to have to get used to it, my friend." His father sat him down at the table and handed him the cup. "I want you to drink half of it."

The child ignored the cup, and his mouth took a stubborn turn that Nathaniel had never seen before. He'd never met with any resistance from his son, only passive compliance, and he'd assumed that was the child's nature. Now he wasn't so sure. There was something about the boy's expression that was uncomfortably reminiscent of himself on occasion.

He held Jake's gaze steadily, exerting his will in silence. If he couldn't win a battle of wills with an exhausted six-year-old, then the world was going to hell in a handcart. To his relief, Jake finally took the cup, and, his nose wrinkled, carried it to his lips. Between chokes and disgusted sips the level in the cup went down to half.

"That's all arranged." Gabrielle spoke as she entered the parlor, clear relief in her voice at the prospect of a few hours of civilized rest and refreshment. "Madame has given me a bedchamber across the passage. There's a truckle bed for Jake, so I'll put him to bed now. Then she's going to bring me dinner." She rubbed her hands with glee. "Saddle of hare with junipers, and a sea bream in parsley sauce. Oh, and a bottle of St. Estèphe."

"You certainly seem to have seen to your own comforts," Nathaniel observed with asperity.

This unmerited grumpiness merely kindled Gabrielle's somewhat perverse sense of mischief. She'd invented a perfectly reasonable explanation for the innkeeper of why mistress and servant would be dining together in the parlor, but now she looked at him in wide-eyed innocence.

"I assumed you would eat with the servants. They're having *tête de veau*, I believe . . . or was it pig's cheek? And Madame said there's a spare pallet in the loft for you. I'm sure they don't have bedbugs; the inn seems very clean and well managed."

"You relieve me," Nathaniel said. "Your consideration is overwhelming."

Gabrielle hid her grin. "Oh, and also I sold the gig and nag for three livres and ten sous and hired a postchaise for the morning. There are plenty of changing posts between here and Paris, so we should make good time tomorrow."

"Such efficiency, countess. I'm in your debt." Nathaniel strode to the door.

"I'm only trying to help," Gabrielle declared, her eyes now flashing with irritation. If Nathaniel wasn't prepared to be joked out of his irritability, then she was fatigued enough to indulge her own.

"Why are you angry? I don't like it when you're angry." This extraordinary statement from Jake silenced them both.

They looked at the child, who was regarding them both with lackluster eyes.

"We're not angry, love," Gabrielle said cheerfully. "Papa's just jealous of my saddle of hare." She smiled at Nathaniel, inviting him to join in with a response that would reassure the child.

But Nathaniel was not to be soothed. "And you have a most misplaced sense of humor, ma'am." He banged out of the parlor, leaving Gabrielle to deal with Jake.

She stared crossly at the closed door and then shrugged. The strain was telling on both of them; it was probably better if they did keep out of each other's way for a while. She turned her attention to Jake and his need for a wash and bed.

Nathaniel's irritation made his role of reclusive servant even more convincing. When their polite inquiries received only monosyllabic responses, the inn servants left him alone to his dinner. Judging from the empty tray brought down from Gabrielle's chamber, she had thoroughly relished her own repast, he noticed. Not that his own tastes were so overly refined that he couldn't enjoy the hearty peasant fare in the kitchen.

He'd eaten a lot worse in his time, and the rough red wine was tolerable.

The pallet in the dormitory loft, however, was a different matter. Nathaniel had not the slightest intention of spending the night suffocated by the garlic snores of unwashed peasants. Clean straw in the hayloft was infinitely preferable.

Gabrielle, from the parlor window, saw him cross the yard from the kitchen door, the swinging agility of his stride unmistakable in the golden glow. Then the door closed and the yard was in moonlight. At the stable he paused, a lantern dangling from his hand. He looked up at the inn toward Gabrielle's window, where she stood in the shadow. Then he went into the stable. The door closed and as she watched, a soft light appeared in the small round window of the hayloft.

She had little difficulty understanding his refusal to share the servants' sleeping quarters. Had he been expecting her to be watching . . . hoping she was, even? It didn't take much imagination to interpret that backward look as an invitation. It had been days and days since they'd lost themselves in the glorious maze of passion.

She turned back to the room, nibbling her fingernail as a current of excitement ran through her, chasing away the fatigue of the long and arduous journey. She could go to him when the inn went to bed. Who would ever know? Jake was so deeply asleep, it would take the last trump to wake him.

She filled the bowl with water from the ewer, stripped off her clothes, and sponged herself from head to toe, shivering in the chill but relishing the sensation of washing away the salt and sweat and wretchedness of the previous night's miserable crossing and the day's jolting carriage ride along muddy lanes.

She'd have liked to wash her hair, but that was impractical with present facilities, so she made do with brushing it until some of the burnished luster had returned, then slipped into a nightgown, thrust her feet into a pair of velvet slippers, and threw a hooded cloak over her shoulders, drawing the hood over her hair.

The inn was dark and silent as she left the bed-chamber, quietly turning the key on the sleeping child and dropping the key into her pocket. She'd opened the window a crack, and if Jake awoke and cried out for her, the sound would carry across the yard to the hay-loft, where Nathaniel would, as always, have his own window open.

A lamp burned dimly on the stairs, and the steep oak steps creaked as she flew down them. Was Nathaniel waiting for her? Her own excitement was such that it was impossible to believe her lover wasn't sharing it a few feet away, across the stableyard.

Nathaniel, however, was sleeping the sleep of the just amid the sweet-smelling hay. Not for one minute had it crossed his mind to expect a visitor hell-bent on indulging an addiction. He was tired himself after the rigors and alarms and excursions of the past twenty-four hours and, since the opportunity for a night's sleep had been forced upon him, he had every intention of taking full advantage of it.

Lust was the last thing on his mind and far from his dreams as he slept lightly under the shaft of moon-light shining through the small round window.

But he heard the faint sounds from the stable be-low. They were not the ordinary shufflings and shiftings and whickerings of a dozen beasts. He didn't take the time to decide how he knew they were not. Without conscious decision he was out of his straw nest and crouching by the top of the ladder that rose from the stables through a hole in the floor. He had a knife in his hand. Not the pocket knife he'd used to cut veal and ham pie, but a wicked stiletto with a blade so thin and sharp, it would slide between a man's ribs and pierce the heart in one smooth insertion.

A dead body would be hard to explain, so fortunately for Gabrielle he was prepared to look before he acted. The hooded head of a cloaked figure emerged at the top of the ladder.

Nathaniel recognized the set of the head a second before the unmistakable scent of her assailed his nostrils. He held his breath on a wild surge of fury that for a moment knew no bounds as he thought of where they were—in the heart of Normandy with his life, his son's life, and the lives of seven agents in France dependent on his safety or, failing that, his ability to keep his tongue still in the ultimate extremity.

What the hell did she think she was doing? She was a spy. She lived on the edge of danger. She knew about unnecessary risks. But he also knew that she took them. He'd told Simon that she was undisciplined and that if she'd proved genuine, then he'd keep his own rein on her.

If she'd been one of his own agents, he knew exactly what he would would have done. And since she was playing the part, then he'd play his. The rage was replaced with a cold clarity of purpose, more ruthless and infinitely more dangerous than the hot flood of anger.

Gabrielle eased herself into the loft on her knees and looked around. And then a hand was clamped over her mouth with suffocating pressure and she was wrestled to the floor, the hand still across her mouth, her face buried in tickling straw. She struggled violently, twisting her body, trying to get leverage with one hip to throw him off, but he threw a leg across her thighs. Her feet drummed on the floor. It didn't seem to matter that she knew it was Nathaniel, that she believed he wouldn't hurt her. She continued to fight in a red mist of atavistic panic at the petrifying knowledge of her own weakness against the strength of this opponent.

She tried to cry out, to tell Nathaniel it was only her . . . Gabrielle . . . only Gabrielle. How could he not recognize her?

She felt him grab a handful of her hair at the back of her head, and her face was pulled roughly upward. She opened her mouth on a sobbing breath, and something was thrust between her teeth, a wad of material that filled her mouth and choked off all sound. Then her head fell forward onto the straw again. His knee on her backside held her pressed to the floor as her hands were jerked behind her, her wrists bound with swift efficiency.

It was all over in a matter of seconds, and she lay bound and gagged on the floor of the hayloft, stunned at the ease with which he'd handled her body, as easily in this assault as he handled her in love.

As instinctive terror receded, she was conscious only of amazement at the strength in Nathaniel's slender frame, the deft competency of his movements, the ruthlessness of it all. Because he did know who she was. He had to have known from the minute he laid hands on her.

And Gabrielle knew what was happening. He believed she'd forgotten the deadly serious nature of their shared enterprise, and the spymaster was punishing an errant recruit in a way that couldn't fail to impress upon her the seriousness of her offense. She lay still and compliant, waiting for it to be over.

She *had* made an unforgivable error. She'd forgotten for a moment in the uprush of desire the true nature of their business there. She'd unforgivably slipped out of role. She'd forgotten Guillaume and Talleyrand and Fouché and thought of herself only as a private citizen with an eager lover.

Nathaniel removed his knee and stood up. "How *dare* you!" he said with soft ferocity. "How *dare* you risk the safety of my son . . . your own safety . . . mine . . . that of my own people?"

Gabrielle, helpless on the floor, winced beneath the ferocious tongue-lashing. She had no defense and resigned herself to justice.

Nathaniel flayed her until he had nothing left to say and then he fell silent, staring down at the prone figure.

"Stand up!" he commanded harshly.

And just how was she supposed to do that with her hands tied uselessly behind her back and her nose pressed into the prickly straw? But compliance struck Gabrielle as the only possible course of action. She rolled onto her side, bent her underneath leg, and levered herself to a half-sitting position with her elbow and knee.

Her eyes spoke rueful appeal as she looked up at him. His expression was less than encouraging, his mouth thinned, the brown eyes hard stones.

"Get up," he demanded as harshly as before, and he stood with his hands on his hips, unmoving as she scrambled to her feet with as much grace and dignity as she could muster.

The tied hands weren't the problem so much as the gag, Gabrielle decided. It dehumanized one in some way. She had no choice but to stand there, mute, under a cold stare that made her feel like a worm. She thought longingly of her bed with its crisp white sheets and feather mattress. Why on earth hadn't she settled for the simple comforts of an uninterrupted night's sleep, instead of reaching for the moon?

"Turn around."

She obeyed, and to her inexpressible relief he unfastened the belt that bound her wrists. She pulled the wadded kerchief from her mouth and ran the back of her hand over her dry lips, trying to moisten her mouth with her tongue. But she kept her back to him, too intimidated by that ruthless display of the spymaster's power to face him as yet.

"Why?" Nathaniel demanded.

"I wanted you," Gabrielle spoke the truth because there was no lie that would be as convincing. "And I thought you probably wanted me too."

Nathaniel's anger seemed to have exhausted itself, and the reality of the situation now hit him. For better or worse, she was there and so far undiscovered.

Gabrielle turned to face him. Her eyes raked his face and detected the slightest softening. "I am truly sorry," she said. "Everyone's asleep. I locked my chamber door. The window's open, so if Jake did cry out, we'd hear him. It didn't seem such a big risk, not when the stakes were so irresistible."

She had a smudge of dirt on her nose where her face had been pressed to the floor, and a wisp or two of straw in her tumbled hair. The cloak had fallen back from her shoulders, and the white nightgown was streaked with dust.

He could still feel the shape of her body in his hands as she'd fought him. He could feel the curve of her thrusting hip as she'd twisted beneath him, and he could smell the soap on her skin.

He was aware of excitement and his body's arousal, the fullness of his loins. Subduing Gabrielle had excited him in some way that he didn't entirely understand.

Her eyes held his.

"God's good grace, woman," he whispered. "What is it about you?"

"Just that, perhaps," she replied as softly. "That I am woman and you are man, and we seem made to fit each other."

Nothing mattered but the need to take her body into his own, to become flesh with her flesh; to hear her murmured words of need, the hungry, earthy words of passion and demand; to feel her skin, alive beneath his hand; to touch and probe in the way that set her body alight; to explore charted territory and discover the bays and the hillocks that he'd missed before; to draw her essential scent deep into his lungs as his tongue translated the scent to taste.

And as he looked at her he knew that his thoughts

were hers . . . that she was as hungry for his body as he was for hers.

Gabrielle moved toward him, impatiently shrugging the cloak off her shoulders. She reached for him, throwing her head back, lips parted in invitation. He circled her throat with his hands, and her pulse beat fast against his thumbs with the energy of arousal.

Gabrielle waited in a state of suspended animation for him to do something other than gaze at her, his face so close to her own, his eyes narrowed with a predatory glitter that she hadn't seen before. A thrill of almost apprehensive excitement jolted her belly. This was a different mood from any they'd shared before, and she had the sense that almost anything could happen.

"What are you looking at?" she whispered when the tension of their silence became unbearable.

"You," he replied simply. And it was as if he were looking through the glowing braziers in her eyes deep into her soul.

But still he made no move. Gabrielle drew a shuddering breath and palmed his scalp, bringing his mouth to hers. His hands stayed at her throat as she kissed him, pressing her aching loins against the hard shaft of his erect flesh. Her hands moved down his back, down to his buttocks, her fingers biting into the powerful muscles, expressing her need and the demand that he make some response to match her own.

Finally she drew back, breathless, her lips reddened, an almost feral glitter in her eyes. His hands on her throat seemed to be imprinted on her skin, and she could feel the pulse in his thumb beating in rapid time with her own as his own blood flowed swift with passion. And yet he was doing nothing to partner her. He just stood there, clasping her throat, and gazing at her with unreadable eyes and impassive mouth.

"What is it?" she asked, her voice sounding strange and thick, as if it emerged through fog. "What do you want?"

"This," he said. His hands went to the neck of her nightgown, and the flimsy lawn parted as he tore through it and down.

The cold air laved her bared body and her nipples grew small and hard on the crowns of her breasts. Her tongue touched her lips and her eyes grew wide. He pushed the torn garment off her shoulders, and it fell to the floor in a puddle of white, silvered in the moonlight falling through the round window.

"This," he repeated softly but with infinite satisfaction as he touched her, drawing a finger down from her throat, between her breasts, down to her navel, slipping between her thighs. Her feet shifted on the straw as the questing finger probed and found what it sought, and all the while his eyes held hers, watching, gauging, as he played upon her, drawing from her the ultimate response that she knew she couldn't have controlled even had she wanted to.

And Nathaniel knew it too. He was mastering her body as assuredly now as he had done in his earlier anger. And Gabrielle, fierce, independent, challenging Gabrielle, was malleable clay and glorying in it as ecstasy ripped through her, tearing her apart, and she fell shuddering against him, for the moment unable to support herself.

He held her tightly and the linen of his shirt rubbed her nipples, the leather of his britches was cool and smooth against her belly and thighs. This time he kissed her, his mouth hard and possessive, his tongue driving deeply within her. Her head fell back under the pressure of his ravaging mouth, her body arching backward against the hands in the small of her back as she bent like a willow before the wind.

Without moving his mouth from hers, he lowered her to the floor. The entire surface of her body was sensitized, every nerve ending close to the surface, so that the prickle of the straw against her bare back and the sensation of linen and leather rubbing her breasts and belly was intensified.

Nathaniel left her mouth. Kneeling astride her, he ran his hands over her breasts, circling the hard buds of her nipples with a fingertip. That same air of detachment clung to him as if he were discovering something entirely new that had to be absorbed, catalogued, understood.

He looked up and met her gaze, and for the first time he smiled. He unfastened his waistband and his flesh sprang free from constraint.

"Come closer," Gabrielle murmured, moving her hand down to enclose him.

He inched up her body so she could take him in her mouth, and he threw back his head on an exhalation of delight, kneeling up, his hands resting unconsciously on his hips as she pleasured him.

When finally he entered her body with a long, slow thrust that penetrated her core, Gabrielle cried out, curling her legs around his hips, her heels pressing into his buttocks as she pulled him into the cleft of her body with fervid urgency.

Nathaniel shook his head in abrupt denial and resisted the pressure, pulling back to the very edge of her body. He looked down at her, that predatory glitter in his eyes again, the tiniest smile touching his lips.

Gabrielle lay still, her body thrumming with expectation as he held himself immobile, and slowly, inexorably, the sensation built deep in the pit of her belly. Still smiling, he watched her eyes, again gauging the progress of her spiraling climb to ecstasy.

When she thought she could bear it no longer, when she thought her body would shatter like crystal under the tension, he drove into her, filling her, becoming a part of her as she became a part of him.

His mouth covered hers, suppressing her cry of joy the instant before it broke from her lips. His body moved in hers, and they rose and fell in mindless union, flesh and bone and sinew joined as one. And then the climactic explosion tore through them and she clung to him like a shipwrecked mariner clutching a broken spar before falling back, barely conscious, on the hard, cold floor, crushed by his body.

"Sweet heaven!" Nathaniel gasped after an eternity. His breath was still an exhausted sob. "What was that?"

"*La petite mort.*" Gabrielle could barely speak.

Nathaniel chuckled weakly. "The French have an accurate turn of phrase." He rolled sideways and lay on his belly, his forehead resting on his forearm as his heart finally slowed and his breathing eased.

Gabrielle struggled up and sat blinking around the moonlit loft. Her ruined nightgown lay in a heap on the straw. "It seems as if I'm going to have to cross the yard stark naked. Whatever possessed you?"

"God knows," he said, sitting up himself. "The devil in *you*, I suspect." He reached for her discarded cloak and wrapped it around her damp body. "You'll catch your death of cold."

"I doubt that." She smiled and then shivered. "Then again, it is March."

"I used to think I was perfectly sane," Nathaniel remarked in tones of mild interest. "But I now realize that I'm heading for Bedlam. Stand up." He pulled her to her feet and cupped her face between his palms. "Driven there by a wanton brigand! What the hell am I going to do with you, Gabrielle?"

"You seem to have done a fair amount tonight," she observed judiciously. "You've wrestled me and manhandled me and tied me up and then dispatched me to the outer limits of bliss. What else is there?" ·

Nathaniel shook his head in mock reproof. "You're an impossible woman, too much for any ordinary mortal to manage. Hurry back now into the warm." He pulled the edges of the cloak tighter around her. "Go on, quickly!" He pushed her to the ladder.

"I'd expected a little more ceremony," Gabrielle grumbled, obeying the hand in her back. "But I can't think why, since this has been a most unceremonious evening, one way and another." She edged backward onto the ladder and grinned at him, blowing him a kiss before the bright head vanished into the darkness below.

Nathaniel stood at the window, watching her run across the yard and slip safely into the inn.

How could someone so open, so gloriously candid in her desires and her needs and her loving, be treacherous? And how could he lose all sense of that when he was within her, when she was a part of him and he of her?

He'd asked himself the question before, and, as before, there was no answer.

17

"The spymaster is in Paris?" Talleyrand most unusually revealed his surprise as he poured wine into two crystal goblets in the study of the house on rue d'Anjou.

"Just so." Gabrielle untied the ribbons of her hat and tossed it onto a leather couch. She peered at her reflection in the glass over the mantelpiece and tucked a straying wisp of hair back into the pins.

"Where?" Talleyrand handed her a glass of burgundy.

"*Merci.*" Gabrielle took the glass with a smile and inhaled the bouquet. "I don't know," she said frankly. "He wouldn't tell me. I'm to wait to be contacted."

"A cautious man, as one would expect." Talleyrand nodded. He made a steeple of his fingers and gazed into the middle distance. "For some reason, your letter gave me the sense that there is a . . . a *frisson*"—his hands opened eloquently—"between you and Lord Praed."

Gabrielle sipped her wine. How had he guessed that? She'd thought she'd been completely emotionless in her letter. But Talleyrand always saw beneath the surface, and there was never any point attempting to pull the wool over his eyes. "Yes," she agreed. "In fact, something rather more than that, I believe."

"I see." The Minister for Foreign Affairs examined her with the searching, assessing scrutiny of a connoisseur of women. "Passion becomes you," he stated after a minute. "It has always been so. You looked thus after your times with Guillaume."

Gabrielle met his gaze steadily. "There are similarities," she agreed.

"They are—were—both master spies," her godfather pointed out dryly. "It would seem you have a fatal predilection toward the devious, *mon enfant*."

"With such a mentor, does it surprise you?"

Talleyrand laughed. "Such a quick tongue, you have. How does your spymaster react to it, I wonder?"

Gabrielle rightly assumed that no response was required.

"So, does this added dimension alter your attitude in any way?" Her godfather shifted the subject, blandly matter-of-fact.

"He was responsible for Guillaume's death," she answered. "I can't forget that, despite—" She shrugged. "Despite physical passion. We have that, certainly, but it alters nothing essential."

Talleyrand stroked his chin. "Let us be sure we understand each other, *ma fille*. You are saying that despite physical passion, you still intend to be avenged on this man for his part in Guillaume's death?"

Gabrielle wandered over to the fireplace, staring into the flames. Guillaume's face rose in her internal vision. He was laughing, his eyes so alive, his beautiful mouth curved. . . .

"Oh, yes," she said, almost to herself. "I will use him, sir, in whatever fashion you dictate."

Talleyrand nodded, satisfied. "There is much at stake. Too much to be sacrificed to blind passion."

"I understand that."

There was a knock at the door, and a footman entered to light the candles, draw the long brocade curtains over the windows as dusk deepened, and make up the fire.

They were both silent as the man went about his work. Talleyrand looked down into his glass as if reading solutions to unanswerable questions in the ruby wine.

"You must be tired after your journey," he said as the servant finished mending the fire and the door closed behind him. "Why don't you go to your apartments and rest. I'm sure Catherine must be eager to greet you."

"Yes." Gabrielle rose immediately. "I'm glad you're in Paris. I'd find it hard to weave my way through this tangle without your counsel." She picked up her discarded gloves and slapped them idly into her palm before saying abruptly, "There's a complication. Nathaniel's son is with him."

"In Paris?" Again Talleyrand revealed his surprise. "How old's the child?"

"Six. He stowed away on the boat and there really wasn't any choice but to bring him. Nathaniel has a safe house where he says the child won't be remarked, but if Fouché were to hear of Jake ..." She fell silent, chewing her bottom lip.

"He mustn't," Talleyrand agreed instantly. "You will have to submit to an interview with him. You must be very careful."

"I know,' she said simply. She bent forward for the avuncular kiss he placed on her forehead. "Will you be dining at home, sir?"

"I hadn't intended to, but in the circumstances, I believe I shall," he said, patting her cheek.

"You do me too much honor, sir." Her eyes twinkled, banishing the seriousness of the last exchange.

"Go and do your duty to Catherine," he said gruffly. "I don't know what your father would say to this habit you have of forming highly improper liaisons.

It's high time you found a husband and started having babies."

"I would if I could," she said, and the twinkle faded. "But I don't seem to be attracted to men who want to lead conventional lives."

"Probably because you don't want to yourself," her godfather observed briskly. "The vicissitudes of war suit you."

"And what does that say about my character?" Gabrielle queried, shaking her head.

"I'm sure you can work that out for yourself." Talleyrand waved her way, reflecting that Gabrielle was one of the people for whom fate had fashioned a twisted destiny, one of great passions and great sorrows. In many ways she was to be envied. She lived on the cutting edge, never in the comfortable safety of the middle, and she'd experience heights and glories that ordinary people would never approach. But such a life had its price, as she already knew. Twenty-five was young to have lost so much.

Gabrielle found the Princess de Talleyrand in her boudoir. Catherine had been married to Talleyrand for five years—a misalliance that shocked society as much as it puzzled. That Talleyrand, a descendent of one of France's oldest families, should have married a woman of inferior birth, his own mistress of four years, and reputed to have been the mistress of anyone willing to keep her, was completely incomprehensible. Catherine was a silly woman with vapid conversation, no companion for the urbane and brilliant Minister for Foreign Affairs, and she was no longer young, although her fabled beauty was as yet barely dimmed.

Gabrielle privately believed that her godfather had married his immensely good-natured mistress because it was as easy to do so as not. As an excommunicated bishop, Talleyrand despised the church, and as an aristocratic intellectual, he despised bourgeois morality. So when Napoleon had conducted one of his periodic moral sweeps through his court, demanding that irregular relationships be regularized, Talleyrand had yielded to imperial pressure simply because he didn't give a tinker's damn one way or the other.

Catherine greeted Gabrielle warmly but rather as if she'd just returned from a shopping expedition instead of an extended visit to England.

"*Ma chère*, how well you look." She lifted her powdered, painted cheek for Gabrielle's kiss. "Have you seen Monsieur le Prince?"

"Just now," Gabrielle said. "He's dining at home, he tells me."

Catherine made a small moue. "What a nuisance. I am engaged to dine at the Bonnevilles and I can't cry off. You'll have to entertain him for me."

Gabrielle hid her smile. Catherine's ability to entertain her husband in any arena except the bedchamber was open to question.

"I have some straw-colored sarcenet," Catherine was saying, examining Gabrielle closely. "It doesn't suit me, I've decided, but it would look very well on you, *ma chère*. Clothilde could make it up for you. There is a perfect pattern for a morning dress—let me see, where did I put it?" She sorted vaguely through a stack of periodicals on a marble-topped Louis XV *desserte* table. "Ah, here it is."

Gabrielle dutifully examined the pattern. Catherine's taste tended to the flamboyant, to match her figure, and the frills and furbelows on the morning dress were not Gabrielle's style at all. However, she made the right noises and promised to take the sarcenet.

Duty done, she went to her own apartments at the rear of the house, intent on ridding herself of the grime and fatigue of a journey that had continued at a breakneck pace for nearly two days.

Nathaniel had had the best of it, riding beside the chaise while she and Jake were jolted miserably over the ill-paved roads. The child had required constant attention and resisted all Gabrielle's attempts to engage his imagination in the journey. The unfamiliar food and the motion of the coach had made him almost as sick as he'd been on the boat, and he'd moaned fretfully whenever he wasn't asleep. Gabrielle had developed a thundering headache by the afternoon of the first day, and Nathaniel, after one look at her drawn face and heavy eyes, had taken Jake up in front of him for a few hours while she slept.

Judging by Nathaniel's tight-lipped relief when he returned the child to the chaise, the arrangement had been less than a success. Jake had whimpered constantly for home, for Nurse and Primmy, for Neddy, for milk and for bread without crusts. His small bladder had required frequent relief, and every attempt his father had made to entertain him had fallen on stony ground.

Nathaniel had handed him back to Gabrielle with the terse comment that it was now his turn to nurse a headache.

However, by the time they reached the outskirts of Paris and clattered through the narrow cobbled streets, Jake had perked up. He'd never been in a city before, and his eyes had grown wide at the sights and the noises and the varied smells. He forgot his nausea, subjecting Gabrielle to a flood of questions that in her fatigue she found almost as exhausting as his earlier complaints.

Gabrielle lay back in the hip bath before the fire and closed her eyes on an exhalation of pure joy as her aching limbs relaxed in the warmth. What were Nathaniel and Jake doing at this moment? It was a safe bet they weren't luxuriating in hot water before a blazing fire.

Nathaniel had directed the chaise to the flower market on the Île de la Cité in the shadow of Notre Dame. There he'd dismounted and lifted Jake from the carriage.

"Here we say good-bye."

"But where are you going?" Gabrielle hadn't expected to part so abruptly in this bustle.

"You'll be contacted," he said. "At rue d'Anjou."

"But when?"

"When the time is right." His response had been implacable and his eyes were already roving the marketplace, assessing, speculating, on the watch. Gabrielle recognized what was happening. She knew what it was like.

"Very well," she said calmly, and then leaned out of the window, lowering her voice to a conspiratorial whisper. "Jake, you're going on a big adventure with Papa. You have to be his helper and not say anything unless he says you can. No one must know anything about us, where we come from, or anything at all. It's a big secret and it's *our* secret. All right?"

Jake, perched on his father's hip, gazed at her, his eyes wide. He'd become accustomed to the fact that Gabby and his father spoke to each other only in French on this journey. He didn't understand what they said to each other, but he could always tell the mood they were in, and now that the strangeness of this journey was wearing off, he was beginning to regain his equable nature.

"Where are you going?"

"That's a secret too," she said.

Jake thought about this, then he nodded. "We'll pretend we're invisible and no one can see us, an' we can walk down the street and no one knows us, an' we can watch them and listen to them and they can't hear us."

"Except when you and Papa are alone," Gabrielle said.

Jake's eyes shone. "Then we can talk like ordinary. When no one's listening."

"Exactly."

"We have to go," Nathaniel said, his voice curt

with anxiety. He held Jake closer to the window so Gabrielle could kiss him good-bye. Then he turned and strode off through the crowded marketplace, and was soon lost to view.

The post boy, already instructed, had mounted the riding horse and they'd continued to rue d'Anjou, where Gabrielle had paid off the coachman and the post boy, who'd conveyed them from the changing post at Neuilly into Paris.

And how long was she to wait here, lapped in luxury, before Nathaniel made contact? Jake's presence obviously meant an end to whatever spying plans Nathaniel had had ... something to do with an agent in Toulouse, he'd said. Would he expect her to work alone in that case?

In the dark back room of a small stone house on rue Budé on the Île St. Louis, three men sat around a table where the stains of old wine were so ingrained as to give the oak a rich patina. Tallow candles cast a dim light over the remnants of a meal of garlic sausage and ripe cheese.

Jake idly picked up bread crumbs from the table with a moistened forefinger and yawned. He was bored. It had been exciting when they'd first arrived at this funny dark house. There were lots of children who'd stared at him and nudged each other and whispered among themselves. One of them had thrust a piece of cake at him, and they'd all giggled when he'd taken a big bite. He'd wanted to play with them, but Papa had said he couldn't today and had hurried him upstairs to a small room under the eaves.

Now the adventure seemed to have lost its novelty. Papa had given him some bread and some of that horrible greasy sausage, but he wasn't hungry enough to eat it. He'd really like some more cake, and milk from the brown cows on the home farm in his china mug with the rabbits on it.

Papa and the two men were speaking French in low voices, and the room smelled of tallow and garlic and ancient damp stone. It was warmed by a charcoal brazier, but it was a stuffy, airless warmth that made Jake even sleepier. He folded his arms on the table and rested his head on his forearms, closing his eyes.

Nathaniel gave him a distracted glance, a worried frown corrugating his brow. The child should be in bed, but the bed he would share with his father was at the far end of a warren of passages that wound its way through the row of stone houses lining the narrow medieval street. Jake couldn't be left alone there, but he looked wretchedly uncomfortable where he was.

He pushed back his chair and stood up, scooping the child into his arms. Jake's eyes opened in startlement, then closed again as his father sat down, settling him into his lap. He pushed his thumb into his mouth and sighed like an exhausted puppy as his body went limp in sleep. Nathaniel, vaguely feeling he should, tried to remove the thumb but gave up as the sleeping child fiercely resisted.

"Poor little devil," one of the two men observed with some sympathy. "He's tired out."

"Yes," Nathaniel agreed shortly, and returned brusquely to the original topic. "One of you will have to go to Toulouse and see what the hell's going on with Seven. I haven't heard from him in weeks. If he'd been captured, we'd have discovered by now, so someone had better track him down. I'd intended to go myself, with the woman, but in the circumstances . . ."

"I'll go."

"Thanks, Lucas." Nathaniel nodded at the fiercely bearded man at the end of the table. Careful not to disturb the sleeping child, he refilled his glass and pushed the wine bottle across.

"So, how are you going to use the woman?" The

second man took a deep gulp from his glass and wiped his mouth with the back of his hand. "I'm not too keen on meeting a double agent, myself." He grinned, showing a mouth from which two front teeth were missing.

"Oh, don't worry, I'll keep her well away from you." Nathaniel sipped his wine and cut a slice of sausage. "We'll establish a channel of communication and you will feed her what we believe she needs to know. I want to flush out their people in England. She'll be told of a meeting to take place with our key agents there. It's to be presumed Fouché won't pass up the opportunity to infiltrate . . . send an observer or two. We'll scoop 'em up."

"And presumably, whatever information she provides us with is suspect."

"Of course. You'll act on nothing without consultation."

"*D'accord.*" The two men drained their glasses and rose. "You will stay with the Farmiers?"

"For the moment. It provides cover for the child. One more brat among their brood isn't going to draw much notice."

Nathaniel remained at the table as his companions wrapped themselves in cloaks and mufflers and slipped out into the bitter night. The candle flared under a gust of wind as the door closed. Jake stirred and mumbled something.

Nathaniel stood up carefully and extinguished all but one of the tallow candles. He hitched the child up against his shoulder and took the last candle, leaving the room. In the narrow passage outside he pressed a stone in the rough-hewn wall and a slab eased back. He stepped through into another room just like the one he'd left at the back of the neighboring house. He progressed in this manner halfway along rue Budé until he entered a room where a narrow bedstead stood against the far wall and a rickety dresser leaned askew against the wall beneath a tiny shuttered window overlooking the narrow street at the back of the house.

It was the house of one Monsieur Farmier, a baker with a large and ever-increasing family who had a nose for an easy profit and a blind eye when it came to the clandestine comings and goings of his various lodgers. They were quiet, unassuming men in laborer's clothes who spoke his own language with perfect fluency and paid handsomely and regularly. He asked no questions and was vouchsafed no information. In the event of a raid, he would have only descriptions to offer Monsieur Fouché's policemen.

Madame Farmier, hugely pregnant, had fussed over Jake, and Nathaniel intended that once Jake had recovered from the journey and was accustomed to the strangeness of this new existence, he would be absorbed into her unruly brood. No observer would notice one extra child running with the Farmiers.

Nathaniel pulled off Jake's shoes, his coat and britches, and tucked him into the cot in his underclothes. Jake flung his arms wide in an expansive gesture. Nathaniel grimaced. It was surprising how much space a six-year-old could take up. He edged into bed beside the child's warm body, rearranging Jake's limbs so that he occupied rather less of the narrow area. However, it was with no great confidence in a good night's sleep that the spymaster composed himself for rest.

18

A lad brought a message to rue d'Anjou the following afternoon. He was a grimy urchin with his cap set crookedly on his unruly thatch of dirt-darkened hair. The footman surveyed him with a raised eyebrow and instructed him to go to the kitchen entrance.

The urchin sniffed and shook his head, thrusting a sealed envelope at the footman before he scampered back down the steps to the street.

The footman glanced at the envelope as if it were something nasty that had crawled out of the woodwork. However, it was clearly addressed in literate handwriting to the Comtesse de Beaucaire.

Gabrielle was sitting with Catherine in a sunny upstairs parlor when the message arrived on a silver salver. She recognized the writing immediately, and her heart jumped against her ribs, her stomach jolting with anticipation.

"Excuse me, Catherine." She smiled vaguely at her companion and left the parlor.

In her own room she tore open the envelope. The message, in the code she and Nathaniel had worked out together at Burley Manor, was similar in content to

many she had received from Guillaume. She was given
a channel of communication: the flower seller in the
flower market whose stall was to the left of the center
pump. She would be selling bunches of primroses.
Gabrielle was to buy a bunch and with the three-sou
payment she could pass on a written message using this
same code.

There was nothing personal in the message, no
greeting and no signature, only the handwriting to
identify the sender. But that was only to be expected.

Gabrielle paced her bedroom, frowning. Nathaniel
intended to keep his whereabouts secret from her.
Why?

She could understand that he'd be extra cautious
with Jake, but she needed to know where he was. For
some reason, the idea of him somewhere in Paris, un-
reachable except through the medium of the flower
seller, made her dreadfully uneasy.

Well, she'd just have to find out for herself where
he was. She sat at the *secrétaire* to compose a missive to
the spymaster. Unfortunately she couldn't think of anything utterly compelling to tell him. She settled for the
simple information that Talleyrand had returned from
Prussia and was likely to be in residence in Paris for
some weeks.

Slipping the sealed envelope into her reticule, she
left the house, hailed a passing hackney, and drove to
the flower market. It was as busy as it had been the previous day, the air moist and heavy with the scents of
flowers, the cobblestones damp from the continual
dousing the merchandise received from prudent sellers.

An old crone in black widow's weeds sat at the stall
to the left of the central pump. She gave Gabrielle an
incurious glance as she selected a bunch of primroses
for her and held out a hand cruelly gnarled with arthri-
tis for the three sous.

She took the envelope and the money without a
flicker in the dull eyes, and Gabrielle moved away,

holding the primroses to her nose, inhaling their spring scent.

She took up a position beside a striped awning across from the primrose seller and waited. After a few minutes she saw a small boy run out from behind a cart and approach the crone. The lad grabbed the envelope and darted off through the throng toward the bridge that connected the small Île St. Louis to its larger cousin, the Île de la Cité.

Gabrielle hurried after him. She couldn't run without drawing attention to herself, but her long-legged stride kept the boy in sight as he raced along the Quai d'Orléans and disappeared round the corner of the rue Budé.

She stood at the end of the street, hidden in a doorway, inhaling the cold air that smelled of garbage and damp stone and mud from the Seine flowing sluggishly around the island. The lad stopped at number thirteen. She couldn't see who opened the door, but in a few seconds the lad was running back up the street. He went past her without seeing her, and Gabrielle walked briskly down the street, glancing casually at the door to number thirteen before making her way along rue St. Louis en l'Île, back to the flower market. At least she knew where Nathaniel and Jake were now. Not that it did her much good.

Nathaniel swore vigorously as he looked at the letter Monsieur Farmier had brought upstairs. He'd instructed the baker to tell the flower seller to deliver any communications to Gerard's bar on the quay, where he'd arrange to have them collected. Farmier had obviously forgotten that instruction; presumably his brain had been fuddled with his midday tippling.

Gabrielle would have followed the lad. It was what he would have done in her circumstances, and she was always resourceful.

He went out into the street. There was no sign of a tall, black-clad redhead. But then, he wouldn't expect her to reveal herself either.

She wouldn't deliberately bring Fouché's men down upon him, not when he had Jake with him, but it was all damnably uncertain. And he couldn't afford uncertainty—not with Jake. He went back into the house and upstairs to his garret room. Perhaps he should change the safe house. Gabrielle could continue to believe he was still there and send her messages. But it was such perfect cover for the child.

Footsteps pounded on the stairs outside and the door burst open. "Papa—"

"It's polite to knock on a door before entering," Nathaniel said, regarding his son with a degree of irritation at this explosive interruption.

Jake fixed his eyes on his shuffling feet, and he became again the timid child of Burley Manor.

"What is it you want?" Nathaniel asked less sharply, catching the child's chin and turning it up. "What's that all around your mouth?"

"Toffee," Jake said, rubbing with the back of his hand. "It's sticky."

"Yes, I can see that. Come here." He drew the child to the dresser, dipped a cloth in water, and scrubbed vigorously.

"There's rabbits in the yard," Jake said, snuffling through the washcloth. "In a cage. Can I go an' see them? Henri has to feed 'em."

"How do you talk to Henri?" Nathaniel turned Jake's face side to side, examining it for any residue of toffee. "He doesn't speak English."

Jake looked confused by the question.

"I suppose actions speak louder than words," Nathaniel observed.

Jake didn't understand this either, but he could feel that his father's annoyance had disappeared. "So can I go, Papa?" He hopped anxiously from foot to foot.

"*May I?*" Nathaniel corrected the child automatically.

"*May I?*" Jake repeated with ill-concealed impatience. "It's only in the yard outside the kitchen door."

"I suppose so, but . . ." Nathaniel was left speaking to empty air, the sound of Jake's feet receding on the stairs.

Nathaniel smiled as he hoped that the child wouldn't associate furry bunnies with his dinner tomorrow. And suddenly he was swamped with longing to see Gabrielle, to share that thought with her, to hear her rich chuckle. He found himself wishing that if she had followed the lad, she'd have thrown caution to the wind and paid him one of her indiscreet visits.

But such thoughts were dangerous madness.

"So, you believe you have gained the English spymaster's confidence, madame?" Fouché rolled an unlit cigar between his stubby fingers and regarded Gabrielle through hooded eyes.

"He has agreed to take me into his service," she responded calmly, leaning back in her chair in Talleyrand's office.

"And how did you travel back to France?"

"By fishing boat from Lymington to Cherbourg."

"And you traveled with Praed." It was not a question but a simple assertion.

Gabrielle controlled her features as her mind whirled. How did Fouché know that? Surely Talleyrand hadn't told him. She glanced at her godfather. His expression was inscrutable.

"Yes," she said.

Fouché's mouth moved in the semblance of a smile. "You seem uncertain, madame."

"No, I'm not in the least uncertain," she retorted. "But I'm wondering how you knew that."

"You were traveling on one of my *laissez passer*,

madame. When you entered Caen, you showed the pass at the city gates. My men take note of such things."

"And they recognized Lord Praed?"

He shook his head. "No, but I was making a lucky guess."

Merde! He was a slimy, tricky bastard! But could they have seen Jake? He'd been asleep in the coach most of that first day, and she was almost positive the city guards hadn't looked inside the carriage. Nathaniel had been riding alongside, of course.

"So, perhaps you could tell me where we might find Lord Praed?" Fouché suggested. He stuck the cigar in his mouth and felt in his pocket for his sulphur matches. Catching his host's eye, he changed his mind and put the cigar on the table, reaching instead for his brandy goblet.

Gabrielle saw Guillaume's body, lying in her arms, the small crimson stain on the smooth, pale flesh of his back. She watched the stain spread and felt her arms grow heavy with his weight as the buoyancy of life left him. She heard again that strange little sound, half protest, half surprise, as the knife found its mark.

Nathaniel Praed had robbed Guillaume de Granville of life and Gabrielle de Beaucaire of a man she'd loved more than life itself.

"Madame?" Fouché prompted, leaning forward in his chair so that his face came close to hers.

"No," she heard herself say, her voice sounding distant, as if it were coming from the rustic pavilion all those months ago. "No, I don't know where he is. He wouldn't tell me. He said I would be contacted."

"And have you yet been?"

Gabrielle had an image of the flower seller in the hands of Fouché's policemen. She shook her head. "Not as yet."

"I see." Fouché was frowning. "Forgive me, madame, but you seem a little uncertain of your answers."

"I detect no uncertainty, Fouché." Talleyrand spoke

for the first time during the interview. His smile was urbane as he refilled his guest's glass. "Gabrielle is always one to weigh her words."

"I am also somewhat fatigued," Gabrielle said. "It was a long journey. I've told you as much as I can about the situation in England, and what I discovered among Lord Praed's private papers. If there's nothing else . . ." She rose from her chair.

"No, you've been most helpful, madame," Fouché said, rising with her, his eyes skimming over her face with a glitter that made her shiver. "You will, of course, inform me the minute the English spymaster makes contact."

"*Bien sur*," she said.

"Well, I must take my leave, Talleyrand." Fouché bowed. "I'll use the rear door, as usual. No, no . . ." he protested as Talleyrand reached for the bellpull. "There's no need to summon a servant. I can find my own way."

"I'm sure you can, my friend, but I wouldn't dream of it," Talleyrand murmured with his calm smile. "Escort Monsieur Fouché to the door, André," he instructed the footman, who'd appeared so fast he must have been standing outside the door.

The door closed and Talleyrand shook his head with a grimace of distaste. "As if I'd be fool enough to let him wander unescorted through my house. He'd probably steal the silver."

Gabrielle's smile was a feeble attempt. "Do you think he believed me?"

Her godfather shook his head. "No. He took you by surprise, as he intended, and I'm sure he learned a lot more than you wanted him to. It's his way."

"But if he doesn't believe me, why did he let it go?"

Talleyrand shrugged. "You're a private citizen with powerful friends. He can't haul you off to his dungeons unless you do something overtly treacherous. I'm sure he'll try to discover why you lied, and you can be certain he'll be watching you."

"Yes." She turned to the door. "I'm sure he will."

"Just as a matter of interest, why *did* you lie? Because of the child? Even if Fouché captures the spymaster, I can protect the child. He'll be of no use to Fouché anyway, once he has Praed in his clutches."

"I know . . . and I don't know why I lied. I didn't think I was going to, when I thought of Guillaume, and then I just did." She shrugged. "I'll have to warn Nathaniel that Fouché knows he's somewhere in the city."

"You will be endangering yourself by protecting him," Talleyrand pointed out.

"But Nathaniel's still more use to you alive than dead, isn't he?"

"Most certainly. But I can always find another conduit."

"And another seductress?"

"If necessary."

"It is a dirty business."

"That can't come as a revelation, *ma fille*."

"No, of course it doesn't. *Bonne nuit, mon parrain*."

In the quiet of her chamber, Gabrielle lay openeyed in bed on her back, arms folded behind her head. The room was lit only by the glowing embers of the dying fire. Why had she lied? Guillaume would have condemned Nathaniel Praed as coldly as Nathaniel had condemned him. Why had she passed up the opportunity to do the same? It would have been a perfectly fitting revenge, and a few short weeks ago she would have jumped at it.

But when she stirred the coals in her heart, searching for that clear, bright spark of hatred and vengeful determination, she found it was no longer there. She hadn't been aware of its passing, so when had it died? She'd told Talleyrand she was still prepared to use Nathaniel to further her godfather's political machinations. How true was that, now? Whether it was true or not, she could no longer imagine causing him direct harm.

Her grief for Guillaume was still a living flame, but it had become somehow detached from the everyday world. Instead of being intrinsic, the one fact through which she filtered everything else, it was now a totally separate emotion that had nothing to do with anything else.

And nothing at all to do with her passion for Nathaniel Praed.

"So where did you find him?" Fouché regarded the sniveling lad held between two burly policemen with an air of mild curiosity.

"In a tavern behind the flower market, monsieur. He's got more money on him than he could expect to earn in an honest lifetime." The speaker backhanded the youth, who cringed, blood already flowing from a split lip, one eye swollen and purple.

"We've been watching the market ever since that tip from One-Eye Gilles."

"Ah, yes." Fouché pulled his chin. "He said he'd heard about some strangers who were throwing their money around rather freely, didn't he?"

"Yes, monsieur. Not that we've seen any signs, and you know old One-Eye. He's so far into the drink, he'd see goblins if he thought you'd pay him for saying so."

"Mmm. So, what have you got to say for yourself, boy?" He turned to the prisoner with a ferocious stare, his voice rising almost to a shout.

"I ain't done nothin' wrong," the lad whispered, trying to back away from the hands gripping his elbows. "I just runs errands for the old besom who runs the flower stall."

Fouché looked with calculated incredulity at the leather purse in his hand. Deliberately, he shook the contents onto the table. A small pile of gleaming silver caught the light from the tallow candles. "Well, well," he murmured. "A few errands for an ancient crone who sells flowers? It seems we have a millionairess in our flower market, gentlemen."

There were dutiful guffaws, and amid them the lad fell to his knees beneath a stunning blow from one of his guards. "He chucked some piece of paper in the river, monsieur, when we nabbed him." A booted foot made contact with the captive's shin.

"Easy, easy," Fouché reproved his men mildly. "Let's not get carried away now." He approached the prisoner and deliberately aimed a kick into his belly. "How about you tell me the truth, before there's any more unpleasantness?" he suggested in the same mild tone.

The lad lay curled in the fetal position on the floor, gasping for breath.

"Pick him up." Fouché lit a cigar, watching as they hauled the youth to his feet. He hung from their hands, his eyes streaming, his mouth half open with pain and shock.

"The truth now." Fouché drew deeply on his cigar and blew the smoke into the prisoner's face. "Tell me about these errands."

"I takes messages," the lad wheezed. "Messages from the flower seller"

"To where?"

"Rue Budé, rue Gambardin, sometimes rue Vallançaires . . . please, monsieur, that's all I does. Really," he gabbled. "It's the truth, I swear it."

"And what do these messages say?"

The boy shook his head miserably. "Don't know. I can't read."

"No, I suppose you can't. And who receives these messages."

The boy wiped blood from his mouth with his

sleeve. His eyes were wild with terror. "Whoever opens the door, monsieur."

"And who pays you?"

"Whoever opens the door. Ordinary folks."

Fouché glanced again at the glittering coins. The inhabitants of the streets the youth had cited were unlikely to possess such riches.

"And where were you supposed to deliver your last message, the one you managed to lose in the river?"

"Rue Budé." The lad looked as if he knew he'd just signed his own death warrant. "But I didn't know it was important, honest, monsieur."

Fouché raised an eyebrow. "Presumably that's why you felt it necessary to dispose of it. What number rue Budé?"

"Number Thirteen, monsieur. Please, I ain't done nothin' wrong. Please let me go, monsieur. You can keep the money, please let me go."

"Are you trying to bribe one of his imperial majesty's ministers?" demanded Fouché. "Dear me, lad. Take him away." He jerked his head to the door, and the two guards dragged their captive out of the small bare room that served Napoleon's Minister of Police as his office.

Fouché nodded to himself, puffing on his cigar. It was at times like this when his policy of direct involvement in all aspects of the police work in the city paid off. His men knew that nothing was too insignificant to be of concern to the minister.

Number 13 rue Budé was clearly worth a visit. It might not turn up anything . . . but it might yield the grand prize. The English spymaster was somewhere in this city and the Comtesse de Beaucaire knew where.

There was a soirée at Madame de Staël's that night. The countess would be there, of course. Maybe, he would drop a little word in her ear and see if he got a reaction.

He would order the raid for the early hours of the following morning. Birds rarely flew their nests before dawn, and it was the best time for invoking terror, when men's spirits were at their lowest. A troop of black-clad secret police wreaking havoc on Île St. Louis would certainly deter its inhabitants from turning a blind eye to strangers, however well the strangers might pay for their cooperation.

Gabrielle was engaged in an animated discussion in Madame de Staël's salon with Prince Metternich, the Austrian ambassador, when Fouché entered.

She felt his eyes on her and glanced up. He was standing in the doorway, surveying the brilliant social gathering with an air of contempt. The Minister of Police was no intellectual, and the refinements of the mind held no appeal.

"Your pardon, comtesse. Have I lost your attention?"

"I beg *your* pardon, sir." She turned back to her companion with a laughing apology. Metternich was a man much like her godfather. One of the ablest politicians and diplomats on the European stage, but still not quite a match for Talleyrand. But they liked and respected each other. "I had the unmistakable sense that Monsieur Fouché was trying to catch my attention."

"Then let us go and greet him." The prince rose with a gallant bow and offered his arm.

Gabrielle took it, finding herself glad of his company. If one was uneasy with Fouché, it was always more comfortable to talk with him in company.

"Monsieur Fouché. You are not often seen in such circles." She greeted him easily. "You are acquainted with Prince Metternich, of course."

"Of course." The two men exchanged bows.

"I was feeling in an expansive mood, countess," Fouché said, smiling. "I think I may have discovered the whereabouts of our elusive friend."

Ice ran in her veins. Gabrielle smiled. "Your pardon, monsieur. Which elusive friend?"

"Why, your traveling companion, madame. It seems possible he's come to rest somewhere on the Île St. Louis."

He watched her with the hawk's eye of an expert interrogator and detected an almost imperceptible flicker in the corner of her eye. "You are to be congratulated, Monsieur Fouché," Gabrielle said calmly. "To have discovered that so quickly."

"I have an ear in every corner of this city, madame," he said with another bow. "If you'd excuse me, I must greet my hostess."

He moved off, sliding through the throng, a slight smile of satisfaction on his thin lips.

"A brutish man," Metternich remarked. "But superlative at his job."

"Oh, yes," Gabrielle agreed. "Superlative. Would you escort me to my godfather, prince?"

"But of course."

Talleyrand saw them approach and frowned. Gabrielle was paler than usual.

"I have the headache, *mon parrain*," she said. "May I take the carriage, and send it back for you?"

"No, I will escort you home." He offered her his arm. "Prince, I would welcome the opportunity for a discussion. Perhaps you would dine with me tomorrow."

"I should be delighted." Metternich bowed himself away and Gabrielle and her godfather left.

"So?" he said once they were ensconced in the carriage.

He heard her out in silence. "You will put yourself at great risk if you warn Praed," he pointed out when she'd finished. "I will ensure the child's safety. That much I can safely promise you. But if you do this, I cannot guarantee to protect you from Fouché."

"I understand." Gabrielle sat back in the swaying carriage, the lights from passing vehicles flickering across the window. Was she about to risk her own life for Nathaniel? She would have done so for Guillaume without thought. But she'd felt differently about Guillaume. He'd been the one great love of her life. There wasn't room in one life for two such overwhelming loves. What she had with Nathaniel was passion. It wasn't love.

"I have to do it," she heard herself say as if her mind and her voice operated separately from each other.

Talleyrand merely nodded.

19

Gabrielle took five minutes in rue d'Anjou to fling off her evening gown and change into her britches. She thrust her pistol into her pocket, wrapped a cloak around her, tucking her hair beneath the hood, and ran back to the carriage, still waiting at the door.

"The flower market, Gaston. As fast as you can."

"D'accord, comtesse." The driver touched the peak of his cap and cracked his whip.

She sat on the edge of the seat as the vehicle swung around corners, the team of horses obeying the urgent encouragement of the driver's whip.

She wouldn't allow herself to think of anything but the immediate plan. She had to get there ahead of Fouché's men. That was all she needed to consider. Nathaniel would have an escape route, just as Guillaume had always had. So long as he had enough warning, he would escape the trap.

The carriage came to a halt in the eerily deserted square that in the daylight was a riot of color and a hubble of noise as the flower sellers jostled and competed for customers. Gabrielle's feet echoed on the cobbles as she jumped down, looking round at the silent buildings flanking the square, the central pump, the wooden struts that supported the canvas awnings. It was a stage set waiting for the drama to commence. It had been raining earlier, and puddles glistened in the faint moonlight and the ground was slippery underfoot.

She ran through the narrow streets at the side of the vast edifice of Notre Dame, its crenelated spires reaching above the pitched roofs, arrowing into the rain-washed sky. She crossed the bridge to Île St. Louis and plunged into the darkness of its central cobbled street, so narrow that the night sky was a mere dark sliver between the opposing roofs.

She splashed in puddles heedless of the debris that clung to her boots and the hem of her cloak, her eyes fixed on the corner of rue Budé ahead.

Suddenly she heard the tramp of booted feet behind her. She dived into a doorway, pressing back into the shadows as she looked up the street. A group of lanterns was advancing. Her heart jumped into her throat. There were six men, all holding lanterns on poles, all bearing staves, all clad in the distinctive black cloak and black cocked hat of Fouché's police.

They were heading toward rue Budé.

Gabrielle dived into rue le Regrattier, her mind racing, her heart thundering in her chest as she ran toward the river. She would have to approach the house from the Quai d'Orléans. Less direct, but she had the advantage of speed and she knew they were there. Fouché's men didn't know they were running a race.

Her pistol was in her hand now as she ran faster than she believed possible, her breath sobbing in her throat. A huddled figure in a doorway yelled something after her, but she ignored him. A dog set up a frantic barking from a backyard and a woman's voice screamed abuse. The dog howled as something struck the ground with a violent clatter.

Gabrielle kept running. Two men lurched out of a tavern, too inebriated to do more than blink bemusedly

as the lithe figure sped past them. Then one of them
lumbered forward in pursuit but quickly gave it up as
Gabrielle disappeared around the corner of rue Budé.

She didn't pause in her headlong dash along the
street, her head down, as if she could reduce her visibil-
ity to anyone approaching. But there was no sign of a
lantern, no sound of booted feet.

Where had they gone? Panic flooded her. Surely
they weren't already in the house. The street ahead was
empty. Could they already be inside? No, it was impossible. They'd have needed wings to overtake her, and
besides, she would have heard the noise. Fouché's men
had no reason to go quietly about their business.

She reached number thirteen and hammered on
the door with her clenched fist, gazing frantically over
her shoulder, down the street, expecting at any minute
to see the sinister group of lanterns wavering toward
her.

But Fouché's men, seeing no need to hurry on their
errand, had made a small deviation into a tavern,
where they were slaking their thirst in blithe ignorance
of their quarry's imminent escape.

Shutters flew open above the door, and Monsieur
Farmier's head, nightcap askew, stuck out. A stream of
obscenities accompanied his demand to know who was
raising the dead at this hour.

"*Ouvrez la porte!*" Gabrielle spat out in an impas-
sioned whisper, her white face glimmering in the darkness. She had no way of identifying herself, but her
urgency must have communicated itself and the baker
withdrew from the window, the shutters banging closed.
She heard feet lumbering down the staircase, then the
bolts screeched as they were pulled back.

"*Merci.* You have someone staying here, where—"

"Gabrielle!" Nathaniel was springing down the
stairs, pistol in hand, before she could finish her sentence.

"Fouché's men," she gasped.

"Where?"

"Behind me ... a few minutes, I think, but they disappeared."

Nathaniel wasted no further time on questions. He grabbed her and pulled her behind him, upstairs, and into the garret, where he began throwing his possessions into the portmanteau. Jake sat up sleepily.

"Gabby?"

"Hush!" Nathaniel swung round on him, his voice barely a whisper but ringing with ferocious authority. "You are to say nothing, not one word, not one sound until I give you permission. Is that understood?"

Jake nodded, gazing in scared silence.

"That goes for you too," Nathaniel instructed Gabrielle. He pressed the wall, and the slab of stone slid back. "Take Jake and get in there."

"But you—"

"Do as I say!"

Gabrielle picked Jake up from the bed, grabbed the blanket, and went through the wall. The slab closed behind her.

Alone, Nathaniel moved with economical efficiency around the tiny space, removing every sign of habitation, shaking out the pillow on the cot, straightening the coarse sheet on the straw mattress. He poured the water from the ewer out of the window, wiped the surface of the dresser with his kerchief, and cast one last look around before grabbing the candle and his portmanteau and pressing open the slab again.

Gabrielle and Jake were standing against the wall, Jake wrapped in the blanket, Gabrielle's arms around him.

Neither of them said anything as Nathaniel opened up the far wall and gestured ahead of him. They had reached the third house along when the sounds of hammering came faintly from number thirteen. Gabrielle jumped, glancing anxiously at Nathaniel, but his expression was impassive as he pushed her ahead of him.

In the last room Nathaniel reached up and removed two rafters from the steeply pitched roof.

"Up you go, Jake," he said softly, lifting the child and thrusting him into the darkness. Jake whimpered.

"Now you, quickly, and keep him quiet." Nathaniel lifted her by the waist and hoisted her up so that she could grasp the edge of the opening. "Use my shoulders."

She scrambled her feet onto his shoulders and pitched herself forward into the dusty crawl space, then leaned down to take the portmanteau and candle from Nathaniel, and then the two dislodged rafters.

Nathaniel swung himself up and through the opening with the agility of an acrobat and deftly replaced the rafters. The space was barely big enough for the three of them. It was inky dark and what air there was was thick with dust.

Jake sneezed and whimpered again. Nathaniel pulled him into his body, turning the child's face into his chest, muffling all sounds.

They seemed to be entombed in silence, and Gabrielle felt the old nightmare terrors nudging at her mind. Once before she'd lain hidden in a roof from a rampaging mob. The musty smell of the rafters, the prickle of dust, was in her nostrils as it had been on that day. This roof pressed down on her as the other one had. In a minute she would fall . . . or she would cry out—

Suddenly she felt Nathaniel's hand on hers in the darkness. It was a connection that grounded her in the present and she pulled herself back from the abyss with a shudder of horror. His grip tightened, and she knew as clearly as if he'd spoken that he understood what had happened and how close she'd been to losing herself in the nightmare again. She squeezed his hand in gratitude and found that despite perching on the pinnacle of hideous tension, she could now listen intently and without panic for the sounds of pursuit.

They could hear banging from the street, and Gabrielle guessed that Fouché's men were waking the inhabitants of every house, prepared to search the entire street when they found number thirteen empty of spies.

They didn't know, then, about the secret doors connecting the attics of the houses. It was a not-uncommon device in these medieval streets where through the ages the persecuted had fled the oppressor. But Fouché's policemen were not known for the subtlety of their thought process or their knowledge of history, only for their ability to wrest information or commit murder without a qualm.

The banging finally came at the door of the last house on the street. It was almost a relief after the terror of anticipation. Gabrielle bit her lip hard, tasting blood, forcing herself to concentrate on the pain and not on the sounds in the house—the banging and scraping and shouting.

Nathaniel stroked Jake's head, holding him tightly against him, his other hand gripping Gabrielle's firmly. He was, as always at such moments, perfectly calm, reserving his strength and the power of fear-engendered adrenaline for when it would be needed. There was nothing more he could do at the moment except wait and impart what strength and reassurance he could to his companions.

Then the sounds were immediately below them. The door was kicked open, boots scrunched on the wooden floor.

Was there a smudge of plaster dust on the floor from when he'd removed the rafters?

The thought flitted across Nathaniel's brain and he felt his heart begin to speed in preparation for action. They would be looking only for him. If they made any move toward the rafters, he would jump down on them, leaving Gabrielle and Jake still hidden. Gabrielle would have the sense to stay put—for Jake's sake if not her own.

But she was in the gravest danger. She must know that. She'd betrayed her own masters to save an enemy spy. He hadn't expected her to betray him on this mission, not when Jake was with him, but he certainly hadn't expected her to risk her own life to protect him either.

Someone flung back the shutters over the tiny window with a resounding clatter and the sound of splintering wood. A woman's wail of protest at this wanton destruction was answered with a string of obscenities. Fouché's men were clearly very put out. Rue Budé had yielded only terrified slum dwellers.

The Farmiers, like most of their kind, were expert at producing a cringing idiocy in the face of violent authority. Once it was clear their lodger and the child had fled, leaving no trace, they had nothing to gain by volunteering information and everything to lose. Ignorance and cupidity were understood by the policemen, who came from their own social ranks and saw nothing out of the ordinary in a man turning a blind eye to the goings-on in his house in exchange for generous payment.

Finally, having vented their frustration by wreaking terror and destruction up and down the street, Fouché's men went on their way to drown their failure in a cask of *vin ordinaire* in the tavern.

Jake was trembling against Nathaniel as the sounds of booted feet receded on the stairs. Gabrielle became aware of an agonizing pain in her shoulders where the muscles were knotted in a violent cramp. She tried to ease it, wanting to scream with the pain, and instead bit hard on her lip again. Nathaniel drew several long, slow breaths and relaxed his hold on Jake so the child could move his head out of the muffling confines of his father's chest.

They remained huddled in silence for an eternity until Nathaniel deemed it safe to move. He put his mouth against Gabrielle's ear, barely whispering his instructions.

"I'm going down. You're both to stay here."

She nodded. The prospect of being alone in the dark crawl space while Nathaniel exposed himself to whatever uncertainties there were outside filled her with dismay, but she was no stranger to dismay in dangerous situations.

Nathaniel removed the rafters again and swung down into the silent room. He replaced them before crossing to the window, where the shattered shutter swung desolately back and forth. He peered down into the courtyard. It was deserted, the house once again dark and silent.

He crossed to the door, opened it gingerly, and stepped onto the landing, listening. There was total silence.

Returning to the room, he dropped the heavy wooden bar over the door, locking them in, before removing the rafters again.

"Come on, Jake."

The little boy's terrified face appeared in the opening, and he half fell, half jumped into his father's arms.

Gabrielle swung herself down awkwardly because of her cramped muscles and stretched with an almost inaudible moan of pain.

"All right?" Nathaniel asked evenly, still holding the child.

She nodded. "A bit stiff . . . nothing worse . . . thank God."

"Let's get out of here," he said in the same even tones.

"Where to?"

"Truly underground," he said with a bleak attempt at a smile. "At least for tonight."

Carrying the child, he led the way back through the houses until they reached number thirteen. They crept downstairs and out through a rear door into the courtyard where the rabbits lay in a somnolent heap in their cage.

"We must hurry," Nathaniel whispered, looking up into the sky where the first faint streaks of gray were showing.

They slipped through a gate into another alley, and Nathaniel strode quickly ahead, his speed unaffected by the child's weight in his arms. Gabrielle half ran to keep up with him.

They came to a small church with cracked, moldering stone walls and slates tumbling from a sagging roof. Its tumbledown air struck Gabrielle as pathetic, like someone whose offers of comfort have been inexplicably spurned. She assumed it had fallen into disrepair during the Revolution, when organized religion was banned and no one had any use for churches.

Nathaniel looked up and down the alley, then walked rapidly around the side of the building. A flight of crumbling stone steps led down into the crypt. Gabrielle followed him down. He felt in a niche in the wall, drew out a key, fitted it into the tarnished brass lock, and the door creaked open, emitting a waft of air, cold as the grave and heavy with the reek of ancient stone and damp earth.

"I don't like it here," Jake whimpered as they entered the dank darkness and Nathaniel pulled the door closed behind them. "I want to go out."

"Hush now, I'm here," Nathaniel soothed. "You're quite safe."

"But it's spooky."

"Yes, it is," Gabrielle agreed, making her voice bright and cheerful. "But I'm sure we can light the candle."

"Can you find it?" Nathaniel asked in the same

easy tones, as if this were all quite normal. "There's flint and tinder somewhere in the portmanteau."

Gabrielle felt in the darkness through the small pile of possessions, found the requisite articles, and in a minute the welcoming glow of the candle threw some illumination.

It was not a cheerful place, Gabrielle thought in understatement, looking around at the oozing stone walls, the cracked greenish slabs beneath her feet.

"Is this another safe house?"

"More like sanctuary," Nathaniel said as if it were perfectly ordinary to make witticisms in such circumstances. "The church is disused and the crypt's an emergency shelter to be used only in *dire* emergency," he added. "We should find some blankets and a lantern somewhere, and some basic supplies."

"Over there." Gabrielle pointed to a tomb where a fully armed stone knight stretched out in perpetuity, hands piously crossed over his breast. A mound of blankets and a lantern with a small jar of oil stood at the base of the tomb. There was a flagon of water and several slabs of chocolate. A slop pail stood on the floor. Apart from that, there was nothing but the graves of the dead.

"A trifle cheerless," Gabrielle observed in what she hoped was a tone to match Nathaniel's. "Let's see if this will make a difference." She filled the lantern with oil and lit the wick.

Jake promptly howled and buried his face in his father's shoulder as the grotesque shapes of armored knights and mitred stone bishops danced on the vaulted ceiling.

Nathaniel gentled him, stroking his back as he sat on the tomb, settling the child in his lap. Jake pushed his thumb into his mouth and rocked himself in his father's arms, suddenly overcome with emotional and physical exhaustion.

Nathaniel regarded Gabrielle, his eyes unreadable in the flickering gloom. "How did you find out about the raid?"

"After I sent you the message telling you that Fouché knew you were in Paris—"

"What message?" The interrogatory crackled in the dank chill. "I got only one, the day before yesterday, and it said nothing about Fouché."

"But I sent you a message via the flower seller this morning . . . well, yesterday morning now."

"I never received it."

"What could have happened to it?"

Nathaniel gazed bleakly over the child's head. "It's a bit late to worry about that now. How did he know I was here?"

"One of his men spotted you, apparently. I assume there are people who would recognize you."

"It's never happened before," Nathaniel said flatly. If Gabrielle had betrayed him to Fouché, why would she then risk her neck to save him? Belated remorse? That seemed too indecisive for Gabrielle. No, probably he'd been recognized at one of the checkpoints on the journey from Cherbourg. It was always a risk.

"Well, it happened this time," Gabrielle declared, tension and fatigue putting a sting in her voice. "And then tonight I was at a soirée at Madame de Staël's and Fouché was boasting about some coup he was going to pull off. I didn't know if he meant he'd found you, but I thought I'd better warn you just in case. And then I ran into his men . . ." She spread her hands, palm up.

"I suppose you followed the messenger yesterday?" She nodded.

Nathaniel stroked Jake's head thoughtfully. Gabrielle had risked her life to save him. It had been a most decisive choice. He wrapped a blanket securely around the shivering child. A permanent choice or simply an emotional response?

"You'd better go back before you're missed," he said. "Jake and I will stay here for today, and move on this evening."

Gabrielle stood looking at him in the gloom as he sat holding the child on the tomb. It was a dreadful place to spend the long hours of the day. The tensions of the night were apparent now in the taut lines of his face, shadowed with the blue tinge of his nighttime beard, and his eyes were sunken with fatigue.

"I'll come back later, then." She went to the door.

"Gabrielle." His voice was soft.

"Yes." She turned back.

"I owe you my life. Mine and Jake's." His face was in shadow, but she could sense his stillness, the deadly seriousness of his statement.

"What else did you expect me to do when my spymaster was in danger?" She tried to invest the question with a lightness, as if it were partly a joke, but it didn't come out right. She sounded ungracious, impatient almost.

"I don't know what I expected," he responded quietly.

"Oh, well, I'm full of surprises." She tried a smile. "I'd better go. I'll come back this evening."

Without waiting for a response, she slipped through the door into the now-clear light of dawn and left Nathaniel and his son in the lantern shadows of the crypt.

Gabrielle de Beaucaire was certainly full of surprises, Nathaniel reflected. She'd made a choice that day that made no sense for the ruthless, skilled, and experienced opponent he knew her to be.

Where did that leave *his* plans?

Impossible to decide at this point. Jake stirred and whimpered in his arms, and Nathaniel stroked his head, murmuring soft words of reassurance until the child was still again.

Nathaniel shifted on the tomb until his back was

against the oozing wall of the crypt. He closed his eyes. Helen's face came to him in the dank, frigid air of this grim tomb . . . her face as it had been on her deathbed. White, bloodless, the lines of suffering smoothed by the hand of death. His hold tightened involuntarily around her child.

20

___

It was eight o'clock that night when Nathaniel emerged from the crypt, holding Jake's hand, the portmanteau slung over his shoulder. He locked the door, replaced the key in the wall niche for the next person in dire need of sanctuary, and climbed the steps.

Jake was silent, clinging to his father's hand. He was frightened, but his relief at leaving their hiding place far surpassed his fear. He was sucking a piece of chocolate, holding it in his cheek, the warm sweetness melting over his tongue. It reminded him of safe and comforting things like his bed in the nursery, and Neddy, and the way Primmy smelled when she kissed him, a faded, sweetish smell like the dried flowers in the still room.

A tall, cloaked figure separated itself from the shadows at the top of the steps.

Nathaniel froze even as recognition hit him. Jake jumped and spoke her name before he remembered he wasn't to speak.

"Shh," Gabrielle said, putting a finger on her lips, smiling at him in the darkness.

"What the hell do you mean, jumping out on me

like that?" Nathaniel demanded in an outraged whisper. "I expected you in the crypt at dusk."

"It took me a while to arrange everything," she whispered, seemingly unperturbed by his anger. "I have a *laissez passer* for you." Her crooked smile gleamed white in the gloom. "With it, you can go anywhere in the city . . . stay at an inn, travel wherever you wish."

She reached into the pocket of her cloak and pulled out the precious document. "See. It's in the name of Gilbert Delors, a servant in the household of Monsieur le Prince de Talleyrand, who's instructed to journey to his master's estates in Périgord and is to be allowed to pass without let or hindrance."

"How on earth did you get hold of this?" He stared at the paper.

"I stole it," she said. "You see, it's signed by Talleyrand's steward." She pointed to the signature. "The real Gilbert Delors has been turning the house upside down looking for it all day. When he came out of the steward's office, I had a most urgent errand for him to run, an armful of parcels that needed to be taken immediately to my chamber. He put the paper on the table when I filled his arms with packages . . . *et voilà*."

Nathaniel turned the document over in his hands. It was Jake's passport to safety. He could leave Paris, travel anywhere in the country without question. He could arrange passage on a regular *paquet* at Calais rather than wait in danger for the eventual return of the fishing boat.

Gabrielle certainly didn't do things by halves, he thought. He had a sudden absurd urge to laugh, to fling his arms around her and dance a jig as relief coursed through his veins, and he felt his muscles relax as he stepped back from the brink of the precipice for the first time since they'd reached Paris.

"Let's go and find some supper," he said. "And a decent bed."

"Ah, well, I have that all planned too," Gabrielle said with a mysterious smile. "There are certain establishments where a man can take a woman, no questions asked." She let her cloak fall open, and Nathaniel's eyes glazed.

Gabrielle was wearing a gown of crimson velvet edged with tawdry lace. The décolletage was so low, it barely covered her nipples, and the skirt was caught up to reveal a petticoat hiked well above her ankles, ankles that were clad in what looked to his astonished gaze to be cotton stockings. On her feet she wore a pair of down-at-heel black shoes with paste buckles.

"Sweet Jesus," he whispered. "What game are you playing?"

"A brigand's game," she said with a roguish gleam in her eye. She too seemed infected with an almost manic edge of delight. "Who's to question a servant and his whore in Pigalle?"

Nathaniel shook his head as if trying to clear the cobwebs from his brain. "Jake . . . ?"

"He'll be quite safe with us. He's too young to understand anything about the place, and it'll be a lot safer and more comfortable than hiding from secret police in crypts."

"And what do *you* know of such places?" Nathaniel demanded.

"Well, if you must know, I had a lover," Gabrielle said nonchalantly. "We used to have our assignations there. Come on, we'll find a carriage at Notre Dame."

"*What?* Come back here!" Nathaniel grabbed her arm as she was about to prance off down the street.

Gabrielle grinned at him. "You're not going to be a prude, are you?" Wisping river mist from the Seine clung to the dark red hair tumbling loose over her shoulders, and the charcoal eyes were alight with the challenge and mischief that he hadn't seen for an eternity, it seemed.

Jake suddenly tugged at his father's hand. He didn't

understand what Gabby and Papa were talking about, but the chocolate had melted in his mouth and now he was cold and hungry and tired again.

"Papa." The single word was a small, undifferentiated plea that caught their attention as nothing else could have at that moment.

Nathaniel bent and picked him up. "I don't know what the hell you're up to, Gabrielle," he said. "But let's get going."

She seemed to have wings on her feet, he thought, following her exuberant progress to Notre Dame. There were several hackney carriages in the square before the cathedral. Gabrielle gestured to one with a vulgar flick of her fingers and, in accents of the streets, engaged the driver in a ribald exchange that had Nathaniel torn between laughter and total bemusement.

She jumped into the carriage, took a bewildered but compliant Jake from him, settling him on the seat beside her as his father climbed in and closed the door.

"Where in the devil's name did you learn to speak like that?" Nathaniel demanded as the carriage lurched forward.

Her eyes glinted in the darkness. "I always wanted to be an actress."

Nathaniel leaned back against the squabs, closing his eyes in defeat. "Brigand," he murmured to himself. "A veritable brigand."

Gabrielle only chuckled, cuddling Jake, who sucked his thumb, rocking with the motion of the carriage, sensing the different atmosphere surrounding him. The fear and the tension were gone; and there was no sign of the anger that often sparked between his father and Gabby. They were behaving in the way that made him feel warm and happy, and Papa had that funny little smile that he only ever wore when he was with Gabby.

The carriage came to a halt in Pigalle. Gabrielle jumped down and informed the driver with a cheeky wave that her escort was paying and he could well afford a good *pourboire*.

Nathaniel handed over the fare and the required tip without demur. The square was busy and well lit, women plying their trade on every corner, potential customers idling by, examining the wares. He glanced down at Jake, who seemed indifferent to the scene, holding Gabrielle's hand, his eyes half closed with tiredness.

"This way." Gabrielle linked her arm in Nathaniel's, allowing her cloak to fall open, revealing her trollop's costume. Her tumbling hair was a startling mismatch with the crimson gown.

The garment was obviously as carefully selected as the rest of her wardrobe, Nathaniel thought with another quiver of amusement as she led them across the square and into a narrow side street where the houses had lanterns outside the doors and in the windows. Women lolled against doorjambs or sat in the windows, displaying their charms.

Gabrielle stopped outside a much more discreet establishment, where a lantern hung over a closed door and the windows were shuttered.

"What *is* this place?" Nathaniel demanded as Gabrielle knocked smartly.

"The madame here used to be Julien's nurse, until she changed professions. He'd kept in touch with her, and he and his army friends used this house for their assignations. Madame is very accommodating and very discreet. It's a profitable sideline for her, I imagine."

Julien was presumably the lover, Nathaniel decided as a grating slid back in the door and an eye filled the gap. But where did the Comte de Beaucaire figure in all this?

He watched, fascinated, as Gabrielle raised her hand to the grating and made a circle with her thumb and forefinger, an identifying sign of some kind.

The door was opened by a very fat woman in a

gown of striped bombazine and a lace cap perched on graying hair. She greeted Gabrielle with a businesslike pleasure that indicated they were old acquaintances but not intimates, then she subjected Nathaniel to an unnervingly close inspection before swooping on Jake with cries of entrancement.

"*Oh, le pauvre petit!*" She enveloped the startled child against her massive bosom, all the while listening with sharp calculation to Gabrielle's request for two adjoining rooms.

She nodded and promptly named a sum that sounded extortionate to Nathaniel. Gabrielle, however, raised her skirt in the manner of her adopted profession and extracted a wad of notes from her garter, counted out the requisite number, replaced the remainder, thanked their hostess warmly, and turned to Nathaniel with a smile.

"There, that's all settled. Jake can have the smaller room, and we can . . . well . . ."

"We might," he agreed dryly.

"Well, that's what you're supposed to do in houses like this," she pointed out. "Oh," she said as if struck by a novel thought. "Perhaps you've never frequented one before."

"Just you wait!" he said in a ferocious whisper.

"I'm not sure I can," she returned, touching her tongue to her lips before turning to follow Madame's expansive rear up the stairs.

The strains of a piano came from behind a closed door, the sounds of laughter, whispers, a little shriek— more of excitement than fear, Nathaniel decided. They were clearly in a rather more salubrious brothel than those they'd passed in the square. The floors were clean, the paint fresh, the decor discreet. And the two bedchambers Madame showed them were clean and well appointed, if somewhat more flamboyantly decorated than the corridors outside. Fires blazed in both grates, an ample supply of logs beside the hearths.

"Will you be wanting anything?" she asked Gabrielle. "Some milk, perhaps, for *le petit*."

"Bread and milk for the child," Gabrielle said. "And we would like champagne and oysters."

"Comme d'habitude," Madame said with a brisk, comprehending nod.

As usual? Just how often had the Comtesse de Beaucaire eaten oysters with her lover in this place? Had the lover been another spy? The husband simply a convenient cover? His death had certainly been the cover story behind her desire to join the English secret service. . . .

"Help me to put Jake to bed." Gabrielle interrupted his reverie and he put the questions aside. There would be time enough for them later.

Jake sleepily submitted to being undressed and washed. The room was warm and cozy, the bed all covered in red satin, and there was a heavy flowery smell in the air that wasn't exactly unpleasant but made his nose tingle. Papa found his nightshirt in the portmanteau and slipped it over his head, then lifted him into bed.

The bread and milk tasted almost like it did when Nurse made it for him, and when he dribbled milk on his chin, Papa wiped it off with his handkerchief.

Feeling warm and safe, Jake snuggled down under the covers. Gabby was smiling and Papa's mouth had a funny twitch to it, as if he were going to laugh. He thought it would be better than anything in the world if they could stay there forever, just the three of them. His eyes closed.

Nathaniel watched the child slide into sleep and felt a deep satisfaction in seeing him, for the first time since they'd left Burley Manor, ensconced in a proper bed with all his accustomed bedtime rituals. The fact that the bed was in a brothel in the city's most disorderly district didn't seem to matter.

He bent to turn the oil lamp low beside the child's

bed and kissed Jake's cheek, brushing the curly hair off his forehead. Jake's heavy eyelids lifted and then dropped again, and he snuggled deeper under the covers. So like Helen ... but he wasn't Helen. He was a separate, discrete entity whose birth had cost Helen her life. But that wasn't Jake's responsibility. It was his father's.

Nathaniel straightened and stood looking down on the sleeping child, the embodiment of his guilt. For nearly seven years he'd carried that guilt. But in the last few days something had happened to the burden. Jake wasn't the embodiment of anything—he was a small boy with needs, both basic and complex. And in his own self-indulgent morass of guilt, the father had failed to address the child's needs.

He turned away from the bed and became aware of Gabrielle standing in the doorway connecting the two rooms. She inclined her head in an almost questioning gesture, her eyes gravely smiling.

She had given him back his son. No, not given *back*. He hadn't had his son in any real sense. Gabrielle had given him Jake. Whatever else she was, whatever else she might have done, she'd shown him the joys and responsibilities of fatherhood and had forged the bond that he now felt so powerfully with the sleeping child.

The lamp from the room behind her set fire alight in her deliberately disheveled hair. Her outrageous, lascivious costume accentuated every luscious curve of her body, and that aura of sensual mischief pulsed around her. A joyous throb of sexual energy coursed through him, obliterating all but desire.

He moved toward her, and she stepped into the room behind.

Her eyes held his as he closed the door gently. For a moment he leaned against it, and the excitement built as they both stood still, eyes held by the invisible thread of pulsating arousal.

Suddenly Nathaniel laughed, a warm, rich sound of joy. He sprang toward her, picked her up, and tossed her onto the bed.

"Brigand!" His mouth came down on hers, his tongue delving in the sweet cavern beneath. "Brigand," he murmured against her lips. "God, I want you. It seems an eternity."

Her answering chuckle was a soft breath on his face, and her hands raked through his hair. He reached down and pulled her skirt up to her thighs, exposing the cheap cotton stockings. His fingers brushed across the remaining notes thrust into her garter.

"Now, just which one of us is for sale, I wonder," he mused, raising his head to look down at her.

"You, if I can afford you," she responded promptly.

He sat back on his heels, astride her thighs, and slowly pulled out the notes, one by one, from their hiding place. He counted them with great deliberation, then pushed them into the pocket of his britches, announcing solemnly, "I can be bought for such a sum."

"I'm relieved, sir," Gabrielle whispered, stretching beneath him, arching her back, pointing her toes, feeling the muscular energy ripple through her. "I have bought *you* in order that you should take *me*."

"The pleasure will be all mine, ma'am."

"Oh, I trust not, my lord . . ."

Gabrielle had worried about how she would feel bringing Nathaniel to the place where she'd shared so much joy with Guillaume, but as the night passed in hours of glory, she realized that it didn't matter.

When Nathaniel pried an oyster off its pearly shell and dropped it into Gabrielle's readily opened mouth, she remembered Guillaume doing the same thing. The memory was precious but not sullied. When he moved the damp stem of the champagne glass in a cold caress over her belly, setting her skin fluttering, she only smiled with languid pleasure at a bodily memory of a similar response long ago.

"So where did your husband fit into the eternal triangle?" Nathaniel asked lazily as dawn began to break.

"It was a marriage of convenience. Julien was already married when we met. I married Roland because one has to be married." She shrugged as if it had been a matter for total indifference.

"And what happened to them both?"

"Roland died of typhus."

"And the lover?"

Oh, no, she wasn't ready for this. Suddenly the euphoria was shattered and she understood that she'd been fooling herself all night. The memories flooded back, and she turned her head aside, reaching across Nathaniel's belly for the champagne glass on the table.

"He was killed," she said. "In the line of duty."

Nathaniel laid a hand on her back and immediately felt the strain beneath the damask skin. "You loved him," he stated quietly.

"Very much. I don't want to talk about it anymore." *Not to you, of all people.*

"You're still mourning?" he persisted.

"I think I always will to some extent. Please, can we go to sleep now?"

Nathaniel took her chin between finger and thumb and brought her face around. Immediately she closed her eyes as if to hide the pain in them. "Look at me," he said, softly insistent.

Her eyes opened reluctantly, and they were sheened with tears. He took the glass from her and gathered her into his arms, holding her against his chest as he'd held Jake, soothing the child's fear.

Gabrielle began to weep. She wept for Guillaume and the love they'd had, but she also wept in confusion and terror because somehow she was beginning to feel just as deeply for the man who had snatched Guillaume from her. How was it possible to feel such a powerful and obsessive and impossible love when one should feel only hate? How was it possible to feel such overwhelming passion when one should desire only vengeance?

Nathaniel stroked her back, bending his head to press his lips to the curve of her neck as his hand smoothed over her buttocks in a caress that imparted warmth and reassurance rather than sensuality. She was jangling, he could hear and feel her discordance. He felt it himself, this terrible confusion of emotions when clear logic and absolute fact was routed again and again by the voracious hungers of lust.

Gabrielle fell asleep first, her head pillowed in the crook of his neck, one arm flung across his body. Nathaniel, despite his own fatigue, lay awake listening to the sounds of a house that worked at night.

He realized that for the first time since Helen's death, he was thinking beyond the present, envisaging a future where the landscape was vibrant and full of promise. But how could the English spymaster be envisaging such a future with a French spy? It didn't make any sense.

He finally fell asleep, no nearer to an answer.

When he awoke, he was alone in the bed, daylight pouring through the unshuttered windows. Jake's chattering voice came from the next room, interspersed with Gabrielle's more measured tones. Throwing aside the covers, he stood up and stretched and yawned. The room was warm, the fire freshly made up. It was an amazing luxury after the cheerless attic on rue Budé, not to mention that dreadful day in the crypt. His body felt good, suffused with the energy that a night of energetic and blissful lovemaking always engendered.

"Did we wake you?" Gabrielle's voice came from the connecting door and he turned with a half-smile. She was wearing her harlot's dress again and still managing to look achingly desirable, although he could detect tiny lines of strain around her eyes and mouth. Something new? he wondered, or just the residue of last night's torrent of weeping?

Jake popped up behind her, neat and tidy for the first time since they'd left England. "*Bonjour*, Papa. Gabby taught me to say that. It means good morning." He beamed at his father, examining his naked body curiously. "Don't you sleep in a nightshirt?"

"Sometimes," Nathaniel said, raising an eyebrow at Gabrielle, who turned aside, hiding her smile. "I'd better get dressed. Any chance of breakfast in this place? Or are they all enjoying a well-earned rest after their labors?"

"I'll ring. I had some hot water brought up, so you can shave if you wish." She gestured to the steaming ewer on the marble-topped dresser, and went to pull the bellrope beside the door.

Nathaniel enjoyed the luxury of a sponge bath with ample hot water in the fire-warmed room. Gabrielle sat on the window seat, her appearance of relaxation just that. The world had reasserted itself this morning as she had known it had to. Last night's interlude had been glorious, but the time for glorious interludes was over.

Jake kept up a stream of chatter and questions, his ordeals apparently forgotten in the warm and fear-free present.

Two maids brought breakfast, laying it on a round table beside the window. If they were aware of Nathaniel shaving, still naked, at the dresser, they gave no sign. Presumably they didn't find it an unusual sight.

"Come and sit down, Jake." Gabrielle lifted him onto a chair. "There's hot chocolate for you and a brioche." She broke a fragrant round brioche and spread it liberally with strawberry jam. "Brioches don't have crusts," she informed him. "But if you have bread, then you should dip the crust in your chocolate. Like so." She suited action to words.

"That's bad manners," Jake said, wide-eyed.

"Not in France," Gabrielle said firmly. "It's very polite. Ask Papa."

Jake giggled. "Is it, Papa?"

"In the nursery it may be," Nathaniel said, pulling on his britches. "But not in serious company."

"Stuffy!" Gabrielle accused, pouring hot milk into two deep bowls before adding the steaming, fragrant coffee. "I dip my bread in my coffee wherever I am."

"Well, we both know how shamelessly you set bad examples." He shrugged into his shirt, tucking it into the waist of his britches before coming to the table.

"What's that mean?" Jake demanded, his eyes bright with curiosity.

"Never you mind." Nathaniel ruffled his hair and sat down opposite him. "We have to decide how best to travel, Gabrielle. If it weren't for Jake, who'll be noticeable, I'd say we'd draw less attention traveling by stage, at least until we get into the countryside."

"It would fit better with your identity as a servant," Gabrielle agreed. "You could pass Jake off as a nephew, or something. I'm sure he'd be able to pretend he was invisible again, wouldn't you, Jake?"

She dipped a crust of bread into her coffee bowl and expertly carried the dripping bread to her mouth, spilling not a drop. Jake watched her, fascinated, his mouth full of brioche.

" 'Course I could," he mumbled.

"And what of your identity?" Nathaniel broke into the brioche. "Perhaps you should travel independently."

"I think I must stay here," Gabrielle said. She tore a hunk off the baguette for Jake, cautioning, "You have to be careful of the drips if you're going to dip it."

"Oh? Why is that?" Nathaniel's voice was calm as he waited to hear how she would explain herself. He now understood the reason for this new strain. She'd betrayed her French masters by saving him. There was no evidence against her at this point, but if she left France at the same time their quarry disappeared, then she'd incriminate herself. Fouché would hunt her down wherever she was. Not even her godfather, even if he was so inclined, could protect her from the knife in the night. He leaned back in his chair, cradling his coffee bowl between his hands, regarding her steadily.

"It would look strange if I were just to disappear," Gabrielle said. "Talleyrand would wonder about it. Catherine is having a ball next week to welcome me back. It would be discourteous, unless there was an absolutely vital reason for leaving, like a death or a wedding with the DeVanes, or something."

Not bad, Nathaniel thought with detachment. Not bad at all.

"So you'll follow when you can?"

"Of course."

Jake shifted in his chair. Something had changed. Gabby was looking sad and Papa's mouth had gone thin again. His tummy tightened and he pushed away his hot chocolate. Gabby wasn't going to come with them. "Gabby's coming with us," he said. If he said it, then perhaps they'd say yes, she was.

"No, love, I can't. Not at the moment." Gabby patted his hand.

"Gabrielle has things to do here," Nathaniel said, his voice flat.

Jake felt his lip tremble. They were going to go on that horrible boat again and Gabby wasn't going to be there. A tear splashed on the table, and he pushed back his chair and ran into the next room before they could tell he was crying.

"I'm sorry," Gabrielle said helplessly. "But I don't see what else I can do."

"No," Nathaniel agreed steadily. "Neither do I." Suddenly he was unutterably weary of this hideous charade. The desire for the clean knife of truth, even though it would sever everything, took possession of his soul. His gaze held hers.

The silence elongated. The fire hissed and the clock ticked. Nathaniel's eyes were for once readable, burning their message deep into hers, and comprehension crept over Gabrielle, lifting the fine hairs on her neck, setting her scalp crawling.

Nathaniel watched shock and understanding flood the dark gray depths of her eyes.

"You know," she said finally.

"Yes."

Gabrielle cupped her chin in her palms. "Since when? I thought I'd been so careful."

"Since Burley Manor. I found your code in the Voltaire."

She raised her eyes and looked at him, her expression swept clear of all emotion. "I wasn't clever enough for you."

"No," he agreed. "Was I clever enough for you?"

"No."

The space between them was a cool, clear wash of cleanliness. He wanted no explanations or excuses, and Gabrielle would not offer them.

"So what now?" Gabrielle asked.

"We go our separate ways. What we know of each other dies here." He stretched his hand across the table.

She put her own in his. "I wish it could be different."

"But it can't."

"I'll say good-bye to Jake and then I'll leave."

"Before you go—"

"Yes?"

"What we know of each other dies here, unless . . . unless you ever oppose me professionally again. You understand that, Gabrielle? If that ever happens, it will be as if we had never met before."

Gabrielle shivered. Despite the bleakness in his eyes, the despairing recognition that matched her own that all was at an end between them, there was unmistakable menace in the statement. The English spymaster would not forgive and forget an enemy a second time.

She nodded silently and went into the next chamber.

Nathaniel heard her voice in the other room, then he heard the door to the corridor close on the sound of his son's sobbing. He heard her footsteps, light on the stairs. He heard the front door open and close. He stood before the window and watched as she disappeared in her black cloak around the corner into Pigalle.

21

On June fourteenth Napoleon defeated the Russians at Friedland and Alexander finally yielded to the wisdom of his brother, Grand Duke Constantine, and sued the French emperor for peace.

The news created great excitement in the salons of Paris, where Gabrielle had passed the past months in a state of limbo. She had passed similar periods—ostensibly taking lively part in court life, talking, smiling, flirting—during her affair with Guillaume, when there had been deserts of time between their meetings, and she'd lived in fear and emptiness, and none of her desolation had shown on her face or in her eyes.

"Now, *mon enfant*, the fun starts," Talleyrand announced three days after the battle. He came into her apartments, flourishing a dispatch bearing the Napoleonic eagle.

"Alexander is sending his plenipotentiary to the emperor requesting a truce, one that I suspect will leave England isolated. I am summoned to Napoleon's side to assist with the terms of the truce. You shall accompany me."

"Me? Why, sir?" Gabrielle stared in surprise.

"I shall need a hostess," he said blandly. "Catherine cannot perform such a task with either discretion or distinction, as you know. So you shall take her place. No one will consider it strange."

"I'd been thinking of going to Valencay," she said. She strolled over to the window, looking down at the street. The plane trees had the dusty look of city foliage in summer, and a mongrel cur lay in the shade, his tongue lolling. She'd been intending to visit Talleyrand's country chateau for a few weeks. She'd often stayed there in the old days, waiting for Guillaume. Once or twice they'd had more than a week together in the idyllic country setting, undisturbed by any but the most discreet staff. They'd fished the river and swam in the deep pool under the bridge. They'd ridden over the countryside under the moonlight, picnicked and picked peaches and greengages in the lush orchards. And they'd made love—under the trees, in the river, in the hayloft, in the fields—whenever and wherever the mood had taken them.

"This will offer you greater distraction," her godfather pointed out.

"You think I'm in need of distraction?" She turned from the window, raising an ironic eyebrow.

Talleyrand made no response to what was a rhetorical question. Gabrielle was a wan shadow of her former self. She had little interest in anything, and none at all in the business of espionage. The bitter end to her encounter with Nathaniel Praed had engendered a deep loathing for anything clandestine. She slept little and ate less, and he'd been an impotent observer of her suffering for too long. It was too much akin to the dreadful weeks after Guillaume's death, and he found himself wishing that she didn't have to feel so deeply, didn't have to throw her entire self, body and soul, into her love affairs. But he also knew that that was Gabrielle's nature and there was no changing it. All he could hope to do was alleviate her pain as and when he could.

Gabrielle smiled in rueful resignation as he merely held out the dispatch to her.

She read it and then shrugged in acceptance. "So when do we leave?"

Talleyrand couldn't conceal his satisfaction. "We travel to Tilsit in the morning. It will be a tedious journey, no doubt. But at least it's summer and the roads are no longer enmired."

Tilsit was on the border of Russia and Prussia, a small town on the River Niemen, and it took a week of hard journeying to reach it. Gabrielle rode beside the carriage whenever she could, but she was soon heartily sick of the primitive way stations where they passed the nights and the rancid meat and hard bread that passed for decent fare.

Her godfather was a poor traveling companion, nursing his aching leg and saying very little, his brain ceaselessly at work on plotting his campaign.

They arrived in Tilsit on the evening of June twenty-fourth. The minister's staff had traveled ahead and had laid claim to a house on the left bank—the Prussian side of the river—to accommodate the Minister for Foreign Affairs and his hostess. It was one of the larger houses in the modest town as befitted the prince's consequence.

The town was taken over by Napoleon's entourage and his Imperial Guard. His victorious army camped in the surrounding fields, as usual living off the land with blithe disregard for the peasantry. They were a conquered people, after all, and Napoleon had little time for his defeated enemies unless they could be useful to him. Alexander, the Czar of all the Russias, he believed, could be useful in the battle he fought against the intransigent English. Therefore, he would treat him accordingly.

"What on earth is that?" Gabrielle exclaimed, wearily dismounting outside the house assigned to them. She stared at the river, where a massive raft was anchored midstream. It bore two lavishly adorned white pavilions, the larger of which carried a massive embroidered letter *N* on the side facing Napoleon's camp.

"Our emperor, *ma chère*, has always had a flair for the dramatic," Talleyrand declared. "He and the czar are to meet tomorrow morning in the large pavilion. I daresay, if you went to the opposite bank, you would see the letter *A* embroidered in the same style on the other side."

Gabrielle shook her head and muttered, sotto voce, "He is a vulgar little man, isn't he?"

Talleyrand tapped her wrist in half-serious reproof. "Be careful where and to whom you say such things, *mon enfant*. I must go now and pay my respects. I'll leave you to inspect the accommodation and make what adjustments you think fit. I intend to entertain quite lavishly at some point in the next few days."

"*D'accord.*" Gabrielle entered the house. The duties of a diplomatic hostess sat easily on her shoulders, and Catherine was always very happy to yield her place at such tedious functions to the younger woman. No one here would think twice about the role of the prince's goddaughter.

She chose a bedchamber for herself overlooking the river and sat in the window for a few moments, looking across the river with its flamboyant raft. On the right bank lay Russia. There was no sign of the Russian emperor or his entourage on the shore, where a crumbling cottage stood in the middle of a field.

A summons to dine with the emperor arrived with Talleyrand's return, and it was late when she finally got to bed. The conversation had all been about the upcoming meeting between Napoleon and his erstwhile enemy, and there was an air of suppressed excitement in the town, as if great things were about to be accomplished.

Midmorning the next day found Gabrielle positioned in her window. She saw a line of barouches arrive on the opposite bank and a small group of men alight and enter the ruined cottage.

At precisely eleven o'clock Napoleon rode to the left bank between columns of cheering troops. His entourage followed, a glittering group of lavishly decorated officers. The contrast between the victor's approach to the raft and the supplicant's struck Gabrielle as more than a little pointed.

This was a purely ceremonial meeting, one that would set the tone for the real negotiations. It was then that Talleyrand would come to the fore.

With the now-familiar wrenching ache, Gabrielle wondered where Nathaniel was. These negotiations were of vital interest to the English. Did he have an agent among the Russians? Or even among the French? She wondered if he had found a replacement for herself, perhaps not so closely attached to the imperial circle, but close enough to watch and listen.

Talleyrand had accepted her return and Nathaniel's departure without comment, and she had no idea whether he was pursuing an alternative method of influencing the English government's actions.

Fouché's rage at the escape of his quarry had resounded throughout the headquarters of the secret police. He had questioned Gabrielle many times, but Talleyrand had always been there, an urbane yet alert witness, and she'd managed, if not to fool the policeman, at least to give him no evidence on which he could act. She knew that one of his men followed her for several weeks after Nathaniel's escape, and she made no attempt to evade him, although she was skilled enough to do so if she'd wished. Monsieur Fouché received dull reports of the blameless and ordinary social life of a widow at the court of the Emperor Napoleon.

Now, as she watched from her window, both emperors from their own side of the river stepped simultaneously into boats, their staff falling in behind them, and teams of rowers bent to their oars, their white-shirted arms pumping in unison under the brilliant summer sun.

Napoleon, in the uniform of the Imperial Guard, the red ribbon of the Legion of Honor on his chest, his hat pulled low over his forehead, jumped lightly from the boat to the raft before Alexander had set foot on the structure. The czar, with his powdered hair, white knee britches, and the green tunic of the Preobrazhensky regiment, was a tall, elegant figure as he stepped onto the raft in his turn.

Gabrielle felt a strange little thrill at the ceremonious panoply despite her earlier remarks about the vulgarity of such a display of power. The stocky little man held out his hand to his willowy counterpart, and the two men embraced.

Talleyrand, standing at Gabrielle's shoulder, pursed his lips at this open sign of friendship. He'd have his work cut out manipulating this burgeoning relationship to his own ends. But it could be done. His hand rested lightly on Gabrielle's shoulder, and she turned her head.

"You'd prefer there to be enmity between them, sir?"

"Make no mistake, *ma chère*, there will be . . . there will be."

There was no indication of such a future when Napoleon and Alexander reappeared from the pavilion arm in arm. Napoleon proposed that the town of Tilsit be declared neutral territory and divided into a French section and a Russian section so that the two courts could meet and mingle and entertain each other, and the serious negotiations, to be conducted on the French side by Talleyrand and on the Russian by Prince Lobanov and Prince Kurakin, could move ahead without a physical boundary separating the two parties.

It was done amid much ceremony and protestations of friendship. Talleyrand greeted his Russian counterparts with urbane courtesy, giving no indication of the contempt in which he held them, and informed Gabrielle that they would be hosting a reception the following evening for the Russian dignitaries.

Gabrielle spent an exhausting day trying to organize a reception that her godfather insisted should be as splendid as any offered in the emperor's accommodations. Since the emperor had his own gold dinner service and his own crystal as well as a traveling cellar and an army of chefs, she was at something of a disadvantage. However, by seven o'clock she had managed to assemble sufficient china, crystal, and silver to serve the fifty guests, and was not displeased with the bowls of caviar on ice, the silver salvers of lobsters, the delicate creamy salmon mousses shivering on Sèvres platters, the oyster patties, and the crystal bowls of syllabub.

"A delicate theme," she informed Talleyrand as he paused in the dining room on his way to dress. "Pink and cream and very light. They will have dined heavily beforehand, so this should tempt the taste buds nicely. And since excellent champagne is one wine that seems in plentiful supply, we have the perfect match."

"Your mother had the same flair," Talleyrand observed, kissing her cheek. "In her wardrobe and in her decor, and she was a superb hostess. Society fought over her invitations."

Gabrielle's smile was sad. "I don't remember."

"By the time you were old enough to remember, *ma chère*, there *were* no parties. Marie Antoinette had told the people to eat cake if they couldn't afford bread, and the Revolution was in full swing."

"I suppose so. I must go and dress. What time will the emperor make his appearance?"

"He and Alexander intend arriving together, a further show of amity," he said dryly. "When all the other guests are assembled, a messenger will run to alert their imperial majesties."

.   .   .   .

At eleven o'clock the two salons were buzzing with officers in the uniforms of the most distinguished regiments of Russia and France. Their ladies glittered, plied fans vigorously in the overheated rooms, and cast sharp, assessing eyes at their counterparts' coiffures, gowns, and jewels.

Gabrielle moved easily through the throng. The Russians all spoke fluent French, so communication was natural enough. Talleyrand was an impeccable host, but Gabrielle noticed that, as always, he stood aside during conversations, rarely participating beyond making the original introductions or subtly suggesting a topic of conversation.

Wily old rogue, she thought with a surge of affection. He was a firm proponent of the principle that the more a man talked, the less he understood, and the less he was worth listening to.

The sound of running feet came from the hallway, and a messenger hurried into the room, making his way to the Minister for Foreign Affairs.

Talleyrand nodded, excused himself, and gestured to Gabrielle. The whisper ran around the room: "*Les empereurs arrivent.*" And the guests moved to either side of the double doors.

Gabrielle was known to Napoleon and had had many conversations with him, so she felt no excitement at making her curtsy to the great man. She was, however, very interested in meeting Czar Alexander.

Their imperial majesties strolled into the salon side by side and their various subjects made ritual obeisance.

Napoleon raised Gabrielle from her curtsy with a smile, and still holding her hand introduced her to Alexander. "*Mon cher ami*, permit me to introduce the Comtesse de Beaucaire, our charming hostess."

Gabrielle curtsied again, murmuring the correct platitudes. As she raised her head, her eyes met those of a man standing some way behind the emperor in a small knot of courtiers in evening dress, who had accompanied Alexander and Napoleon.

The room spun; her stomach turned to water, her knees to jelly, her blood seemed to stop flowing. Nathaniel's cool brown gaze held hers with absolute command. If he was as numbed by seeing her as she was by seeing him, he wasn't showing it. And it would be death to show it.

The crisp dark hair with the silver swatches at his temples was now all silver, and he wore a small, neat beard that accentuated the leanness of his face, the angularity of his features. But no superficial changes could alter the magnetism that flowed from him, or disguise the lithe agility of the slender frame, or the power in the long, white hands—those long, slow, arousing hands. . . .

Gabrielle was aware that she was breathing rather fast and her palms were moist within her silk gloves. She was also aware that Czar Alexander was talking to her.

The need to respond to the emperor was her salvation. She murmured about honor and pleasure and made polite inquiries as to his health and contentment. Alexander held her hand for rather longer than strictly necessary and complimented her on her gown and the elegance of her salon. Then their imperial majesties moved down the twin lines of guests, Talleyrand limping beside them, presenting his guests.

Gabrielle turned to greet the knot of civilian courtiers who had accompanied the emperors. Alexander's aide-de-camp performed introductions, bowing deeply with each presentation.

Gabrielle held out her hand to one Benedict Lubienski, introduced as a Polish acquaintance of the aide-de-camp's.

For a moment she was mute, her mind as frozen as her tongue. He bowed over her hand. His fingers tightened on hers in powerful warning, and she found her voice.

"Are you here in an official capacity, sir?" she inquired, managing a flickering smile of courteous welcome.

"Not really, madame. The fate of Poland is dear to my heart, but I can't expect it to be under consideration during these negotiations."

"No, I imagine not." She withdrew her hand and turned to greet the next man, vaguely aware that she was smiling inanely and nodding her head as if she were a marionette with a slack string.

Nathaniel moved away, greeting acquaintances, smiling agreeably, saying little, and drawing even less attention to himself. He took a glass of champagne from a footman and joined the outskirts of a group standing beside the long windows that stood open to a terrace overlooking the river.

The broad sweep of water glittered under the myriad lamps of the town, and the raft with its white canvas pavilions was ablaze, strains of music coming from an orchestra playing in the smaller pavilion for the pleasure of Monsieur Talleyrand's guests.

He watched Gabrielle unobtrusively as she moved around the room. For one terrifying minute he'd thought she was going to give them away. Her hand in his had been shaking like a leaf in a gale, and her face had gone so white, he'd thought she was about to faint. If he could have warned her, he would have, but he'd discovered she was there only when he was on the way to the reception. It had been casually mentioned that Talleyrand's goddaughter was acting as the minister's hostess.

Forewarned had been forearmed, and yet he hadn't been totally prepared for her, for the moment when his eyes had locked with hers. It had taken all the years of living on the edge of danger to withstand the annihilation of reason and control, to keep from putting his hands on her body, from covering that wide, crookedly smiling mouth with his own.

The bodily memory of her, the thick, rich silk of her hair, the cool smoothness of her skin, the sweet fragrances of her honeyed core had haunted his lonely nights since he'd left her. But greater than passion's loss had been the absence of the essence of Gabrielle—of her laughter, and her temper, and her warmth, and her generous impulses, and her challenges.

And here she was, in the same room with him, as striking as ever, in a gown of deepest blue taffeta, sapphires at her throat, the dark red hair drawn up through a sapphire-studded comb, then tumbling in artful ringlets on either side of her face.

And he wanted her with the overpowering bodily hunger she had always aroused in him. He wanted to put her down on the parquet floor, raise those elegant rustling skirts, part the creamy, impossibly long thighs, lay his hand on their moist, heated apex. . . .

He turned abruptly aside, stepping through the window onto the terrace, desperately hoping the cool air would dampen his now-embarrassing ardor. Of all the insane self-indulgences!

"How long have you been at the Russian court, Monsieur Lubienski?"

Gabrielle spoke at his shoulder, and he turned very slowly, a social smile on his lips.

"Several weeks, comtesse. I have many friends there, since I spent some months in Russia three years ago."

"I see." Presumably, before he became spymaster, he'd been an English agent in St. Petersburg. A Polish cover would be perfect. The Polish nobility mingled freely with the Russian, and it would explain both any lack of facility in the Russian language and his ease with French, since it was the lingua franca of both Russia and Poland.

"How are we to manage?" she demanded in a sudden urgent whisper, her hand brushing his black silk sleeve, her eyes molten lava. The past was forgotten in the desperation of their longing, the agony of their separation, the wonder of this meeting.

Nathaniel glanced around the terrace. Groups of people were drifting away from the overheated salons to enjoy the cool river breeze. Without answering, he clicked his heels and inclined his head in a formal bow, offering her his arm.

She laid her gloved hand on his arm, and they strolled the length of the terrace, Nathaniel making innocuous comments on the loveliness of the night, Gabrielle responding as best she could, but she was on fire, as if in the grip of a devastating fever, at the feel of his body so close to hers, the music of his voice, the special scent of his skin.

When they'd twice made public promenade of the length of the terrace and everyone was perfectly accustomed to the sight of them arm in arm, Nathaniel directed their steps toward a shadowy corner screened by a group of bay trees in wooden tubs.

Gabrielle forced herself to keep her pace to Nathaniel's slow, idling stride as she saw where he was heading. She wanted to leap forward into the dim privacy of the trees and lose herself in his body, but the spymaster, in the grip of the same compulsion, knew what he was doing. No one took any notice of them as they slid unobtrusively into the shadows.

"Dear God," Gabrielle whispered. "I can't bear it another minute." She flung her arms around his neck.

He wrapped her in his arms, lifting her off the ground as their mouths met, crushing her against him. Bearing her backward, he pressed her against the stone parapet of the terrace, his tongue driving into her mouth as they drank of each other's sweetness. Her body bent backward as he leaned over her as if all the better to devour her, and his hands pushed her skirt up to her waist, holding it there with his body. A fingernail snagged the delicate silk of her stocking, and his flat palm pushed up inside the leg of her drawers. This was no slow and easy exploration, but a rough and hungry revisiting of her body, damp and aching with its own passionate arousal.

She groaned against his mouth and bit his lip as his fingers delved deep within her. She pressed her loins against the hard mound of his erect flesh as if she could somehow achieve the fusion that was now such a desperate need.

"Come into me," she whispered. "You have to, *now*, Nathaniel."

"No . . . no . . . sweetheart. *No*." He withdrew his hand, pulled away from her, gazed at her in the dimness from his own passion-filled eyes. "Not here—it's not possible."

She sagged against the wall, her breathing ragged, her heart racing, her eyes closed as she fought to control the conflagration of her senses.

Nathaniel straightened her skirt, barely touching her as he did so, as if she were a burning brand that would set him alight.

"Where?" she breathed finally.

"Outside the town, along the river," he said with soft-voiced urgency. "Walk north, and I'll wait for you."

She nodded slowly as if the physical effort was almost too much for her.

"Go back now, ahead of me," he instructed, adjusting his cravat, smoothing his hair.

"But what must I look like?" She touched her lips that still sang with the memory of that consuming kiss.

"A little disheveled, that's all," he reassured. "Nothing that a couple of minutes in the retiring room won't put right. Now, off you go, before you're missed."

She left him, gliding out from the screen of trees but keeping in the shadows of the house as she made her way inside, hurrying through the brilliantly lit salons, keeping her head down so that she wouldn't catch anyone's eye.

Nathaniel took his time about emerging. He leaned on the parapet and breathed deeply until his aroused loins were once again comfortable and his head was clear. Madness . . . utter madness. But he hadn't been able to help himself, and for two pins he'd have yielded to Gabrielle's desperation and joined with her there and then, standing against the parapet of a terrace in the midst of the two most illustrious courts in the world.

Madness! But he wanted to laugh aloud. And that was not the prudent reaction of a man who walked in the lion's den and whose life presently depended upon a mixture of good fortune, experience, cool nerves, and utter discretion.

He'd half hoped, when he left her in Paris, that distance would lend detachment, but it had done the opposite, merely intensified his addictive passion. She continued to obsess his dreams, both sleeping and waking.

And here, on the banks of the River Nieman, in surroundings that would be more suited to a theatrical drama, she was with him again and it was the stuff of fantasy.

Gabrielle somehow managed to get through the rest of the evening without any obvious signs of insanity. The two emperors left together as they'd arrived, in perfect unity. Benedict Lubienski made his farewells with a group of others, his lips brushing her gloved hand, his eyes opaque.

"Well, that went off very well," Talleyrand declared as the last guest left. "Congratulations, *ma chère.*"

"On what?" she asked swiftly.

Her godfather's eyebrows rose. "On what do you think?"

Flustered, Gabrielle waved a vaguely dismissive hand. "I didn't mean to be obtuse. I'm rather tired."

"I imagine you might be." He examined her thoughtfully for a second. "You seemed to enjoy the company of Monsieur Lubienski."

The crafty old fox never missed anything! "Did I, *mon parrain?*" She met his shrewd gaze and sighed; there was no point in prevaricating with Talleyrand.

"You forget that I know how you are with your lovers, *mon enfant.*"

"Just two," she reminded him.

"More than enough for a woman who loves as hard as you, Gabrielle."

"Yes," she agreed with a subdued smile.

"You were not expecting him?" His glance was suddenly sharp.

"No." She shook her head helplessly. "I feel as if I'm in some dream world. I never expected to see him again."

"*D'accord.*" He kissed her cheek, and then stood back, holding her shoulders lightly.

"I won't insult either of you by recommending caution."

"No," she agreed.

The door closed on the Minister for Foreign Affairs, and Gabrielle gave a little involuntary skip of excitement. Nothing now lay between her and the rendezvous on the riverbank.

22

Nathaniel strode north along the riverbank away from the town. The air was fragrant with wild thyme, and a field of sunflowers hung their heavy golden heads, turned to the east, ready to greet the rising sun. The moon was a perfect circle in a black velvet sky, its reflection sailing over the dark waters of the river.

The silvery fronds of an ancient weeping willow on the bank hung to the water's edge. Nathaniel pushed through the veil of leaves and found what he sought—a perfect secluded bower where the grass was cool and fragrant, protected from the burning summer sun that during the day dried the ground to a crisp and shriveled the grass to brown spikes.

He spread his cloak on the grass at the base of the gnarled trunk and sat down to await Gabrielle, ears pricked for the rustle of hasty footsteps outside his bower.

Gabrielle let herself out of the house and ran straight into a soldier from the garrison patrolling the street outside. She'd somehow not taken into account the fact that the town would be crawling with guards, with two such precious personages asleep within its walls.

She identified herself and said she was going for a walk along the river. The soldier seemed nonplussed. Unescorted ladies didn't ordinarily take walks at three o'clock in the morning. Gabrielle subjected him to a haughty stare and demanded to know whether he wished to awaken the Minister for Foreign Affairs to verify her credentials? Or the emperor, perhaps?

The soldier coughed apologetically and bowed her on her way.

She sped along the riverbank, barely aware in her eagerness of the beauty of the night, the balmy air, the harvest moon.

She was in such a hurry, her eyes straining into the distance for some sign of Nathaniel, his shadow in the moonlight perhaps, that she didn't see a flat stone in her path and tripped, falling headlong with a vigorous expletive.

"Don't make such a noise!" Nathaniel sprang out of his willow cave a little way ahead as the shocked curses filled the quiet night. "Oh, dear, what are you doing down there?"

Gabrielle pushed herself onto her knees. "Don't laugh," she demanded crossly. "There's a great big boulder sticking up in the path. It has no right to be there."

"No, of course it doesn't," he said soothingly. "And you've just told it so in no uncertain terms. I'm sure it won't do it again."

Gabrielle grinned reluctantly and held up her hands. "Kick it for me, will you?"

He pulled her up, laughing. "I might stub my toe if it's as vicious as you say."

"Such chivalry!" She held him at arm's length, examining him with her crooked smile. "I suppose I'll become accustomed to the beard, and the silver hair is *très distingué.*"

"It's only temporary." He subjected her to his own assessing scrutiny. "You look well. But thinner."

"Pining will do that," she said, still smiling.

"Have you been?"

"Pining? Oh, yes."

"So have I."

They stood for a minute in silence, still holding themselves away from each other, almost as if they were afraid to move closer, as if the other would prove to be only the dream phantom of the long, lonely nights of the past two months.

Then Nathaniel said softly, "Come here." He pulled her in toward him and she came with playful reluctance. He pushed off the hood of her cloak and ran his hands through the silky dark red mane, drawing it forward over her shoulders.

"Whenever I've tried to remember the color of your hair, I haven't been able to," he mused, frowning as he stroked it. "It changes color according to the light. Here, for instance, under the moonlight, it's like a charcoal brazier, all glowing embers. But when we go under the trees, it'll be almost as dark as the night. And in the sunlight it flames so that sometimes it looks too hot to touch."

Gabrielle chuckled. "It goes with my temper, I'm afraid."

"So they say." He traced her mouth with his finger. "But yours is no worse than mine, and I've no hint of the devil's color in my hair."

"Nathaniel, I don't mean to be importunate, but how long must we continue this conversation," she said, the mock-plaintive tone doing little to disguise the husky throb in her voice. "We started something earlier, and I'd dearly like to finish it."

"Postponing gratification is good for the soul, they say," he murmured mischievously, trailing his finger along the curve of her cheek.

"To the devil with my soul," Gabrielle declared.

"My body is already on fire, so my soul might as well join it."

"In that case . . ." Taking her hand, he led her through the veiling fronds of the willow tree. "My parlor, madame. I trust you find it to your satisfaction."

"Quite frankly, I'd find the open road to my satisfaction at this point," she said, flinging off her cloak before slipping her arms around his neck, reaching against him.

"I am possessed with the most violent need, my love," she whispered, all teasing abruptly vanished beneath the urgency of her demand. Her hands ran over his back, remembering every curve, every muscular ripple, every knob of his spine. Her eyes closed and the scent of his skin and hair filled the air around her. She inhaled greedily, her lips parting as he kissed her, gently at first, as if he wanted to rediscover her taste and the wonderful feel of her mouth.

Her breasts pressed against his chest, and his hands moved to cup her bottom. The firm, rounded flesh was warm against his hands, and he realized with a shock of amusement and delight that she wore no underclothes beneath the fine muslin gown.

He drew back, taking a deep, steadying breath. "Wanton brigand," he said with soft satisfaction. Obeying the peremptory hand on her shoulder, she sank down on the cloak he'd spread earlier, her hands reaching for him impatiently.

He dropped to his knees beside her, and without preliminary drew her skirt up to her waist. Her tongue touched her lips as the cool night air laved her bared belly and thighs.

Her thighs parted for him as he unfastened his britches and pushed them off his hips. Her hips lifted to meet him as he lowered himself upon her. He entered her, penetrating to her very self in one deep thrust. It was the culmination of their passion on the terrace and the long, tantalizing hours of anticipation ever since. A rich liquid fullness spread through her loins, her inner muscles contracted around him, and she was instantly lost in an explosion of joy that sent her spinning into the star-filled night.

The piercing descant of a nightingale brought them back to an awareness of their surroundings. Nathaniel hitched himself on one elbow and smiled down at her transported countenance.

"I do believe I've just made love in my boots," he said with an exhausted chuckle. "I've never done that before."

Gabrielle was too spent to do more than stroke his face with a languid hand, brushing back the lock of hair that flopped damply onto his forehead.

Slowly, he caressed the length of her exposed thighs, his fingers playing in the curly tangle at the base of her belly, moving over the mound beneath, taking his time now that the desperate urgency of lust had been slaked.

"Don't do this," she pleaded weakly. "I am already dissolved."

"But I want to," he said simply. He placed his hand over the moist, pulsing warmth of her core and bent to kiss her belly, tickling his tongue into her navel. His breath whispered over the taut skin of her abdomen and his hand seared her.

"Please," she whispered, uncertain what she was asking for as, despite dissolution, she lifted and twisted on the cloak beneath the devastating power of his touch. And when his mouth replaced his hand, her little sobbing cries filled the dim green grotto beneath the willow as the rapturous tide swept her yet again into momentary oblivion.

"Cruel," she gasped when she could find breath. "When you knew I couldn't bear any more."

"But you did," he said, kneeling astride her again. "It's what happens to wanton brigands who roam the countryside at night without any underclothes."

Gabrielle's chuckle was more of a groan. "I thought they might get in the way."

"Such a hurry you were in," he reproved, tracing the curve of one breast beneath the muslin.

"That was your fault for starting something on the terrace and not finishing it," she retorted.

"I suppose I have an irrational desire to keep my head on my shoulders," he responded, flicking the dark smudge of her nipple until it rose against the bodice of her dress. "Even under the influence of near ungovernable lust."

"What are you doing with the Russians anyway? It seems madness." She tried to marshal her thoughts for a coherent conversation but sensed that the reprieve was going to be short-lived.

"Someone needs to eavesdrop on these negotiations," he told her blandly, transferring his attentions to the other breast. "And I have the best cover of anyone. It took a lot of work developing it, so whenever there's a particularly delicate job to be done among the Russians, I usually do it myself."

"But it's so dangerous." Her hand clasped his wrist, whether to stop his caresses or to encourage them, she didn't know. It didn't much matter anyway, since Nathaniel shook off her hold and continued regardless.

"Spying generally is," he reminded her evenly. "And what are you doing here?"

"Acting as my godfather's hostess," she said.

"And what else?" His hand ceased its delicate maneuvers and he grasped both her wrists strongly, his eyes seeming to run her through as he knelt over her.

"Let's have it in the open, Gabrielle. If you're involved in espionage, then we can have nothing more to do with each other after tonight. It should never have happened. I swore it never would again, but I seem to be in the grip of some madness when I'm with you."

His hold on her wrists tightened almost painfully and the glitter in his dark eyes intensified. "It won't happen again, Gabrielle. It can't. We say good-bye now."

"I'm not involved in anything," she said. "Talleyrand needs a hostess and I'm better at it than his wife."

"And Fouché?"

"This isn't his field of operations," she said. "His territory is internal not international diplomacy. That's my godfather's sphere. If Fouché's men are here, it's only as bodyguards."

Nathaniel looked down at her in frowning silence, still holding her wrists captive. He had no reason to doubt her . . . not this time. She smiled up at him, the gray eyes candid.

"Why would I lie to you?" she asked quietly. "I've had no part in spying since you left."

"Why not?"

"I couldn't seem to find the stomach for it," she said with utter truth.

His frowning scrutiny continued for minutes, then he nodded. "Very well."

His eyes were suddenly hooded, but she could read the resurgence of passion in them as she could feel him rising hard against her thigh.

She reached down to enclose him in her hand, her fingers fluttering in an erotic dance along the stem of flesh, sliding between his thighs to play a tune of yet deeper resonance before guiding him within the warm, welcoming portal.

This time, with the utmost delicacy Nathaniel held himself poised at the very edge of her body before sheathing himself slowly within the silken chamber. He knelt upright between her wide-spread thighs and stroked with firm rhythm, watching her face, watching for the moment when the charcoal eyes would deepen to ebony and a look of joyous wonder would cross the mobile features. He knew her so well, he thought, every facet of her body, every play of emotion, every response, and yet each lovemaking was a revelation, a glory of newness.

Gabrielle smiled up at him, and he knew she was sharing his thoughts, that she too found each experience unique in its wonder.

Slowly he withdrew, holding them both on the edge of delight. Expectation thrummed in her veins, and he could feel it in his own flesh buried deep within her.

"Gabrielle," he whispered, and took her with him into the inferno.

"How's Jake? I've been meaning to ask ever since I saw you, but something else always distracted me." She smiled indolently, her head resting in the crook of his shoulder. "How was he on the boat?" She plucked a succulent stem of grass from the base of the tree and sucked it with the same dreamy smile.

Nathaniel grimaced. "The only way I could get him aboard was to carry him bodily, kicking and screaming blue murder. If anyone had been around to hear, they'd have accused me of torturing the poor mite. Fortunately, it was a calm crossing, so he quietened down; I don't think he holds it against me," he added with a wry grin.

"And you left him at Burley Manor?" She tossed aside the chewed stem and plucked a fresh one.

"Yes, in the arms of an overjoyed Primmy and Nurse. The entire household was frantic. They thought he'd been abducted. Miles had called in the Bow Street Runners, and they were swarming all over the countryside."

"I can imagine," she said, adding casually, "is Primmy still there?"

Nathaniel pulled down a strand of foliage from their canopy and tickled her nose. "Yes, she's still there, Madame Interference. But so is Jeffrys."

"I suppose that's all right so long as he still has Primmy," she said, wrinkling her nose under the tickling leaves.

"Your qualified approval overwhelms me, ma'am." He released the frond, letting it spring back into the canopy, and dislodged her head from his shoulder. "It's time to make a move." He stood up and bent to catch her hands, hauling her to her feet.

"How are we to manage?" Gabrielle asked as she shook down her skirt. She was stunned with fulfillment, warm satiation flowing like honey in her veins, and yet the need to establish some plan of campaign before they parted couldn't be postponed.

Nathaniel picked up his cloak and shook it free of grass and leaves. "I want you to leave that up to me," he said, as calm and matter-of-fact as if they hadn't passed two transcendent hours under the moon.

"How?" She tossed her hair back over her shoulders, combing her fingers through the tangled ringlets. "Where are you staying?"

"In the town. Six Vilna Street. I have lodgings with a widow."

"Alone?"

"Yes." He picked up her discarded cloak and shook it out.

Gabrielle filed this information away for future reference. "How will we meet?"

"At every reception, dinner, and social engagement," he said, draping the cloak over her shoulders.

"I mean, how will we *meet*?" she said, fastening the clasp of the cloak.

"Ah ... is that what you meant? I didn't quite understand."

"Oh, don't tease!" Playfully she punched him in the ribs and he caught her wrist, clipping it behind her as he pulled her into his body, pushing up her chin with his free hand.

"I said, leave it to me."

"I'm to wait for you to tell me what to do?" The look in her eyes seemed to indicate that she didn't find the prospect particularly appealing.

"I may not tell you in so many words, but the message will be clear enough if you use your wits and watch me and listen to me very carefully whenever we're together."

He was quite serious now, and Gabrielle quashed the inclination to challenge his assumption of authority. It was his life on the line, after all.

"You must understand," he was saying in the same matter-of-fact tone, "that if I'm discovered at any point, then you too will be in danger if there's anything to connect us."

"You hardly need to tell me that," she said dryly.

"But do I have to tell you to be discreet?" He pulled up the hood of her cloak, tucking her hair away. "In public, there are to be no double entendres, none of your wicked looks, no indications at all—I mean *at all*, Gabrielle—that we have any interest in each other."

"What do you take me for?" she demanded.

"A reckless, wanton, lamentably undisciplined brigand," he said roundly. "Without a discreet bone in your body when it comes to games of passion."

Gabrielle grimaced, obliged to admit that she'd given him enough ammunition in the past to justify such an opinion. "I'll treat you with lofty disdain," she said. "Unless you'd prefer active dislike?"

"Ordinary civility will do fine," he said, circling her throat with his hands, his thumbs pushing up her chin.

"That's never been easy between us," she teased. "I'm not sure I'll be able to manage it."

"I'm serious, Gabrielle."

"Yes, I know you are."

He nodded and kissed her eyelids. "You'd better be on your way. It's already getting light."

"There's no law against taking a dawn stroll," she said. "Just as long as you don't stroll into town on my heels."

"I won't. Off you go now." He turned her with a pat and thrust her through the veil of leaves onto the path. "And be careful of lurking stones."

"Why can't we meet here again tonight?" She paused, squinting against the rosy ball of the rising sun.

"Maybe we can. It depends what the day brings. I'll tell you if we can."

"Very well, my lord." She laughed and blew him a kiss, then turned and walked away, a skip to her step despite the sleepless night.

Nathaniel waited in the willow grotto for over an hour before following her. He sat on the grass, leaning against the tree trunk, his eyes closed as he rested in a half-sleep that he knew would be as refreshing as several hours of deep sleep.

So Gabrielle had given up espionage. Was it for good?

He let the thought warm him as the sun's heat grew, filtering through the silvery fronds of the willow.

"The Comtesse de Beaucaire's a striking woman," observed Count Nicholas Tolstoy, letting his lorgnette fall and helping himself to a dainty oyster barquette from the tray proffered by a footman.

"Indeed," Nathaniel agreed somewhat indifferently. "Although I confess I find Princess Kirov more to my taste."

"Oh, do you like fluffy blondes?" the count said. "I prefer a little spice to my meat." He laughed with a hearty masculine complacence that grated on Nathaniel's nerves.

"I understand you have the task of inquiring after Napoleon's health every morning," he commented, changing the subject.

"Oh, yes. The czar is most anxious to know that his dear friend and ally has passed a restful night," Tolstoy said. "Just as General Duroc trots up to our door on the same errand from Napoleon at nine o'clock every morning."

"How touching," Nathaniel said dryly, and the count laughed.

"Good evening, gentlemen. Did you enjoy the ride this morning?" Gabrielle glided across the salon toward them. Her gown of dove-gray Italian gauze flowed around her, hinting at the length of leg beneath, the soft curve of her hips.

"More than the King of Prussia, madame," Count Tolstoy said with an ironic smile.

"Yes, poor man." Gabrielle looked across the room to where the unhappy Frederick William of Prussia stood on the outskirts of the group centered on the two emperors. "Napoleon was making fun of his uniform this morning. He asked him how he managed to button so many buttons on his tunic."

"He shouldn't have come," Nathaniel said. "He knows Napoleon despises him and he was simply setting himself up for further humiliation."

"That's harsh, my friend," Tolstoy remonstrated. "It's only natural that he'd hope for some concessions for Prussia out of these negotiations."

"A fond and foolish hope," Nathaniel declared. "And his pathetic wife, trying to flirt with Napoleon as if her womanly charms could soften him."

"She's very lovely," Gabrielle said. "But it's true that the emperor's impervious to her charms. He was cruel at dinner. He wanted to know why she was wearing a turban. He said it couldn't be in homage to Alexander, since the Russians were at war with Turkey. She didn't know where to look or how to reply."

"Perhaps I'll go and comfort her," Tolstoy said with a smile. "I am far from impervious to her flirtatious ways, so if you'll excuse me, comtesse." He bowed and strolled off toward the disconsolate Queen Louise.

"You have sharp ears, madame," Nathaniel observed coolly, his eyes darting around the salon to see if they were being observed with any unusual interest.

"And sharp appetites," she whispered, her tongue touching her lips, her eyes glowing. She took a step closer and he could feel the warmth of her thigh beneath the gauze of her gown.

"Careful," he warned, smiling at an acquaintance who was trying to catch his eye. "May I procure you a glass of champagne, comtesse?"

"Thank you, monsieur." She took his proffered arm and they walked casually toward the supper room. "My godfather is of the opinion that Alexander's negotiators haven't a brain between them," she said in a normal voice.

Nathaniel inclined his head courteously toward her. "Is that so, comtesse."

She smiled. "It seems to be the received opinion, sir."

"By all but Alexander and his negotiators," Nathaniel agreed blandly. "I imagine your godfather's running rings around Prince Lobanov and Prince Kurakin at the treaty table."

"He runs rings around most people," she responded with a touch of asperity.

She bowed and smiled to Madame Duroc and paused to exchange pleasantries, casually introducing Nathaniel. "Monsieur Lubienski has kindly offered to procure me a glass of champagne."

"Perhaps I may fetch something for you also, Madame Duroc."

"Why, thank you, monsieur, a glass of negus, if you please. Now, tell me, Gabrielle, what is your opinion of poor Queen Louise." The general's wife took Gabrielle's arm and drew her aside.

Nathaniel went to fetch the required refreshment,

somewhat amused by Gabrielle's comments. He knew now how fond she was of her godfather, but she was very clear-sighted when it came to her assessment of his ambition and his scheming.

He returned with the two glasses. "It seems too mild a night for negus, Madame Duroc." Smiling, he handed her the glass of warm spiced wine. "More a night for strolling under the moon."

"A glass of negus makes me nice and sleepy," Madame Duroc said. "And at my age, a good night's sleep is infinitely more valuable than a stroll under the moon."

"Oh, but I find a walk before bed has the same effect," Gabrielle said. "Particularly after an evening spent in an airless, crowded room. It's so hot in here, it gives me the headache in no time."

"We all have our own remedies," Nathaniel said pleasantly. He bowed and excused himself, sauntering into the card room, confident that Gabrielle would appear under the willow tree later that night.

23

Gabrielle was dressing for a ball at the Prussian residence the next evening, when her godfather knocked and entered her apartment. He had just returned from the day's negotiations and had not yet changed into evening dress.

"Leave us," he ordered the maid, who, looking startled, dropped a curtsy and departed.

Talleyrand closed the door and regarded Gabrielle gravely for a minute. Then he spoke. "What I am going to tell you now will have the most far-reaching effect on the outcome of this war. It's vital that the English government should hear it without delay. It's providential that Lord Praed is here. He will understand the importance of the information immediately and will know how to convey it to the right ears with all due speed."

Gabrielle had turned on her dressing stool at his entrance, and now stared at him, uncomprehending, her fingers stilled in the act of screwing a diamond drop in her earlobe.

"There are certain secret articles to be appended to the treaty," Talleyrand said, taking a pinch of snuff. "Listen to me very carefully."

In stunned silence Gabrielle listened, and when he'd finished said, "I don't understand what you want of me." But she did understand.

"You will inform Lord Praed of the details of the secret articles," her godfather stated.

Gabrielle shook her head. "No ... no, I can't do that. I am no longer a spy."

"I am not asking you to spy on the English spymaster," Talleyrand said patiently. "I am asking you to give him some information that his government will find invaluable. I am asking you to spy *for* him, not against him."

Gabrielle closed her eyes as she saw the inexorable logic of her godfather's thought processes.

"Why do you not simply tell him yourself?"

"Don't be naive, Gabrielle. If the English knew that I was plotting against Napoleon, there's no telling what they'd do with the information. They could discredit me with the emperor with the merest hint. I am not particularly popular with the English, *ma chère*." His smile was mildly sardonic. "And I am a great deal more useful to everyone if I remain in the emperor's confidence."

"I have done with this dirty business, *mon parrain*," she said slowly. "You know that. I've told Nathaniel I'll play no further part in espionage."

"This is a different kind of espionage," Talleyrand pointed out with the same patience. "You will give your lover this information as a gift."

"And how would I explain betraying my country?"

"People have been known to switch loyalties for deeply personal reasons," he observed mildly. "You will not be harming your lover, *ma chère*, you will be doing him the greatest service."

"But I will be deceiving him," she said wretchedly.

"For the good of France, of England, of the whole of Europe," he said, and there was a ringing conviction in his tone. "This time I'm not asking you to be a dou-

ble agent. I want no information from you. I have no
interest in hearing English secrets. I simply want you to
tell Lord Praed something that he and his government
desperately need to know.

Gabrielle stared at the diamond drop in her hand
without seeing it. She felt as if she were teetering on
the brink of a snake pit.

"How will you feel, Gabrielle, if you withhold this
vital information from Lord Praed? It will bring him
only credit and advancement and the deepest professional satisfaction. Do you have the right to deny him
those opportunities?"

She looked up at him then, her expression bleak.
"You are an arch manipulator, sir."

Talleyrand's countenance was impassive. "I am a
statesman, a tactician, a diplomat, Gabrielle. If that
also makes me a manipulator, then so be it. I believe in
the stability and peace of Europe. That will not be
achieved without Napoleon's downfall. If you don't
share my goals, then there is nothing more to be said."

An end to war, Gabrielle thought, a war that had
been fought almost continuously for the last fifteen
years. An end to the killing. She knew her godfather
was right, just as she knew the depths of his convictions. He was a manipulator, a man with few personal
ethics, a man of deep and abiding ambition. But he was
passionately loyal to his country and, like most men
born and educated in the last century, he understood
the need for a balanced Europe. Without a balance of
power, chaos would reign, as indeed it now did.

"How am I to explain how I came across such information?"

Talleyrand showed no indication of his satisfaction
at her tacit acceptance. He stroked his chin. "It is a difficulty, I admit. I would hardly tell you such a thing in
conversation, or leave a paper lying around with the articles described. I believe you must have overheard my
discussion with Duroc and the emperor."

"How?"

He frowned, considering. "As we were leaving the emperor's ceremonial gathering this afternoon, I remembered that I'd left my cane in one of the parlors. Like a considerate goddaughter, you offered to fetch it for me. When you brought it back, the corridor where you'd left me was deserted, all the other guests departed, servants about their business elsewhere. Then you heard my voice from one of the window embrasures in the long drawing room. Not thinking anything of it, you came forward with the cane and then heard something that gave you pause. You listened, because you're trained to do so, and you heard a great deal more than you bargained for. When you thought you'd heard enough, you retreated to the corridor, and then reentered the drawing room noisily, calling my name."

He looked across at her and nodded. "That will serve, I believe."

Gabrielle nibbled her lip. "I suppose so, but will he accept that I've changed my allegiance so suddenly?"

"It will be for you to convince him," he said somberly. "He is your lover—that's compelling enough reason for many people. And he will also understand that working for Napoleon's downfall is not necessarily the act of a traitor to France. The man is no fool."

"No," Gabrielle agreed. "Nathaniel's no fool."

"Then I'll leave you to make your own plans." He walked to the door. "But don't delay, Gabrielle. It's vital the information reaches London as fast as humanly possible."

"I understand. Do you have today's password for the Russian zone?"

Talleyrand gave it to her without so much as a questioning eyebrow. "I'll send your maid back."

The maid bustled in immediately. "Your gown, ma'am. Are you ready for it?" She held up a delicate gown of cream crepe de chine. "Or do you wish to finish your coiffure first?"

"Help me with these feathers first." Feathers were de rigueur for formal attendance at court, even if the court was only that of the ignored and despised king and queen of Prussia.

Annette picked up one of the three black ostrich feathers and carefully inserted it into Gabrielle's high-piled hair, fixing it in place with a diamond-headed hairpin. The other two were as reverently placed, and Gabrielle examined her reflection with a critical frown before nodding her satisfaction.

She shrugged out of her tiring robe and stepped into the dress, turning to allow Annette to fasten the hooks at the back.

"Oh, you look lovely, madame," Annette breathed. "Those black feathers against your hair, and then the dress . . . so delicate."

"Thank you, Annette." Gabrielle smiled briefly at the wide-eyed girl. "And there's no need to wait up for me." She drew on her long silk gloves, easing them over her fingers, smoothing out wrinkles. She was doing everything with a curious detachment, a careful deliberation, as if the body she touched, the possessions she handled, were nothing to do with her at all.

Her skin was cold and clammy, as if she'd walked through a cold mist as she went downstairs. She knew exactly how she was going to approach Nathaniel—in a manner that would sweep all questions and objections from his mind, that would add overwhelming credence to the gift of love brought by a lover. She had never had to feign passion with him, but she wondered with chill apprehension whether she would have to this time . . . and if so, would he be able to tell?

She directed the coachman to Vilna Street. As they crossed into the Russian zone, the hussar at the guard post stepped forward, hand raised. "Password?"

Gabrielle leaned out of the window. "Alexander, Russia, greatness."

The soldier saluted and waved them through. Each

day the password was chosen alternately by Napoleon and by Alexander. Today it had been Napoleon's choice. A nice piece of flattery that Alexander would emulate tomorrow.

She sat back in the darkness, drumming her fingers on the velvet squabs. She felt sick. She was doing what had to be done, but it didn't seem to help. It was only a technical deception, but it didn't seem to matter how many times she told herself that. She had told Nathaniel she was not engaged in any form of espionage, and now that was a lie. She couldn't betray her godfather's plot without endangering his life. So she must writhe on the horns of her dilemma.

She jumped from the coach as it came to a halt before the house on Vilna Street. Two officers in the green tunics of the Preobrazhensky regiment were walking down the street, deep in conversation. They stopped and stared at the woman emerging from the carriage. This part of the Russian zone was occupied only by single officers and less important aides. The married quarters and the apartments of the senior members of the czar's entourage were close to the royal residence. A lone woman on this street could mean only one thing—an assignation.

Gabrielle became aware of their stares. She turned and stared them down, her chin lifted, haughty arrogance in every line of her body.

They took in her evening dress, the glitter of diamonds, and nonplussed, they both bowed. Gabrielle didn't acknowledge the salute. She turned her back and walked up to the door of number six, banging on the knocker.

The woman who came to the door stared in as much astonishment as the two officers had. "Madame?"

"Monsieur Lubienski, please," Gabrielle said with the haughtiness of before.

Intimidated by the brilliance of her dress and the

arrogant glitter in the dark eyes, the woman backed into the hall, giving Gabrielle room to step inside.

The hall was small and sparsely furnished. A flight of wooden stairs led upward. There was a smell of boiling cabbage in the air. "Upstairs," the landlady said. "Second door on the left, madame."

"Thank you." Gabrielle went swiftly up the stairs, her step light. At the second door she raised her hand to knock, then changed her mind. Boldly, she lifted the latch and pushed open the door onto a narrow room furnished with a single cot, a plain dresser, and a massive oak table beneath a small, high window.

Nathaniel was in the process of dressing for the evening. He spun away from the spotted mirror as the door flew open. Gabrielle stood there. Energy seemed to pulse from her, creating a sparking halo around the dark red hair; the dark eyes had an almost febrile glitter, her lips were parted, the faintest flush glowed beneath the habitual translucent pallor.

"What the *hell* are you doing?" he said with a surge of anger.

"Fraternizing with the enemy," she said with one of her crooked, wicked smiles.

"By God, Gabrielle, you have done this just once too often. I told you I would not tolerate indiscretion—"

"I *had* to come," she said. "No one knows who I am. I sent the carriage away and told it to come back in an hour." She stepped toward him, pushing the door shut behind her.

She was an image of glinting diamonds, smooth, undulating cream silk, black feathers flowing in startling contrast to the vibrant hair massed on top of her head.

"I want you," she stated, coming toward him across the plain, unvarnished floorboards, her hands outstretched. "I wanted you with such an overpowering hunger that I had to come."

She seized his hands, pulling herself forward against him. A smile hovered on her lips, and the febrile glitter in her eyes intensified.

He could feel the power of her sensuality emanating in waves, lapping him, enclosing him. And he was lost as he always was when she came to him in this way.

She laughed softly, reading his capitulation, clipping her bottom lip with her teeth, moving her lower body against his loins with an urgent sinuous pressure that set his blood on fire.

"Now," she said. "I want you *now*, Nathaniel."

Catching her around the waist, he lifted her onto the table beneath the window. His hands circled her throat, covering the emerald collar, and he brought his mouth to hers. Her lips parted in eager response, her tongue fencing with his, her breasts pressing against his chest as she leaned into him.

Slowly he bent her body backward with the pressure of his own until she lay stretched out on the cool, hard surface of the table, her mouth still joined with his, her hands on his shoulders.

He reached beneath her skirt. At the brushing touch of his fingers, she leaped beneath him, and he knew it would take but a whispering breath to carry her over the edge of bliss.

Why? he wondered. Why this desperate passion tonight? But the questions were fleeting as his own body responded to Gabrielle's urgency.

He drew back long enough to pull down her lacy undergarment, to release his own body from confinement.

Gabrielle's eyes held his, and they were filled with the wonder of anticipation.

He gathered her against him, crushing her to him as the turbulence raged around them, swallowed them, then receded, leaving them stranded on the sands of fulfillment.

Nathaniel let her fall back on the table and slowly straightened, his breathing ragged, his head whirling. Gabrielle lay unmoving in an abandoned sprawl, her rich skirts rucked up around her waist, long, bare thighs gleaming pale against the dark wood beneath her, diamonds glittering in the lamplight, the dark red hair tumbling loose, the black feathers escaping from the securing pins.

She looked like some wildly exotic bird come to rest after a long and exhausting flight. Leaning over, he stroked the curve of her cheek with one finger. "Come back, sweetheart."

Her eyelashes fluttered and her eyes opened. She looked up at him, her expression dazed, then she smiled. "I think I just died again."

"You were possessed by some madness," he said, taking her hands and pulling her into a sitting position. "How dare you come here, Gabrielle." But there was little force behind the statement. Shaking his head, he pulled up his britches. "Do you have any idea how you've compromised us both?"

Gabrielle struggled to regain her senses after that explosion of sexuality. How could she ever have been afraid she might have to feign a response?

"Nonsense," she said after a minute. "This kind of thing is going on all over Tilsit. People are crisscrossing the town, hopping from bed to bed—"

"How do you know that?"

"I heard," she said loftily.

Nathaniel examined her with a puzzled frown. She seemed completely unaware of her semi-nakedness, and the contrast of that dishevelment with her elaborate dress and those priceless diamonds. "Just what, in the name of goodness, brought that on so suddenly? Or don't you know?"

"I've brought you a present," she said. "You might find it strange . . . but—"

"I don't think I can concentrate until you tidy

yourself up." Nathaniel picked up her discarded drawers and slipped them over her feet, then he lifted her off the desk and pulled them up over her hips. "Straighten your skirt."

Gabrielle shook down the crumpled silk and put her hands to her head, where unruly ringlets escaped in a cloud. She plucked out the feathers and tossed them onto the table, then released her hair from its pins and shook it free to her shoulders, combing her fingers through the tangles. The routine process calmed her and gave her time to collect her thoughts.

"Any better?"

"Some," he said. "I think the problem really lay with the feathers. They were more than a little incongruous." He picked one up and ran it through his fingers. "You're going to need the attentions of your maid again before you go to the Prussian residence."

"I don't think I'm going," Gabrielle said. "Do you have a glass of wine?"

"I managed to persuade Tolstoy to part with some of his precious supply of port." Nathaniel opened a cupboard in the dresser and took out a bottle and two thick, rather dusty glasses. "This place lacks for amenities, I'm afraid." He wiped the glasses with his handkerchief before filling them.

"The bed's a little small," Gabrielle observed, taking the glass from him.

"But the table compensates," he observed with a half-smile. A tumult of speculation was going on behind his eyes, but there was no indication on his face. What strange gift lay behind this wild visit? Gabrielle was deeply disturbed, and by a lot more than the exigencies of lust.

"So?" he prompted. "Where's my strange present?"

Gabrielle sipped her port and then said, "It's a gift of information."

A great stillness entered Nathaniel, but his eyes remained calmly on her face.

"There are some secret articles to be appended to the treaty. One of them commits Alexander to mediate a peace between England and France. If the English refuse, then Russia will declare war on England and join France and her allies in the Continental Blockade, bringing Denmark and Sweden with her."

Nathaniel said nothing for a long time. Napoleon had forced all the nations subjected to France to join a naval blockade designed to starve England into submission. Her prosperity, indeed her lifeblood, depended on overseas trade. With all the ports of Europe closed to her, she would be unable to trade, and the nation of shopkeepers, as Napoleon referred to them, would be brought to their knees. The blockade was already biting deeply into the nation's economic foundation, but while Russia was at war with France, the Baltic ports had remained open to English commercial shipping. If the Scandinavian nations in hegemony to Russia were forced to join the blockade, then they could close off the Baltic and there would be no outlets for British trade. She would indeed starve to death.

Nathaniel also knew that no amount of Russian mediation would convince the English government to make peace with Napoleon, so war with Russia and the closing of the Baltic ports was inevitable under the terms of the secret articles.

Gabrielle had just given him a piece of information of such outstanding value that for a minute he couldn't fully comprehend its consequences.

"Why would you tell me this?" he asked finally.

"It's a gift, I told you." She twisted the stem of her wineglass. "A lover's gift."

"You would betray your own country?"

She shook her head. "I told you once I didn't believe Napoleon was good for France."

"But you spied for France." It was a flat reminder.

"I spied with my lover for France. Now I give you the lover's gift of a piece of priceless information." Was he believing her? He should; it was only the truth. She didn't want to look at him, to read his expression, but she forced herself to do so.

So the lover *had* also been a spy. He'd wondered about that in the brothel in Paris. Knowing Gabrielle as he did, it seemed inevitable that she would have embraced every aspect of her lover's life.

Nathaniel leaned back against the table, his glass in his hand, his eyes resting unwaveringly on her face. "A gift of love?" he asked.

"I love you," she said simply. "I know now that I can't endure to be separated from you. And I can't be with you when we're on opposite sides in this war. I've always been torn between two allegiances. Now I have chosen."

Nathaniel drew a deep shuddering breath. The power of that simple declaration shook him to his core, and for the moment he was unable to absorb it, to see how it affected them both. "How did you discover this?" he asked as if she hadn't said what she'd said.

Gabrielle gave him her explanation.

"You're very fond of your godfather," Nathaniel probed, still unable to accept the simplicity of her declaration. "Why would you choose to betray him?"

"I don't believe this does," Gabrielle replied steadily. She wondered absently if Nathaniel had heard what she'd said. He wasn't reacting to it in any way.

She kept her voice calm and matter-of-fact as she offered an explanation as close to the truth as she could get without revealing Talleyrand's true goals. "He too believes in a strong, united Europe. I have no idea what deep plans he has, except that he's not in favor of an alliance between Russia and France. He's attempting to circumvent the Russian negotiators—I know that for a fact—and from what I do know of Talleyrand, I'd lay any odds that he's no more in favor of the secret articles than England would be."

Gabrielle's reasoning was devious, but from what

Nathaniel knew of Talleyrand's reputation and ambitions, it was sound. Whatever reasons she had had for bringing him this information, the information itself was pure gold and only a fool would debate its authenticity. From his own observations during this meeting of the two emperors, it was clear that Alexander was willing to court Napoleon as assiduously now as he'd been prepared to fight him before.

"I must leave for England immediately." He pushed himself away from the table.

"Now?"

"By dawn."

"I'm coming with you."

"Don't be absurd." He dismissed her statement with a brusque gesture.

"I told you I loved you," Gabrielle said quietly. "Will you give me nothing in return?"

Nathaniel looked at her in silence, allowing her declaration to replay in his head. When he spoke, his voice was unusually hesitant, as if he was feeling for words. "It's a gift so precious that I don't know if my own love is sufficient return," he said. "I don't have your generosity of spirit, Gabrielle, and I'm afraid, terrified, that I'll hurt you in some way."

Gabrielle shook her head. "You won't," she said. "You didn't hurt Helen."

"I was responsible for her death," he said bleakly. "I didn't think about her, I thought only of my own needs, and those needs killed her. I don't feel entitled to another chance at that happiness."

"But that's silly," she said, reaching for his hands, holding them tightly. "You can't pay forever for one mistake. I'm not afraid you'll hurt me."

When he said nothing, merely let his hands lie in hers, she said, "Do you love me, Nathaniel?"

"Oh, yes," he said softly.

"Then I see no difficulty." She smiled her crooked smile.

"Let me deal with this information first," he said, drawing her tightly against him. "I have to go to England at once and I can't give *us* the attention I must. I'm overwhelmed. It's something I want more than anything, but I can't get my mind around it. You have to give me time."

Gabrielle heard the sincerity behind the plea, and she knew she could push him no further. "Very well." She kissed him lightly. "I understand . . . I think." She moved away from him, and he stood still, his hands hanging at his sides as if he'd just dropped something.

Gabrielle picked up her feathers. "How do you intend to travel?" she asked cheerfully.

Some of the intensity left Nathaniel's face at this ordinary, matter-of-fact question and her easy tone. "Ride to Silute and take ship from there to Copenhagen, if possible. The sea is safer than the land, and generally quicker."

"Then I'll wish you godspeed."

He ran his hands through his hair in a gesture of frustration. "This isn't right, Gabrielle, but I don't know what else to do. Will you come to England?"

"Yes, of course," she said. "Very soon."

She blew him a kiss and left him, closing the door quietly behind her.

24

Silute, on the mouth of the Neimen where it opened into the Baltic Sea. A few hours ride. Nathaniel intended to leave by dawn; presumably it would take him until then to make his preparations, construct appropriate reasons and farewells. He wouldn't want to destroy such a useful cover by acting in haste. She, on the other hand, could be away within the hour.

Gabrielle sat impatiently on the edge of her seat as the carriage took her back into the French zone and home.

Talleyrand had already left for the Prussian ball, so she scrawled him a note explaining what she'd done and what she intended to do. She put the note on the desk in his study and then rummaged through the pigeonholes until she found the imperial seal that Talleyrand used for all his official documents. She wrote herself a suitably officious set of instructions, folded the document, and sealed it with the imperial eagle. It could well prove a useful passport or protection as she journeyed through Napoleonic Europe.

It took her a few minutes to change into her britches and throw a few necessities into a cloak bag.

She dropped her pistol into the deep pocket of her cloak. A leather purse with a substantial sum of money went inside her shirt, close to her skin. Brigandage was rife among the disaffected population in the small towns of invaded Prussia.

She slipped quietly out of the house and round to the stables, where a sleepy lad saddled her horse. He was Prussian, a native of Tilsit, and regarded Gabrielle in her strange costume with scant interest.

It was still an hour to dawn when she left the town and turned her horse toward the sea, following the river to its mouth.

As dawn broke, the hamlets and villages she passed came to life, women opening doors, shooing out dogs, plying brooms. Children ran with buckets to the river and men appeared in the fields, anxious to start work before the blistering heat took hold.

No one took any notice of the black-clad rider. Prussia was an occupied land, and the peasantry plodded about their daily business, hoping only to be spared a ravaging column of French infantry who would pick them clean, chop down their woods for their own braziers, and trample the fields so that they were fit for nothing but to lie fallow for several years. If a lone rider offered no threat, then he could pass among them without hindrance.

The second rider, following an hour on the heels of the first, engendered the same lack of interest.

Gabrielle rode into Silute just before noon. Away from the open countryside, the atmosphere was different. The narrow, muddy streets were smothered in refuse that steamed and stank in the broiling heat. The houses were cramped and dark, the people pinched and scrawny, generally barefoot and clad in grimy rags.

Here a stranger riding a piece of prime horseflesh drew immediate and unwelcome attention.

Gabrielle rode straight to the small harbor, where fishing boats and several larger vessels were docked, waiting for the tide to turn. The smell of rotting fish seemed an almost palpable miasma on the hot, still air. She examined the assorted fleet critically, looking for one large enough to make a sea crossing.

A group of men surged out of a tavern and came toward her. They were silent except for the sound of their heavy clogs on the cobbles of the quay.

Gabrielle's heart thumped, and she reached inside her pocket for her pistol, backing her horse against the water's edge so that she wouldn't be surrounded.

They formed a half circle and examined her in the same menacing silence. One of them put out a hand and touched the fine embossed leather of her bridle. He looked up and grinned, his teeth blackened stumps. Money, she decided, would incite rather than appease. Her pistol would probably do the same. She couldn't deal with six men with one shot, and there'd be no time to reload.

Slowly, she withdrew from her pocket the one talisman that in occupied Europe spoke louder than anything else. It was the document with the Napoleonic eagle. She held it up and the group fell back. One of them spat on the quaystones, but the danger was over. It was more than their lives were worth to interfere with an imperial courier.

Taking advantage of her ascendancy, Gabrielle asked in her halting Prussian if they knew of a vessel bound for Copenhagen. She had the emperor's message to deliver. Silver now glittered on her palm as she waited.

There was a guttural, staccato exchange, and then one of them gestured toward a small frigate anchored in the bay. A second coin on her palm produced the information that the master was to be found in the tavern. A third produced the master himself, a Dane, who, to Gabrielle's relief, spoke French.

He held a tankard of ale as he listened to her request for passage for two and named an extortionate sum, one eye disconcertingly squinting to the right while the other looked straight at her.

Gabrielle frowned, then said that for that price she'd expect him to accommodate their horses.

The master hesitated, examining Gabrielle's mount with his straight eye, then he drained the contents of his tankard and nodded. "High tide's at three. Ferry'll be at the quay at two. If you're not here, we go anyway." He returned to the tavern without a backward glance.

That left an hour and a half to kill and hopefully sufficient time to bring Nathaniel. Gabrielle was hungry and thirsty but didn't dare risk leaving her horse anywhere in this den of thieves while she went in search of sustenance. She wondered where best to await Nathaniel's arrival and decided to position herself at the end of the quay, facing the alley he'd have to use to reach the harbor. She decided it was not pointful to consider what she would do if he didn't arrive before the surly Dane's ferry left the quay, just as it was not pointful to anticipate his reaction to her presence. The man needed a serious push, and he was going to get one.

Nathaniel rode into the reeking town just after half past one. He was instantly aware of the eyes on him as he guided his horse through the narrow, ordure-ridden lanes toward the waterfront. Hollow-eyed children gazed from doorways at the well-dressed stranger on his glossy stallion. Men lounging against walls in the shade picked their teeth and spat as he rode past.

As he turned down a particularly dark, narrow lane, where a slice of water and a change in the quality of the light at the end indicated the quay, a stone flew through the air and thudded against his shoulder. He swore and turned his head. A group of men advanced on him from behind, cudgels and rocks in their hands. Another stone hit his horse's neck, and the animal squealed and reared.

Suddenly there were men all around him, emerging from passageways so narrow, they were barely wide enough for a man's shoulders, moving out of shadowed doorways, all bearing staves and knives.

It was, Nathaniel thought, about the ugliest mob he'd ever encountered, and he was its sole target.

His pistol was in one hand while the other loosened the cane he carried attached to his saddle; his eyes never left the gathering rabble. He pressed a catch in the handle of the cane, and a wicked blade sprang forth. Another stone flew, catching him full in the chest, almost winding him.

He fired his pistol straight into the line of men in front of him. A man went down with a scream, and for a second the line faltered. He put spur to his horse and charged through them, bending low over the saddle as he slashed with his sword. For a moment he thought he was through, and then his horse caught a hoof on an uneven cobble and as the animal struggled to regain his balance, a knife plunged into his neck, severing the carotid artery. Blood leaped in a pulsing fountain as the horse died instantly. Nathaniel flung himself sideways off the saddle before the animal rolled on him, and spun on the balls of his feet, his sword slicing through the mosaic of grim faces bearing down upon him. On his feet and with no time to reload his pistol, he hadn't a chance against such a number.

It seemed ironical that after a career of circumventing danger and treachery for the highest stakes he should meet his death in a squalid alley in a reeking port in Eastern Prussia at the hands of a starving mob.

And then he heard the sound of a pistol shot and a wild cry of fury. A horse plunged through the mob, rearing, caracoling, hooves flailing, forcing men to fall back or be trampled. There was a moment when he saw clearly through the bodies surrounding him to the glitter of water at the end of the alley. He flung himself toward the gap before it closed, and Gabrielle leaned low over her saddle, holding out her hand. He grabbed it and sprang upward with the same acrobatic agility he'd shown when he'd leaped into the rafters in the attic in Paris.

And then they were out in the sunlight of the quay and the milling horde was left behind with a dead horse, leather harness, and Nathaniel's portmanteau as prize.

Gabrielle rode her horse straight onto the flat-bottomed ferry waiting at the quayside. The Danish master of the good ship *Kattegat* was already on the ferry, supervising the loading of supplies. He glanced at the horse and its two riders and then came over to Gabrielle.

"Two horses, you said."

"Yes, but now there's only one."

"Same price," he declared, squinting ferociously.

"*D'accord*," she replied with an impatient shrug, swinging off her mount. "I'll tether him to the rail."

Nathaniel said nothing. What he had to say couldn't be said on an open deck. Gabrielle had simply followed her own impulses as she always did, and he wondered vaguely why he hadn't expected this. She'd accepted his refusal in Tilsit with too much docility, and he should have been warned. Then he noticed that blood was dripping from her arm, leaving a sticky trail across the bottom of the ferry. Presumably, as she'd plunged into the fray, one of his assailant's knives had nicked her arm.

He pulled off his cravat. "You're bleeding all over the place. Let me bind it for the moment and I'll look at it properly when we get where we're going." He fastened the cravat tightly around the gash. "Just where are we going?"

"Copenhagen," she said with a weary sigh. "That vessel in the middle of the bay . . . the *Kattegat*."

Nathaniel sank down on the bottom of the ferry, propping his back against the rail, and lifted his face to the sun. A slight breeze offered some relief from the scorching heat and carried away some of the noxious stench of Silute. Gabrielle tethered her horse and came and sat down beside him.

She wasn't fool enough to believe that Nathaniel's present silence meant that he had nothing to say. The storm would break when he was good and ready, so she kept her own counsel until then.

Rowers pulled the ferry across the short stretch of water to the *Kattegat*. Gabrielle followed the master up a swinging rope ladder, Nathaniel on her heels.

"We'll manage the horse," the master said. "There's a cabin to starboard for you two . . . uh—" His straight eye rested on Gabrielle in open speculation, running down her figure. Her cloak was thrown back from her shoulders, and the britches and shirt offered little concealment to the rich curves of her tall body. "Gentlemen . . ." he added with something suspiciously like a leer.

Gabrielle kept her expression haughtily impassive, and Nathaniel stared out to sea, apparently stone deaf.

The master shrugged. "Not that it's any of my business. You pay your passage and I ask no questions." He held out his hand. "Forty livres, I believe was agreed upon."

Nathaniel's breath whistled through his teeth, but Gabrielle calmly withdrew the pouch from inside her shirt and shook out the required sum into the master's open hand. "I believe you'll find that to be correct. Be careful with my horse."

The master solemnly counted the coins, then turned and shouted orders to his seamen. Within half an hour Gabrielle's terrified horse had been hoisted aboard in a canvas sling and securely tethered in the stern of the boat.

Only then did Nathaniel speak. "Come below." It was a sharp command.

Gabrielle followed him down the companionway

and into a small, sparsely furnished but clean cabin with a small porthole and two bunks set into the bulwark.

Nathaniel closed the door with a controlled slam and stood with his shoulders against it, regarding Gabrielle in fulminating silence. "Dear God," he exclaimed at last, "you ought to be beaten, Gabrielle!"

"Well, that's a fine thing to say, when I've just saved your skin," she retorted. "And for the second time too."

"I wonder why it is that my skin needs saving only when you're around," he declared dourly.

"Oh, that is so unjust," she protested. "It has nothing to do with me, and you know it."

He did, but was not yet ready to admit to anything. "I forbade you absolutely to come with me."

"Did you?" She glanced around the cabin with an air of interest. "Which bunk do you want?"

He ignored this. "Just what story did you spin to explain leaving your godfather?"

"The truth," she said, smiling blandly.

"*What!*"

"My godfather has infinite tolerance for the weaknesses of the flesh," she told him in perfect truth. "I told him I wished to pursue a liaison with Benedict Lubienski. I told him we were intending to spend some private time in Danzig, and I would decide where I would go next when we had satisfied each other."

Nathaniel stared at her. It was so damnably reasonable. She was no ingenue. She was a widow who'd had lovers in the past. Talleyrand was a man of the world. Napoleon had his Marie Walewska. Josephine wrote to him daily with endless protestations of jealousy. Talleyrand had innumerable liaisons. There was absolutely no reason why such a story shouldn't be believed . . . particularly when it bore the mark of truth.

"So I rode out ahead of you," she continued into his stupefied silence. "And arranged passage to Copenhagen on this ship. And then I assume we'll be able to get passage on an English commercial vessel to London, don't you think?"

She had simply put his own plan into operation. Simply and most efficiently.

"Come here and let me take a proper look at that gash on your arm," he said.

"Oh, it's all right ... it's just a flesh wound," she responded cheerfully, recognizing his tacit acceptance and agreement in this oblique change of subject and perfectly prepared to settle for just that.

"I said *come here!*" Nathaniel bellowed, his temper finally loosened from the reins.

Gabrielle crossed the small space in two hasty steps. "There's no need to shout at me like that."

"I don't seem to have any other way of expressing my frustration," he gritted, unwrapping the cravat from her arm.

"I love you," Gabrielle said calmly. "And I've made my choice, and I'm afraid you're stuck with me. I'm quite happy to wait while you become accustomed to the idea, but I'm afraid you'll have to get used to it in my company. Because where you go, I go."

Nathaniel observed judiciously, "This may be a flesh wound, but it needs washing."

"Does it?" she responded, regarding him with her head on one side. "Have you become accustomed to the idea yet?"

Nathaniel dropped her arm and took her head between his hands, his fingers twisting in her hair. "Yes," he said savagely. "I know when I'm defeated. I accept the fact that I'm stuck with you. We'll see if that Danish robber on deck has the authority to perform a marriage service."

"Is that a proposal, sir?"

"No, it's not a proposal. It's a damn statement. It's past time I took the initiative around here."

"Oh, well, be my guest," Gabrielle said. "I must say I'm getting a little tired of making all the decisions."

His fingers tightened in her hair, holding her head in a viselike grip. His eyes burned with a passionate intensity. "You are sure, Gabrielle? Sure you love me . . . sure you embrace all I stand for? Sure you're willing to trust me with your love?"

"Yes," she affirmed. "I'm certain of all those things. Are you also certain?"

Nathaniel nodded. "I'm still terrified, but I know that I love you and I will do everything I can to make you happy."

He brought his mouth to hers, and Gabrielle thought, the instant before she was lost in the hard assertion of his kiss, that it was only the smallest white lie, the most technical of deceptions on which their future rested.

25

An ant was crawling up the back of Mr. Jeffrys's rusty black gown. In a minute it would reach his shoulder and then crawl onto his neck. He had a scrawny neck, like a chicken's, and it was dirty too. His white collar always had a dark ring around it.

Jake dreamily watched the ant's progress, wondering what the schoolmaster would do when it touched his skin. Perhaps he wouldn't notice and it would crawl down inside his shirt and bite him.

Jake grinned to himself, hugging this pleasurable thought. Perhaps it was a poisonous ant and the bite would swell up and Mr. Jeffrys would have a fever and have to go to bed. Perhaps it would be so bad, he'd decide to leave Burley Manor and go back where he came from.

A fly buzzed against the windowpane, and Mr. Jeffrys's chalk squeaked on the blackboard. Jake frowned at the long series of numbers appearing beneath the chalk. In a minute Mr. Jeffrys would tell him to come up and work the sum out for himself and he wouldn't be able to do it because he didn't understand long division. He thought he might have been able to understand it if the schoolmaster didn't drone on and on in that horrible thin, flat voice.

It was warm in the schoolroom. Mr. Jeffrys had a loathing of fresh air—he said it was bad for his chest or something. Papa and Gabby loved to be outside. Papa had been away for a long time now. Jake wondered where Gabby was. Papa had said she had to stay in Paris and it wasn't anything to do with Jake that she couldn't come back with them. But Jake sometimes thought Papa had been fibbing. . . .

Tears pricked behind his eyes and he blinked them away rapidly. He always felt like crying when he thought of Gabby. She was so warm and she was always laughing and she had such lovely clothes and she smelled of roses. . . .

"Ow!" He sat up with a cry of pain, rubbing his knuckles. Mr. Jeffrys stood glaring at him, tapping his swishy stick on the edge of the desk.

"Master Praed, perhaps you would favor me with your attention," the schoolmaster said with one of his nasty yellow smiles that wasn't a smile at all. He gestured to the blackboard with his stick. "Perhaps you would do me the great honor of completing the sum I've begun."

Wiping his eyes with the back of his smarting hand, Jake went reluctantly to the board and picked up the chalk. The figures meant nothing to him, and he stared at them blankly.

"Dear me," murmured Mr. Jeffrys, coming up behind him. He was standing so close, Jake could feel his breath stirring his hair and he could smell that sour-milk smell that seemed to hang around him. "We haven't been listening to a word I've said the entire afternoon, have we, Master Praed?"

Jake wrinkled his nose, trying not to breathe in too deeply. His stomach knotted with tension as he waited for the inevitable tirade. The words were not so much angry as hurtful, like little darts that buried themselves in his skin. It made him feel sick, and he stared at the white chalk figures, holding himself very still.

The sound of carriage wheels on the gravel below carried faintly through the sealed window. Mr. Jeffrys paused in full sarcastic flood and walked to the window.

"It seems his lordship has arrived," he observed, tapping the stick in the palm of his hand. "I'm sure he'll be very grieved to hear of your lack—" He stopped in astonishment as Jake abandoned his chastened position at the blackboard and ran to the window. He jumped on tiptoe to look out.

"Gabby! It's Gabby!" Before the outraged tutor could say or do anything, he'd bolted from the room, his feet resounding on the stairs as he hurled himself down them.

Mr. Jeffrys gathered his gown around him and marched downstairs in the wake of his errant pupil.

"Gabby ... Gabby ... Gabby ..." Jake catapulted into Mrs. Bailey as he flew across the hall. Bartram had the front door open and jumped aside as the child shoved past him, almost tumbling down the steps to the gravel sweep.

Gabby had just alighted from the chaise and was leaning in to reach for something. His father stood behind her. There was another chaise standing on the gravel, but Jake didn't take this in at first in his joy.

"Gabby!" he bellowed again.

She spun around. "Jake!" Her arms went around him as he leaped against her, and she lifted him off the ground. "My, you have grown," she said, kissing his cheek. "I can hardly lift you now."

"That's 'cause I'm seven," the child gabbled. "Where've you been? Have you come back to stay?"

"I realize I run a poor second after Gabrielle," Nathaniel said, sounding amused, "but how about a greeting for your father."

Laughing, Gabrielle set Jake on his feet. There was the barest hesitation in the boy's manner as he looked up at his father, but when Nathaniel smiled and bent to pick him up, he put his arms tightly around his neck and hugged him with a silent wealth of emotion that filled Nathaniel with a warm, deep joy.

"Lord Praed, I really do apologize." Mr. Jeffrys's accents, both obsequious and outraged, broke into the reunion. "Jake had no right to leave the schoolroom in such a discourteous and impetuous fashion. I will deal with him at once. Come here, young man." He moved purposefully, obviously prepared to wrest his pupil from Nathaniel's arms.

"Are you still around, Mr. Jeffrys?" Gabrielle turned to look at him, her lip curled in disdain. "You really are the most odious toad. I suggest you pack your bags and leave as soon as you can do so. Lord Praed will give you a month's wages in lieu of notice and the gig will drive you into Winchester, where you can catch the stage to take you back from whence you came."

She brushed her hands together with an air of great satisfaction.

Mr. Jeffrys's mouth opened and shut, and he looked just like the big old carp in the fish pond, Jake thought delightedly, unable to believe what he'd just heard.

"My lord?" Jeffrys turned in appeal to Nathaniel. "I don't know what to say—"

"We'll discuss it later, Jeffrys," Nathaniel said calmly, setting Jake on his feet. "You may be sure there'll be a generous settlement."

The tutor clutched the lapels of his gown in a convulsive grip as if trying to hang on to some symbol of his authority, then he turned and went back into the house.

Jake gave a gleeful shriek. "You sent him away, Gabby! Gabby sent old Jeffrys away!"

Gabrielle grinned down at him. "Mothers can be remarkably useful on occasion."

Jake blinked and then said in an awestruck voice, "You going to be my mother?"

"Would you like that?" She came down to his level, catching his chin in her hand.

Jake just gazed at her, speechless. Then he gave a loud whoop of joy and dashed away, racing round and around the gravel sweep, his arms flapping wildly in a violent imitation of a massive bird.

Georgie, who'd just alighted from the second chaise, regarded Jake's exuberance with a tolerant eye. "He seems to like the idea," she observed.

"Did you just give that tutor his walking papers, Gabby?" Simon was looking half shocked, half amused.

"Odious toad, she called him," Miles said with a grin. "Mind you, he did seem to be singularly lacking in attraction, even for a tutor."

"I suppose it was too much to expect you to wait for the ink to dry on the marriage license before you started throwing your weight around," Nathaniel remarked with a degree of resignation.

"When it comes to Jeffrys, yes," she responded firmly.

Nathaniel shook his head with a half-smile and called to his son, still tearing around the circle loudly whooping.

"Jake! Jake, come here now and greet our guests in proper fashion."

Jake turned and came swooping toward them, flapping his wings. His father reached out and collared him, hauling him to a standstill.

"You remember Lord and Lady Vanbrugh, don't you?"

Jake nodded, too out of breath to speak. His face was scarlet with his exertions and his hair stuck damply to his forehead.

"Make your bow," Nathaniel prompted.

Panting, Jake obeyed, jerkily sticking out his damp hand. Taking a gasping breath, he asked Gabrielle, "Are you married to Papa now?"

"Almost," she said, wiping his face with her handkerchief. "That's why Georgie and Simon and Miles are here. We're going to be married in the church tomorrow."

"Can I watch?"

"Of course. That's why we came here," she said, taking his hand. "Shall we go and tell Primmy that Mr. Jeffrys is going?"

Miles watched them walk off hand in hand, Jake's bubbling voice continuing almost without pause for breath. "It's funny, but I'd never have thought of Gabby as a mother," he said. "She seems too exotic, somehow."

"Oh, that's nonsense," Georgie declared. "Gabby's wonderful with children. You should see her with my baby brothers and sisters. And little Ned dotes on her."

"Shall we go inside?" Nathaniel said abruptly, his countenance suddenly dark. He strode ahead of them into the house.

Simon and Miles exchanged a rueful look. "Did I say something wrong?" Georgie murmured, slipping her arm through her husband's.

"No," Simon reassured. "He's just a bit sensitive on the subject of children because of Helen."

"But that was seven years ago!"

"He'll get over it. Gabby'll make sure of that," Miles said with confidence as they entered the house.

Gabrielle came running down the stairs as they went into the library. "Oh, there you all are. Georgie, come and help me choose my wedding dress. Ellie's unpacking my things and I can't decide whether to wear flaming crimson, since I am a scarlet woman about to be made an honest one, or some niminy-piminy sprigged muslin."

"You don't have any sprigged muslin," Nathaniel said, pouring wine for his guests, his expression once more equable. "At least, not that I've seen."

"I suppose I could wear my britches, like I did when the Danish captain married us."

"What Danish captain?" Simon asked, fascinated.

"Oh, on a boat to Copenhagen. Nathaniel asked him to marry us and he did his best, poor fellow, but I don't think he knew what he was doing, so we decided we'd better do it again, properly. Just to be on the safe side. We don't want any little ones born on the wrong side of the blanket, do we?"

"Gabby!" Georgie exclaimed, for once shocked.

Gabrielle just laughed. She glanced at Nathaniel, expecting to see amusement on his face, and suffered a shock. His face had closed, his mouth tightened, his eyes flattened. He looked at his most intimidating.

"I don't find that amusing," he said in cutting accents.

"Why not?" Gabrielle perched on the arm of the sofa. "Maybe it wasn't a piece of scintillating wit, but it wasn't *that* awful."

"It was tasteless and unfunny. Do you want a glass of wine?"

"Not if you're going to be such a stuffy scold." She stood up. "Come to my room, Georgie, and help me go through my wardrobe."

Georgie left the men in the library with a degree of relief. Nathaniel was looking thunderous and the other two embarrassed.

"I haven't seen Nathaniel look so ominous in ages," she said in the privacy of Gabrielle's apartments.

"He doesn't like talking about children," Gabrielle said. "He feels that Helen's death was caused by his own thoughtlessness. I suspect he's not going to want any more."

"Oh." Georgie frowned. "But what about you? Do you want children?"

"Yes," Gabrielle said. "I want lots of them."

"What will you do?"

"I'm hoping that once he gets used to being married again, he'll stop worrying about it and it'll just happen naturally."

"But what if it doesn't?"

Gabrielle shrugged. "I'll cross that bridge when I come to it." She flung open the wardrobe, where Ellie had hung her gowns. "Now, what's it to be? I suppose I really can't wear black, not to my own wedding."

"No, of course you can't," Georgie said indignantly. "Not even you could do something that outrageous." She riffled through the dresses. "What about this?"

Gabrielle put her head on one side, frowning at the gown of lilac crepe. "No, I don't think so. There's an ivory silk in there with black velvet ribbon knots on the sleeves. . . . Oh, it's you, Nathaniel." She turned at the sound of the door opening. "Do you think I can wear a dress with black velvet ribbon?"

"I wouldn't presume to have an opinion when it comes to your wardrobe," he said, his tone constrained, his eyes still frowning. "I wanted to consult you about Jeffrys, but I see you're busy."

"I'm just going," Georgie said hastily. "I have to decide what *I'm* going to wear to this wedding."

"I believe Mrs. Bailey has had your luggage taken to the red suite," Nathaniel said with some of the stiffness of the old days, holding the door for her.

"Thank you." Georgie whisked herself into the corridor, wondering again just what it was her cousin saw in Nathaniel Praed. Sometimes he could be quite approachable, but usually he was downright intimidating.

In her bedroom Gabrielle regarded Nathaniel quizzically. "Why do I have the feeling you're about to be unpleasant?"

"What possessed you to make such a vulgar and indiscreet remark?" he demanded, striding to the window. "It embarrassed everybody."

"No, *you* embarrassed everybody," she corrected, "by scolding me like that."

Nathaniel said nothing for a minute as he stared out the open window. A flock of swifts were diving and circling through a cloud of midges hovering over the river, and the evening air was hot and heavy.

He didn't want to have this discussion, but he knew it had to come out in the open, for Gabrielle's sake. He hadn't realized until then how strongly he felt. "Gabrielle, I don't want any more children," he said finally.

Gabrielle sat on the bed. "I think you mean that you don't want me to become pregnant."

"It's the same thing." He turned to face her, his eyes troubled but his face set.

She shook her head. "No, it's not at all the same thing. And I'm telling you now that I am not Helen. I'm strong as a horse, as you well know, and—"

"I don't want to discuss this further, Gabrielle," he interrupted. "I am not prepared to father any more children. I'm sorry."

"Don't you think this is a bit premature?" Gabrielle said. "To be quite so definite before—"

"I wanted to bring it up now," he interrupted again. "If you can't accept this, then I'll understand if . . . if—" He broke off, running his hands through his hair, his eyes anguished. "If you don't want to go through with the wedding," he finished in a rush.

He was serious! Instinctively, she attempted to lighten the atmosphere. "But we're already married," she pointed out, raising her eyebrows.

Nathaniel shook his head. "I think we can forget that ridiculous ceremony," he stated. "God knows if it was legal, but I'm prepared to forget it ever happened."

"Well, I'm not," Gabrielle said firmly. "And I think it's most unchivalrous of you to suggest I might become a bigamist."

"Don't make a joke of this."

"Well, I don't know what else to do," she retorted. "You're being absurd."

"I'm being honest," he snapped. "And I'm trying to save you from making a mistake."

"Oh." She stood up, her eyes flashing. "Well, let me tell you, Nathaniel Praed, that I don't need saving from anything, and I'll make whatever mistakes I choose. And if that includes marrying an arrogant, miserable, self-willed, ill-tempered, misanthropic bastard, then so be it."

"You are a termagant," Nathaniel declared as honey-eyed relief flowed in his veins.

"Well, maybe you'd like to think twice about marrying me, in that case."

"Oh, I have," he said with a slow grin. "Many times. It doesn't seem to make any difference though."

"Bastard," she said again, but with a responding grin, relieved in her turn that the painful intensity had dissipated. He'd change his mind once he was secure in their marriage. There was plenty of time.

"And as it happens, I do have an opinion on black ribbons," Nathaniel said. "I won't permit them. This is a wedding, not a wake." He pulled her to him, pushing up her chin. "And once we're married, I won't tolerate being savaged by a disrespectful virago either. Is that clear?"

Before she could respond, he sealed the statement with his mouth on hers, his hands sliding around her body to cup her buttocks, pressing her hard against him until he felt the playful resistance leave her. Her mouth was soft and yielding beneath his, her body moving against him of its own accord.

The door burst open at this inopportune moment. "Gabby . . . Gabby . . . can I . . . oh—" Jake stood openmouthed in the doorway, staring.

Nathaniel released Gabrielle and turned slowly, bending a stern eye on his blushing son. "I believe you forgot something," he said. "What do you normally do outside a closed door?"

Jake shuffled his feet. "Knock."

"Precisely. I suggest you go back outside and start again."

"It's easy to forget in all the excitement," Gabrielle said.

Jake shot her a grateful look and rapidly disappeared.

"You shouldn't make excuses for him," Nathaniel said, frowning.

"Oh, but he was so embarrassed, poor lad."

"It could have been a great deal more embarrassing . . ." Nathaniel's frown deepened as he regarded the closed door. "Now what's he doing?"

"Perhaps he's too uncomfortable to try again."

Nathaniel shook his head and impatiently opened the door. Jake was standing in the corridor, chewing his lip. "Did you want to talk to Gabrielle?" his father demanded.

"Yes, sir." Jake nodded.

"Well, come in, then." Nathaniel waved him in and Jake scuttled past him. Clasping his hands tightly, he gazed intensely up at Gabrielle and spoke in a rush.

"Primmy says that when people get married they have page boys," he blurted out. "Can I be your page boy when you marry Papa?"

"Yes, of course you can." Gabrielle bent to kiss the earnest little face. "I would be honored . . . and so would Papa." She glanced up at Nathaniel and Jake's anxious eyes followed hers.

"Yes, I would," Nathaniel said gravely. "In fact, I'd like you to do something very important. I need someone to hold the ring and give it to me at the right moment. Do you think you could do that?"

Jake's face was scarlet, his brown eyes huge, and he could only nod vigorously. Then abruptly he turned and ran from the room, and they could hear his shrieking whoop of excitement receding down the corridor as he headed for the nursery stairs.

"Now, that, Papa, was an inspiration," Gabrielle approved, smiling. "And it deserves a kiss."

"More than that, I believe," Nathaniel said. "But I think I'll lock the door."

The next afternoon Jake stood behind his father in the dim, musty light of the village church, waiting for Gabrielle. He clutched the gold circle that Papa had given him so tightly that it seemed to be ingrained in his hot, sticky palm.

Papa had said there wouldn't be anyone there but their three guests and Primmy and Mrs. Bailey, and any of the household who might want to give up part of a Saturday afternoon to see Lord Praed married, but in fact the church was full. The entire village had turned out, as well as the estate workers and tenants.

Jake's stomach was fluttering. Supposing he missed the right moment, or, horror of horrors, dropped the ring. He stared down at the uneven flagstones at his feet and imagined the bright little circle of gold rolling away under one of the pews among all those feet.

He took a step closer to Papa and tugged his coat with his free hand. "What happens if I drop it," he said in a loud whisper that reached the front pews.

"We'll just pick it up again," Nathaniel said with a calm smile.

Jake nodded, but kept hold of his father's coat. It made him feel better.

There was a rustling in the church, people turned their heads toward the door, and Jake looked too. Gabby was walking up the aisle with Lord Vanbrugh. She was smiling, acknowledging the people in the pews, and when she reached Jake, she bent down and kissed him.

"I might drop it," he whispered.

"Then we'll pick it up," she said, just like Papa, and he knew it wouldn't matter. He let go of his father's coat and looked confidently around as Reverend Addison began to speak in his Sunday voice.

"I think I'm going to cry," Georgie said matter-of-factly to Miles. "Doesn't Gabby look wonderful?"

She did, Miles agreed. Nathaniel had prevailed over the black ribbons and she wore a blue-gray gown opening over a half-slip of Valenciennes lace, her hair piled high and held in place with a pearl-encrusted silver fillet. Pearls encircled her throat and wrists, and their creamy pallor seemed to blend with her skin, accentuating the dark eyes and the vivid fire of her hair.

Nathaniel's head whirled. He wondered if he would ever become so used to her that she would no longer take his breath away. And then she gave him her crooked little smile and there was a gleam of mischievous invitation in her eye, and he knew that she would never lose the power to enchant him.

"With this ring I thee wed," the Reverend Addison intoned.

Jake instantly stuck out his hand, open-palmed. His father peeled the ring off his palm and ruffled his hair. Gabby winked at him, and he squeezed one eyelid shut, wrinkling his nose in imitation.

"With my body I thee worship . . ."

Gabrielle's hand in Nathaniel's quivered, her fingers tightening imperceptibly around his, her eyes locked with his.

Georgie gave up the struggle and snuffled pleasurably into her handkerchief and even Miles blinked rapidly. The powerful magnetism between the couple at the altar was almost palpable in the still, attentive church.

And then it was all over and the organist began to play and Lord and Lady Praed went into the vestry to sign the register.

"Jake, I want you to run an errand for me," Nathaniel said, "if I can find some paper—oh, thank you." He took the sheet of paper and quill offered by the vicar and wrote swiftly. "I want you to take this note to Mr. Stewart, the bailiff. He was in the church, but I expect he's outside now, waiting for us to come out. Can you do that?"

Jake nodded importantly, took the note, and ran off.

"What was all that about?" Gabrielle scrawled her signature in the ledger and stepped aside to make room for Nathaniel.

"I hadn't expected such a turnout," he said. "I thought I'd better host a reception. Stewart will put it about that the Red Lion is open for business and the drinks are on Lord Praed."

Gabrielle smiled to herself. She'd noticed that winter day on the river that a different side of Nathaniel was revealed when he was in character as lord of the manor; it was a role at which he was naturally adept, inspiring both affection and loyalty.

Outside, they were engulfed in the throng of well-wishers, women bobbing curtsies, men twisting their hats between their hands, offering awkward but genuine congratulations, children shyly smiling, pushed forward by their parents.

It seemed to put a seal on the marriage that Gabrielle hadn't thought she needed or wanted. And yet this public acknowledgment filled her with a deep sense of satisfaction and contentment. She was well and truly married to Nathaniel Praed. A convoluted past of deception and fear behind her, a simple conventional future lying ahead.

Talleyrand would be smiling.

"Honeymoon time," she whispered as the crowd thinned and they began to walk toward the lych-gate.

"So it is," Nathaniel said. His hand drifted down her back, coming to rest on her bottom.

"There are people around!" she hissed, moving forward. The hand followed her.

"So what? I can touch my legal wedded wife if I wish . . . wherever and however I wish." He smiled with such complacency that Gabrielle went into a peal of laughter.

"Why do I have the feeling our hosts are about to find us surplus to requirement?" Miles murmured.

"I think we should dine in Lymington," Simon agreed. He looked behind him. "Where's Jake? Oh, there he is." He called the boy, who came running over, still glowing with self-importance. "How would you like to come into Lymington with us, Jake?"

"With Gabby and Papa?"

Georgie shook her head. "No, just with us."

Jake frowned. Papa and Gabby were walking very close together. He remembered the previous afternoon when they'd been kissing. A blush spread over his cheeks and he nodded. "Yes, please. If Papa says I can."

"Don't worry about that," his godfather said cheerfully, taking his hand. "I doubt your father will have an opinion on the subject."

26

"They've captured the entire Danish fleet! Bombarded Copenhagen and the *entire* fleet captured!" The Emperor Napoleon paced the council chamber at the Tuilleries Palace, carrying his rotund belly high over his short legs, his hard eyes glaring at the select gathering of ministers.

"It would appear so, sir," Talleyrand agreed, taking snuff. The newly entitled Vice Grand Elector of France was standing in a window embrasure, leaning against the broad sill, resting his crippled leg as the debate raged around him.

The English government had responded to Talleyrand's artfully directed intelligence at Tilsit with both speed and efficiency. There was now no Danish fleet to enforce a blockade of the Baltic ports. Of course, the Danes weren't too happy about it, in fact rabidly anti-English as a result, but it certainly took the teeth out of the secret articles to the Treaty of Tilsit.

Talleyrand looked down idly on the gardens of the Tuilleries bathed in the late September sun. The leaves of the plane trees were turning russet, and from the

Seine came the frantic barking of a dog in the stern of one of the long barges slipping beneath the Pont Neuf.

"Monsieur Talleyrand, what is your opinion of the Portuguese government's refusal to enforce the blockade?" The new Minister for Foreign Affairs posed the question somewhat hesitantly. He was still accustomed to deferring to the former minister but felt that perhaps he should be asserting his own opinions rather more definitely.

"Inconvenient, in the light of the Danish catastrophe," the Vice Grand Elector said.

"Inconvenient! You call it inconvenient!" exploded the emperor. "I tell you it's the epitome of treachery." He fell into a fulminating silence, examining Talleyrand with steely hostility. The man was too clever by half. Every diplomatic court in Europe hung on his opinion and advice, and if it came to a disagreement between the emperor and Talleyrand, Napoleon had the uneasy suspicion that the former's opinion would count in such circles for more than his own.

If only he could do without the man's cleverness and expertise himself. It was both disagreeable and inappropriate for an emperor to be dependent on the assistance of anyone, and most particularly a man who had distinct views of his own and didn't hesitate to impart them. But the fact remained that the Emperor Napoleon could not manage to govern his vast empire without the help of Charles-Maurice de Talleyrand-Perigord.

"It would ruin Portugal to enforce the blockade, sir," Talleyrand pointed out as he'd done often before. But this was another instance where the emperor refused to listen to Talleyrand's doctrine of moderation when it came to dealing with opposition. The emperor never looked ahead, anticipating consequences, but acted only according to the dictates of his ambition. His genius lay in turning circumstances to his own advantage, but Talleyrand saw only disaster in increasing France's liabilities at this point.

"We shall enlist the help of Spain," Napoleon announced. "We will suggest to her a partition of Portugal. That will bring Portugal to heel. Champagny, send a message to the Spanish king, inviting him to send emissaries to Fontainebleau for a secret convention next month. We shall hold court there."

Talleyrand turned back to his contemplation of the garden beneath the window. The English government needed to know what Napoleon was up to now. The subjugation of Portugal was only an excuse for gaining French control of the entire Iberian Peninsular. Napoleon might well deceive the Spaniards with his offers of false friendship, but they'd discover the treachery of their assumed ally once they gave him free passage across their country to gain access to Portugal. Once in, Napoleon would secure the most important strategic positions and they'd never see the back of him.

The English couldn't afford to stand by while the Peninsular was peacefully incorporated into the French Empire and the killer blockade extended to its ports.

Gabrielle was now married to her spymaster, and Fouché was beside himself. The policeman had a long reach, but he couldn't be revenged on Gabrielle without jeopardizing his uneasy alliance with Talleyrand, an alliance he needed at the moment more than he needed revenge for being duped. While Gabrielle remained in England, she would be safe.

Safe and perfectly placed to be useful, her godfather reflected, if she could be persuaded.

He'd send the intelligence to her, suggesting she pass it on to the right quarters. She was clear-headed and pragmatic; he couldn't imagine she'd refuse to do again what she'd once done so successfully. She would see that she would only be helping her friends and her husband's country that was now her own.

•   •   •   •

Gabrielle leaned back against the stone seat of the garden bench, Talleyrand's encoded letter lying open on her lap. The ground at her feet was a carpet of copper leaves that still wafted down from the beech tree behind her. The air was sharp with the acrid smell of burning leaves from the gardener's bonfire, reminding her of roasting chestnuts and eating buttered toast on winter afternoons before blazing log fires. Comforting, secure images of childhood in the DeVane schoolroom.

Damn Talleyrand! Damn this goddamned war! She folded the letter and pushed it into the pocket of her pelisse. Her godfather had offered no suggestions as to how she was to pass on the information, merely reiterated that his identity must be kept absolutely secret. The envelope had been addressed in a feminine hand and had arrived on the London mail coach. There was nothing to connect it with the author of the letter.

She shivered. It was getting cold, and the evening star was already visible in the metallic sky above the river. She stood up and began to walk back to the house.

She could always ignore the letter.

She kicked at a pile of leaves, and suddenly a memory rose as vivid and clear as if it had been yesterday. Guillaume, at Valançay one October, lying on his back in a pile of leaves where she'd pushed him. He was laughing, holding his arms up in invitation. . . .

It still happened occasionally, this upsurge of memory, but the sadness usually had a sweetness to it. The images were like the pictures and memorabilia of long-lost childhood that one looked at in attics: dusty portraits, forgotten toys, scraps of material, pressed flowers. But not this one, not this time. She felt only a deep well of loss, an awareness, sharp and bitter as aloes, of a squandered life.

Guillaume had always seen the war through Talleyrand's eyes, and he would expect her to do this. He would see it as her duty.

"Gabby ... Gabby ..." Jake came hurtling down the path toward her. "You look sad," he said with habitual directness. "Are you sad? Don't be." He took her hand, looking anxiously up at her.

"No," she said, dredging up a smile of reassurance. "I was just remembering things. Have you finished your lessons?"

Jake pulled a face. "I don't think it's fair I have to go to the vicarage on Saturday afternoons, do you?"

Jake now did his lessons in the vicarage schoolroom with the vicar's children, an arrangement that suited everyone and provided the child with much-needed company of his own age.

"Why don't you talk to Papa?" Jake now said with a crafty sideways glance. When Gabby took up his cause with his father, things usually changed for the better.

Gabrielle couldn't help laughing. "You're a sly one, young Jake. If you do lessons in the vicarage schoolroom, then you must abide by their rules. That's only fair, isn't it?"

"Perhaps you could talk to Reverend Addison," he suggested a little less confidently. Gabrielle's power over the vicar was so far unproven.

"I'll talk to Papa, but I'm not making any promises."

Jake was content and trotted beside her as they entered the hall, where the candles were already lit and the air was filled with the scent of dried lavender and rose petals from the bowls scattered on every surface.

"You'd better run along for your tea," Gabrielle said, shrugging out of her pelisse. Jake scampered off in the direction of the nursery stairs, and Gabrielle stood for a minute, indecisive. She wanted to go up to her own apartments and think in private about the letter and what options she had, but she knew in her heart that there was no decision to be made. She had only one option.

She turned aside to the library. She might as well fulfill her promise to Jake while it was fresh in her mind.

Nathaniel looked up from his papers as she came in, and smiled involuntarily. Gabrielle seemed to become more beautiful and more desirable day by day.

"Come and be kissed," he said, pushing back his chair.

She leaned over the back of his chair and brushed his lips with her own.

"That's not much of a kiss," Nathaniel grumbled, reaching for her arm and pulling her around his chair and onto his lap. He frowned. "What's the matter?"

"Matter? Nothing," Gabrielle said, moving to stand up.

His arm tightened around her waist. "Something's upset you, Gabrielle. I can feel it."

"It's this time of year," she improvised, not totally without truth. "It always makes me feel sad. For some reason it reminds me of my parents. It was October when I arrived at the DeVanes and I still couldn't absorb what had happened." She leaned back against his shoulder, playing with his fingers linked at her waist.

"Would you like to go to London for a couple of months? The Season should be getting under way by now."

"You hate London," she said, smiling slightly.

"I can endure it until Christmas."

It would be easier in London to do what she had to. Much easier to practice deception in a crowd.

"Yes, I'd like that." She twisted her head and kissed his mouth before untangling his hands at her waist and pushing herself off his knee. "We could take Jake, couldn't we?"

Nathaniel stroked his chin. "What about his lessons?"

"I have lots of friends with children his age. I'm sure we can find a temporary schoolroom for him to share. Incidentally, he doesn't think it's fair he should do lessons on Saturday afternoons. Behold in me his emissary."

Nathaniel chuckled. "The crafty little monkey. So what do you think?"

"I think there are many educational and certainly more amusing pursuits for a Saturday afternoon," she declared.

"Well, if we're taking him to London, the issue is moot for the time being."

"Such a just and reasonable Papa," Gabrielle said in tones of mock awe. "It does seem a waste for all that justice and reason to be expended on one small boy."

The light faded from Nathaniel's eyes. He pushed his chair away from the table with an angry scrape and gathered together his papers. He said nothing, but the silence was all too eloquent.

She wasn't making any headway on the subject of children. He was the most infuriatingly obstinate individual! He refused to be drawn on the issue, maintaining this steadfast silence whenever she offered the slightest opening.

Frustrated, Gabrielle watched him open the safe and deposit the papers, the tense silence wreathing around them.

But she had a bigger and more immediate problem on her plate at the moment.

"So, when should we go to London?" she asked cheerfully, as if the last tense minutes hadn't happened.

Nathaniel turned from the safe, clear relief in his own eyes, and responded in the same tone. "Next week . . . if you like."

"The Vanbrughs have been in Grosvenor Square for three weeks. I'll write to Georgie and let her know we're coming—oh, and shouldn't we send Mrs. Bailey, and perhaps Bartram, on ahead to get the house on Bruton Street ready?"

"Whatever you think best, madam wife." Gabrielle had the reins of his household firmly in her own hands, and he knew she was asking for his opinion only for politeness's sake.

Gabrielle gave a nod of acknowledgment and left the library. Ellie was drawing the curtains when she went into her boudoir, and the maid immediately began a gossipy account of some village scandal.

Gabrielle listened with half an ear. She didn't discourage Ellie's gossip in general because she often heard of trials and tribulations that could be alleviated by the manor, but this evening the girl's light tones grated and the story held no interest.

"Ellie, be a dear and fetch me some tea," she interrupted. "I feel as if I'm developing a headache."

"Oh, yes, my lady. I'll fetch it right up." Ellie's good-natured face expressed genuine concern as she hurried from the room.

Gabrielle sat by the fire, resting her feet on the fender. She was going to give Talleyrand's intelligence directly to Simon. He'd share it with Nathaniel, of course, but no one would know where it came from. She was going to create an anonymous character, a mole who had sensitive information from France. It should be simple enough to arrange for the delivery of an anonymous letter to Simon's government office at Westminster, particularly once she was living on Bruton Street.

In one way, she would be making up for her earlier deceit when she'd used Simon to introduce her to Nathaniel. Grief and the need for vengeance then had subsumed guilt at deceiving her friends, but she was still uncomfortable with the memory. Nathaniel had never referred to it because they never talked about that time; she had made her choice of loyalties and they both accepted it. She knew he must have done similar distasteful things in his own career; it went with the territory.

That night, for the first time in many months, she had the nightmare again.

Nathaniel held her, stroking the damp ringlets from her forehead as she wept, her body a tight bow of pain. She clung to him, shivering in her sweat-soaked nightgown, and he didn't know how to comfort her except to hold her, trying to infuse her with the warmth of his own body, the deep steadiness of his own heartbeat. He remembered he'd felt some strain, some unhappiness in her that afternoon, and she'd ascribed it to these old dreadful memories of childhood terror and loss.

When her sobs lessened, he drew her nightgown over her head and gently sponged and dried her body. And she lay still as he did so, her forearm covering her swollen eyes as if the soft glow of the candle hurt her. He moved her arm and bathed her eyes, then kissed her eyelids, her nose, her cheeks, her mouth, his hands visiting her body in long, healing strokes, seeking to exorcise her demons in the only way he knew. And slowly she relaxed beneath his touch and welcomed the warm length of his body measured along hers, drawing strength and renewal from a tender possession that gave much more than it took.

Two weeks later Nathaniel drew his horses to a halt in front of an imposing mansion on Bruton Street. "I'll visit Tattersalls tomorrow and purchase something for you to drive," he observed to Gabrielle as he assisted her to alight. "Do you fancy a phaeton?"

"No, a curricle," she said promptly, standing on the pavement, looking up at the double-fronted façade of Praed House. "A handsome house, my lord."

"I trust it will meet with your approval inside." He gave her a mock bow, then offered her his arm to mount the steps.

The door opened before they reached it, and a smiling Bartram bowed them within. Mrs. Bailey greeted them in the hall with the information that she'd taken the liberty of hiring two footmen and three parlor maids. But she thought her ladyship would prefer to hire the cook herself. The agency would send suitable candidates to be interviewed as soon as Lady Praed was rested from her journey.

"I'll see them first thing tomorrow morning, Mrs. Bailey," Gabrielle said immediately, looking around, noting the highly polished banister, the gleaming marble beneath her feet, the sparkling chandelier. "You have done a wonderful job. Everything looks splendid."

Mrs. Bailey permitted herself a smile of satisfaction. "Nurse and Miss Primmer will be arriving with Master Jake this evening, I understand, my lady."

"Yes. In a couple of hours, I imagine. The postchaise is no match for Lord Praed's curricle." Gabrielle cast Nathaniel a sideways smile. "Or perhaps I should say for his lordship's driving skill." They'd had a friendly competition on the way up, alternating between changing posts. Nathaniel was a vastly superior whip.

"Perhaps you'd like to inspect the nursery quarters, my lady. I trust everything is in order, but I expect Master Jake will be tired, and Nurse does suffer so from her rheumatism cramped in a carriage, and poor Miss Primmer is a martyr to the headache."

The old Nathaniel would have offered the caustic observation that he provided his retainers with the most comfortable vehicles available and they should be grateful for it. Instead, he said relatively mildly, "I'll leave you to look to the comforts of the staff, Gabrielle. I'm going to the mews."

"Don't forget we're engaged to dine with the Vanbrughs," Gabrielle reminded him as she stripped off her gloves. "Show me around, Mrs. Bailey, and we'll see what needs to be done."

By the time the schoolroom party arrived two hours later, the house was ready to receive an excitable if slightly fractious Jake, a drawn but bravely suffering Miss Primmer, and a groaning Nurse.

"Thank God we're dining elsewhere," Nathaniel declared, watching the progress of bandboxes and trunks ascending the stairs. "How could one child require so much paraphernalia?"

I don't think two requires much more than one. But on this occasion, Gabrielle kept the observation to herself.

"I'm going to dress for dinner. Look in on the nursery, will you? Someone needs to pour a little cold water on Jake's high spirits. I don't think Primmy and Nurse are quite up to it tonight."

Nathaniel grimaced but went off as requested and Gabrielle went up to her own apartments. Ellie had finished unpacking and was laying out Gabrielle's evening dress. "Bartram's fetching up bathwater for you, my lady."

"Oh, lovely. I could do with a bath after the journey," she said absently, unlocking her writing case that lay on the dainty Sheraton *secrétaire.*

She ran her eye down the note she'd arrange to have delivered to Simon's office in the morning. She'd written the message in anonymous block letters on a piece of heavy vellum that could have come from any stationer's. The contents were short ... were they too succinct? Had she left anything out?

Her eye flickered to Voltaire's *Lettres philosphiques* on the bookshelf. She must encode a letter to Talleyrand, telling him what she'd done.

"I don't know what the hell's the matter with that child!" Nathaniel's voice, half exasperated, half amused, came from the doorway and she jumped, her hands suddenly shaking.

She was out of practice! "Why, what he was doing?" Her voice was steady, though, as she nonchalantly replaced the paper and closed the lid of the writing case, turning the tiny silver key in the lock.

"Running naked around the nursery, when he wasn't leaping in and out of his bath, saying he was a porpoise."

Gabrielle turned to face him, casually slipping the key into her pocket. "He's never been to London before. It's not surprising he's excited."

"Well, he's not so excited now, I can tell you," Nathaniel said, moving to the connecting door to his own apartments, shrugging out of his coat as he did so.

"You weren't cross, were you?"

"No." He tossed his coat through the door and began to unbutton his shirt. "Just somewhat dampening . . . as instructed, ma'am." He raised a quizzical eyebrow before disappearing into his own room.

The next morning a scruffy urchin handed a sealed paper to a liveried, powdered flunkey at Westminster Palace. The paper was addressed in block letters to Lord Simon Vanbrugh.

The flunkey barely noticed the lad and couldn't offer a description when summoned by Lord Vanbrugh a few minutes after his lordship had received the paper.

"Did he say where it came from?"

"No, my lord."

"Did you ask him?"

"No, my lord."

"Well, someone must have given it to him."

"Yes, my lord." The flunkey stared rigidly out of the narrow, slitted window in the ancient stone wall overlooking the river.

Simon scratched his head. If the intelligence in the note was genuine, then it was of incalculable importance. As important as the information about the secret articles to the Treaty of Tilsit.

He dismissed the flunkey, picked up his hat and cane, and left Westminster, hailing a hackney. "Bruton Street."

Nathaniel, in buckskin britches and top boots, was leaving the house as the hackney drew up. "Simon, what brings you in the middle of the day?" He greeted his friend cheerfully. "Affairs of state not too pressing?"

"On the contrary," said Simon. "I need to discuss something with you."

"Oh, well, let's go to Brooks' in that case. I was thinking of going to Mantons Gallery for some target practice, but Brooks' will do as well. Gabrielle's interviewing cooks and the house is Bedlam. Jake's just slid down the banisters and twisted his ankle, which seems by any standards to be only justice, but Miss Primmer is wailing and gnashing her teeth, and Gabrielle insists on sending for the doctor. One more minute in that madhouse, and I shall seriously take to drink."

Chuckling, he flung an arm around Simon's shoulder, turning him toward Piccadilly.

Simon, despite his preoccupation, couldn't help reflecting with pleasure that his old friend had finally reemerged from the dour carapace of grief and guilt. But then, no one could live with Gabrielle for any length of time and remain morose. Outraged, perhaps, but never sullen or aloof.

In the hushed masculine seclusion of Brooks', Simon handed Nathaniel the paper. "This arrived by some mysterious messenger this morning." He reached for the decanter of port on the table between them and filled two glasses while Nathaniel perused the document.

"A secret convention at Fontainebleau with the Spanish," he murmured, sipping port. "We knew about that."

"But not about the threat to Portugal."

"No." Nathaniel sat back, crossing his legs. "Who the hell supplied this?" It was a rhetorical question, and Simon offered no answer.

"Do we believe it?" he asked.

Nathaniel nodded. "Can't afford not to, as I see it.

Boney's had his eye on Spain for a long time. We need to support Portugal if we're to keep the entire Iberian Peninsular out of his clutches."

"You'll put some of your people into the field?"

Nathaniel nodded again, setting down his glass. "I've several agents in Madrid who can be deployed to Lisbon. In fact," he added almost to himself, "I might go myself."

"You could talk directly with the Portuguese regent," Simon said. "You'd have more authority, carry more weight than one of your agents."

He stood up. "I'll see the prime minister immediately. I expect he'll want to consult with you without delay." He drew on his gloves. "I wonder if this mysterious source will produce anything else."

"If he does, make damn sure the messenger is held at the gate until I can interview him. I have every intention of getting to the bottom of this," Nathaniel declared. "If there's one thing I can't tolerate, it's manipulation, even if it is to our benefit. If this source is above board, then why the devil doesn't he show himself? Surely he must want something in exchange?"

"You're a cynic," Simon said. "Maybe his motives are of the purest . . . loyalty, patriotism . . ."

"In a pig's ear," Nathaniel retorted. "If they were, he'd show himself. No, something about this stinks to high heaven, Simon, and I intend to find out what."

He strode back to Bruton Street, his head full of dispositions and plans, and a deep sense of unease. All his instincts told him that something was badly wrong. Espionage by definition involved clandestine informers, but this intelligence was too important for a mere dabbler to have acquired. And Nathaniel was convinced he knew all the experienced players in the international field. And if it was a newcomer, how did he know to pass on his information to Simon? Simon's close government connections with Nathaniel's secret service were known to no one apart from the spymaster and the prime minister, not even Georgie or Miles.

Gabrielle knew, of course. He paused outside Hatchard's bow window, frowning, as a past world of suspicion reared its ugly head. Once a spy always a spy? No, that was nonsense. She had given up espionage with irrefutable conviction, and he had no justification for doubting her. Besides, there was no way she could be involved in this. Her marriage had defined her loyalties and cut her off from all access to such privileged information. And even if by some weird happenstance she had had such access, she'd simply have given the information to him. It was only logical. She'd gain nothing by this devious approach.

He walked on, convincing himself of this logic. A line of black-clad candidates for the post of cook snaked out of the door and down the steps of his house. With a fresh wash of irritation he stopped on the pavement. Surely Gabrielle should have finished this tedious business by now.

He marched in and entered the morning room, where Gabrielle was conducting her interviews.

"For God's sake, the house looks like an employment exchange," he declared. "Haven't you found someone suitable yet?"

"Thank you, I'll be in touch with the agency," Gabrielle said to the woman sitting on a straight-backed chair against the wall. The woman bobbed a curtsy and left.

"What's the matter with you?" Gabrielle demanded of Nathaniel. "That was so inconsiderate."

"What's going on in my house is inconsiderate," he said. "There must be twenty women out there."

"Well, I can't send them away without seeing them," she said reasonably. "I don't know why there are so many unemployed cooks in town at the moment. I should have told the agency to screen them first, but it slipped my mind."

She regarded her husband closely. He was in one of his impatient, preoccupied moods, and it wouldn't take much to trigger an explosion. "Something's upset you."

Nathaniel ran a hand through his hair in an impatient gesture. "I've just seen Simon, that's all."

Had Simon consulted Nathaniel about the information already? She'd expected him to consider the message, consult his cabinet colleagues, and certainly the prime minister, before involving Nathaniel. Was Nathaniel Simon's first call? The lad couldn't have delivered the paper much more than a couple of hours earlier.

"Is that all?" she said lightly. "Seeing Simon doesn't usually put you out of sorts."

"I hate mysteries," he said. "And I cannot abide the feeling that I'm being used in some way." His eyes skimmed her face, took note of her hands lying calmly in her lap.

Gabrielle's palms dampened. So it *was* about the information. "Who's using you?"

"I don't know . . . yet," he added, beginning to pace the room. "But I intend to find out."

"You're not being particularly informative." Gabrielle rose and went to the fire, bending to warm her hands, although she was uncomfortably hot. She had the feeling her cheeks might be flushed and the warmth of the fire would offer explanation.

Nathaniel looked at her, the graceful curve of her tall body, the flickering lights in her hair, caught by a spurting flame, the slenderness of her waist, the flare of her hips, outlined under the creamy beige cambric of her morning gown.

Gabrielle had nothing to do with the events of the morning.

A familiar urgent sweep of lust carried all unease and irritations from his mind.

He approached her softly, encircling her waist with one arm, holding her steady across one outthrust thigh, his free hand molding the curve of her buttocks beneath the gown, slowly drawing up the soft material, revealing the length of her legs inch by inch, the hollow behind her knees, the expanse of smooth thigh, the pale flesh above her stocking tops.

Gabrielle made no attempt to straighten her body, relaxing into the supporting hold of the arm around her waist, feeling the hardness of his buckskin-clad thigh beneath her belly. His hand slid under the ruffled hem of her drawers, and a shudder of delicious expectation rippled through her as the fingers insinuated themselves into her moistening cleft, searching her out in an ever-spiraling dance of erotic intimacies.

"This isn't going to get a cook hired," she murmured in a desperate attempt to keep herself from sliding too soon into the inferno.

Nathaniel removed his hand and whacked her bottom. "Not an appropriate response in the circumstances, wife." He flicked her skirt down so that it fluttered back to her ankles, and released his hold.

Gabrielle straightened, flushed, her eyes glowing. "That was hardly appropriate behavior in the circumstances." She gestured eloquently around the salon. "Anyone could have walked in."

The idea seemed to amuse him, judging by his complacent grin. "I didn't hear too many objections, my love."

"No, well, you wouldn't, would you?" she said with feigned resignation. "You know my weaknesses all too well."

His grin broadened. "I'll lock the door and then I can finish what I started without fear of interruption." He suited action to words and then leaned back against the door, regarding her with hooded eyes.

"What is it?" she whispered, her voice thick, as if the sounds were coming through treacle.

"I'm trying to decide how I want you." he replied.

Gabrielle glanced around the room at the available

props, now so engrossed in their game that she gave no thought to her earlier anxiety. "Chaise longue?" she suggested. Nathaniel shook his head. "Table?" Another headshake. "Chair?"

"Perhaps," he said consideringly, pushing himself away from the door. With a swift economical movement he toppled her forward over the back of an armchair.

"I might have guessed," Gabrielle said into the velvet cushions, laughter mingling with arousal in her voice. "You're in one of your dominant moods."

"So it would seem," he said affably, throwing her skirts up over her head and slipping her drawers down over her hips. "Are you comfortable?"

"Perfectly," she assured, chuckling, shifting her feet to brace herself.

His hand moved over her, long, slow sweeps caressing her buttocks and thighs, repeating the voluptuous intimacies of the moment by the fire, and all desire to laugh vanished as they both entered the closed world of passion.

He drove against her womb in a deep probing thrust, and she reached back, wanting to enclose him totally within her, to lose all sense of their separateness. His fingers curled into her hips in a biting grip that expressed his own need for this knowledge of completion. Her flesh was his. The rhythmic throbbing deep within her grew to envelop her in the crimson-shot blackness behind her eyelids. He had a strong hand on the nape of her neck, exerting warm pressure as he moved within her, and his other hand was teasing, nipping at the exquisitely sensitive bud of her sex. Her climax ripped through her in a devastating, mind-numbing tidal wave. Somewhere in the distance she heard her voice, and then Nathaniel's hand on her neck pushed her into the cushions, muffling the involuntary sobbing cries of bliss, and his length fell against her back, his hands on her breasts as he held her through his own explosive moment of joy.

"Sweet heaven!" Nathaniel straightened slowly, leaving her skin feeling cold and exposed as he peeled his body from hers. He ran a hand down her back.

Gabrielle pushed herself upright. "Tell me it's eleven o'clock on a Monday morning," she demanded weakly, fumbling with her clothes as she attempted to put herself back together again.

"It is," Nathaniel refastened his britches. "What is it about you?" He shook his head in bemusement. "Devil woman." He answered his own question.

"I don't think I had anything to do with that," Gabrielle declared, examining her reflection in the mirror above the fireplace. "Look at my hair, it's all over the place. How am I supposed to show myself outside the room like this?"

"I can't imagine," Nathaniel said with callous insouciance, unlocking the door. "But do something about those women. I want my house back."

"Yes, my lord. We *are* feeling assertive this morning, aren't we?" Gabrielle stuck her tongue out at him in the mirror as she hastily tucked errant ringlets back into their pins.

Nathaniel raised a hand in mock threat and left her, unaware of the smile hovering on his lips or the bounce in his stride.

Gabrielle rang the bell for Mrs. Bailey and asked her to send in the next candidate.

Nathaniel went into his book room. He sat down at his desk, pulling a sheaf of reports toward him. He had to decide which of his agents could best be sent to Lisbon ... or should he go himself? The Portuguese king was a pathetic, childlike individual, unable to govern; his regent was a coward, unfit to govern. They would crumple before a French advance. A British presence in Portugal was now vital. . . .

Idly, he picked up his quill, noticing that the end

was splitting. He looked for the small knife he used to sharpen his pens, but it wasn't on his desk and he remembered that Gabrielle had borrowed it the previous evening.

He didn't need it right now, but his mind was racing and he was too restless to sit in contemplative silence, so he strolled upstairs, pausing at the foot of the nursery stairs, thinking he would go up and see how Jake's twisted ankle was progressing. Perhaps he'd retrieve his penknife first.

Gabrielle's sitting room was quiet, sun-filled. It had been Helen's favorite room and the wallpaper and furnishings were distinctively her choice. He wondered if Gabrielle would decide to change anything. It was a very pastel foil for her vibrancy.

The *secrétaire* was open, his penknife lying on the blotter. He picked up the knife and his eye fixed on the markings on the blotter.

Curious marks, back-to-front letters, numbers. He felt an enormous reluctance to pick it up, and yet he did so. He picked it up and held it in front of the mirror on the dresser.

Gabrielle had been playing with the Voltaire code.

27

It wasn't possible that she was still involved in espionage. She couldn't be. It wasn't logical.

Nathaniel looked across the dining table to where Gabrielle sat in animated conversation with her neighbor. As if aware of his scrutiny, she glanced up briefly, her eyes flickering across the expanse of glowing rosewood, the glistening silver, the puddles of golden candlelight. Her lips twitched into her crooked little smile that imparted a special intimacy among the buzzing voices of their fellow guests. Then she turned back to her neighbor and Nathaniel heard her laugh, that deep, warm sound of merriment that had never failed to delight him even when he was angry with her.

His own neighbor offered a tentative conversational sally, and he realized that he'd been sitting in brooding silence for the better part of the second course. He went through the motions for a few minutes but was as relieved as his partner when she was drawn into a conversation on her other side.

Absently, he helped himself from a dish of quail in aspic, remembering too late that he disliked the fiddly little birds and couldn't abide aspic.

He'd asked her about the notations on her blotter—a genial, casual question—and she'd responded in the same manner, saying it had been such a long time since she'd exercised her mind in that way and she'd been testing herself to see how much of the code she could remember.

It was a perfectly reasonable explanation.

Why on earth was Nathaniel eating quail? Gabrielle frowned, watching him dissect one of the birds and then push it to the side of his plate with an impatient gesture. He loathed aspic and despised quail. And didn't he realize how discourteous he was being, sitting in morose silence? Poor Hester Fairchild looked as uncomfortable as if she were sitting next to a hungry tiger.

But he'd been in an unpredictable mood for the past ten days, ever since his meeting with Simon. As luck would have it, he wasn't satisfied with merely receiving and acting upon such valuable information. There was a mystery attached to it, and the need to solve it had become a near obsession. For some reason, she hadn't considered that possibility.

He didn't know that solving it would do nothing for his peace of mind, quite the opposite. And it would do nothing for Gabrielle's peace of mind either. The prospect of his reaction to the truth filled her with a healthy fear. However useful her information, she was still manipulating him at Talleyrand's bidding.

Lady Willoughby rose from her chair at the foot of the table, signaling that the ladies should withdraw, and Gabrielle's neighbor stood to pull back her chair for her. She noticed that Nathaniel moved a fraction too late for courtesy to render his own partner the same service. Something had to be done . . . but what?

Nathaniel lingered in the dining room with Lord Willoughby, long after the other men had left to join the ladies over the teacups in the drawing room. Lord Willoughby was more than happy to find one of his guests prepared to match him glass for glass as the port decanter circulated, particularly when the guest was disinclined for conversation and as content to ruminate in silence as his generally reclusive host.

"Is Nathaniel still in the dining room, Miles?" Gabrielle crossed the drawing room as Miles came in.

"Yes, the last one. He and Willoughby are partnering each other in sullen silence. He's in one of his vile moods tonight. What's the matter with him, Gabby?"

"I don't know." Miles was ignorant of Nathaniel's true working life, so she couldn't offer even a vague explanation about pressure of work. "It's probably London. You know how he hates all this." She gestured around the room with a half-smile. "The inane gibbering of a troupe of monkeys . . ."

Miles chuckled. "I thought he'd recovered from his misanthropy."

"I think it's an innate characteristic," Gabrielle said seriously. "But in general he keeps its manifestations in check."

"Mmmm. Let me fetch you a cup of tea." Miles strolled over to where his hostess was dispensing tea and brought back two cups. "So what do you think of your godfather's new position as Vice Grand Elector? It would seem a position of title rather than power."

Gabrielle laughed. "If you believe that, you don't know Talleyrand, Miles. You can be sure he's peddling his influence as much now as he ever did as Minister for Foreign Affairs. I'll lay any odds he was at Fontainebleau last month. . . . Oh, Georgie, I was hoping to have a word." She held out a hand to her cousin, who was weaving her way through the knots of tea drinkers toward them. "I need your advice. Should I invite your mama and papa to dinner with the prime minister? Or do you think they would prefer a group of their own friends?"

Her voice rose and fell, and Nathaniel, who'd come quietly into the room, stood frozen in the shadows behind her. What did Gabrielle know of Fontainebleau? He'd told her no details of the mysterious message, and she'd accepted his refusal to discuss it with what now struck him as unusual compliance.

If she knew what the message was, then she wouldn't need to pursue it.

His head felt as if it were about to burst. Fat grubs of suspicion heaved in his brain. But it still made no sense. There was no logical reason why, if in some extraordinary fashion she'd come across such information, she shouldn't be honest about it. And it was always possible Simon had mentioned Fontainebleau to her. She was often at the house on Grosvenor Square and he and Gabrielle were great confidants. He talked to her with complete freedom.

No, Gabrielle couldn't reasonably be the source of that intelligence. She had no contacts in France anymore. Or did she? Was she still part of the network of French agents in London?

Suddenly she turned, and the candid gray eyes filled with pleasure at the sight of him.

She had sworn to him that she loved him, that she forswore all previous allegiances. She had brought him her loyalty as the gift of love. She had pursued him, saved his life, forced him to accept his own love as he accepted hers. She had done nothing to warrant his suspicions. And yet . . .

"Nathaniel, there you are. I was beginning to think I'd lost you permanently to the port decanter." There was a hint of rebuke in her voice, although her eyes smiled.

"Come, I wish to go home," he said. He hadn't meant to say that, or at least not in that curt manner. Why was it that he could dissemble in his work, never show a hint of his thoughts and feelings, and yet in the everyday world he found himself speaking straight from his heart without any mental filtering?

A slight flush touched Gabrielle's translucent

cheeks and her chin lifted in ominous fashion. Miles and Georgie exchanged glances and stepped backward, blending into the group behind them.

"Then I suggest you go," she said icily. "As it happens, I'm not ready to leave yet."

He wasn't going to leave her there. While the doubts and mistrust swirled in his head, he wanted—no, desperately needed—her under his eye. It was an instinctive but nonetheless compelling reaction.

"Nevertheless, we are leaving." He drew her arm through his, and she was immediately aware of the muscular power clamping her arm to his body.

She had no choice but to submit if this was to be a dignified exit. Nathaniel whisked them through the salons in search of their hostess. Gabrielle glanced at his tight-lipped countenance and struggled for the sake of politeness to keep her own anger from showing as she made her farewells, trying to compensate with her own warmth for Nathaniel's taciturn mutter.

They stood in the hall while a maid went in search of her cloak and the footman ran to the mews for their carriage. Gabrielle tapped one foot on the parquet, her eyes blazing. Nathaniel still held her arm in the vise of his own, and when she attempted to pull free, he smacked his other hand over hers so that she was held fast.

The carriage drew up and the footman bowed them out. Nathaniel released her at the footstep, but instead of handing her in, he put a flat palm on her bottom and propelled her unceremoniously upward.

She turned on him before the door was shut behind him. "Just what the devil was that all about? How dare you drag me out of there like some misbehaving child! And how could you behave so badly yourself?"

Nathaniel said nothing, just leaned his head against the leather squabs, his face turned to the window. Light from a night watchman's lantern flickered momentarily over his set countenance and Gabrielle could see a muscle twitching in his cheek.

"Answer me, damn you!" Her palm itched to slap him into a response, but Nathaniel was not a good man to hit. He gave as good as he got.

"There's nothing to say." He spoke finally, sounding ineffably weary. "I'm tired and I'm sick to death of these damn parties."

"That's it?" She stared at him. "You behave in the most ill-mannered fashion the entire evening, embarrass and humiliate me beyond bearing, and your only excuse is that you're *tired*. Well, let me tell you, Nathaniel Praed—"

"*Be quiet!*"

The sharp command so surprised her that for a moment she was silenced. She closed her eyes, struggling for reason and control, and then said more moderately, "What's the matter, Nathaniel? What's behind this?"

He regarded her bleakly in the dimness. What if he asked her outright? What if she admitted it? He couldn't bear it. It was as simple as that. He couldn't court that destructive admission. Better to live with these maggots of suspicion than have to deal with the knowledge that his wife had reasons other than love for marrying him.

Cowardice . . . arrant cowardice, and yet he couldn't help it. He rubbed his eyes with the tips of his fingers and sighed heavily. "Forgive me. I have a crushing headache. I could think only of getting out of there."

"Perhaps you should have gone easier on the claret and the port," she said with asperity, not a whit appeased by this explanation.

She turned her head toward the window, feeling her own temples tighten. His attack had not been simple petulance, Nathaniel in a bad mood taking it out on a safe object—wives were supposed to fulfil that function occasionally. No, it had been directed at her as the cause of his anger.

Could he suspect anything? But there was no proof and there never would be. Just that carelessness with the blotter, and that was easily explained. Even if he did suspect something now, it would die away in time when nothing happened to confirm those suspicions. She would just have to keep cool and calm until that happened. And accepting his treatment this evening was not consonant with the presumption of innocence.

"If you ever do anything like that to me again, Nathaniel, I'll create such a scene, you won't want to show your face outside your own door for a six-month," she declared in a low, fierce voice.

"Don't threaten me, Gabrielle." But he sounded more weary than menacing. "If I embarrassed you, I beg your pardon. I was desperate to get away."

"You could have gone home on your own."

"I needed the comforting company of my wife." Again without volition, the declaration emerged as sardonic as the feeling behind it.

The carriage drew up in Bruton Street before Gabrielle could come up with an appropriate response. Nathaniel jumped down and held out his hand to assist her down. Gabrielle ignored the hand, stepped down to the street, and stalked past him into the house. Her hands shook as she stripped off her silk gloves.

"I'll bid you good night, my lord. I suggest you take a powder for your headache. I can't think what to suggest for your temper, however."

In a rustle of emerald silk skirts she marched up the stairs, leaving Nathaniel in the hall.

He swore a savage oath and went into his book room, slamming the door behind him. He poured a glass of cognac from the decanter on the pier table, then tossed the fiery spirit down his throat and reached again for the decanter. He seemed to have a great cold hole in his chest that he could neither warm nor fill. It was a long time before he went up to bed.

Gabrielle slept badly and awoke late the next morning. She lay in bed, wondering for a minute why she felt so leaden and melancholy, and then she remembered. Last night's scenes replayed themselves with depressing accuracy. How long was it going to continue . . . and how long could she keep quiet and put up with it?

Damn Talleyrand!

She pulled the bellrope beside the bed and waited for Ellie to come up with her hot chocolate.

"Miserable day, it is, m'lady." Ellie greeted her cheerfully, placing the tray on the bedside table before pulling back the rose velvet curtains on a gray, overcast sky. "I'd best light the candles," she said, bustling around.

Gabrielle hitched herself up on the pillows and reached for the cup of chocolate. The rich scent came up and hit her, and her stomach rose into her throat. "Dear God, I'm going to be sick!" She flung herself from the bed and behind the commode screen.

Ellie was plumping the pillows when Gabrielle re-emerged, paler than usual.

"Maybe tea would suit better than chocolate, m'lady," the maid said matter-of-factly. "Folks take agin different things . . . sometimes it's coffee, sometimes tea—"

"What are you talking about?" Gabrielle climbed back into bed. "I must have eaten something last night that disagreed with me. It was probably the crayfish pudding. I thought it tasted a bit odd."

"I don't believe so, m'lady," Ellie said, smoothing the coverlet over Gabrielle's knees. "It's been near six weeks since you last 'ad your time."

"What?" Gabrielle lay back on the pillows, absorbing this. "That long?"

"Yes, ma'am."

"Sweet heaven." She touched her belly fleetingly.

"Shall I fetch some tea?"

"Yes, please ... anything but that revolting stuff." Gabrielle's mouth twisted in distaste. "And, Ellie—"

"Ma'am?"

"For the moment this is just between the two of us. I don't want to say anything to his lordship until I'm certain."

"Of course, m'lady." Ellie bobbed a curtsy and disappeared with the tray of chocolate.

Gabrielle closed her eyes, a smile on her lips. Nathaniel was not going to be overjoyed, not at first, but he'd have to realize that however scrupulously careful he'd been, in the excess of passion that so often shook them like an earthquake, it was not surprising that his caution had been insufficient.

Anyway, this news should serve to divert his thoughts from his present obsession. It would give him something else to worry about, something much easier for her to handle.

She'd have to pick her moment to tell him. And soon. She touched her belly again, and the sweet hope became a certainty. There was no need to wait for further signs. She knew that Nathaniel's seed had been well planted.

Ellie reappeared with tea. "A little dry toast often 'elps in the morning, m'lady," the maid observed. "So I took the liberty of bringin' a piece. It worked a treat for me mam when she was 'avin' our Martha."

"I can see I'm going to be relying on your experience, Ellie," Gabrielle said, nibbling the toast. She took a sip of tea. "So far so good."

"Other best thing is rose hip tea, Mam always says." Ellie poked the fire and threw kindling on the sparking embers. "What gown will you be wearing this morning, m'lady?"

"Oh, a riding habit, please. I'm engaged to ride in

the park." Gabrielle threw aside the covers and stood up. No nausea. Tea and dry toast in the morning from now on.

Nathaniel was in the breakfast parlor when she went downstairs. He looked up without smiling from the *Gazette* as she entered.

"Good morning. I trust you slept well."

"Not particularly," Gabrielle said, finding no desire to smile herself in the face of this patent unfriendliness. "How about you?"

"All right, I suppose." He resumed his reading.

The shadows under his eyes told another story, Gabrielle reflected, surveying the chafing dishes on the sideboard with an unconscious moue of distaste. Nothing appealed. A dull nausea had settled in her belly. She glanced across at Nathaniel and decided this was not the moment to share her news.

She sat down and took a piece of toast, buttering it lightly before cutting it into thin strips. Idly, she dipped the finger of toast into her tea and ate it with relish.

"What on earth are you doing?" Nathaniel stared in disbelief.

"What?" Startled, she looked up in the act of dunking another finger. "Oh." She looked at the piece of toast with some surprise. "I don't know, it just seemed like a good idea. And it tastes lovely."

"It's disgusting," Nathaniel declared. "Pure slop. Anyone would think you hadn't got any teeth."

"Well, I'm sorry if it offends you, but—"

Her words were cut off by the violent shattering of glass as something flew through the long window and crashed against the far wall.

"What the hell!" Nathaniel sprang to his feet as the cricket ball rolled beneath the sideboard. "That's the second window in three days! I told him he was not to play anywhere near the house!"

Gabrielle rose from her chair. "Easy now, Nathaniel," she cautioned swiftly. "It's only a window."

But if Nathaniel heard her, he made no acknowledgment. He flung open the window. "Jake! Come in here at once."

A stricken Jake appeared at the breakfast room door a couple of minutes later. "I b-beg pardon, sir," he said. "I was practicing bowling overarm, and it sort of slipped."

"What did I tell you the last time?" Nathaniel demanded furiously, towering over the child.

Jake looked in anguished appeal toward Gabrielle, who could tell that he was about to run to her. She realized that this was one occasion when no one would benefit from her intervention; any such action would only exacerbate his father's anger. Deliberately, she turned aside, picking up the discarded newspaper.

"Well?" Nathaniel demanded when Jake stood, tongue-tied.

Two large tears trickled down Jake's cheeks, and he snuffled miserably. "I was waitin' for Primmy to take me to the square garden to play," he offered with a gulp. "It was only one throw."

"I will not tolerate disobedience," his father stated. "You may spend the rest of the day in the schoolroom, and there will be no visits to the garden for the rest of the week."

Jake's eyes widened in horrified dismay. "But, Papa—"

"Did you hear what I said?" Nathaniel thundered.

Jake turned and fled upstairs.

"Oh, Nathaniel," Gabrielle said in soft protest. "He was to go to Astley's this afternoon with the Bedford children. He's talked of nothing else for days."

It was clear from Nathaniel's expression that he'd forgotten this. But he only said curtly, "Then it's to be hoped he'll learn the lesson well." He returned to his unfinished breakfast.

Gabrielle sat in frowning silence for a minute. If it weren't for the trip to Astley's, it didn't qualify as a particularly severe sentence, but Jake was such a sensitive child that a mild rebuke was usually enough to ensure penitence.

After a minute she said, "Couldn't you reconsider, Nathaniel? If he believes he's going to be denied the treat for the next three hours, it'll be sufficient punishment. You know how tractable he usually is."

Nathaniel raised his eyes from his plate, and a chill ran down her spine. He was looking at her as if he didn't know her.

"Jake's my son," he said coldly. "This isn't your business."

Gabrielle felt winded, as if someone had punched her in the stomach. How could he say such a thing? In all essentials Jake was as much her child as Nathaniel's. It was one of their greatest shared joys, one of the inextricable ties that joined them.

It felt as if he was cutting those ties.

Without a word she pushed back her chair and left the room.

Nathaniel dropped his head into his hands under a wash of misery. He couldn't go on like this. Either he confronted her with his suspicions, or he put them from him. But he seemed to be in the grip of some satanic influence that forced him to cut and wound with every breath as if such inflictions could lessen his own pain. Instead, they increased it.

Perhaps if he went away, took some time, put some distance between them, then things would fall into place. He *would* go to Lisbon. There was a job to be done there, one he could do better than anyone. It would distract him. And when he came back, perhaps he'd have an answer to this horrendous dilemma.

He spent the morning making the necessary arrangements and returned to the house at noon, after a meeting with the prime minister. The house seemed very quiet, unpleasantly quiet.

"Is her ladyship in?"

"I believe so, my lord." Bartram took his hat and cane. "I understand she's having nuncheon with Master Jake in the schoolroom."

"I see. Has the glazier fixed the breakfast room window yet?"

"Yes, my lord." Bartram coughed. "It was a capital throw, my lord. Very good form. I saw it from the landing window. He'll make a first class bowler one of these days, if you don't mind me sayin' so."

Bartram's expression was wooden, except that he had a twinkle in his eye.

"He's going to have to learn to aim better first," Nathaniel observed, but there was a hint of amusement in his voice. The prospect of action had gone some way toward restoring his equilibrium.

He mounted the stairs to the third floor, pausing outside the schoolroom door. Gabrielle's cheerful voice reached him through the oak, but there was no sound from his son.

He opened the door. Gabrielle and Jake were sitting at the table in the firelit room. They turned and regarded him in wary silence. Nathaniel felt like an ogre. It was as bad as the days before Gabrielle.

Jake's eyes were red and swollen, Gabrielle's gaze was unreadable, but he knew that she was both hurt and angry.

"Jake, you may go with the Bedfords," he said.

The child leaped to his feet with a delighted cry, his wan countenance transformed. He ran to Nathaniel and flung his arms around his waist, hugging him.

"Hey." Nathaniel caught the small, round chin, tilting it up. "It had better not happen again, do you hear?"

"Oh, yes." Jake nodded solemnly, but he couldn't help the grin that immediately split his face. "Thank you ... you're ... you're the *best* papa in the whole wide world!"

Nathaniel shook his head in amused denial. "You'd better hurry and get ready. Cut along now."

Jake scampered off to the nursery, calling for Primmy to help him find his coat.

Gabrielle rested her elbows on the table. "What brought on the change of heart?"

"You," he said. "As usual. I need to talk to you." He closed the door.

Her heart went cold. Was he going to confront her?

"I'm going away for a few months," Nathaniel said, his shoulders resting against the door at his back.

"Away?" She couldn't hide her dismayed surprise. "Where to?"

"To Lisbon," he said, watching her closely, but her expression didn't change.

"Why?"

"There's work to be done," he said noncommittally.

"Why don't I come with you?" She stood up, her eyes suddenly alight. For the moment she'd forgotten about her pregnancy, and could think only of the thrill of being together again through the excitements and dangers of such a journey . . . of how such an adventure would cure the present grimness, would put paid to all suspicion and doubt.

"Don't be absurd!" Nathaniel said. "If Fouché got his hands on you, your life wouldn't be worth a day's purchase." *Unless she was still in his pay.*

"The same applies to you," she pointed out. "Oh, come on, Nathaniel, remember the last time, that journey from Tilsit. Wouldn't it be wonderful to do it again?"

Nathaniel pushed himself away from the door, and his face was black, his eyes as hard as stone. "Now, you listen to me," he said with soft but deadly menace. "If you so much as think of following me, Gabrielle, I will make your life a living hell. I swear it on my mother's grave."

Gabrielle took an involuntary step back from the ferocious figure. "All right," she said, lifting her hands palm up in a gesture of acceptance. "It was a bad idea ... all right." It was, of course. Reality reasserted itself. Racketing around the Continent in the early months of pregnancy was asking for trouble.

Nathaniel's eyes bored into her during a brief, tense silence, as if he were reading her mind, then he exhaled through his mouth, apparently satisfied.

"I'm going to Burley Manor in the morning," he said in more level tones. "I've some estate matters to deal with before I leave. I expect to sail for France toward the end of the week."

"Shall I come to Burley Manor?" she asked very tentatively.

"No. There would be no point. I'll be far too busy."

"Oh ... right." She shrugged with an assumption of carelessness. "I don't suppose you know how long you'll be away."

"A few months, as I said."

"Two ... three ... four?"

"I've no idea. You know how hard it is to be precise." He sounded impatient.

It's a question of how pregnant I'll be when you get home. "Yes, I know," she said with another shrug. Damn the man! How could she possibly tell him, when he was being so hostile and distant?

"I'll miss you, though." She tried to inject some warmth into the conversation.

Nathaniel's eyes softened. "I'll miss you too, Gabrielle." He meant it. Even when she was twisting him into knots, he couldn't bear to be away from her. "But it's something that I have to do."

"I understand."

Maybe it was time for a separation, she thought. Maybe when he was away from her, whatever suspicions lay behind this estrangement would be put to rest.

He left early the next morning, driving his curricle. Gabrielle stood at the window, watching as he disappeared down the street. Her body felt bereft, as if she'd been abandoned in the middle of making love. And perhaps that wasn't an inaccurate analogy.

28

Two days later another letter arrived from Talleyrand. It was short and terrifying. Fouché had arrested an English agent in Calais. The man had been broken and the Minister of Police believed he was now in possession of vital facts that would endanger the entire English intelligence network in Europe.

Most particularly, he knew the names and types of the boats used to transport agents across the Channel, and he knew most of the safe landing spots they used along the Brittany and Normandy coasts.

Gabrielle read the letter twice. Black spots danced before her eyes and she couldn't think. It was as if her brain were paralyzed. Her hand was numb, she was clutching the letter so tightly, and she forced herself to breathe deeply, to relax her fingers. The letter fluttered to the carpet.

> I give you this information, *ma fille*, to do with as you think best. It is in the way of returning a favor. You will understand what I mean. As always, it is imperative that I am not involved. I trust in your ingenuity to ensure this.

She stared down at the lines at her feet. Ingenuity!
Did he know what he was asking ... *demanding*. But
she knew that he didn't. Talleyrand had no understanding of the complexities of emotional relationships. He
had no time for them. Oh, he loved, he was fond, he
was capable of affection. Why else had he sent her this
intelligence? But individuals and the whole labyrin-
thine maze of feelings could never be allowed to come
between the man and his purpose.

Gabrielle bent to pick up the letter. The movement
made her head spin and her gorge rise into her throat.
She straightened rapidly, one hand stroking her throat,
praying that the wave of nausea would recede. The sensation never left her except when she was nibbling on
some plain and undemanding food, but she dreaded the
times when it would sweep over her in an invincible
wave and she'd have to run for the commode.

Mercifully, it faded from an acute presence to normal queasiness, and she read the letter for the third
time. But now her head was clear and alternative
courses of action tumbled and sorted themselves in her
brain.

There was only one possible course of action. She
had to warn Nathaniel before the *Curlew* sailed from
Lymington. He'd said they would sail at the end of the
week. Today was Friday. Did he mean today or Saturday?

No point speculating, or worrying. She had to
leave immediately. If she rode, she could be in Hampshire by early evening. It would be hard riding. She
touched her belly. Dear God, she couldn't deal with the
nausea on horseback, at least not in its acute version.
But she'd noticed that fresh air seemed to help, and she
had a feeling that panic might well keep a lesser problem at bay.

She couldn't leave the house without a word. She
needed to take someone into her confidence—Primmy.
She'd listen to what she was told, would ask no ques-

tions, and would ensure that no one was alarmed. And a fuller explanation to Simon, just in case something went wrong.

Don't think like that. Guillaume had taught her never to anticipate the worst until she needed to. She didn't need to yet.

She wrote at length to Simon, telling him everything except the source of her information. He could make what guesses he wished. If anything did happen, if she and Nathaniel didn't return, then at least the intelligence would be in the hands of someone who would know what to do with it.

Primmy, as Gabrielle had expected, accepted that Lady Praed was going into the country for a few days. She didn't question the directive that she was to consult Lord and Lady Vanbrugh in the event of any difficulties.

Jake grumbled a bit that he wasn't to go with her, but was easily reconciled when reminded that it would mean forgoing a promised excursion to the lions at the Exchange.

By mid-morning Gabrielle was on the road to Kingston. She had a groom with her who, when she changed horses halfway, would take her own tired mount back to London by easy stages.

They rode into the yard of the Green Man in Basingstoke in the early afternoon. Gabrielle's back was aching, as it did after a long day's hunting, but she ignored it. She was ravenous but stayed only to select a fresh mount. The inn provided a picnic of bread and cheese wrapped in a checkered napkin, and she rode out of the yard ten minutes after entering it, leaving the groom thankfully resting his weary bones before the fire in the taproom and addressing a substantial mutton chop.

Gabrielle now rode harder than she'd ever ridden in her life, pressing the fresh horse to its limit, and delving deep into her own physical resources to find the last vestiges of endurance.

It was six o'clock when she rode up the driveway of Burley Manor. The front of the house was in darkness and her heart sank. If Nathaniel was in residence, there would be some light, in the library at least. The weary horse stumbled on the gravel and came to a halt as she reined him in at the front door. He stood hanging his head, sweat glistening on his neck.

Gabrielle pounded the door knocker, trying to keep the rising panic at bay. Perhaps he was on the estate somewhere and hadn't yet returned. But she knew that was wishful thinking.

A bolt scraped back. "Why, my lady, we wasn't expectin' you." A startled elderly retainer, one of the skeleton staff left to take care of the house, stared at her in the light of the lantern he held high. The hall behind him was in darkness, just a glow of lamplight coming from the open door into the kitchen regions.

"His lordship . . . where is he?" She offered no explanations, clinging to the doorjamb as her legs threatened to give way.

"He be gone, m'lady, two hours since. Said 'e wouldn't be back for a few months."

"What time is high tide?" The sea was such a factor in the lives of these people of the tidal marshes along the Hampshire coastline that most people knew the tide table as they knew the days of the week.

The man stepped outside and looked up at the sky, where a crescent moon swung low over the river. "Ten o'clock, I believe, m'lady."

The relief was so great that Gabrielle almost sat down on the step. But she knew that once she stopped moving, she wouldn't be able to get up again for hours.

"Take this horse to the stable and saddle me another," she commanded. "Quickly!"

"Aye, m'lady." The old man shuffled off with infuriating slowness, and Gabrielle dug deep for a strength she didn't think she had, but found something.

"Never mind, I'll do it," she said, taking the horse's bridle. "Just follow me and look after this one."

Fifteen minutes later she rode out of the stableyard, one of Nathaniel's hunters moving eagerly beneath her. Her fatigue now enclosed her in a mind-numbing grayness, and she could feel herself swaying, her thighs barely exerting any pressure on the saddle. If the hunter decided he didn't have a master on his back, he could well charge off on frolics of his own and she'd be helpless to prevent him. Fortunately he was a well-mannered animal and cantered easily down the lane, responding to the barest guiding nudge of her thighs or flicks of the reins.

Lymington Quay was quieter than Gabrielle had expected, but her blood sang with relief when she saw the *Curlew* tied up in her usual spot at the quayside. She was dark with no sign of her crew, but the sound of raucous voices, laughter, and singing came from the Black Swan. Maybe Nathaniel was in the tap room with the *Curlew*'s crew. It would be like him.

High tide was an hour away. She slipped from the hunter's back and leaned against him for a minute, resting her forehead against the saddle, smelling the rich leather and the pungency of warm horseflesh. Curiously, it seemed to soothe the nausea.

Should she go into the inn and seek out Nathaniel?

But the thought of confronting him in her present weakness in the midst of a crowd of probably inebriated strange men was more than she could manage. She would go aboard the *Curlew* and wait for him there. It was going to be a grim encounter at best; at least it would be relatively private there, and there'd be no fear of her missing him.

She beckoned a yawning lad standing in the light spilling from one of the inn's windows, and handed the hunter over to him, to be stabled until she collected him later. Then she went aboard the *Curlew*.

Immediately the combined odors of tar, fish, and the crude oil they used in the lamps swamped her, and she retched feebly over the side until the spasm passed. She dug into her pocket and pulled out a hunk of bread from her picnic. Breaking off a piece, she chewed it slowly and it had the usual soothing effect.

She stumbled down the companionway into the small, well-remembered cabin, the scene of Jake's hideous sickness. The cot beckoned, and with a groan she tumbled onto it, heedless of the rough ticking of the straw mattress beneath her cheek, or the smelly wool of the thin blanket that she dragged over her. . . .

She awoke to a dimly lit, moving, alien world that made no sense. Her sleep had been so heavy that for minutes she couldn't move her limbs although her brain was giving the right orders. Finally she was able to turn her head and open her eyes.

Nathaniel was sitting at the small table in the middle of the cabin, a glass of cognac in his hand, watching her with a face of granite, and everything rushed upon her in a dizzying flood of memory and panic. She tried to sit up and the nausea hit her. With a groan she fell back again.

Nathaniel spoke, every soft word weighted with lethal menace. "You were warned. And by God, Gabrielle, you're going to pay for this. Get up!"

She couldn't get up, not yet, not without throwing up. "You don't understand—"

"*Get up!*"

Oh, God! She thrust her hand into her pocket and found the last piece of bread.

Nathaniel stood up in one swift, angry movement, sweeping the glass to the floor. It crashed against the metal bolt of the table and broke.

"If I have to put you on your feet, Gabrielle, you are going to wish you'd never been born!"

Gabrielle crammed the bread into her mouth as he advanced on her, and with one desperate, fervent prayer that her stomach would behave, sat up, swinging her legs over the edge of the cot.

"On your feet." Nathaniel stood over her, his face a mask of fury, his eyes deadly.

She swallowed the bread almost whole. Her head was spinning and she was suddenly more frightened than she had ever been in her life. If he was like this now, when he believed she'd merely defied his prohibition, what was he going to do when he learned the truth?

"Listen," she said, her voice thin. "You have to listen to me . . . why I'm here."

"On your feet," he repeated with the same soft savagery.

Gabrielle stood up slowly as the words tumbled in desperate explanation from her lips. "Fouché . . . Fouché has broken one of your agents in Calais. He knows all the landing places in Normandy . . . the boats you use . . . I came to warn you."

Nathaniel face was bloodless in the dim lamplight, his eyes now dark holes in his ghastly complexion. "So you *are* working for Fouché," he said in a voice devoid of emotion.

"No!" Gabrielle shook her head vigorously. "No, not Fouché, never Fouché."

"Then you're working for Talleyrand," he stated in the same flat voice.

"Yes. But—"

"*Whore!*" He hit her with his open palm, and she fell back on the bed, her hand pressed to her cheek, her eyes stunned.

"Whore," he repeated. "I trusted you. I believed in you. I loved you, God forgive me." He bent and grabbed her arms, pulling her up.

He was submerged in a rage so wild, Gabrielle couldn't recognize him. This was not the Nathaniel

Praed she knew—father, lover, husband, friend—a man of humor and great passions, abiding loyalties and deep privacies. This man had moved into a world where ordinary rules didn't apply and where ordinary human sensibilities were suspended.

Somehow she had to bring him back before something dreadful, irrevocable, happened.

"Please, Nathaniel," she cried as his fingers bit deep into her arms and his unseeing eyes blazed with a ruthless rage. "*Please.* I'm having a baby!" It was a desperate plea, and for a minute she thought he hadn't heard. And then his hands dropped from her arms and Nathaniel reinhabited his eyes.

"You're pregnant?"

She nodded, relief washing through her, turning her legs to jelly. She sat on the cot, conscious of the stinging in her cheek and the deep ache in her arms where his fingers had bruised.

"Please, will you listen to me. I have to tell you everything and maybe you'll understand a little."

Nathaniel stepped back from her. There was still bitter hostility in his eyes, but he was in control of himself. He said nothing. Gabrielle swallowed. She was about to betray her godfather, but this time she must think only of herself—and Nathaniel, and Jake—and the child she carried.

"It begins with a man you knew as *le lièvre noir.* . . ."

Half an hour later the story was told and the silence in the dim, fusty cabin was weighted with the words and emotions of that half hour.

"You used me," Nathaniel said finally. "You've been using me from the first moment we met. Even your gift of love, the allegiance you swore . . . everything. It was all part of it."

Gabrielle gazed down at the floor. She had no words of defense. He spoke only the truth. "Yes," she said in a low voice. "You're entitled to see it like that.

But there is another way to look at it. I have—had—old loyalties to Talleyrand, to the memory of Guillaume, as well as new ones. I tried to find a way to reconcile them both."

She looked up, meeting his eye, reading the great hurt and bitterness. "Nathaniel, we're both spies. It's a vile business . . . but necessary. We both know that. I did what I thought best."

He opened his mouth to speak, and suddenly the quiet was shattered by the sound of a musket, followed by another, and then a volley of shots. The fishing boat lurched violently and there was a cry of pain from the deck.

Nathaniel, his pistol in his hand, was already at the companionway.

"Fouché!" Gabrielle murmured. How long had she been asleep? Were they already out of the protection of the Solent? The horrified realization dawned that despite everything, she'd failed in her mission. If she hadn't fallen asleep, they wouldn't have sailed unwarned. And she must have slept for hours, her exhaustion had been so overpowering. Why hadn't Nathaniel woken her? How long had he sat there, feeding his anger, watching her, while they sailed into danger?

She had her own pistol, as usual, in the pocket of her riding habit and leaped for the companionway on Nathaniel's heels. The scene on deck was nightmarish. Dan and his crew lay in a heap by the deck rail, and the deck seemed to swarm with black-clad figures, moonlight glittering off their knives and cutlasses.

The French boat stood off their bow, a boarding net covering the short distance between the two vessels. How had it happened so fast? They must have appeared out of the darkness, that volley of musket shot the first warning. The *Curlew*'s crew must have been overpowered almost without resistance.

Nathaniel sprang forward. His pistol spoke and one of the boarders fell to his knee, clutching his shoulder.

Nathaniel had a knife in his hand now, and was in the midst of the group, slashing, kicking with deadly accuracy, whirling from side to side with the grace of a dancer and the savagery of a warrior.

Gabrielle fired her own pistol into the fray, reducing Nathaniel's opponents by one. She grabbed a broken spar from the deck and brought it down on the head of one of the men grappling with Nathaniel. But the two of them were vastly outnumbered and unable to reload their pistols.

Gabrielle struggled in the grip of two men, their faces blackened with cork. She kicked sideways, drove her elbows into the belly of the man holding her from behind, but it was futile. Her arms were wrenched behind her, twisted upward, and she screamed in pain.

Nathaniel with a cry of fury spun from his own deadly combat at the sound, and a man behind him brought the barrel of his musket down on his head with skull-shattering force.

Nathaniel dropped to the deck. The man kicked him in the belly, but he lay unmoving.

"Nathaniel!" Gabrielle surged forward against her captors' hold and screamed again at the agonizing jolt in her arms. She swore at them, calling them every vile name she could think of, heedless of nothing but her terror that Nathaniel, lying so still with a livid swelling on his forehead, was dead.

Someone silenced her with a brutal blow across her mouth, and she tasted blood from a split lip. Then she was being bundled below. They threw Nathaniel down the companionway behind her, and she gave another scream of outrage, struggling with renewed strength. But she could do nothing to save herself from the ropes. They bound her wrists behind her and tied her ankles and dumped her on the floor. She lay watching as they bound Nathaniel in the same way, and she took some comfort in the reflection that if he were dead, they wouldn't bother to bind him.

She listened to them talk as they completed their work. They were going to leave four men aboard the *Curlew* to bring her with the prisoners into Cherbourg harbor. Their own cutter, the *Sainte Elise*, would continue to sweep the sea along the French coast for any other vessels on their list.

Gabrielle kept very still and silent even when they kicked at Nathaniel's inert body on their way out of the cabin. Her head was now very clear. If there were only four of them, they'd have a chance to overpower them with the advantage of surprise. How many of Dan's men were alive? They'd be bound too, of course. But if she could just get free . . .

She was lying on her back against the table. Nathaniel lay some three feet away from her, on his side, his back to her. She could see the ropes around his wrists. They were thick and tight, tighter, she thought, than the ones at her own wrists. She had enough play to move her wrists against each other, although not a hope of sliding a hand free.

Nathaniel groaned and her heart leaped. He was still alive, but when she called his name softly, there was no response.

She turned her head gingerly on the hard floor and her eye caught a glint under the table. It took her a minute to realize what it was. The glass Nathaniel had swept from the table in his anger. The glass that had broken against the steel bolt of the table.

Her heart began to beat fast, the blood pounding in her temples as she thought what this meant. Broken glass, a jagged edge—a cutting edge. If she could reach it . . .

She stared at the glinting glass, fixing its position in her mind's eye; then she rolled awkwardly onto her side, so her back and her hands were toward the glass. The table legs prevented her reaching the glass with her whole body, but she stretched her joined hands as far as she could, ignoring the renewed pain in her wrenched arms.

She couldn't reach it. Her fingers scrabbled futilely in the dirt and dust under the table and made contact with nothing. Drawing her knees up tight against her chest, she pushed her curled body backward, edging between the table legs. Her fingers searched, encountered something sharp, and she gave a little cry of pain that turned rapidly into a crow of triumph.

Very, very gently her fingers closed around the jagged chunk of glass. She mustn't drop it, but she couldn't hold it too tightly without cutting her hands to ribbons, and she was going to need her hands.

She squirmed out from under the table, stretching her body with a sigh of relief, keeping on her side, holding her arms as far from her body as she could.

Now to reach Nathaniel. But she couldn't roll on her back without injuring herself with the glass. Drawing her knees up again, she levered herself across the cabin until she was lying beside Nathaniel. Now she would have to roll so that her back was against his.

Closing her eyes tightly, she inched over onto her back, raising her hips as far from the ground as she could, arching the small of her back away from her hands. One jerking heave, and she was over, lying back-to-back with Nathaniel.

Now. She ran a finger over the edge of the glass, finding the sharpest, most jagged point. Then she felt for the rope at Nathaniel's wrists. Sweat broke out on her forehead despite the dank chill in the cabin, and a wave of sickness broke over her, but it was anxiety rather than pregnancy this time.

An agonized scream came from on deck, and then another. She took a deep breath, trying not to imagine what was happening. She must concentrate.

Gently at first, she began to saw at the rope at Nathaniel's wrist. But gently took too long. Biting her swollen lip hard, she sawed faster. There was blood on her hands now; she could feel its stickiness, and her nausea increased. Was it Nathaniel's or hers? Impossible to tell.

She stopped, her breath rapid and shallow as she tried to master her terror.

"Keep going, Gabrielle." Nathaniel's voice was calm and steady but so startling in the intense silence of her own private world that she jumped in fear.

"I didn't want you to come to until I was finished," she managed to whisper through dry lips. "I'm afraid I'm hurting you."

"Keep going," he repeated steadily. "I'm holding my wrists as far apart as I can."

"But what if I cut a vein?"

"You won't."

He sounded so confident that she was able to continue despite the blood that now seemed to cover her hands.

"All right," Nathaniel said softly after a long silence when the only sound was the strange rasping of glass on rope. "You're almost there. I can feel it fraying."

"Oh, God," Gabrielle whispered. Her arms were a mass of aching muscle, her wrists cramping with the strain, her fingers so numb, she was afraid she'd drop the glass. She closed her eyes again; it helped her to concentrate, to see nothing but the rope fraying strand by strand beneath the glass.

And then it was done. The rope parted.

"That's my girl," Nathaniel said softly. He sat up. His hands were smothered in blood, but he took no notice, inching his way across to the portmanteau against the bulkhead. Gabrielle was too exhausted to roll over to see what he was doing. He withdrew a knife with a wicked rapier blade and sliced through the rope at his ankles in one stroke.

Then he was kneeling beside Gabrielle. "Hold still." Her wrists were freed and she gave a groan of relief, bringing her hands round, flexing her fingers, massaging her wrists.

"You're bleeding like a stuck pig," she said in horror as he cut the rope at her ankles.

"Bandage them for me," he said matter-of-factly. "There are cravats in the portmanteau."

She found the cravats and wrapped them tightly around his slashed wrists. "There are only four men. Here, put your finger on the knot."

"Only four, you're sure?"

"That's what I heard them say—the other one now—there, that'll do for the moment." She looked up from her handiwork. "They kicked you when you were unconscious."

"I can feel it," he said grimly. He went back to the portmanteau and took out the twin of the knife he still held.

"You've been taught to use one of these." It was more of a statement than a question.

"Yes. And a garrote," she added as he took out the length of rope weighted at either end. She didn't say she'd never used any weapons outside a training session.

His nod was matter-of-fact as he handed her the knife. "I'd like to reduce the odds on deck. Lie on the floor as if you're still tied and start shouting." He moved into the shadows behind the companionway, the length of rope held lightly between his hands.

Gabrielle curled up, facing the door, her feet tucked under the table so that at first glance her lack of bonds wouldn't be immediately apparent. Then she began to scream, one high-pitched cry after another, shivering the timbers of the deck above her head.

Feet sounded above and the hatchway thudded open, filling the cabin with the gray light of dawn. They must be dreadfully close to the French coast, she thought as she screamed again.

Cursing, a man pounded down the companionway.

"Stop that racket, *putain*." He thundered toward her, hand clenched in a fist.

Nathaniel swung the rope, and the man fell back, clutching his throat. Nathaniel lowered him to the floor.

"Jacques . . . what's going on down there?" A voice yelled down the companionway.

Nathaniel gave her a nod and stepped back.

Gabrielle's bloodcurdling scream rose again. A figure jumped down the ladder. As his feet touched ground he seemed to realize that something was wrong. He spun around, and the edge of Nathaniel's right hand chopped against the side of his neck and he dropped to the floor.

Nathaniel swung himself onto the ladder, the knife in his hand. Gabrielle was on his heels. The dawn air, cold and salty, hit her in the face, clearing her head, stinging her swollen lip.

The man at the wheel gave a warning shout as he saw them. Nathaniel had crossed the deck in four bounds, and there was a glint of steel as the Frenchman drew his own knife. His partner lunged from behind the mainsail. He didn't see Gabrielle, who stuck out a foot, and he went sprawling on the deck.

Now she was supposed to use the knife. To hell with it. This was a dirty business, but there were limits. She grabbed up a marlin spike from a coil of rope and brought it down across his shoulders as he struggled onto all fours.

"Much better!" She permitted herself a grim smile of satisfaction at the prone figure before she raced to the grappling couple at the wheel, the marlin spike raised like some Viking club.

Nathaniel's opponent had his back to her for an instant and she brought the spike down onto his shoulder. He screamed as the bone cracked, and dropped to his knees.

Nathaniel glanced down at him and then up at Gabrielle. "You got the other one too, I see."

"Yes, but he's not dead. At least I don't think so." She pushed her hair away from her face, bracing herself unconsciously on the slippery deck as the fishing boat heaved and pitched with no guiding hand on the wheel.

She was bruised and bloody, her eyes black-shadowed, sunken in her white face. And Nathaniel didn't think he'd ever loved her more than he did at that moment. He knew he'd never understood her as he now did.

He grinned tiredly. "You're quite a fighter, aren't you, Gabrielle?"

"I fight for what I believe in," she said. "I fight for what I love . . . in whatever way I must."

Her eyes held his in a passionate plea for his understanding, and in the dawn stillness he nodded in simple but complete acknowledgment. Then he said briskly, "See what you can do for Dan and the others. I'm going to put her about and I'll need a hand with the mainsail."

She left him at the wheel and approached the three figures of Dan and his crew, tied to the rail, gags in their mouths. Dan was bleeding from a gash in his forehead, one of the others, a youngster of maybe seventeen, slumped unconscious in his bonds, the other had a broken arm, the splintered bone sticking jaggedly through his flesh.

They were unnecessary wounds, the work of Fouché's men, and a red wave of hatred surged over Gabrielle as she cut them loose.

"Bastards!" Dan exploded in soft ferocity. "They've been playing their foul games with young Jamie here for hours." He gently eased the unconscious lad to the deck. Gabrielle remembered the agonized screams and turned her eyes away from the pattern of knife marks on his chest.

"Nathaniel needs help with the sails," she said as calmly as she could. "Are you able to do it?"

"Aye." Dan walked stiffly and painfully toward Nathaniel while Gabrielle went below to see what she could find to bind up the broken arm.

She glanced at the men on the cabin floor and was surprised to find them both breathing. She had thought Nathaniel had killed the one with the garrote. There was livid bruising around his throat, but he was breathing in stertorous gasps.

She went back on deck and did what she could with the broken arm, binding it tightly and fashioning a sling so that at least the pieces of bone wouldn't scrape together and the arm was supported.

The man smiled wanly, but he was clearly incapable of doing anything.

"Gabrielle!"

"Yes?" She went over to the wheel.

"Come here." Nathaniel took her shoulders and drew her in front of him. "Hold the wheel. Do you remember anything I taught you on the river that day? What I told you about keeping the wind abaft the mainsail."

"I think so, but this is so much bigger than the dinghy."

"The principle's the same. Look up at the sail. The edge mustn't flutter. Try to keep the wind on the side of your face—here." Gently he touched her cheek. Then he bent and brushed his lips over the spot, and she knew he was remembering how he'd struck her earlier.

She reached up and grasped his bandaged wrist. "I'll manage."

"Yes, I know you will. Come on, Dan, let's get these swine off this boat."

They tied the four unconscious men, lowered the rowboat over the side, and heaved the bodies into it.

"They'll probably get picked up, more's the pity," Nathaniel said, squinting through the morning mist to the rocky cliffs of the French coast. "Let's hope we get the hell out of here before anyone else comes along."

"We'll fly the French colors," Dan said. "That might give us some leeway."

Nathaniel looked across at Gabrielle. Her hands were steady on the wheel, her feet braced wide apart, her eyes on the mainsail. She was like no other woman. And she had more courage in her little finger than a regiment of marines.

The courage of her convictions too. It still hurt to think that she'd deceived him, that he'd been duped by Talleyrand. But he thought how it had begun. He knew Gabrielle's passion. He understood her need for vengeance for her lover's murder. He would have felt it himself. And he now understood the curious logic that had brought them to this point. Gabrielle *was* loyal. In fact, her fault, if it was one, lay in too much loyalty. By an accident of birth she had a foot in both camps. A tempestuous and passionate nature would not allow her to abandon either one.

And he loved her. He loved her for that courage and that loyalty as much as he did for her passion and her warmth and her generosity.

And she was carrying his child.

He went over to her. "Let Dan take the wheel now."

She relinquished it with a weary shrug of her shoulders, trying to ease the aching stiffness, the residue of the night's ordeal. "I'll make a sailor yet," she said, smiling.

The smile was such a brave attempt that his heart turned over anew. He reached for her, but suddenly she clutched her throat, murmured, "Oh, no, why now?" and fled to the rail, retching miserably. But she'd eaten almost nothing in the past twenty-four hours and the spasm eased, although the queasiness didn't.

"What is it, love?" Nathaniel drew her against him. "The sea's like glass."

"I seem to have time to feel sick again," she said. "I don't suppose you have a piece of bread on you?"

"Bread? No. Why?"

"It's the only thing that helps. It's the most horrid inconvenience, Nathaniel. Was Helen sick?"

"I don't believe so." He leaned against the rail, and his expression was both somber and confused. "Just *how* did it happen?"

She gave him another wan smile. "You mean there's more than one way?"

"You know what I mean." He rubbed the back of his neck, frowning in frustration. "How could you—"

"Hey," she interrupted. "It takes two, I'll have you know."

"Yes, I know." He pulled her against him, pushing her hair off her forehead. "But I'm frightened."

"What of?" She smiled, touching his mouth. "I rode without stopping for ten hours. It's been a night of trial by ordeal. And I'm still here, aren't I? Still pregnant? I'm tough, Nathaniel. It may not be a particularly feminine characteristic, but I grew up in a hard school."

"I know that." He caught her chin. "Your poor mouth." Tenderly he kissed her swollen lips.

"And do you understand what ... why ..." She needed his words although she knew he did understand now.

He laid a finger over her mouth. "It's over, Gabrielle. We both made mistakes. We didn't trust each other enough, and maybe with cause," he added gravely. "Trust comes with knowledge. It's taken us a long time to know each other."

"But you know me now?" She leaned into him.

"As I know myself."

"That's what *I* find frightening," Gabrielle said. "We're so alike. Can one fight with oneself?"

"All the time," he said with a wry smile. "And I suspect we're going to be the living proof."

29

Jake stood outside Gabrielle's closed bedroom door, listening. He could hear voices, people moving around, but nothing to give him an idea of what was going on in there. He couldn't picture what was happening. He'd asked Primmy and she'd said he wasn't old enough to understand. He'd asked Mrs. Bailey and she'd blessed him and given him a jam tart and told him to run along. He didn't think there would be any point asking Nurse. She didn't know much about anything except keeping things clean and generally fussing.

He slid down the wall at his back until he was sitting on the floor, facing the door and hugging his drawn-up knees. He was scared, but everyone else in the house seemed excited. They went around smiling and whispering in corners, and he'd heard Ellie giggling about a book that Milner was keeping in the stables about whether it would be a boy or a girl. Why would he keep a book about that in the stables?

His eyes fixed on the cream-painted door, willing it to open. Papa was in there. He wished he would come out and tell him what was happening.

Behind the closed bedroom door Nathaniel stood

in the shadows of the bedcurtains, out of Gabrielle's direct line of sight but close enough to respond if she wanted him. He didn't know what else to do. If he touched her or spoke to her when she was distracted, she cursed him like a trooper, but when he'd tried to tiptoe from the room, she'd called him back urgently, telling him she needed to know he was there.

There was nothing concrete he could do. The doctor, the midwife, and Ellie were all moving around with unhurried efficiency, talking softly to Gabrielle, ignoring her occasional oaths.

He wasn't frightened, Nathaniel realized. This was nothing like Helen's time. The woman on the bed was a tigress, hissing and spitting at the pain of this ghastly ordeal, yielding to her body and yet never losing herself in the violent paroxysms. Her spirit was hovering way above the suffering body on the bed, and despite six hours of this, she didn't seem to be weakening. If anything, she grew ever more peppery as the contractions increased.

"Goddammit, Nathaniel," she said with sudden clarity. "If you ever do this to me again, I'll kill you. . . ." She gasped, sweat breaking out on her forehead, and then relaxed, turning her face toward him. To his amazement, her crooked smile touched her lips. "That was a piece of rank injustice, wasn't it?"

"Even for you," he agreed with an answering smile. He wiped her forehead with a lavender-scented cloth.

"I wish I knew who'd coined the phrase Mother Nature," she said in another moment of respite. "No female would have inflicted this on women."

She grabbed his hand suddenly, clinging to it as the pain tightened unmercifully, impossibly, gripped for an eternity, and then slowly receded.

"Jake's outside the door," she said, her voice weaker than before. "He needs reassurance."

"How do you know he's there?"

"Because he would be." She was lost again, and

Nathaniel stood helplessly for a minute, and then went to the door.

Where did she get her strength from? It far exceeded his own at the moment. She was keeping up this banter to make *him* feel better. And she was worrying about Jake, when he hadn't given the child a thought.

He opened the door and his heart went out to his son, sitting wide-eyed, scared, and uncomprehending, on the floor.

"What are you doing here, Jake?" he asked gently, closing the door behind him.

"I don't know what's happening." Jake stood up. "Is Gabby going to die?"

"No, of course not." Nathaniel squatted on his heels so that he was on a level with the child. "Everything's going just as it's supposed to. Gabrielle is fine, although she's a little cross because it's not very comfortable having a baby."

"My first mother died." Jake's eyes were big brown pools of anxiety and confusion. "She died because of me."

Nathaniel shook his head. "No, not because of you, Jake. You must never think that." He drew the child against him in a fierce hug. "And I promise you that Gabrielle is *not* going to die. She's too busy being rude to me." He drew back with a teasing smile, pushing the child's hair off his forehead.

"I want to see her."

"Not just now."

"Why not?"

"Because she's not feeling well enough for visitors. But as soon as she is, you'll be the first one she'll want to see. You know that."

Jake did know that. He chewed his lip for a minute. "She's really not going to die?"

"No. I promise you." Nathaniel stood up. "Now, I

want you to go back to Primmy and stay in the school-room until I send for you."

"Can't I stay here?"

"No," his father said firmly. If Gabrielle lost control, the child would be terrified. And God knows, she was entitled to scream her head off if it would help.

"Off you go." He turned him with a pat on his rear and watched him walk with dragging step down the corridor.

He returned to the bedroom and was immediately aware of a tension in the atmosphere replacing the calm efficiency of before.

His heart was in his throat, his blood running cold. "Is something wrong?"

"No, my lord," the doctor said, rolling up his sleeves. "Everything's quite normal."

"Nathaniel!" Gabrielle's voice was urgent.

"I'm here, love." He took her hand.

She gripped it fiercely, and then her body convulsed and a cry as much of triumph as effort broke from her lips.

Nathaniel watched as his daughter fought her way into the world, a waxy, blue, blood-streaked scrap. There was a thin cry and the scrap turned pink.

"A daughter, my lady," the midwife said. "A beautiful baby."

"I don't think it's quite over," Gabrielle said with a gasp, her eyes startled.

"Well, well," the doctor murmured, turning back to his patient. "It seems she has a sibling."

"I don't believe this," Nathaniel murmured as his daughter's brother entered the world with a lusty bellow.

Gabrielle fell back against the pillows, her eyes closed. "Give them to me," she said.

"I'll wash them first, my lady," the midwife said, sounding shocked at this unconventional demand.

"No, you won't," Gabrielle declared. "You'll give them to me this minute."

The midwife looked as if she was going to protest, but Lord Praed moved to take the infants from her, even more of an outrage to proper procedure, as if it wasn't bad enough that he was in the room at all. With a sniff she hastily laid the babies naked on their mother's breast.

"You don't do anything by halves, do you, my love?" Nathaniel said, his eyes wet, a smile of wonderment on his lips as he gently touched the tiny heads.

Gabrielle chuckled weakly. "Aren't they beautiful?"

"They'll be even more so, my lady, when they're washed and dressed." The midwife reasserted her authority. "Now, come along, we don't want them to get cold, do we?"

Gabrielle relinquished her babies with a grimace at Nathaniel, who bent to kiss her.

"You are miraculous," he whispered against her mouth.

"Now, my lord, we need to tidy her ladyship up a little," the midwife said, gesturing toward the door. "I'm sure everyone's very anxious to hear of her ladyship's safe delivery of two such healthy babes."

"No." Gabrielle put out an imperative hand. "Jake must be the first to know."

"Of course," Nathaniel said. "I'll just sit over here and wait until you're ready to receive him."

Ignoring the sniffs of the midwife, he sat down on the window seat, stretching his legs in front of him, linking his hands behind his head, a dreamy smile on his lips as he contemplated his family. How had he ever thought he didn't want any more children?

The bustle continued around him for a half-hour, and then Ellie pulled back the bedcurtains and announced, "Her ladyship is ready for visitors, my lord."

Nathaniel went over to the bed. Gabrielle was propped up against piled pillows, and her translucent pallor blended with the embroidered white linen. Black shadows smudged the thin skin beneath the charcoal eyes, but there was life and laughter in her eyes and her hair had been brushed into some semblance of its usual fierce vibrancy.

"Fetch Jake," she said. "And I'm sure the doctor would appreciate a glass of something . . . to wet the babies' heads." An eyebrow lifted quizzically as she reminded him of his role.

Nathaniel shook his head ruefully. There'd been no joyous celebrations of birth around Helen's deathbed; perhaps it wasn't surprising he'd neglected the ritual.

It was easily rectified, however, and the doctor was soon appreciating a glass of the finest cognac from the decanter in Nathaniel's adjoining apartments.

Jake jumped to his feet as his father entered the schoolroom.

"My lord?" Primmy put down her tambour frame, her faded eyes both apprehensive and excited.

"All's well," he said. "Come, Jake. Gabrielle's waiting for you." He held out his hand and the child ran to him.

"But, Lord Praed? What . . . what . . ." The question went unanswered as Nathaniel left the schoolroom hand in hand with his excited son.

Jake dropped his father's hand as they neared the Queen's Suite and ran ahead, bursting through the door. "Gabby . . ."

He stopped in the doorway, staring at the bed. "There's two of 'em," he said with more indignation than pleasure.

"Yes, it *was* rather a surprise," Gabrielle said cheerfully. "Come and meet them."

Jake approached the bed somewhat cautiously. He peered into the shawls Gabby held, one in each arm. "Which is which?"

"Well, this is your sister." Gabrielle indicated the left shawl. "And this is your brother."

Jake squinted at the two wrinkled beings, commenting, "One of each."

"Just so." His father leaned over. "But don't ask me how you can tell when they're all swaddled like this."

"It's easy," Gabrielle said. "Jake's sister has a curl on her forehead."

"An' the other one's got no hair at all," Jake pronounced, hitching himself onto the bed. "Can I hold him?"

Gabrielle handed over the right-hand bundle, smiling as Jake struggled to accommodate the living shawl in his arms.

"Now, who's that?" Nathaniel strode to the window, opened onto the soft warmth of the July evening. Carriage wheels crunched on the gravel below.

"Georgie, I expect," Gabrielle said calmly, playing with her daughter's tiny fingers.

"But how could she have known?"

Gabrielle smiled, tickling the infant's chin. "We've always known when important things are happening to the other. It's very mysterious."

"She has Lady DeVane with her," Nathaniel observed in mild resignation, leaning out of the window. "I can only imagine Simon and Miles and Lord DeVane are not far behind."

Gabrielle chuckled. "Probably not Lord DeVane. He's not too enamoured of babies. But I'm sure you're right about Miles and Simon."

Nathaniel scooped his younger son from the arms of the elder and said, "Run downstairs, Jake, and welcome Lady Vanbrugh and Lady DeVane, and escort them up here."

Jake blinked. This was a novel responsibility. He looked at the bundle that was his brother. Such a baby.

"Yes, Papa. Can I tell them it's two?" He slid from the bed and ran from the room before Nathaniel could answer him.

"Let me hold her too," he said, his eyes gleaming with pure pride.

Gabrielle handed over her own bundle and lay back, smiling. The extent of Nathaniel's pride and joy took her by surprise, and she wondered why as she watched him holding his children, waiting to present them to their first outside admirers.

"Gabby ..." Georgie exploded through the door first. "Was it all right? I was so worried about you." Ignoring Nathaniel and his bundles, she flew to the bed and flung her arms around her cousin. "Look at you," she said between laughter and tears. "You look no more tired than after a day's hunting!"

Gabrielle hugged her tightly. "Believe me, love, I'd rather hunt."

"Yes, it is awful, isn't it?" Georgie straightened, feeling for her handkerchief. Misty-eyed, she turned to Nathaniel, who was reluctantly relinquishing his infants to the arms of Lady DeVane.

"Congratulations," she said, standing on tiptoe and kissing his cheek with a warmth that startled him.

He put an arm around her and hugged her with a fierceness that startled both of them.

"Well, if this isn't just like you, Gabby dear," Lady DeVane observed placidly, rocking the babies in her arms. "Always full of surprises."

"Quite so, ma'am," Nathaniel agreed, sitting on the bed beside Gabrielle, drawing Jake between his knees, rubbing the child's neck.

"Have you named them?" Lady DeVane asked, handing one infant to her eager daughter.

Gabrielle opened her mouth but Nathaniel spoke first. "Imogen."

"Oh, yes. For Gabby's mother. Very appropriate. ... Would you like to hold your sister, dear?" Lady DeVane bent her vague smile on Jake.

Jake wanted to ask how this lady could know which one she was giving him. She didn't know about the curl. But it wouldn't be polite to ask. He held out his arms.

"And what of the boy?"

"William," Nathaniel said quietly.

Gabrielle was suddenly very still. That was not a name they'd discussed.

"Is that a family name, Lord Praed?" Lady DeVane looked mildly curious.

"No," Nathaniel said. "It honors a lost life." He looked at Gabrielle, and she smiled her crooked smile, her eyes filled with love.

Guillaume's death had begun this. Her son would celebrate his life.

About the Author

JANE FEATHER is the *New York Times* bestselling, award-winning author of *The Least Likely Bride*, *The Accidental Bride*, *A Valentine Wedding*, and many other historical romances. She was born in Cairo, Egypt, and grew up in the New Forest, in the south of England. She began her writing career after she and her family moved to Washington, D.C., in 1981. She now has over five million copies of her books in print.

Don't miss Jane Feather's newest

captivating romance

The Widow's Kiss

a Bantam hardcover on sale in January 2001.
Read on for a special sneak preview. . . .

DERBYSHIRE, ENGLAND
SEPTEMBER 1536

THE WOMAN STOOD by the open window, the soft breeze stirring the folds of her blue silk hood as it hung down her back. She stood very still and straight, her dark gown shadowy against the dense velvet of the opened window curtains.

She heard him in the corridor outside, his heavy, lumbering step. She could picture his large frame lurching from side to side as he approached. Now he was outside the great oak door. She could hear his labored breathing. She could picture his bloodshot eyes, his reddened countenance, his lips slack with exertion.

The door burst open. Her husband filled the doorway, his richly jeweled gown swirling about him.

"By God, madam! You would dare to speak to me in such wise at my own table! In the hearing of our guests, of the household, scullions even!" A shower of spittle accompanied the slurred words as he advanced into the chamber, kicking the door shut behind him. It shivered on its hinges.

The woman stood her ground beside the window, her hands clasped quietly against her skirts. "And I say to you, husband, that if you ever threaten one of my daughters again, you will rue the day." Her voice was barely above a whisper but the words came at him with the power of thunder.

For a second he seemed to hesitate, then he lunged for her with clenched fists upraised. Still she stood her ground, a slight derisive smile on her lips, her eyes, purple as sloes, fixed upon his face with such contempt, he bellowed in drunken rage.

As he reached her, one fist aimed at her pale face beneath its jeweled headdress, his only thought to smash the smile from her lips, to close the hateful contempt in her eyes, she stepped aside. Her foot caught his ankle and the speed and weight of his charge carried him forward.

For a second he seemed to hover at the very brink of the dark space beyond the low-silled window, then he twisted and fell. A shriek of astounded terror accompanied his plunge to the flagstones beneath.

The woman twitched aside the curtain so that she could look down without being seen. At first in the dark depths below the window she could make out nothing, then came the sound of upraised voices, the tread of many feet; light flickered as torchmen came running from the four corners of the courtyard. And now, in the light, she could see the dark, crumpled shape of her husband.

How small he looked, she thought, clasping her elbows across her breast with a little tremor. So much malevolence, so much violence, reduced, deflated, to that inert heap.

And then she seemed to come to life. She moved back swiftly to the far side of the chamber, where a small door gave onto the garderobe. She slipped into the small privy and stood for a second, listening. Running feet sounded in the corridor beyond her chamber. There was a loud knocking, then she heard the latch lift. As the door was flung wide she stepped out of the garderobe, hastily smoothing down her skirts.

An elderly woman stood in the doorway in her nightrobe, her head tucked beneath a white linen cap. "Ay! Ay! Ay!" she exclaimed, wringing her hands. "What is it, my chuck? What has happened here?" Behind her, curious faces pressed over her shoulder.

The woman spoke to those faces, her voice measured, calming. "I don't know, Tilly. Lord Stephen came in while I was in the garderobe. He called to me. I was occupied . . . I couldn't come to him immediately. He grew impatient . . . but . . ." She gave a little helpless shrug. "In his agitation, he must have lost his balance . . . fallen from the window. I didn't see what happened."

"Ay . . . ay . . . ay," the other woman repeated, almost to herself. "And 'tis the fourth! Lord-a-mercy." She fell silent as the younger woman fixed her with a hard, commanding stare.

"Lord Stephen was drunk," the younger woman said evenly. "Everyone knew it . . . in the hall, at table. He could barely see straight. I must go down." She hurried past the woman, past the crowd of gaping servants, gathering her skirts to facilitate her step.

Her steward came running across the great hall as she came down the stairs. "My lady . . . my lady . . . such a terrible thing."

"What happened, Master Crowder? Does anyone know?"

The black-clad steward shook his head and the unloosened lappets of his bonnet flapped at his ears like crows' wings. "Did you not see it, my lady? We thought you must have known what happened. 'Twas from your chamber window that he fell."

"I was in the garderobe," she said shortly. "Lord Stephen was drunk, Master Crowder. He must have lost his footing . . . his balance. It was ever thus."

"Aye, 'tis true enough, madam. 'Twas ever thus with his lordship." The steward followed her out into the courtyard, where a crowd stood around the fallen man.

They gave way before the lady of the house, who knelt on the cobbles beside her husband. His neck was at an odd angle and blood pooled beneath his head. She placed a finger for form's sake against the pulse in his neck. Then with a sigh sat back on her heels, the dark folds of her gown spreading around her.

"Where is Master Grice?"

"Here, my lady." The priest came running from his little lodging behind the chapel, adjusting his gown as he came. "I heard the commotion, but I . . ." He stopped as he reached the body. His rosary beads clicked between his fingers as he gazed down and said with a heavy sigh, "May the Lord have mercy on his soul."

"Yes, indeed," agreed Lord Stephen's wife. She rose to her feet in a graceful movement. "Take my lord's body to the chapel to be washed and prepared. We will say a mass at dawn. He will lie in state for the respects of the household and the peasants before his burial tomorrow evening."

She turned and made her way back through the crowd, back into the house, ducking her head as she stepped through the small door that was set into the larger one to keep the cold and the draughts from invading the hall.

Lady Guinevere was a widow once more.

"HOW MANY HUSBANDS did you say?" The king turned his heavy head towards Thomas Cromwell, his Lord Privy Seal. His eyes rested with almost languid indifference on his minister's grave countenance, but no one in the king's presence chamber at Hampton Court believed in that indifference.

"Four, Highness."

"And the lady is of what years?"

"Eight and twenty, Highness."

"She has been busy, it would seem," Henry mused.

"It would seem a husband has little luck in the lady's bed," a voice remarked dryly from a dark, paneled corner of the chamber.

The king's gaze swung towards a man of tall and powerful build, dressed in black and gold. A man whose soldierly bearing seemed ill suited to his rich dress, the tapestry-hung comforts of the chamber, the whispers, the spies, the gossip-mongering of King Henry's court. He had an air of impatience, of a man who preferred to be doing rather than talking, but there was a gleam of humor in his eyes, a natural curve to his mouth, and his voice was as dry as sere leaves.

"It would seem you have the right of it, Hugh," the king responded. "And how is it exactly that these unlucky husbands have met their deaths?"

"Lord Hugh has more precise knowledge than I." Privy Seal waved a beringed hand towards the man in the corner.

"I have a certain interest, Highness." Hugh of Beaucaire stepped forward into the light that poured through the diamond-paned windows behind the king's head. "Lady Mallory, as she now is . . . the *widowed* Lady Mallory . . . was married to a distant cousin of my father's when she was sixteen. He was her first husband. There is some family land in dispute. I claim it for my own son. Lady Mallory will entertain no such claim. She has kept every penny, every hectare of land from each of her husbands."

"No mean feat," Privy Seal commented. "For a woman."

"How could she do such a thing?" The king's eyes gleamed in the deep rolls of flesh in which they were embedded like two bright currants in dough.

"She has some considerable knowledge of the law of property, Highness," Lord Hugh said. "A knowledge the bereaved widow puts into practice before embarking on a new union."

"She draws up her own marriage contracts?" The king was incredulous. He pulled on his beard, the great carbuncle on his index finger glowing with crimson fire.

"Exactly so, Highness."

"Body of God!"

"In each of her marriages the lady has ensured that on the death of her husband she inherits lock, stock, and barrel."

"And the husbands have all died . . ." mused the king.

"Each and every one of them."

"Are there heirs?"

"Two young daughters. The progeny of her second husband, Lord Hadlow."

The king shook his head slowly. "Body of God," he muttered again. "These contracts cannot be overset?"

Privy Seal lifted a sheaf of papers from the desk. "I have had lawyers examining each one with a fine-tooth comb, Highness. They are drawn up as right and tight as if witnessed by the Star Chamber itself."

"Do we join Hugh of Beaucaire in his interest in these holdings?" Henry inquired.

"When one woman owns most of a county as extensive and as rich in resources as Derbyshire, the king and his Exchequer have a certain interest," Privy Seal said. "At the very least, one might be interested in adequate tithing."

The king was silent for a minute. When he spoke it was again in a musing tone. "And if, of course, foul play were suspected with any of these . . . uh . . . untimely deaths, then one could not leave the perpetrator in possession of her ill-gotten gains."

"Or indeed her head," Privy Seal murmured.

"Mmm." The king looked up once more at Lord Hugh. "Do you suspect foul play, my lord?"

"Let us just say that I find the coincidences a little difficult to believe. One husband dies falling off his horse in a stag hunt. Now, that, I grant Your Highness, is a not uncommon occurrence. But then the second is slain by a huntsman's arrow . . . an arrow that no huntsman present would acknowledge. The third dies of a sudden and mysterious wasting disease . . . a man in his prime, vigorous, never known a day's illness in his life. And the fourth falls from a window . . . the lady's own chamber window . . . and breaks his neck."

Lord Hugh tapped off each death on his fingers, a faintly incredulous note in his quiet voice as he enumerated the catalogue.

"Aye, 'tis passing strange," the king agreed. "We should investigate these deaths, I believe, Lord Cromwell."

Privy Seal nodded. "Hugh of Beaucaire, if it pleases Your Highness, has agreed to undertake the task."

"I have no objection. He has an interest himself, after all . . . but . . ." Here the king paused, frowning. "One thing I find most intriguing. How is it that the lady has managed to persuade four knights, gentlemen of family and property, to agree to her terms of marriage?"

"Witchcraft, Highness." The Bishop of Winchester in his scarlet robes spoke up for the first time. "There can be no other explanation. Her victims were known to be learned, in full possession of their faculties at the time they made the acquaintance of Lady Guinevere. Only a man bewitched would agree to the terms upon which she insisted. I request that the woman be brought here for examination, whatever findings Lord Hugh makes."

"Of what countenance is the woman? Do we know?"

"I have here a likeness, made some two years after her marriage to my father's cousin. She may have changed, of course." Hugh handed his sovereign a painted miniature set in a diamond-studded frame.

The king examined the miniature. "Here is beauty indeed," he murmured. "She would have to have changed considerably to be less than pleasing now." He looked up, closing his large paw over the miniature. "I find myself most interested in making the acquaintance of this beautiful sorceress, who seems also to be an accomplished lawyer. Whether she be murderer or not, I will see her."

"It will be a journey of some two months, Highness. I will leave at once." Hugh of Beaucaire bowed, waited for a second to see if the sovereign's giant hand would disgorge the miniature, and when it became clear that it was lost forever, bowed again and left the chamber.

It was hot and quiet in the forest. A deep somnolence had settled over the broad green rides beneath the canopy of giant oaks and beeches. Even the birds were still, their song silenced by the heat. The hunting party gathered in the grove, listening for the horn of a beater that would tell them their quarry had been started.

"Will there be a boar, Mama?" A little girl on a dappled pony spoke in a whisper, hushed and awed by the expectant silence around her. She held a small bow, an arrow already set to the string.

Guinevere looked down at her elder daughter and smiled. "There should be, Pen. I have spent enough money on stocking the forest to ensure a boar when we want one."

"My lady, 'tis a hot day. Boar go to ground in the heat," the chief huntsman apologized, his distress at the possibility of failing the child clear on his countenance.

"But it's my birthday, Greene. You promised me I should shoot a boar on my birthday," the child protested, still in a whisper.

"Not even Greene can produce miracles," her mother said. There was a hint of reproof in her voice, and the child immediately nodded and smiled at the huntsman.

"Of course I understand, Greene. Only . . ." she added, rather spoiling the gracious effect, "only I had told my sister I would shoot a boar on my birthday and maybe I won't, and then she will be bound to shoot one on hers."

Knowing the Lady Philippa as he did, the chief huntsman had little doubt that she would indeed succeed where her sister might not and shoot her first boar on her tenth birthday. Fortunately he was spared a response by the sound of a horn, high and commanding, then a great crashing through the underbrush. The hounds leaped forward on their leashes with shrill barks. The horses shifted on the grass, sniffed the wind, tense in expectation.

" 'Tis not one of our horns," the huntsman said, puzzled.

"But it's our boar," Lady Guinevere stated. "Come, Pen." She nudged her milk-white mare into action and galloped across the glade towards the trees, where the crashing of the undergrowth continued. The child followed on her pony and Greene blew on his horn. The leashed dogs raced forward at the summons, the huntsmen chasing after them.

They broke through the trees onto a narrow path. The boar,

his little red eyes glowing, stood at bay. He snorted and lowered his head with its wickedly sharp tusks.

Pen raised her bow, her fingers quivering with excitement. The boar charged straight for the child's pony.

Guinevere raised her own bow and loosed an arrow just as another flew from along the path ahead of them. The other caught the boar in the back of the neck. Pen in her mingled terror and excitement loosed her own arrow too late and it fell harmlessly to the ground. Her mother's caught the charging animal in the throat. Despite the two arrows sticking from its body, the boar kept coming under the momentum of his charge. Pen shrieked as the animal leaped, the vicious tusks threatening to drive into her pony's breast.

Then another arrow landed in the back of the boar's neck and it crashed to the ground beneath the pony's feet. The pony reared in terror and bolted, the child clinging to its mane.

A horseman broke out of the trees at the side of the ride and grabbed the pony's reins as it raced past. As the animal reared again, eyes rolling, snorting wildly, the man caught the child up from the saddle just as she was about to shoot backwards to the ground. The pony pawed and stamped. Other men rode out of the trees and gathered on the path facing Guinevere's party.

Pen looked up at the man who held her on his saddle. She didn't think she had ever seen such brilliant blue eyes before.

"All right?" he asked quietly.

She nodded, still too shaken and breathless to speak.

Guinevere rode up to them. "My thanks, sir." She regarded the man and his party with an air of friendly inquiry. "Who rides on Mallory land?"

The man leaned over and set Pen back on her now quiet pony. Instead of answering Guinevere's question, he said, "I assume you are the Lady Guinevere."

There was something challenging in his gaze. Guinevere thought, as had her daughter, that she had never seen such brilliant blue eyes, but she read antagonism in the steady look. Her friendly smile faded and her chin lifted in instinctive response. "Yes, although I don't know how you would know that. You are on my land, sir. And you are shooting my boar."

"It seemed you needed help shooting it yourself," he commented.

"My aim was true," she said with an angry glitter in her eye. "I needed no help. And if I did, I have my own huntsmen."

The man looked over at the group of men clustered behind her. He shrugged, as if dismissing them as not worth consideration.

Guinevere felt her temper rise. "Who trespasses on Mallory land?" she demanded.

He turned his bright blue eyes upon her, regarding her thoughtfully. His gaze traveled over her as she sat tall in the saddle. He took in the elegance of her gown of emerald-green silk with its raised pattern of gold vine leaves, the stiffened lace collar that rose at her nape to frame her small head, the dark green hood with its jeweled edge set back from her forehead to reveal hair the color of palest wheat. Her eyes were the astounding purple of ripe sloes. The miniature had not done her justice, he thought.

His gaze turned to the milk-white mare she rode, noticing its bloodlines in the sloping pasterns, the arched neck. A lady of wealth and discrimination, whatever else she might be.

"Hugh of Beaucaire," he said almost lazily.

So he had come in person. No longer satisfied with laying claim to her land by letter, he had come himself. It certainly explained his antagonism. Guinevere contented herself with an ironically raised eyebrow and returned his stare, seeing in her turn a man in his vigorous prime, square built, square jawed, his thick iron-gray hair cropped short beneath the flat velvet cap, his weathered complexion that of a man who didn't spend his time skulking with politicos in the corners and corridors of palaces.

"This is my son, Robin." Hugh gestured and a boy rode out of the group of men behind him and came up beside his father. He had his father's blue eyes.

"I claim the lands between Great Longstone and Wardlow for my son," stated Hugh of Beaucaire.

"And I deny your claim," Guinevere replied. "My legal right to the land is indisputable."

"Forgive me, but I do dispute it," he said gently.

"You are trespassing, Hugh of Beaucaire. You have done my daughter a service and I would hate to drive you off with the dogs, but I will do so if you don't remove yourself from my lands." She beckoned the huntsmen to bring up the eager hounds.

"So you throw down the glove," he said in a musing tone.

"I have no need to do so. You are trespassing. That is all there is to it."

Pen shifted in her saddle. She met the gaze of the boy, Robin. He was looking at least as uncomfortable as she was at this angry exchange between their parents.

"Greene, let loose the dogs," Guinevere said coldly.

Hugh raised an arresting hand. "We will discuss this at some other time, when we are a little more private." He gathered his reins to turn his horse.

"There is nothing to discuss." She gathered up her own reins. "I cannot help but wonder at the sense of a man who would ride this great distance on an idle errand."

She gestured back along the path with her whip. "If you ride due west you will leave Mallory land in under an hour. Until some months past, you would have found hospitality at the monastery of Arbor, but it was dissolved in February. The monks seek shelter themselves now." Her voice dripped contempt.

"You would question His Highness's wisdom in dissolving the monasteries, madam? I would question *your* sense, in such a case."

"No, I merely point out the inconvenience to benighted travelers," she said sweetly. "Farewell, Hugh of Beaucaire. Do not be found upon Mallory land two hours hence."

She turned her horse on the ride. "Come, Pen. Greene, have the boar prepared for the spit. It will serve to furnish Lady Pen's birthday feast."

"But I didn't shoot it myself, Mama," Pen said with the air of one steadfastly refusing to take credit that was not her due. Her eyes darted to Robin. The lad smiled.

"But you shot at it," he said. "I saw your arrow fly. The boar went for your pony's throat. You were very brave."

"My congratulations on your birthday, Lady Penelope." Hugh smiled at the child and Guinevere was brought up short. The smile transformed the man, sent all his antagonism scuttling, revealed only a warmth and humor that she would not have believed lay behind the harsh soldierly demeanor. His eyes, brilliant before with challenge and dislike, were now amused and curiously gentle. It was disconcerting.

"I bid you farewell," she repeated as coldly as before. "Pen, come." She reached over and took the child's reins, turning the pony on the path.

Pen looked over her shoulder at the boy on his chestnut gelding. She gave him a tentative smile and he half raised a hand in salute.

Hugh watched Guinevere and her daughter ride off with their escort. The huntsmen followed, the boar slung between two poles.

The miniature had not done her justice, he reflected again. Those great purple eyes were amazing, bewitching. And her hair, as pale and silvery as ashes! What would it be like released from the coif and hood to tumble unrestrained down her back?

"Father?"

Hugh turned at Robin's hesitant voice. "You found the little maid appealing, Robin?" he teased.

The boy blushed to the roots of his nut-brown hair. "No . . . no, indeed not, sir. I was wondering if we were leaving Mallory land now?"

Hugh shook his head, a smile in his eyes, a curve to his mouth. This was not a particularly pleasant smile. "Oh, no, my son. We have work to do. Lady Mallory has only just made my acquaintance. I foresee that before many hours are up, she will be heartily wishing she had never heard the name of Hugh of Beaucaire."